STEVEN STATTON

A VERY WORKING-CLASS SPY

GORDON HENDERSON

Steven Statton - a very working-class spy

Published by The Conrad Press Ltd. in the United Kingdom 2024

Tel: +44(0)1227 472 874

www.theconradpress.com

info@theconradpress.com

ISBN 978-1-916966-23-9

Typesetting and Cover Design by: Charlotte Mouncey, www.bookstyle.co.uk

The Conrad Press logo was designed by Maria Priestley.

Printed and bound in Great Britain by Clays Ltd, Elcograf S.p.A.

AUTHOR'S NOTE

My first novel, *Operation Seal Island*, which was set in 1982, had as its main character David Statton, who was an ex-intelligence agent who became a mercenary when he was sacked by the Department for Covert Operation (DFCO).

Statton was hired by the CIA to rescue a Russian nuclear scientist, Gregori Zamyatin, who had been captured by the South African government and imprisoned on Robben Island by the South African.

During the ensuing operation to release Zamyatin, Statton was blackmailed by members of the ANC into rescuing Nelson Mandela at the same time as Zamyatin. However, although Statton succeeded in reaching Mandela's cell, the ANC leader refused to be rescued, saying he was more use to his people in prison, than as a fugitive in exile.

My second novel, *The Mandela Project*, also featured David Statton. It was set eight years later in 1990. By then Statton had been recruited back into the DFCO by the department's new Director-General, Rupert Disraeli-Astor.

In this book Statton was tasked with protecting the newly released Nelson Mandela during his historic visit to London, where he attended a tribute concert at Wembley Stadium, and visited the Houses of Parliament, where he gave a speech to a joint assembly of members of Parliament and peers. Statton foiled an assassin who tried to shoot Mandela as he was leaving Westminster Hall.

And so we come to my latest novel, *Steven Statton – a very working-class spy*, which is set twenty years later in 2019-20. Statton had by then retired from the DFCO, but his son Steven worked for the department, which has been renamed the Special Security Agency (SSA), although many of those working for the department still refer to it by its old name.

Steven Statton – a very working-class spy, tells the story of Steven Statton's efforts to counter an Iranian plot to use the Mafia to destabilise Britain by flooding its streets with heroin from Afghanistan. Unfortunately, Statton's task is made almost impossible when he is betrayed by somebody working in one of the British security agencies.

I am now in the process of writing my next Steven Statton novel, provisionally titled *Danger In The Deep*, which I am hoping to get published in 2025.

Watch this space!

Gordon Henderson, January 2024

PART ONE

WORKING-CLASS HERO

There's room at the top they are telling you still
But first you must learn how to smile as you kill
If you want to be like the folks on the hill

A working-class hero is something to be
A working-class hero is something to be
If you want to be a hero well just follow me
If you want to be a hero well just follow me

John Lennon

1

Monday, 30th December 2019. St James's, London.

The jewellery shop was in a small shopping precinct, located close to St James's Park. The shop rubbed shoulders with a high-class gentlemen's outfitters and an upmarket art gallery selling abstract paintings that looked as if they could have been painted by a six-year-old. Maybe they were.

The jewellery shop itself was like one of those expensive joints that has sturdy metal grilles on its windows and keeps its front door locked, which it only opens for customers who make an appointment and can afford to pay its exorbitant prices without having to take out a second mortgage.

This shop had grilles and a locked front door, but had no customers, rich or poor.

I peered through the window and saw a security guard sitting on a chair in a corner reading *Bodybuilding Monthly*. The man looked as if his photograph might appear in the magazine sometime.

The only other person visible was an elderly shop assistant in a smart suit and white shirt, who stood behind a wooden counter staring intently at an upright glass display cabinet positioned at the end of the counter. Every so often the old boy flicked the cabinet with a yellow duster, but he looked distracted and his heart did not seem in it.

Displayed on the cabinet's shelves were several black velvet trays containing rows of rings, each inset with large sparkling stones. They looked like diamonds, but I knew better. The stones were made from cubic zirconia. Not exactly valueless, but hardly worth such ostentatious security arrangements.

I tapped on the window and the guard glanced up from his magazine. When he saw me he rose unhurriedly to his feet and came lumbering over to the door. The shop assistant glanced at me, said something to the guard, and then went back to flicking his cabinet.

The guard regarded me suspiciously with eyes that were as black as his face. Plainly he didn't recognise me. I wasn't offended because I didn't recognise him either.

He mouthed silently from behind the hardened glass window with exaggerated movements of his mouth, looking for all the world like a gurning competitor. I couldn't make out what he was saying, but I guessed he wanted to see some form of identity. I took out my police warrant card and held it against the window.

The guard studied the small photograph carefully, then stared intently at my face. When he was satisfied the two matched, he opened the door to let me in. Once I was safely inside, he locked the door behind me and returned to his seat in the corner. He did this without saying a word and with little emotion.

I headed for an internal door located next to the counter.

'Morning, Mr S,' the shop assistant said, without looking away from the small portable television set that was now visible behind the display cabinet. He was watching the BBC News Channel.

'Morning, Plummy,' I replied. 'What's in the news?'

'Fires are still raging in Oz; Sudan is sending troops to West

Darfur; the PM is being urged to cut foreign aid to India; North Korea's been 'acking Microsoft; and there's talk of some sort of lurgy in China,' Colin Plum reeled off these news items as if by rote. Up close, his smart clothes looked as frayed as his cockney accent, with a loose thread visible on the cuffs of his shirt for every aitch he dropped.

'Anything else?'

'Yeah, President Trump is being a right arse'ole.'

'That's hardly news.' I nodded towards the security guard, who was once again immersed in his magazine with a serious expression on his face. 'Who's the heavyweight?'

'That's Bruno. 'e's standing in for Kenny,' Plum explained.

'He doesn't look much fun.'

"e's from an agency,' he said, as if this was explanation enough. "e ain't spoke more than 'alf a dozen words since 'e arrived.'

'Perhaps he's shy. Have you tried talking to him?' I punched my pin number into the keypad on the door's security lock.

'Yeah, but I don't fink 'e understands our lingo. I fink 'e's foreign.'

'He's reading an English magazine,' I pointed out.

'I know, but I fink 'e just likes looking at pictures of blokes with big muscles. If you get my drift, Guv.'

I got his drift. 'Where's Ken?'

"e 'ad an 'ospital appointment. Somefink to do wiv 'is piles, 'e'll be back tomorrow.' Plum glanced back at the TV, where a shapely weather girl, in a low-cut blouse, was forecasting rain for that evening.

'I ain't seen much of you recently, Mr S. Where you been?' he said without looking away from the television screen.

'Berlin.'

'What's going on there then?'

'A funeral.'

'Anyone I know?'

'That depends if you know the German Chancellor.'

That grabbed his attention. He dragged his eyes away from the weather girl's cleavage and looked at me instead. 'Was it what's 'er name's funeral?'

'Yeah.'

'But she was on the telly just now, complaining about Brexit.'

'So that explains why there was a voice coming from her coffin.'

He eyed me suspiciously. 'Are you winding me up again, guvnor?'

'Like a clockwork orange.'

'What's one of them?'

'Like clockwork lemons, but sweeter.'

'Clockwork oranges and lemons? I ain't never 'eard of them.'

'They come from the clockwork bells of St Clements.'

Colin Plum was not renowned for his sense of humour or speed of thought, but the penny finally dropped, 'You catch me every time, don'tcha, Mr S? 'ow d'ya manage to keep such a straight face?'

'Years of practice.'

'I guess you're 'ere for the meeting?'

'I guess I am.'

'In that case you're gonna be late.'

'What time does the meeting start?'

'Ten.' Plum knew everything that went on in the building.

I pointed at the TV screen where the BBC digital clock was showing the time as 09.59. 'I'm early.'

'Yeah, but you gotta get down to the wine-cellar yet, aintcha?'

I found it difficult to counter this indisputable logic, so I changed the subject by asking: 'Who's with the boss?'

'Mr Brewer and a few other guys.'

'How many is a few?'

'About 'alf a dozen.'

'Any idea who they are?'

'Well, there's some blonde bint I ain't never seen before, and that cop with the nice bristols[1] oozed tipped to be the next Commissioner. Then there's a couple of geezers each from Six[2] and Five[3], including that bloke you 'ad the big bust-up with last year.'

'You mean Gerry Draper?'

'That's 'im, although somebody told me 'e don't like being called Gerry. It seems 'e gets right uppity when people don't call 'im Gerald.' Plum did not explain who shared this information with him, or why.

Wonderful! Dickhead Draper is all I need on a Monday morning, I thought as I opened the security door, stepped through, and carefully closed it behind me.

I was now in the home of the Secret Security Agency[4], still known by most people who work there as DFCO, which was the SSA's name in a different era of espionage. Some people in the department believed it was a better era. I was one of them.

I headed down to the wine-cellar, which had long since seen its last bottle of Châteauneuf-du-Pape gathering dust in the wooden wine racks that had now been relocated, along with the wine, to a temperature-controlled basement room in the Foreign and Commonwealth Office.

The cellar had been converted into an operations-room,

cum small in-house cinema, but if you got close enough to the room's brown-stained brick walls, you could still detect a slightly musty smell, with hints of oak, cork, stale wine, and cigar smoke.

In the centre of the room was an oblong boardroom table, around which were positioned a dozen chairs, eight of which were currently occupied, including one by my boss, Dame Alexandra Nichols, the Director-General of DFCO, who sat at the head of the table.

As I entered the room, Dame Alexandra glanced at me and then made a point of looking at her watch. 'Thank you for taking the trouble to join us, Steven,' she said, making no attempt to disguise her irritation. 'Perhaps now we can start.'

On the wall directly behind my boss was a 75-inch flat screen television. Standing under the TV was a narrow table, on which were laid out cups, saucers, a plate of biscuits, and three chrome coloured, pump-action thermal flasks.

Each flask had a little white sticky label stuck to its front. One read COFFEE, the next TEA, and the last WATER. There was also a milk jug and sugar bowl on the table, but those were not labelled. I suppose the catering staff assumed attendees would have the intelligence to work out which of those was which. I had my doubts. I had been forced to listen to some of the mindless drivel spoken at such meetings.

'Don't wait for me. I'll just get myself a cup of coffee.' Ignoring my boss's glare I wandered over to the refreshments table.

'We cannot start, Steven, you're standing in front of the screen,' she said with a heavy sigh.

I stopped pumping coffee into my cup for a moment and

looked at the television. 'Sorry, boss,' I apologised, but carried on filling my cup. 'I didn't realise we were here for a film show.' When my cup was full I took a handful of biscuits and balanced them on the rim of my saucer. I headed for an empty seat at the far end of the table.

'Morning, Gerry,' I said to Draper, who had manoeuvred himself into a seat next to Dame Alexandra. I was not surprised. This was Draper all over. It would make it easier for him to suck up to the D-G.

The MI5 man was facing me, but he refused to make eye contact. Instead, he found something interesting to look at in his empty coffee cup. He did mumble something through pursed lips. It could have been good morning, or perhaps he was telling me to drop dead. Either way I would not be lying awake that night worrying about it.

I exchanged nods with the Deputy D-G of DFCO, Sam Brewer, who was sitting next to Draper, then took the seat opposite Joseph Onura, who was Draper's senior colleague from the International Counter-Terrorism branch of MI5, which investigates terrorist activity in the UK.

'Hi, Joe. It's good to see you.'

'You too, Steve,' Onura responded with a friendly smile.

I looked round the table to see who else was in attendance. Next to me sat James Bannerman, who was an MI6 senior operational manager. I had worked with Jimmy in the past and he was somebody with whom I got on well. Next to him was a man I did not know. Bannerman introduced him as Nadhim Kazemi, an intelligence officer from the MI6 Iranian desk.

Sitting between Sam and Onura, was a uniformed police officer. DAC[5] Jane Manning oversaw the Metropolitan Police's

Special Operations Drugs Task Force. I knew her well. She was a good copper.

Sitting opposite Draper, to the right of the D-G, was a blonde-haired young woman I had not met before. I wondered who she was.

As if reading my mind, Dame Alexandra looked up the table. 'I would like to introduce our young friend here.' She reached out and laid her hand gently on the young woman's arm. 'Harriet Barratt is an intelligence data analyst from the Middle East and North Africa Section at the Foreign and Commonwealth Office.'

The D-G squeezed the girl's arm and offered her a warm smile. This was a revelation. I knew from personal experience that receiving any sort of smile from my usually undemonstrative boss, let alone a warm one, was a rare privilege indeed.

'Now ladies and gentlemen, down to business,' the D-G went on. She picked up a television remote control from the table in front of her, then swivelled her seat so she was facing the screen.

She pressed a button on the control and the TV screen lit up, showing a Microsoft File Explorer menu. Under a blue cloud icon with the name One Drive – SSA, was a list of directories. She clicked on a directory tagged Foreign and Commonwealth Office, and a list of files showed on the screen.

'This file was compiled by Miss Barratt, with the help of our friends from MI6,' Dame Alexandra explained as she clicked on a file named Operation QS. A list of documents and JPEGs was revealed. She clicked on one of the latter and a photo filled the screen. A group of men stood in a line, looking directly at the camera. None of them was saying cheese.

'This photograph was taken a few weeks ago, outside the Tehran headquarters of the Islamic Revolutionary Guard Corp. The men were attending a meeting,' the D-G explained, before turning to the blonde girl. 'Perhaps you would like to tell us something about the attendees, my dear.'

Harriet stroked the keyboard of a laptop that was open in front of her. An arrow shaped cursor moved from the corner of the TV screen and glided quickly across the photograph, ending up pointing at the first member of the group. The man was dressed in a bottle-green uniform and had dark eyebrows that contrasted sharply with the whiteness of his short, well-groomed hair and beard.

'I imagine most of you will recognise Major General Qasem Soleimani,' the young woman said in a self-confident voice. 'However, if anyone has spent the last few years on a desert island, I should explain that Soleimani is Commander of the Quds Force, which is the division of the Islamic Revolutionary Guard Corps responsible for undertaking extraterritorial military and clandestine operations.'

I certainly recognised Soleimani, who was the second most powerful man in Iran, after Ayatollah Khamenei. However, looking down the table I could see from the blank look on Draper's face that he had no idea who the Iranian was. I guessed he was not alone.

'Because the meeting was held in Tehran, we assume Soleimani instigated the meeting and is behind any action being planned against us, which is why we named the Operation QS file after him,' Harriet explained.

The cursor moved to point at the next man.

'This guy is less well known. His name is Sabawi al-Barak

and he's head of the Iraqi National Intelligence Service, which was created when Saddam Hussein's Intelligence Service, Jihaz Al-Mukhabarat Al-Amman, was disbanded by the transitional government, following the Coalition invasion seventeen years ago.'

The cursor moved again.

'Next we have Jalaluddin Haqqani, who was the Taliban's military commander in the Baghlan Province, which, as I'm sure you know, is north of Kabul. Two years ago it was reported that Haqqani had died from an unspecified disease and had been buried. However, as you can see, he's very much alive. In fact, we have firm evidence that he's currently heavily involved in poppy cultivation, and the production of heroin in Afghanistan. The proceeds from which we assume go to help fund the Taliban, of which we believe Haqqani is still a leading member.'

The girl paused and took a sip from the glass of water that stood next to her laptop. As she placed the glass carefully back down on the table, a strand of blonde hair dropped across her face. She flicked it away with a casual movement of her delicate fingers, before continuing her monologue.

'This is Giuseppe Navarra.' She used the cursor to point at a short, chubby man, dressed in a shabby, ankle length overcoat. He had a swarthy, Mediterranean complexion and a bald head with a halo of greying hair round its rim, which made him look like Friar Tuck. 'He's the underboss of an organised crime group called the Mala del Brenta.'

'Who are they?' DAC Manning asked. 'I've never heard of them.'

'You might know them better as the Mafia Veneta, or the

Venetian Mafia,' Harriet explained.

'I've certainly heard of the Mafia,' the policewoman acknowledged.

'Well, the Mala del Brenta is behind most of the drug trafficking that takes place in Northern Italy and Navarra oversees its smuggling pipeline. Part of his role is to liaise with suppliers and customers, which we believe is highly significant in the context of the meeting.'

Standing behind Navarra were three other men. All were much taller than the Mafia underboss and all had the hard eyes of killers.

'And who are the heavies?' the policewoman asked.

'I'm sorry, ma'am, I didn't receive any information about them from MI6 and I haven't had time to research them myself yet,' Harriet said. 'However, I do know Navarra goes nowhere without bodyguards, so it's likely they're also members of the Mala del Brenta.'

'Thank you,' Manning said.

The cursor moved again and settled on the final figure in the group. The man stood next to Navarra, although noticeably apart, as if deliberately trying to distance himself from the Italian.

The policewoman gave a sharp intake of breath. 'I recognise that guy,' she said, just beating me to it.

The man was an imposing figure, about the same height as Navarra's bodyguards, but much beefier. He had a cruel face and short, plastered-down black hair, which looked as if it had been painted onto his cannonball of a head.

The man's left hand was tucked inside the lapel of his expensively cut suit jacket. He looked as if he was about to reach for a gun but I knew better. His hand was hidden from view because he was self-conscious about the two missing fingers bitten off in a pub brawl.

The man's right hand was also out of sight; thrust deep in his jacket pocket to hide the heavy gold rings he wore on every finger. Those rings were used as a makeshift knuckle duster to mess up the face of anybody who was unlucky enough to cross swords with him.

I knew all this because, like Jane Manning, I recognised the man. 'What the hell is the Balham Butcher doing in Tehran?' I asked her, but she shook her head and gave an expressive shrug.

Harriet Barratt leaned forward and looked up the table at me. She raised an eyebrow. 'You know him?'

'Yes.'

'Who is he?'

'His name is Tommy Cassidy,' Manning answered for me. 'He's a South London thug who is involved in a range of criminal activity. The trouble is, we've never been able to pin any crimes on him.'

'Why's that?' Harriet asked.

'Because he's the worst kind of thug,' Manning replied.

'What kind is that?'

'A clever thug.'

'Before you get the wrong idea,' I interjected. 'I don't suppose Cassidy gave much work to exam certificate printers when he was at school.'

'None,' Manning agreed. 'As far as I know Cassidy never took any exams, let alone passing them.'

'So, what did you mean about him being clever?' Harriet asked her.

'He's sly-like-a-fox-clever,' Manning replied. 'He has an

instinct for self-preservation and has always managed to keep one step ahead of the chase. We've only once ever come close to pinning a crime on him.'

'Would that have been the Wilder family murders?' I asked her.

'Yes.'

'Who were the Wilders?' Dame Alexandra asked. 'I recognise the name from somewhere.'

'That's probably because their murder made the front page of all the national newspapers about twelve years ago, ma'am,' Manning said.

'Remind me of the circumstances,' the D-G said.

'Kevin and Marion Wilder, and their nine-year old son, Jason, were hacked to death on Clapham Common,' the police-woman explained.

'Of course, the Clapham Common massacre.' Dame Alexandra said. 'Wasn't there a second child involved?'

'Yes. Jason's twin sister Kylie,' Manning replied.

'What happened to her?' Harriet Barratt asked.

'She escaped.'

'That's strange. I seem to recall the newspapers reported the girl was killed too. Am I wrong?' the D-G queried.

'No, ma'am, you're right. The press did report Kylie's death, but that was because we fed them that line,' the policewoman said. 'We were worried about the girl's safety, so we staged a mock funeral for her, at the same time the other members of her family were buried.'

'What became of Kylie?' Dame Alexandra asked.

'She was placed on our witness protection scheme and moved down to Wales, where she was given a new name and put into foster care,' Manning replied.

'This is news to me,' I told her. 'Do I take it that you fed us the same bullshit you gave the press?'

Manning nodded. 'I'm afraid so. It wasn't something we liked doing, but we were being extra cautious. We didn't want any leaks that might put Kylie's life at risk.'

I nodded my understanding. Even Britain's security services are not entirely leak free. 'How did the girl escape?'

'The killers didn't see her. She was asleep on the back seat, covered in a blanket.'

'So she didn't see what happened?'

'No, but the killers wouldn't have known that. That's why we took the steps we did to protect her identity.'

'Were there no witnesses to the murders?' the D-G asked.

'Just one, ma'am. A rough sleeper who was dossing down on a bench in Clapham Common. He saw everything that happened.'

'So what did happen?' Harriet asked.

'Wilder was driving through Clapham Common with his family, when he was ambushed by two cars, which forced him to stop. Three men jumped out of the cars. Two of them pulled Wilder from his seat whilst the third man used a machete to hack him to death. It was over in seconds. Marion Wilder tried to protect her children by locking the car doors from the inside, but when she reached over to close the driver's door, the killer sliced off her head.'

'Oh, my God! What about the little boy?' Harriet asked quietly.

'Hacked to death like his parents.'

'That's appalling. How could anyone be so heartless and brutal?'

'Tommy Cassidy could,' Manning replied.

'How do you know Cassidy was the killer?'

'Because the attack took place under a streetlight and our witness gave a photo-fit description that fitted Tommy Cassidy's identity.'

'What was the motive for the murders?' Dame Alexandra asked.

'Kevin Wilder was leader of the Yamyam Boys, who are a gang that controls the drugs trade in the Black Country,' the policewoman explained. 'We think Cassidy suspected Wilder was in London sniffing round with a view to muscling in on his drugs business and he decided to take out his rival before the Yamyam Boys could get themselves organised.'

'But why was Wilder's family killed?' This was the first of several further questions from Harriet.

'We think a couple of reasons. Firstly, because they were potential witnesses to his murder, and secondly, Cassidy hoped killing the family would show a ruthlessness that would act as a warning to any other gang that might be tempted to invade his manor.'

'And is that what Wilder was planning?'

'We'll never know one way or the other,' Manning admitted.

'If you had a witness, why wasn't Cassidy arrested?'

'He *was* arrested, but the day after our witness formally identified Cassidy in an identity parade, he was found dead on a bench in the park,' the policewoman explained sombrely.

'How did the witness die?' It was my time to ask a question.

'A drug overdose. He was a junkie with arms like a pin cushion.'

'Not all drug addicts die,' I pointed out.

'That's true, but then not all addicts inject themselves with heroin heavily laced with strychnine,' Manning said.

'Is that what happened?'

'That's what the post-mortem result suggested.'

'How dreadful. That must have been a painful death,' Harriet said sadly.

'Very painful.'

'It was lucky for Cassidy that the rough sleeper died.'

'People like him never rely on luck, Miss Barratt,' Manning said.

Harriet frowned. 'Are you suggesting that Cassidy killed the witness?'

'Not personally, but certainly indirectly. We're convinced Cassidy arranged for our witness to be supplied with a wrap of heroin mixed with a lethal dose of strychnine.'

'Was Cassidy prosecuted?'

'Sadly not. We tried to pin the Wilder killings on him, but unfortunately the CPS[6] decided that with only circumstantial evidence, and no witnesses, there was little chance of a successful prosecution, so they refused to take the case to court,' Manning's angry voice reflected her frustration.

'So, why did you call Cassidy the Balham Butcher?' Harriet asked me.

'Because when he left school he went to work in his local Dewhurst shop in Balham, where he trained to be a butcher,' I explained.

'Tommy Cassidy still owns a string of butcher shops in South London, which he bought in the mid-Nineties, including the Balham branch he trained in,' Manning added. 'He also owns an abattoir in Peckham, where he still loves to keep his hand in by personally slaughtering some of the animals.'

'He sounds like a right animal himself,' the girl said sourly as she started tapping away on her computer. 'I'll update his file. He was another of the group I didn't have time to research properly.'

'I was surprised to see Cassidy in Tehran, Steve,' Manning said. 'He rarely leaves London.'

'I know. How he managed to find his way there is beyond me. I don't suppose he can even spell Iran.'

Dame Alexandra switched off the TV and swivelled her chair so she was looking down the table again. She was a tall, slender woman, with cropped grey hair and steely-blue-eyes that seemed to drill through you like lasers, particularly when she was displeased, or worried. On this occasion it turned out to be the latter.

'How Cassidy got to Tehran is irrelevant, Steven,' she said. 'The important thing is that he got there and is part of a conspiracy that could do untold damage to our country.' She looked round the table to ensure she had our attention. She did.

'Our friends in MI6 have discovered that the Iranians, and their Iraqi allies, are planning to flood our streets with heroin, which is why I invited DAC Manning to this meeting.'

'Why would the Iranians do that, ma'am?' Draper asked, although, like me, he had probably worked out the answer already and was just trying to be clever, or perhaps my cynicism was the result of prejudice.

'Because they believe easy access to drugs will increase the influence of county lines gangs, create many more young addicts and, eventually, destabilise our society.'

'Was the meeting in Tehran about that plan?' Draper asked.

'We don't know for sure, but it seems likely. As Miss Barratt

22

said earlier, the presence of Navarra at the meeting was highly significant, particularly with Haqqani in attendance also,' Dame Alexandra replied.

This did not satisfy Draper. 'If the Iranians really are planning to flood our streets with drugs, do you know how they propose to achieve their aim?'

'Sadly not. In fact, we know very little about their plans.'

'If the meeting took place a few weeks ago, drugs could already be being smuggled into the country,' I suggested.

'That is true, Steven. Which is why Mr Bannerman and his team are trying to find out what is going on.'

'So, what has Six found out so far?' Draper asked. I guessed where his probing was heading.

'Only what you have been told today, Mr Draper,' the D-G said tetchily, probably thinking the same as me.

'With all due respect, ma'am. All we have been given is the names of a few people suspected of being involved in a conspiracy. That seems to be very little information,' he said.

'That is as maybe, but sadly it is all we have.'

'But is the lack of intelligence not worrying?' Draper persisted.

I glanced at Bannerman. I knew there was no love lost between him and the MI5 intelligence officer and this was confirmed in the way the MI6 man was staring down at his hands and biting his bottom lip in anger.

'I am not sure you can blame Six entirely for that, Mr Draper,' Dame Alexandra said, choosing her words carefully.

Bannerman looked up. 'Thank, you ma'am. I can assure you we're doing our best in the circumstances.'

'I am sure you are, Mr Bannerman, and I am sure there are

valid reasons for the lack of information. However, Mr Draper is right about one thing. For whatever reason, the situation in which we find ourselves *is* rather worrying.' She paused as if to add emphasis to her next words. 'Particularly for the Prime Minister. Which is why he has asked us to take the lead on Operation QS.'

Out of the corner of my eye I saw Bannerman stiffen at this news.

'By us, I assume you mean the SSA?' Sam Brewer asked our boss.

'That is the agency we work for, Samuel.'

Bannerman looked sideways at me and raised an eyebrow.

'I know nothing, Jimmy,' I whispered in his ear.

Nor it seems did Dame Alexandra's deputy. 'You didn't tell me,' Sam said tightly, not happy about being kept in the dark.

'It has all been quite a rush, Samuel. I was only informed myself this morning,' the D-G explained. 'The PM is very concerned and wants us to help find out exactly what is going on as quickly as possible.'

'Did the PM say why he wants you to take over our operation?' Bannerman asked, sounding no happier than Sam.

'I did not speak to the PM, Mr Bannerman. His instruction was relayed via the Cabinet Secretary, and we are not taking over Operation QS, we will simply be helping you.'

'But you said you're taking the lead,' Bannerman pointed out.

'That is true, but only because my team has a certain unique operational advantage over the country's other security agencies,' Dame Alexandra said smoothly.

'What advantage is that?' Harriet Barratt asked.

It was Draper who answered. He spoke in a distinctly disapproving voice. 'The SSA is the only security service in the UK with a licence to assassinate people without prior political permission.'

'I would not describe what we do as assassination, Mr Draper,' Dame Alexandra said. 'We prefer to call it Extreme Retribution.'

'No matter what you prefer to call it, what you do is little short of state sponsored murder,' Draper said acidly.

'I beg to differ,' the D-G said, before stressing in an earnest voice, 'and of course we use our ER powers only very rarely.'

I had to use my hand to hide the instinctive smile at the way my boss was able to deliver this lie with such sincerity. I looked down the table at her, but she avoided my eyes.

'However, I cannot deny that ER is a very useful weapon to have in our armoury,' Dame Alexandra went on quickly. 'The fear of it can sometimes act as a powerful deterrent to our enemies.'

'Yeah. The Iranians will be wetting their pants,' I muttered loudly. Obviously too loudly because Dame Alexandra glanced my way, but this time, surprisingly, she agreed with me.

Looking round the table she said, 'For once Steven's natural cynicism is warranted. Although the knowledge we will not hesitate to use ER makes some of our enemies wary, the truth is that the threat of such reprisals will not worry people like General Soleimani. He and his ilk are fanatics who will stop at nothing in pursuit of their agenda.'

'Would that be the same agenda the guys from MI6 have failed to discover anything about, Dame Alexandra?' Draper asked, putting the knife in once again, this time the blade stabbed deeper. 'A failure, I might add, that raises questions about the competence of our colleagues.'

This led to an embarrassed silence, during which the only sounds were the hum of Harriet Barratt's laptop, the tick-tock of the wall clock, the nervous rustling of paper and my loud harrumph.

I did not share the embarrassment, all I felt was irritation at Draper's comments. 'I suppose you think you could do better, Gerry?'

'Perhaps I could,' he responded tightly.

'You're delusional.'

Draper glared at me angrily. 'Are you questioning my ability, Statton?'

'Not at all. Your ability is beyond question. However, I am questioning your grasp on reality.'

'How dare you,' he spluttered, but was interrupted temporarily when Sam Brewer restrained him by touching his arm.

'Ignore him, Gerald,' Sam said gently. 'He's just winding you up.'

'No. I will not ignore him, Samuel,' Draper insisted, pulling his arm away. 'I have every right to express an opinion.' He pointed at the two MI6 men. 'If I think they are falling down on the job, I will say so.'

'Drop it, Gerald,' Joseph Onura ordered as he leaned back in his chair and looked round Sam. 'Rather than picking a fight with our colleagues, it might be better if you gave them an opportunity to explain why they haven't been able to come up with more information.'

'That makes a lot of sense,' Dame Alexandra stepped in smartly before the disagreement could escalate further. 'Are you able to tell us the reason for the lack of information, Mr Bannerman?'

Bannerman was silent for a few moments before he spoke. 'Yes, ma'am, I can.'

'In that case we are waiting.'

'The truth is we have something of a problem in Iran.'

'What sort of problem?'

'If you don't mind, ma'am. I'd prefer to let Nadhim explain that. Iran is his area of expertise.'

'I have no preference who explains,' Dame Alexandra said. 'As long as I find out what is going on.' She looked at Bannerman's MI6 colleague. 'It seems it is down to you, Mr Kazemi,' she said.

'Yes, ma'am,' Kazemi said. 'But before I tell you about the situation in Iran, would it be helpful if I explain something of my background to those who don't know me?'

'That is an excellent idea,' the D-G said. 'I am sure Miss Barratt, in particular, would be most grateful.' She managed to use her words as an excuse to give the girl's arm another affectionate squeeze.

The younger woman showed no sign of objecting to this intimacy. Instead, she just sat with an enigmatic smile on her face, as if amused by some secret thought.

Sam Brewer caught my eye and offered me a knowing wink. I had no idea what he knew, but he was obviously hinting Dame Alexandra and Harriet Barratt were in some sort of secret relationship. It was only much later that I discovered he was right.

'My father was a senior advisor to Shah Mohammad Reza Pahlavi,' Kazemi was saying. 'My family was forced to leave Iran in 1979, when the Shah was deposed following the Islamic

Revolution. At first we fled to Egypt, but four years later, when I was five years old, we moved to Britain.'

'I'm sure this is all very interesting, Mr Kazemi,' Draper butted in, 'but what relevance does it have to your current problem in Iran?'

Kazemi looked across the table at the MI5 man and offered him a smile that was about as warm as a Siberian winter. 'As it happens what happened to my family is very relevant, Mr Draper. As you will find out if you let me finish.' He spoke softly and patiently, as if talking to a small child and this mild-mannered rebuke was far more effective than any angry retort.

Draper tightened his lips at the obvious put down, however, he made no other comment, perhaps warned off by the glare Dame Alexandra gave him.

'Please continue, Mr Kazemi,' she said.

'Thank you, ma'am. As I was saying, we moved to Britain when I was five years old, over thirty years ago.' Kazemi looked at Draper to make sure he was not about to interrupt him again, but the MI5 man was once again staring sullenly into his empty cup.

'Although many of my father's extended family, and his Sunni friends, shared his hatred of the new Shi'a regime, they decided to stay in Iran,' Kazemi continued his story. 'They kept their views to themselves, worked hard, and managed to build successful careers, including senior positions in the civil service, the police, and the military.

'However, despite their success, those friends and relatives never supported the regime and they became increasingly unhappy with the hard-line policies being pursued by the mullahs. Eventually, some of them got together to form a small dissident group, which was so select and secretive it had no formal structure or name.

'When the British Government decided to set up an intelligence network in Iran, the MI6 intelligence case officer who was in charge of recruitment at the time, approached my father for advice. It was the same case officer who had helped my family flee Iran, so my father offered to put him in touch with members of the dissident group.

'That case officer, who was a very experienced field agent, accepted the offer immediately, because he knew members of the group would understand that the key to a successful clandestine cell is having agents who keep their eyes and ears wide open, but their mouths tightly shut.'

'When was the network set up?' Dame Alexandra asked.

'About seventeen years ago, just before the start of Operation Telic[7].' Kazemi replied. 'The cell was given the code name January 16th.'

'Any significance in the name?' Harriet Barratt asked.

'Yes, it was the date on which the Shah left Iran.'

'How big is your January 16th network?' Draper piped up, seemingly taking an interest in Kazemi's story for the first time. Perhaps he was hoping to pick holes again.

'It's very small as clandestine cells go,' Kazemi said. 'However, despite its size, Jan 16th has provided some useful information over the years. For instance, we were given a number of excellent briefings both on the regime's attitude to the Coalition's invasion of Iraq, and the effect on the morale of Iranian civilians when sanctions were imposed by the United Nations Security Council ten years ago.'

'Is the cell still operational?' Draper asked.

'It was until recently. In fact, it was one of the Jan 16th agents who supplied the Soleimani group photograph that Miss Barratt showed us just now.'

'Who was the agent?' Draper asked.

'I'm afraid that's classified information,' Kazemi said firmly.

'Don't be ridiculous,' Draper snapped. 'Classified or not, surely you can share the information with us?'

Sam Brewer weighed in to support Draper. 'Come on, Nadhim. Everyone sitting round this table has DV[8] clearance.'

Kazemi looked to Bannerman for guidance. His senior colleague gave a slight shrug and nodded. 'Very well, our agent's code name is Cuckoo. However, I cannot tell you their real name because I'm not party to that information myself.'

'How did your agent get hold of the photograph?' Draper asked.

'We don't know that either. However, the photo was taken outside the Iranian Revolutionary Group Corp HQ, so make of that what you will.'

'Are you saying Cuckoo has access to IRG files?' Sam asked.

Kazemi shrugged, but said nothing. Despite Sam's earlier comments, he was obviously very uncomfortable giving away any information, no matter how little.

Sam recognised the Iranian's discomfort. 'Don't worry, Nadhim,' he said reassuringly. 'Anything you say is safe with us and will stay strictly within these four walls.'

'Yeah, it'll be like storing your information in the Hatton Garden safe deposit vault,' I said.

Kazemi looked at me and smiled. 'As I recall, a bunch of old lags broke into that vault five years ago and stole valuables worth millions of pounds.'

'Fourteen million to be precise,' I told him.

'So, not the best example of security then, Mr Statton,' the Iranian said with another wry smile.

'Quite,' I said simply.

'Come on, Steve. This is out of order,' Sam protested angrily. 'There's simply no comparison between the Hatton Garden heist and sharing information between internal security services.'

'Is that so?'

'Yes, and anyway they caught the guys who robbed the vault.'

'Yeah, but most of the goods are still missing.'

'That's irrelevant.'

'Tell that to the companies that insured them.'

'Look, whatever you say, I'm very confident everybody in this room can be trusted,' Sam insisted.

'You sound just like Harold Macmillan when he was Foreign Secretary,' I said.

'What do you mean?'

'I mean Macmillan stood up in the House of Commons and told MPs that Kim Philby[9] could be trusted, but Super Mac's ringing endorsement didn't stop the treacherous bastard scarpering to Moscow with a suitcase full of secrets.'

'Are you suggesting…' Sam started but was interrupted by Dame Alexandra.

'This is getting us nowhere, gentlemen,' she said sharply. 'Let us move on. Is there anything else, Mr Kazemi?'

'Yes, ma'am. It's about the Jan 16th cell. We think there's a problem.'

'What sort of problem?' she asked.

'We received that photograph from Cuckoo two weeks ago, and nothing has been heard from any of our agents since.'

'You think something has happened to them?' the D-G asked.

'Yes, ma'am. But we're not sure what.'

'So what makes you think there is a problem?'

'The lack of any communication.'

'Explain.'

'All members of Jan 16th have to report to the cell's Principal Agent once a day. If an agent fails to do that, the cell automatically goes into emergency lockdown mode.'

'Has that happened?'

'We think so, ma'am.'

'But you do not know why?'

'No, ma'am.'

'So, what does your Principal Agent say about the situation?'

'That's part of the problem, ma'am. In an emergency, our Principal Agent has to follow the same lockdown protocol as all the other agents, which means our usual communication channels are now suspended.'

'I think I am beginning to get the picture. The lack of intelligence information about how the Iranians are planning to get drugs into our country is because of this problem with Jan 16th. Yes?'

'Yes, ma'am.'

'Are there no emergency arrangements for such circumstances?'

'There are, ma'am, and as soon as our Jan 16th Case Officer became aware of the problem, he flew to Tehran to make use of those arrangements in order to contact the Principal Agent.'

'Who is the Case Officer?' I asked.

'Will Berry,' it was Bannerman who answered.

'He's a good man,' I offered.

'Yes,' Bannerman agreed.

'Is Mr Berry still in Iran?' the D-G asked.

'Yes, ma'am.'

'When is he due back?'

'We're not sure. It depends what the situation is like on the ground.'

'Very well. When he returns, I would like him to brief everybody who needs to know straight away,' the D-G said and then added: 'Including Steven's team.'

'Which team would that be?' I queried. 'The last time I held a section rollcall, my team consisted of my secretary and me. Personally, I'm happy to be briefed about Jan 16th, but I don't suppose Marion is interested in anything other than the current fashions in Tehran.'

'That situation has changed,' the D-G said.

'Has it?'

'Yes, somebody else is joining your team.'

'Who would that somebody be? Is it Bruno?'

'Who is Bruno?'

'He's the security guard who let you in upstairs.'

'Do try not to be so frivolous, Steven,' she said with another heavy sigh.

'So who is this new member?' I asked, unabashed.

'It is Miss Barratt here,' the D-G gave the blonde girl's arm another affectionate squeeze.

'Miss Barratt?' Sam sounded surprised.

'Yes.'

'But I thought Miss Barratt worked for the FCO.'

'Not anymore. She is being transferred to us.'

Sam looked at me. His face was expressionless, but his eyes betrayed the irritation he felt at not being consulted about the girl's transfer.

'I have assigned Miss Barratt temporarily to the Operations Section, where she will assist Steven working on Operation QS.'

'Since when was I working on Operation QS?'

'Since now,' Dame Alexandra replied in a voice that broached no argument.

I gave a resigned shrug. I had no intention of arguing with her, not least because the news did not come as a surprise. It was obvious the D-G had not invited me to the meeting just to make up the numbers.

'I would like you to take Miss Barratt under your wing and show her the ropes,' the D-G told me.

'Oh, joy of joys. I can't wait,' I muttered loudly.

If the young woman heard me she did not respond, but when I glanced her way, she was studying me intently with shrewd eyes and still wore the same enigmatic smile.

The last time I saw a smile like that was in a painting in the Louvre Museum in Paris. Robert Orben once said Mona Lisa's smile reminded him of a journalist listening to a politician.

Looking at Harriet Barratt's face now, I knew exactly what Orben meant.

1   Bristols: Bristol Cities, i.e. cockney rhyming slang for 'titties'.
2   Six (MI6): Military Intelligence Section 6 is also known as the Secret Intelligence Service (SIS) and operates only outside the UK. It reports to the Foreign Secretary.
3   Five (MI5): Military Intelligence Section 5 is the United Kingdom's security service responsible for counterespionage within the UK. It reports to the Home Secretary.
4   The Special Security Agency (SSA) started life as the Military Intelligence Section 13 (MI13), which was taken over by MI6 in 1945. However, it was resurrected as a stand-alone agency in the early 21st Century, when the small and very secretive intelligence agency, the Department for Covert Operations (DFCO), was expanded into a larger specialised security service. It should be noted that the SSA is the only British intelligence service that can operate both inside and outside the UK. It reports directly to the Cabinet Office and, unlike its sister security agencies, MI5 and MI6, its field agents are licensed to kill, internally and externally, without prior political approval..
5   DAC: Deputy Assistant Commissioner.
6   CPS: Crown Prosecution Service.
7   Operation Telic, or Op TELIC, was the code name used for the UK's military operations during the Invasion of Iraq on 19 March 2003.
8   DV is the abbreviation of Developed Vetting, which is the highest form of security clearance in UK government. It is needed for frequent and uncontrolled access to Top Secret assets or information.
9   Harold Adrian Russell 'Kim' Philby was a British intelligence officer and a double agent for the Soviet Union. In 1963 he was revealed to be a member of the Cambridge Five, a spy ring which passed information to the USSR.

35

2

Tuesday, 31ˢᵗ December 2019. Shepherd's Bush.

When I entered Dame Alexandra's office she was standing in front of the window with her back to me. I did not recognise her at first because she was dressed in a calf length Laura Ashley floral dress and sling-back shoes. It was only her tall, lean body and close-cropped grey hair that gave her away.

I watched as she pulled closed the heavy red satin curtains, shutting out the last of the fading winter sunlight that had shone weakly through the window. The office was now lit only by three candles, stuck in holders on a marble fireplace set into the side wall.

Dame Alexandra walked over to a plush chaise longue that stood in the corner of the office. She looked down lovingly at Harriet Barratt, who lay on the couch wearing nothing more than her Mona Lisa smile. The D-G reached down and stroked the girl's bare shoulder.

This was all very odd.

I had only ever seen my boss dressed in trouser suits and starched white blouses; her office window had no curtains, red or otherwise; there was no fireplace in her office, only radiators to provide heat; and to the best of my knowledge, her office had never contained a plush chaise longue, with or without a naked blonde girl draped over it.

I was trying to make some sense out of this weird scene when the telephone on the D-G's desk started to trill. A light on the front of the telephone pulsed in time with the ring tone.

Harriet turned her head and stared at the phone with wide blue eyes.

'Ignore it, my dear,' the D-G said, as she continued to caress the girl's shoulder. But the phone refused to be ignored, instead its tone increased in volume and the light pulsed ever more urgently.

As I drifted out of my end-of-sleep dream, and forced open my eyes, I saw my mobile phone flashing on my bedside table. I picked it up and recognised the number displayed on the screen, which also showed the time as 07.24.

'What do you want, Sam?'

'Did I wake you?' he asked cheerfully.

'Is that supposed to be some sort of sick joke?'

'What do you mean?'

'I mean, it's the middle of the bloody night.'

'Not for most normal people.'

'Most normal people weren't up until the early hours of the morning putting together a briefing paper on the threat to our economy from Russian cyber-attacks, which I might add, Mr Deputy Director-General, you were supposed to be writing.'

'I know, but you are an expert on the subject.'

'If you think flattery is going to make me feel better about being woken at this ungodly hour, then you're as delusional as your mate Draper.'

'He's not my mate.'

'Well you seemed pretty close yesterday.'

'We aren't close,' Sam said hastily. 'I just feel sorry for him. Nobody seems to like him.'

'That's because he's a dickhead. Now why did you ring me?'

'Look, I am grateful for your help with the Russian cyber report, and I'm sorry about disturbing your beauty sleep,' Sam said, sounding neither grateful, nor apologetic. 'But I wanted to catch you before you left home.'

'You did that all right,' I grumbled. 'So, what's so urgent it can't wait until I get into the office?'

'It's the Iranian business we discussed.'

'What about it?'

'I had a phone call from James Bannerman about an hour ago.'

'And?'

'Remember Kazemi told us Berry was in Tehran?'

'Of course I remember. It was only yesterday and I'm not bloody senile.'

'My, you are touchy!'

'I don't do civility at this time of the morning, Sam, so don't try my patience. Now, what about Will?'

'He's flying back from Iran today.'

This surprised me. 'Today? Why didn't Jimmy tell us that yesterday?'

'Because he didn't know. Berry only informed Kazemi late last night.'

'Has something happened?'

'Bannerman didn't say, he just said that Berry is catching a flight just after midday local time and says he has some important news. I'm setting up a meeting for tonight, so he can brief us.'

I tried to remember how long a flight from Iran took, and what the time difference was between Tehran and London. I started to do the calculation, but it was too early in the morning for mental arithmetic. I gave up and instead asked, 'What time's he expected back?'

'I'm not sure. His plane is due to touch down at eight o'clock this evening, but then he has to get from Gatwick to London.'

'Great! And there was me looking forward to seeing in the New Year at Ronnie Scott's. So, where's the meeting taking place?'

'Westminster.'

'Westminster is a large borough. Where exactly?'

'Sorry, the House of Commons.'

'Why there?'

'Because Benedict Fletcher wants to attend.'

'How did our new Minister for Intelligence and Home Security find out so quickly?'

'I briefed him on Operation QS last night and he asked to be kept in the loop. When I heard from Bannerman this morning, I contacted Benedict before I rang you.'

'Great! We now have a bloody politician attending our meeting. All of a sudden, what was looking like a crap evening just got a whole lot worse.'

Sam laughed.

'It's no laughing matter,' I moaned, but this only made him laugh louder. 'Tell me something,' I said, breaking into his laughter. 'If the honourable member for West Berkshire plans to be in attendance, why isn't the meeting being held at Marsham Street[1]?'

'Because he's arranged for some of his constituents to watch the New Year's Eve fireworks display from the Commons Terrace and he wants to join them as soon as the meeting ends.'

'Of course he does. His dedication to those who pay his wages knows no bounds.'

'Are you being sarcastic?'

'Does it show?'

'Yes.'

'That's a relief. I was worried I might be losing my touch.'

'I think you're being harsh, Steve. I've known Benedict for years and I can assure you he feels a real sense of loyalty to his constituents.'

'Wow, a loyal MP. That's a first.'

'Is that what you think of our political masters?' he asked, with a hint of disapproval in his voice.

'As it happens, I prefer not to think of them at all, even those you're on first name terms with. So, what time is this bloody meeting and where?'

'10.30pm in Room 60, Lower Ministerial Corridor. Do you know where that is?'

'No, but I'm sure I'll find it.'

'Ring me if you get lost and I'll send a Saint Bernard to rescue you.' Sam laughed at his own joke.

'In that case I'll make sure I bring some extra-large dog biscuits with me.'

He laughed again and then said, 'All joking aside. Please don't be late. I know what you're like.'

'Don't worry. I'll be on time. My parents gave me a new Mickey Mouse watch for Christmas.'

'I never know when you're being serious, Steve.'

'That's because I like to keep people guessing. It's a trait I inherited from my old man.'

'I'll bear that little gem in mind if ever I meet him,' Sam said, in a tone that made clear meeting my father was the last thing he wanted. 'Now, was there anything else?'

'Yeah, I have a couple of questions.'

'Ask away.'

'Okay, why couldn't you wait and tell me about this evening's meeting when we're in the office?'

'Because I won't be in the office today. I have a meeting at GCHQ[2]. In fact, I'm on the train to Cheltenham as we speak. Next question?'

'Who else will be at tonight's meeting?'

'Pretty much all those who attended yesterday's meeting except for Jane Manning and Dame Alexandra.'

'But Draper will be there?'

'Yes.'

'Wonderful,' I groaned.

'What's the problem?'

'No problem, except I'm not sure I can stomach him twice in one week without puking up.'

'In that case bring a sick bag with you. I don't want you embarrassing the department by making a mess on the minister's carpet.'

'Very funny. So why won't the boss be there?'

'She's on her way to Rome.'

'What's happening in Rome?'

'She's staying with Luigi Campisi[3] over the New Year holiday.'

'I didn't know Luigi and her were friends.'

'Despite what you might think, you don't know everything that goes on in the world. Apparently the boss is bosom buddies with Luigi's wife,' he lowered his voice when he told me about the friendship, managing to make it sound scandalous. 'They were at Cambridge together,' he added, as if this made the scandal worse.

'So, she won't be with us tonight?' I asked, refusing to react to Sam's bit of gossip.

'No, but I've invited our latest recruit.'

'You mean the gorgeous, pouting Miss Barratt?'

'Yes, but don't get any ideas, Steve. She's not your type.'

'How do you know what my type is?'

'I meant you're not her type.'

'I ask the same question. How do you know?'

'Because I have it on good authority that she's not into men.'

'You mean she's a lesbian?'

'Yes.'

'That's going to disappoint an awful lot of men.'

'Maybe, but not women of a certain age. Did you notice the way Dame Alexandra was all over her?'

'That's an exaggeration, Sam. She only touched the girl's arm a few times. There was nothing in it.'

'Trust me, there's more to those touches than meets the eye.'

'Are you suggesting the boss is gay?' I asked, but there was no reply. I guessed Sam's train had gone into a tunnel and he had lost his mobile signal. As I headed for the bathroom to have a shower I thought about Dame Alexandra and Harriet Barratt.

Despite what I told Sam, I had noticed the affectionate way the D-G behaved towards the girl, which is probably what triggered last night's strange dream. However, all thought of the two women was driven from my mind when I reached the bathroom and discovered there was no hot water.

A quick check of the combination boiler showed the pilot light had blown out. This kept happening recently and I suspected there was something wrong with my gas supply. I really had to get it sorted out.

After a miserable cold shower and shave, I got dressed and went through to the kitchen where I popped a couple of slices of bread in the toaster and made a cup of instant coffee. I resolved to ring my gas supplier when I reached the office.

I heard a rustling noise in the hall. It was my mail coming through the letterbox and hitting the doormat. I walked through and collected a handful of envelopes. I took them back to the kitchen and settled down to open them as I ate my breakfast.

Most of it was junk mail. One of the larger envelopes contained an unsolicited brochure from a travel agency I did not know, offering me winter-break deals to faraway countries I had no desire to visit.

A second large envelope was from a mail order company promising money off a range of products in their "Once in a lifetime" January Sale. This company sent me a brochure every year. I have no idea how I got onto their mailing list and I had never been attracted by any of their offers, the discounts of which were mostly much less than the "Up to 60% off" they advertised.

There were also three bills, and an envelope with a Government crest embossed on the back. I opened it and found inside a smaller envelope with a Croydon postmark, addressed to me at the SSA address in St James's. I did not recognise the scrawled longhand writing that had been used to mark the envelope Private and Confidential.

The back of the small envelope had been stamped with an official Government mark before being forwarded to my home address. The mark certified the envelope had been screened by the Government's off-site security contractor and contained no dangerous materials. Despite this assurance I still opened the envelope very cautiously.

Most envelopes these days are self-sealing and can be peeled open easily, but this was one of those old-fashioned types with an adhesive flap the sender had to lick. It was stuck tight and I had to use my breakfast knife to cut the envelope open. I peered inside it and saw it contained a folded newspaper page.

I went through to the bathroom, took a pair of tweezers from the wall-cabinet, and returned to the kitchen. Using the tweezers, I pulled out the newspaper and carefully unfolded it.

It was a page from the Surrey Advertiser. Somebody had ringed an article with a pink felt tip pen. It was a report about the theft of a horsebox from a service station on the A3.

The horsebox was transporting a horse from Italy to the Grange Polo Club in Hinkley Green. There was little other information of any real interest in the article, which ended with an appeal by the police for witnesses to come forward if they saw the horsebox parked at the service station, or had seen it since.

There was no clue as to who had sent the article to me, or why. But I carefully folded the page back up, again using the tweezers, and returned it to the envelope, which I put into my briefcase. I threw the bills in a kitchen drawer and the junk mail in the recycling bin.

As I drove to the office I mulled over a couple of things. Firstly I wondered about Sam's relationship with Fletcher. I could understand him keeping the minister in the loop, but I could see no reason to tell him about an internal meeting. After some thought, I concluded Sam invited Fletcher because it would benefit him in some way. But how?

And then there was the newspaper article. I had no idea why it had been sent to me, but that in itself did not concern me. Finding out more about the missing horse would be a perfect research job to dump on the desk of my new assistant. If nothing else, it might keep her out of my hair.

However, what did concern me was that the article was sent to my office address. I had no idea who had sent it, nor, more worryingly, how the sender knew I worked for DFCO.

1   Marsham Street, London, is where the Home Office is located and where the Minister for Intelligence and Home Security is based.
2   GCHQ is the Government Communications Headquarters, which monitors all types of communication activity around the world and uses it to provide intelligence information.
3   Luigi Campisi was the resident MI6 intelligence officer in Rome.

3

Tuesday, 31ˢᵗ December 2019. Westminster.

It was 9.45pm when I left my office and headed for the Palace of Westminster. There was no public transport available, because many of the roads in Central London had been closed to traffic since early afternoon, so I walked across St James's Park and down Birdcage Walk.

I was not alone. By the time I reached Bridge Street several groups of pedestrians were making their way past Portcullis House[1] towards the Embankment, where thousands more people were already waiting for the start of the fireworks display that would herald in a new decade.

I headed towards two stewards wearing Day-Glo yellow tabards, who stood behind metal barriers that had been erected to ensure people kept to the correct side of the road.

One of the stewards saw me coming and pointed towards Westminster Bridge. 'That's the way to the fireworks, sir. Keep to the pavement and hurry up or you won't find anywhere to watch the show.'

'Police,' I told her. This was not true, but my lie was backed up by the fake warrant card I confidently brandished in her face. 'I'm heading over there.' I pointed towards the Houses of Parliament.

The steward took the warrant card from me and studied it carefully. 'Where exactly are you going, Inspector Statton?'

'The Commons.'

'Are you going to watch the fireworks display from the Terrace?'

'No, I have a meeting.'

'On New Year's Eve?'

'Is that what it is?'

'Yes.' She looked at me doubtfully. 'Didn't you know?'

I shrugged. 'When you're in a job like mine, one day is much the same as another.'

'I suppose so,' she conceded as she handed the warrant card back to me. 'Do you know where you're going?'

'I told you, the Commons.'

'I know you did, sir,' she said patiently. 'But are you aware that Carriage Gates and St Stephen's entrances are closed?'

'No,' I admitted.

'Well they are. So you can only access the palace via Black Rod's Garden entrance. Do you know where it is?'

'Yes.'

'That's good,' she said and turned to her companion. 'Open up Billy.'

We both watched as Billy moved one of the barrier's aside to create a gap for me.

'Shame you're not going to the fireworks display. You would have got a fantastic view from the Terrace.'

I shrugged. 'Once you've seen one fireworks display, you've seen them all,' I told her and set off across Parliament Square towards the House of Lords.

As I reached Black Rod's Garden entrance my mobile vibrated. It was Sam Brewer.

'Where are you?' I asked.

'The Commons. Why?'

'Because I was hoping you were ringing to say you were delayed at GCHQ and the meeting was cancelled.'

'No, I got back about three hours ago.'

'So why did you ring me?'

'I wanted to let you know the minister has changed the venue.'

'Why?'

'When he found out how many people were attending, he realised his office was too small, so he's moved the meeting to the Lower Ministerial Conference Room. Do you know where it is?'

'I'm sure I'll find it. Has Will Berry arrived yet?'

'No, but he rang a few minutes ago to say he's reached Chelsea Embankment and reckons he'll be here by ten-thirty.'

'Only if he's hitched a lift on a helicopter. Did you remind him all the local roads are closed to traffic and the closest he'll get by car is Vauxhall Bridge?'

'Yes, but he still insists he'll be here on time.'

It was a long walk from Vauxhall Bridge and the MI6 man had to find somewhere to park first. 'He'll be late,' I said with certainty.

Sam gave a little laugh. 'Oh, ye of little faith.'

'My lack of faith is as a result of being let down by too many people who promised me the earth, but gave me sod all,' I countered.

In the event, my scepticism was well founded, because Berry did not arrive at the conference room until a quarter to eleven, by which time the Minister for Intelligence and Home Security's well-rehearsed good humour was beginning to wilt.

Benedict Fletcher was one of life's natural leaders, who had been gifted with an easy charm that he used to great effect. An ex-military man, he wore his invested authority like an invisible coat of armour, and had the supreme self-confidence that only an expensive public school education buys.

In addition to providing the young Fletcher with a first class education, which saw him sail through the entrance exam for Sandhurst, his school nurtured in him the ability to mix easily with everybody with whom he came into contact, from dukes to dustmen, and the social graces that enabled him to treat them like bosom buddies, whether or not he liked them.

When we arrived, Fletcher greeted each of us with a firm handshake and a smile that never quite reached his eyes. He had abandoned his ministerial pinstripe suit, starched white shirt, and regimental tie. Instead, he was dressed casually in a Ben Sherman shirt, fashionable Ted Baker Squishy slimline trousers, and a pair of Kurt Geiger loafers that he wore without socks.

There were nine of us sitting at the table. In addition to the minister, Sam, Harriet, and me; Jimmy Bannerman and Nadhim Kazemi were there from MI6; and Joe Onura had turned up from MI5 with Derek Draper in tow.

It was a good turnout, considering it was New Year's Eve, and I wondered fleetingly if any of the attendees had a life outside their work. This was a stupid question, because like me, work *was* their life.

The only other attendee was a man I had never met before. He was tall and rangy, and what excess weight he carried looked like muscle rather than fat.

The man was dressed as an Ivy League graduate, but talked like a cowboy when he introduced himself as Troy Olsen. He told us proudly he was from Texas, and said he was a military attaché from the US Embassy. This admission made me smile to myself. In my book that nailed him as a CIA spook[2].

The minister took a seat that allowed him to glance surreptitiously at the wall clock from time to time, whilst maintaining an air of studied interest in the inconsequential chatter that swirled around him.

Every so often Fletcher added to the conversation an anecdote from his time in the Army, or a barrack room joke, all of which Harriet Barratt seemed to find hilarious. However, apart from laughing at the minister's jokes, she made no further contribution to the meeting, although I could tell from her shrewd eyes she was taking careful note of everything that was said.

But the longer we sat twiddling our thumbs, the harder it became for Fletcher to disguise his growing irritation, and slowly the anecdotes and jokes dried up. I was not surprised. Like many ex-military officers, the minister was a stickler for time keeping and hated being kept waiting.

When Will Berry eventually arrived, I thought he was in for a rollicking for being late, but I was wrong. Benedict Fletcher greeted him like a long-lost son, offering him the same well practiced smile he had gifted the rest of us.

The minister's cultured voice showed none of his earlier irritation. 'It's a pleasure to meet you, Mr Berry. I trust you had a smooth flight from Tehran.'

'I've had worse, minister,' Berry said.

'With whom did you fly?' Fletcher asked, managing to make it seem that knowing this snippet of useless information was one of the most important things in his life.

'Qatar Airways.'

'Very good! Well done!' Fletcher said and gave Berry a friendly pat on the back as he directed him towards an empty seat at the table. 'An excellent choice if I may say so!'

'It wasn't my choice, sir,' Berry admitted, as he took his seat. 'Flights, and that sort of thing, are arranged by one of our business support officers.'

'In that case, MI6 is lucky to have such discerning administrators in its ranks,' Fletcher said, before going on breezily: 'Now, I'm sure you're on a very tight schedule, Mr Berry, so perhaps we can get started. What information do you have for us?'

'Bad news I'm afraid, minister.'

'What bad news?'

'Are you familiar with our January 16th cell?'

'Yes, I was briefed on it yesterday by Mr Brewer. Has something happened to it?'

'Yes, sir.'

'What's the problem?' Kazemi asked.

'Jan 16th has definitely been compromised, Nadhim,' Berry replied.

'How?'

'Two weeks ago Cuckoo was arrested by PAVA.'

Fletcher held up his hand. 'Who or what is PAVA?'

'Sorry, minister,' Berry apologised with a diffident smile. 'PAVA is an acronym for the Persian name for the Iranian Intelligence and Public Security Police, which is a sub-division of the Law Enforcement Force of the Islamic Republic of Iran.'

'Thank you,' Fletcher said. 'As you can see, I still have a lot to learn about the intelligence agencies of other countries.'

'You're not alone, sir,' Berry assured him. 'Even we struggle sometimes to keep up to date in an ever-changing world.'

'That makes me feel slightly better, thank you. Now you were saying that Cuckoo has been arrested.

'Yes, sir, which is why Jan 16th went into lockdown,' Berry said.

'Lockdown?' Fletcher asked.

'Didn't Mr Brewer brief you about that?' Bannerman asked.

Sam answered for Fletcher. 'No, I told the minister there was a problem with Jan 16th, and Will had gone to Iran to investigate, but I didn't want to go into too much detail until he got back.'

'That makes sense,' Bannerman agreed and then explained to Fletcher about the emergency arrangements that were put in place should a member of the cell be arrested.

'Thank you,' Fletcher said when Bannerman had finished. 'So what has happened to Cuckoo?' he asked Berry.

'48 hours after his arrest he was found guilty of treason at a Military Revolutionary Court secret trial.'

'Is he in prison?'

'No, sir. He was executed the same day.'

'How dreadful. What a tragic loss.'

'Yes, sir. He was a very good agent.'

'What affect will his death have on your network?'

'Hopefully there will be no permanent damage. Cuckoo will almost certainly have been interrogated by PAVA before his trial. However, he appears to have held out for at least 24 hours, because none of his colleagues have been arrested.'

'How do you know that?'

'Because I managed to contact our Principal Agent in Tehran, who told me what had happened.'

'How were you able to meet your agent?'

'I didn't meet our agent, sir. Once the emergency protocol was activated, I had no means of contacting Eagle other than through a dead drop box[3] located in Tehran, hence my visit.'

'Who is Eagle?'

'Our Principal Agent.'

'I realise that. I meant what is his real name?'

'Unfortunately, that is a question I can't answer.'

'Can't or won't?'

'Can't.'

'Why not?' Fletcher asked sharply.

'Because for security reasons, the identity of each member of the cell is known only to the person who recruited that member. That way, if one of our agents is caught, they can only reveal the identity of their recruiter, and anyone they themselves recruited. So I have no idea what the Principal Agent's real name is, in fact Eagle could be a woman for all I know.'

'But you referred to Cuckoo as a man. How do you know that?'

'Eagle told me, sir.'

The minister raised an eyebrow in query.

'Cuckoo was dead, so protecting his identity was no longer necessary,' Berry explained.

'Of course. I should have realised that. So, how did Eagle know Cuckoo's identity?'

'Because Eagle recruited him.'

'I see,' Fletcher said and then studied Berry silently for a few moments before adding: 'However, what I don't understand is why you don't know Eagle's identity. You are his, or her, case officer. How can you not know the identity of your Principal Agent?'

'Because I didn't recruit Eagle, sir.'

'Who did?'

'It was the case officer who set up the January 16th cell in the first place. He retired several years ago,' Berry replied.

'Didn't the case officer share Eagle's identity with anybody else before he retired?'

'No, sir.'

'Why not?'

'He refused, sir, on the grounds of confidentiality.'

'That's nonsense. Surely as his case officer it would make your job a damn sight easier if you knew Eagle's identity.'

'It might, sir,' Berry said cautiously.

'Can't we talk to this chap again? Perhaps put a little pressure on him? What's his name?'

'David Statton.'

Fletcher glanced at me. 'Any relation?'

'Yeah. He's my dad.'

'In that case can't you ask him about this Eagle?'

'I could, but I'd be wasting my breath.'

'Why's that?'

'Because he wouldn't tell me anything.'

'But you're his son.'

'That makes no difference. My dad promised his agents anonymity when he recruited them. He never broke that promise when he was working, and he won't break it just because he's now retired.'

'That's what made David such a successful case officer, minister,' Bannerman chipped in. 'He was trusted by everyone he recruited because they knew he would keep his word.'

Fletcher nodded his understanding. 'Your father is a man

after my own heart. He deserves respect.' He turned back to Berry. 'I have another question.'

'Ask away, sir.'

'You mentioned Cuckoo held out for 24 hours.'

'Yes, sir.'

'Is the time lapse significant?'

'I can answer that question, minister,' Draper piped up.

'Can you really?' Fletcher asked with a coolness in his voice that Draper did not appear to notice.

'I certainly can, sir,' Draper replied with a self-important smile.

I could only guess what Fletcher thought of that smile, but it just made me want to punch the MI5 man on the nose.

'How many field agents do *you* have in Iran?' Fletcher asked.

'These days we prefer to call them covert human intelligence sources, or CHIS for short.'

The minister looked unimpressed. He viewed Draper silently for a few moments. 'I see,' he said eventually. 'So, how many CHIS do you have in Iran?'

Now Draper sensed the minister's hostility and shifted uneasily in his seat.

'In fact, does MI5 have any such sources, Mr Draper?' the minister persisted.

'Not exactly.'

'What does "not exactly" mean?' Fletcher's voice had now dropped a few degrees and was sinking fast.

'I think you'll find MI5 have no agents in Iran, sir,' Bannerman chipped in.

'Jimmy's right, minister,' Joe Onura agreed. 'Although we have our fair share of CHIS, who, personally, I still prefer to call snitches, they are all based in this country, because we are responsible for counter-terrorism and counter-espionage activity only within the UK.'

'That's what I thought,' Fletcher turned back to Draper and sliced him up with a few sharp words. 'Do not patronise me, Mr Draper. I might be new to my role as the Minister for Intelligence and Home Security, and I might not be up to speed with the intelligence setups in other countries, but I can assure you that I'm not a complete idiot. I certainly know the difference between the responsibilities of MI5 and MI6.'

The minister's putdown wiped all signs of smugness from Draper's face, now all he wore was an embarrassed blush. Seeing the MI5 man's flushed cheeks, almost persuaded me to set aside my life-long distrust of politicians. Almost.

'Now, perhaps we can hear from somebody who knows what they're talking about,' Fletcher continued in the same vein, and then turned to the MI6 case officer. 'Mr Berry would you be good enough to answer my question?'

'Certainly, sir. Actually, the importance of Cuckoo holding out for longer than a day cannot be overstated. As I'm sure you will understand, the biggest risk to any intelligence gathering network is the threat posed if one of the cell's agents is captured and interrogated.'

'Yes, I get that. It's pretty obvious that a captured agent might reveal the identities of any other members of the network he happens to know,' Fletcher agreed. 'So tell me more about how you combat that risk.'

'Well as I explained before, Jan 16th has a warning system in place to counter the possibility of a domino effect when an agent is captured. It's based on an encrypted WhatsApp group, on which each member of the cell must post a predetermined one-time codeword once a day. To increase security, members are not allowed to use the group for any other purpose.'

'What happens if a member fails to post the code word? Does the cell close down?'

'Yes, sir. The mandatory procedure is that all the other members of the cell must assume the network has been compromised; go into an immediate lockdown situation; stop all covert activities; and get the hell out of Dodge City until given the all-clear.'

'I see. So your agents need to resist the pressure of interrogation for at least 24 hours to give their colleagues time to disappear and cover their tracks?'

'Yes, sir.'

'So, we have to assume that January 16th has been compromised?'

'Yes again, sir.'

'Does that mean the flow of information will dry up?'

'Not entirely. We are certainly unlikely to see the same level of activity, but hopefully the cell will still be able to get some stuff out to us. One encouraging sign, is that two of our agents are still operating normally.'

'I assume one of them is Eagle, since you were able to contact him or her?' Fletcher asked.

'That's right.

'And the other?'

'An agent whose code name is Raven, who works at the Iranian Ministry of Defence and Armed Forces Logistics. She's been a very useful source of information,' Berry explained.

'She? I thought you didn't know the identity of the agents?'

'I don't generally. However, I know Raven is a woman because Eagle let slip by referring to her as "she" in one of the messages he sent me.'

'How do you know Raven is still operating?'

'Eagle told me she had decided to carry on working because she doesn't feel under threat.'

'Why's that?'

'Because Cuckoo didn't know Eagle, and Eagle is the only person who knows Raven's identity.'

Fletcher nodded his head thoughtfully to acknowledge he understood.

'We should be grateful Raven decided not to shut down,' Berry went on.

'Why's that?'

'Because she was able to provide us with some very interesting information.'

'What information?' Bannerman asked.

'Qasem Soleimani is currently in Venice.'

'What the hell's he doing in Italy?'

'I asked Eagle that question, but he didn't know. I can only assume he's there to meet Guiseppe Navarra. Perhaps Luigi Campisi can do some digging.'

'Of course. I'll get onto him tomorrow,' Bannerman said. 'Do you have anything else, Will?'

'Yes. Raven gave us more information about Soleimani's future movements.'

'Go on.'

'When he leaves Venice, his next stop is Baghdad,' Berry said.

'Baghdad?' Troy Olsen asked. 'Are you sure?'

'Yes.'

'Do we know when?'

'Yes. He'll be flying from Italy on an Iranian military plane. His flight is scheduled to leave on Thursday evening at twenty-one hundred hours local time, and is due to touch down in Baghdad at around oh-oh-forty-five hundred hours local time.'

The American made a note of this information. His keen interest in Soleimani's movements set off alarm bells in my brain and I thought about challenging him, but then decided it was not important. How wrong I was.

'That's good stuff, Will,' Sam said. 'Do we know why Soleimani is going to Baghdad?'

'Yes, he's visiting Sabawi al-Barak.'

'Is he by God? Now that really is interesting, particularly if he's meeting Navarra in Italy.'

'Yes,' Berry said simply.

'Who is this Navarra character?' Olsen asked in his soft southern drawl.

'He's a Mafia underboss,' I explained.

'You think the Eye-ranians are tied up with the Mafia?'

I shrugged.

'It wouldn't surprise me if they were. Those mothers are planning something,' Olsen said.

'And what would that something be?' I asked, wondering how much the American knew about Operation QS.

'They're gonna shaft us,' Olsen said, not giving anything away.

'Who is "us"?' I asked.

'All of us in the West, and that includes you, pal,' he replied, then, pointing at the others one at a time he intoned: 'and you, you, you, you, you, you, you, and particularly you, sir,' he ended with the minister.'

'Me?' Fletcher asked.

'Absolutely you, minister.'

'Did Soleimani's flight details come from Raven?' Draper asked.

'Yes,' Berry confirmed.

'So how did she get hold of such sensitive information?'

'I told you earlier. She works in the Ministry of Defence and Armed Forces Logistics.'

'Excuse me for being sceptical, but how did some ministry pen-pusher get such detailed travel information?' Draper asked disparagingly.

'Because that pen-pusher, as you put it, is the senior logistics clerk who organised Soleimani's flights,' Berry explained.

That shut Draper up again.

'Is that all, Will?' Bannerman asked.

'Yes.'

Benedict Fletcher cleared his throat. 'Gentlemen and lady, I have some information myself in which you might be interested. I think we have another problem.'

'What sort of problem, minister?' Bannermen asked.

'Three weeks ago a missile was fired from a drone at a car in Tehran.'

'That's news to me, sir,' Bannerman said. 'Where did the information come from?'

'From my counterpart in the US State Department,' Fletcher said.

'So how's that a problem?' Olsen asked.

'Because the missile took out one of the leaders of al-Qaeda who was in the car.' He looked at Olsen. 'It was an American missile.' The politician made this last piece of news sound like an accusation.

Olsen shrugged, but did not admit to knowing about the attack, instead he asked, 'I still don't see why that's a problem? Surely it's just one less rag-head terrorist to worry about?'

'If only it were that simple, Mr Olsen,' Fletcher said. 'The reason it's a problem is because also in the car was the Iranian Home Security Minister, Islam Houshian.'

Olsen shrugged off this revelation just as nonchalantly.

The rest of us were less complacent. We recognised the danger. However, after chatting through the implications of Houshian's death, we were unable to agree what action should be taken. So, we decided to postpone our deliberations until we had more information. A few minutes later, after a short closing speech from Fletcher, the meeting ended.

'Can you hang on a minute, Steve,' Sam said as everyone started to leave the conference room. 'I'd like a quick word with you.'

'Take as long as you like. I'm in no hurry,' I replied, hanging back as Fletcher and Harriet made their way to the door. Apart from Sam and me, they were the last to leave.

I watched as the minister stepped aside to allow Harriet through the door before him. At first I took this as an old-fashioned, gentlemanly gesture, but changed my mind when I realised Fletcher had made the manoeuvre to give himself a better view of the girl, who looked sensational in her tight, scarlet cashmere jumper; black jeggings, that clung to her long, shapely legs; and red, high-heeled ankle boots.

Harriet Barratt must have been pushing six-foot tall in those boots, but she was still a few inches shorter than Fletcher.

'Did you notice our political master was getting an eyeful,' Sam said when the pair were out of earshot.

'Are you surprised?'

'No, but if he tries anything on, he's going to be very disappointed.'

'I don't know, our new colleague seemed quite taken with him.'

'Laughing at a guy's jokes doesn't make a gal straight,' he said, affecting an American accent.

'You still reckon she's gay?'

'Absolutely.'

'What about Dame Alexandra?'

'That's what I've heard.'

'That's crap. The boss is happily married with two grown up children.'

'That means nothing these days. It takes some people time to accept they've been living a sexual lie. I can mention a least half a dozen current members of Parliament who've done that.'

'Dame Alex seemed happy enough the last time I saw Angus and her together.'

'That mean's nothing. The word on the street is that she swings both ways.'

'She's bi-sexual?'

'So I understand.'

'Who told you that, Sam?'

'Let's just say I have a source who told me all about her other young conquests.'

'What about the girl? How do you know she's gay?'

'I have a couple of sources in the FCO also,' he replied cryptically.

'Your trouble, Sam, is that you have more sauces than Heinz, but they're just not as reliable as tomato ketchup. Now, what do you want to talk to me about? I'm sure it's not the boss's sex life.'

'Well, actually it is,' he replied and then looked over his shoulder as if to make sure there was nobody listening. This was a quite unnecessary melodramatic gesture because we were clearly alone in the room, but it was typical of Sam. He lowered his voice to add to the sense of drama. 'Dame Alexandra's behaviour has come to the attention of the powers that be.'

'What powers would that be?'

'The Cabinet Secretary[4] and he's not a happy bunny.'

'You mean Sir Mark is unhappy with Dame Alex's sex life?'

'No, not all of it. Just her involvement with Harriet Barratt.'

'That's total bullshit, Sam. We're living in the 21st century, for Christ sake. Even if the boss is gay, members of the LGBTQ community are no longer treated like lepers in our country.'

'Oh, don't get me wrong. Sir Mark has no interest in the boss's sexuality, the Civil Service has more than its fair share of people wearing rainbow lanyards. However, he disapproves strongly of senior staff being intimately involved with junior staff, whatever their gender, particularly when the offender is head of one of the nation's security services.'

'I see.'

'Do you?'

'No. What are you getting at?'

'It means the knives are out for the D-G.'

'It's that serious?'

'If you think that looking for a way to get rid of Dame Alex without causing a political scandal for the new Government is serious, then yes, it's that serious.'

'You mean the PM[5] wants rid of her too?'

'Apparently.'

That was when I began to realise that Sam was on career enhancement manoeuvres. 'Let me guess. If the PM and the suits in the Cabinet Office manage to force out the boss, you want her job. Am I right?'

'Well, nothing is definite. She might see off her critics.'

'But if she doesn't escape a knife in the back?'

'Well, in those circumstances, yes, I would apply for her position.'

'So it's a case of et tu, Brutus?'

'Certainly not.' He avoided my eyes. 'I'm just covering all eventualities.'

'Of course you are. So why are you telling me this?'

He smiled. 'Well, if Dame Alexandra *is* forced out, I'm confident I'll have some political support if I go for her job.' He nodded towards the door where Fletcher had just exited. 'However, it will enhance my chances immeasurably if I have the support of my senior staff also.'

'*Your* senior staff?'

'Yes. As Deputy D-G, technically everybody in SSA works for me, except Dame Alexandra of course.'

'Of course.'

'And I would like the support of those staff.'

'Including mine?'

'Particularly you.'

'Really?'

'Yes. Backing from the head of the Operations Section could swing it for me.'

'Sam, if you're relying on the likes of me to get you promoted, then you really are scraping the bottom of the barrel.'

He laughed. 'Don't under-estimate yourself, Steve. You're very highly regarded in certain places.'

'Which places?'

'The Red Lion for a start.' He grinned. 'One of the barmen told me you're one of his best customers.'

'Was this barman Polish by any chance?'

'I'm not sure, but he did have a foreign accent and a thin waxed moustache.'

'Yeah. That would be Oskar. He does tend to exaggerate everything.'

'So, you're not a regular in the Red Lion?'

'Well, I do go there occasionally, but I'm not really fussed where I drink, as long as there's ice in my G and T and the beer is warm.'

'In that case, let's head over to Strangers Bar and I'll buy you a beer,' he offered.

'If you're trying to bribe me, Sam, a pint of bitter isn't much of an inducement.'

'What about a large single-malt whisky?'

'Now you're talking.'

---

1   Portcullis House is the building opposite the Houses of Parliament in which many MPs have their offices.
2   CIA spook. US Central Intelligence Agency spy.
3   A dead drop box is a method used to pass messages using a secret location known only to those intended to use it.
4   The Cabinet Secretary is also Head of the Civil Service and responsible for overseeing the appointment of, and disciplinary matters relating to, departmental permanent secretaries, Director-Generals and deputy Director-Generals.
5   Prime Minister.

4

Wednesday 1st January 2020. Westminster.

The House of Commons Terrace was packed with revellers waiting for the New Year's Eve fireworks display. Sam and I made our way up the steps clutching our drinks, and managed to make our way through the crowd to the low wall fronting an area that stretches almost the full length of the Palace of Westminster.

Below us on the River Thames, a flotilla of half a dozen boats was positioned in a line, providing a floating viewing platform from which to watch the fireworks. The display was due to start in a few minutes time, and the fireworks would be set off from the London Eye and barges moored on the water alongside.

On board one of the larger boats, a party was in full swing. The well-lit galley was full of revellers and a small group of young men had spilled out onto the deck, bringing with them bottles of lager, laughter, and the smell of cigarette smoke.

In front of the flotilla was a police launch, which moved slowly up and down the line, ensuring the bows of the boats did not creep over an invisible boundary in the river, which kept the craft away from Westminster Bridge and prevented them from edging closer to the London Eye.

Every so often the strong tide would push one or other of the craft closer to the bridge, forcing its helmsman to reverse the boat until it was back in line.

Opposite the Palace of Westminster, on the south bank of

the Thames, lights shone out from St Thomas' Hospital. Dark silhouettes flitted across the upper-floor windows, as staff and ambulatory patients looked for a suitable position from which to view the fireworks that would soon be heralding in another New Year.

I looked down the length of the Terrace and saw the tall Benedict Fletcher standing with his head and shoulders above the crowd.

He was in a section reserved for members of Parliament and their guests. That part of the Terrace was smaller, but less packed than the area in which Sam and I were standing. But then everything is relative. Although Fletcher's group had slightly more breathing space than we did, they were still surrounded by scores of jostling people, some holding glasses above their heads to reduce the risk of somebody's elbow spilling the contents.

'I can't see our new colleague anywhere. I half expected to see her with Fletcher,' I said.

'She's not here. I invited her to join us, but she told me fireworks were boring,' Sam explained.

'A woman after my own heart.'

'So why are you here?'

'For the single malt.' I took a generous sip of my drink and felt the comforting warmth as the whisky hit my stomach.

'I promised to meet up with Gerald Draper. He's over there somewhere.' Sam pointed towards the House of Lords' Terrace. 'He was coming with one of his friends, who's a senior executive officer in the Cabinet Office. Let's go find them and have a chat. Gerald's friend might know what's happening about the boss.'

'No thanks, I'll leave the departmental politicking to you. Anyway, I'd rather swap this very nice malt whisky for a glass of hydrochloride acid, than have to exchange pleasantries with your pal Draper.'

'In that case, I'll leave you to hate the fireworks in peace.' Sam dived into the crowded smoking section that led to the Thames Pavilion and, beyond that, the Lords' Terrace.

I finished off my whisky and was about to head for Strangers' Bar to get a refill, when a female parliamentary security guard came up the steps that led from the Medals Corridor.

When the guard reached the top step, she stopped and turned her head slowly from side to side, like a lioness surveying a herd of wildebeest, looking for the easiest prey to target.

Hanging by a strap over one of the woman's shoulders was a black leather bag, which she clasped tightly to her side, as if frightened somebody might snatch it from her. This seemed an unusual precaution for a security guard, which I found both ironic and puzzling.

I put my glass down on a nearby table and headed towards the steps. However, by the time I reached the spot where I saw the guard standing, she had moved away and was pushing purposefully into the heaving throng, but she was very petite and I soon lost sight of her in the crowd.

As midnight approached, an excited voice blared out of the massive loudspeakers that were located somewhere on the other side of the Thames. The voice started a countdown that was picked up by the thousands who lined the Embankment. Many in the crowd on the Terrace turned towards the London Eye and joined in the chant: 'Ten... Nine...'

To my right, people edged forward to try and get a better

view, and as they moved closer to the river a gap opened in the crowd.

'Eight… Seven…'

That's when I spotted the tiny security guard again as she entered the section reserved for MPs.

'Six… Five… Four…'

I moved quickly after the woman, elbowing my way across the packed Terrace, ignoring several angry cries of protest, and had almost caught up with her when she stopped close to Benedict Fletcher's group.

'Three… Two…'

The guard opened her handbag, reached into it, and took out a handgun.

Instinctively, I reached for my own Glock 17[1], but quickly abandoned any idea about drawing it because the Terrace was too congested, I had no clear line of fire, and the chance of collateral damage was too high to take the gamble. Instead, I continued pushing my way through the crowd, praying I would reach the woman in time.

'One!' The crowd roared in unison as Big Ben announced the death of the Old Year.

As the iconic clock struck twelve, music started pounding out from the loudspeakers and Calvin Harris began singing *Let's Go!* as hundreds of fireworks soared upwards, filling the sky with a succession of bangs, flashing multicoloured explosions of light, and billowing clouds of coloured smoke.

As if on cue, the security guard pointed her gun up at Fletcher, who towered above her and was staring up at the sky with a rapt look of childlike enjoyment on his face. I suppose some people never fully grow up.

I was close enough to see the look of sheer hatred on the woman's face as she stared at Fletcher, and the way the woman's hand was shaking badly as she screamed: 'Allahu Akbar!²'

The minister turned to look at her and immediately snapped out of his dreamlike state. His eyes widened in alarm when he saw the pistol pointing at his head.

Roughly I shoved a couple of startled people out of harm's way, threw myself at the woman, and managed to push her arm upwards just as she pulled the trigger.

Very few people heard the crack of the pistol, or the whine of the bullet as it ricocheted off one of the Clipsham stone walls and veered into the air. Those noises were drowned out by the cacophony of sound from the blaring music, and the loud bangs and cracks that accompanied the constant explosions of colour filling the sky.

I spun the woman round, knocking off her hat in the process, until she was staring at me with eyes that still blazed with hatred as she struggled to pull free.

I gripped her arm tightly with one hand, as, with the other, I wrenched the gun from her. However, at the very moment I had both her and the weapon under my control, I slipped on a half-eaten sandwich somebody had dropped on the ground.

As I fell in an untidy heap, the woman twisted out of my grasp. Side-stepping a half-hearted attempt to stop her by one of Benedict Fletcher's entourage, she darted into a gap in the crowd of revellers, some of whom were watching our little drama with wide eyed alarm.

As more people sensed something was wrong, the gap in the crowded Terrace widened, like the Red Sea for Moses, forming a human passage that allowed the security guard to reach the parapet unimpeded.

Despite her small size, the woman clambered up onto the wall before anybody could react, then, without looking back, she jumped.

By the time I managed to limp to the wall the security guard had disappeared beneath the swirling, black waters of the Thames, just as the sound of Lady Leshurr singing *Where are you now?* started blasting out from the speakers. It was morbidly appropriate.

Somebody on the police launch must have seen the woman jump because it moved quickly away from its position controlling the line of boats and headed to the spot where she fell into the river. On its arrival, the launch trained its searchlight on the surface of the water, but there was no sign of the guard.

'Who was she?' Fletcher asked as he joined me at the wall, he had to shout to be heard above the sound of the fireworks and blaring music.

'Asma Malik.'

'Did you know her?'

'No, she was wearing a name badge.'

We stood side by side looking down at the dark, swirling water.

'They won't find her alive,' Fletcher shouted. He did not sound particularly unhappy at this prospect.

'I know.'

'The water will kill her. It's ice-cold at this time of year.'

'I know,' I repeated. The woman would have been dead seconds after hitting the river, because when the cold hit her

71

face, the shock would have forced her to inhale water involuntarily.

We watched as the police launch worked its way slowly forwards and backwards across the watery grave.

'They're wasting their time,' Fletcher said. 'They won't find her.'

'I know,' I agreed again.

'Her body will already have been dragged downstream by the strong undercurrents,' Fletcher went on. 'She'll probably be found down Wapping way sometime next week.'

'I know.' Okay, so I sounded like a broken record, but what more could I say? The minister was right on every count.

1   Glock 17 is the standard pistol used by the Metropolitan Police and the UK security services.
2   Allahu Akbar: God is great!

5

Thursday 2ⁿᵈ January 2020. St James's.

When I entered Dame Alexandra's office she was standing with her back to me. However, she was no longer dressed as a Laura Ashley model, there was no plush chaise longue with a naked Harriet Barratt draped across it, nor were there red satin curtains on the window out of which she was looking.

But then this was no dream. What I could see through the window now, was not the fading winter sunlight, but the eerie light cast by a six-day old moon.

The slim white crescent was just visible above the roof of the building opposite and had somehow managed to escape from the thick blanket of cloud that covered London, hinting at another mild night in the capital.

'Thanks for agreeing to come at such a late hour, Steven,' the D-G said as she turned to face me.

'Agreeing? I didn't realise my attendance was optional. If I'd known there was a choice, instead of dragging myself halfway across London to meet you, I'd have gone to my Farsi For Beginners class at the Holland Park Language School.'

'Is there a language school in Holland Park?' She asked with a questioning frown.

'Not as Farsi know.'

'That's really not very funny, Steven.'

'Nor is receiving a text ordering me to come to your office for a meeting when I'm having a quiet drink in my local pub.'

73

Dame Alexandra sat behind an uncluttered, highly polished oak desk, on which stood a Polycom conference phone; a large faux leather pad with a white blotter that had no hint of ink to be seen on it; and a gold stand, positioned parallel with the top of the blotter pad, on which was perched an expensive Montblanc fountain pen.

'It was not exactly an order,' she said. 'It was more an invitation. You could have refused.'

I raised an eyebrow at her. 'I'll remember that next time you contact me out of hours.'

She held up her hands in a sign of appeasement. 'Look, I apologise for dragging you away from the pub and spoiling your evening. However, since you are here, can I offer you a drink?' She pointed at the Nespresso machine sitting on a side table positioned against one wall.

'I'd prefer a proper drink.' I nodded my head in the opposite direction, towards a large globe in a wooden frame that stood on top of a low bookcase on the other side of the office.

'If you must,' she said with a resigned sigh.

I walked over to the globe and tipped its hinged-top backwards until it split at the Equator to reveal half a dozen bottles. Standing next to the globe was a tray on which was an assortment of crystal glasses. I selected the Glenfiddich malt whisky and poured two fingers into a tumbler that was engraved with thistles.

'What about you?' I asked, but she declined with a shake of her head. With a shrug I took my glass and settled into one of the chairs that stood in front of her desk.

My seat was not as plush as the high-backed, padded, executive swivel-chair in which Dame Alexandra sat, but it was comfortable enough for me to relax and enjoy my drink. 'So why am I here?' I asked after I had taken a generous sip.

'We have a problem.'

'What sort of problem?'

'It is our American cousins.'

'What have the Yanks done now?'

She reached for her Montblanc, picked it up, and studied it thoughtfully. 'Earlier this evening GCHQ intercepted two encrypted messages sent between Baghdad and Tehran,' she said eventually.

'That's what the Cheltenham techies are there for,' I said, then had another quick sip of my whisky before asking: 'What did the messages say?'

'The first was from the Iraqi Ministry of Defence claiming that an American drone strike near Iraq's International Airport killed four members of the PMF[1], including Abu Mahdi al-Mu-handis.'

'Wasn't al-Muhandis the PMF's head honcho?'

'Yes.'

'Well, the Iraqis won't be happy about that and it will set the whole region alight.'

'That is an understatement,' she said, 'because the situation gets worse. Much worse.'

'What could possibly be worse than killing a senior Iraqi military commander and three of his colleagues?' I asked.

'What would you say if I told you that in addition to al-Muhandis and his colleagues, the missile took out Qasem Soleimani.'

'I would say a can of petrol has been thrown on the bonfire and turned it into an inferno.'

'Which, if you will excuse the mixed metaphors, means a storm could be heading our way,' she said.

'A bloody big storm if *you* will excuse my French.'

'I can think of a stronger word to use.'

'What, like hurricane?' I asked and was rewarded with the hint of a smile. I took another sip of my whisky.

'As you might expect, the Iranians are even angrier than the Iraqis,' she went on.

'Oh, there's no "might" about it,' I agreed. 'In addition to Soleimani being the second most powerful man in Iran, the Mullahs will already have been smarting following the drone attack on Tehran last month that wasted their Home Security Minister. I assume you heard about Houshian's death?'

'Yes, Minister Fletcher rang to inform me as soon as he found out.' She said and then looked at me intently before asking: 'So you agree we have a problem?'

'Yeah. If the Yanks definitely did kill Soleimani, both the Iranians and their Iraqi allies will be out for revenge.'

'Trust me, Steven. Soleimani is definitely dead, and he was definitely killed by the Americans.'

'Has that been verified?'

'Yes, the Foreign and Commonwealth Office sought clarification from the US State Department as soon as the message was deciphered.'

'How come we weren't warned in advance about the drone attack?'

'That is the very question the Prime Minister asked when he was told. He was absolutely livid when the FCO admitted they had no idea the US were planning either this drone strike, or the one last month.'

'I bet he was,' I said and knocked back the rest of my Glenfiddich.

'The PM was even more upset when it became apparent the Pentagon deliberately kept us out of the loop.'

'Why'd they do that?' I asked, but she did not answer. 'I thought Boris and Trump exchanged mobile phone numbers so they could keep in touch?'

'They did.'

'So why didn't The Donald ring the PM?'

'Perhaps the battery on his phone ran down,' she replied with a twinkle in her eye.

'I'm supposed to be the cynic in this department,' I said.

'Cynicism is just a state of mind, as an old work colleague of mine would have said.'

'Who was this philosophical old work colleague?'

'His name was Rupert Disraeli-Astor.'

'My old man plays wargames with somebody called Disraeli-Astor. Is it the same guy?'

'Most likely,' she said, but did not seem keen to discuss the matter further. 'Now can we move on?'

'Can I have another drink first?' I showed her my empty glass.

'I suppose so,' she replied reluctantly.

'Don't sound so begrudging, boss. Rewarding me with a couple of whiskies is a small price to pay for my presence at this little tête-à-tête.' I got to my feet and walked over to recharge my glass. 'What did our friends in Five and Six say about the drone strike?' I asked when I had returned to my seat.

'They were both taken as much by surprise as us.'

'Not for the first time,' I pointed out and took a sip of my whisky before asking: 'How have the Iranians reacted so far?'

'They are screaming blue murder and threatening revenge on America for what they are calling an act of state terrorism against a sovereign, peace-loving country.'

'Would that be the same peace-loving country that we believe is conspiring with Iraq and the Mafia to flood our streets with drugs?' I asked.

'Yes and the assassination of Soleimani by the Americans will make them even more determined to make the West pay.'

'Do we know why the Yanks decided to take out Soleimani?'

'Their line is that the drone strike was to prevent an imminent attack on their assets in the region.'

I took another sip of malt whisky and rolled it round in my mouth as I thought about that for a moment. 'For what it's worth, my own view is that the drone strike had something to do with Operation QS,' I said eventually.

'What makes you say that?'

'You heard about the meeting Sam called on New Year's Eve?'

'Yes, he briefed me.'

'Did he tell you there was a guy called Troy Olsen at the meeting?'

'No. Who is he?'

'He introduced himself as a military attaché at the US embassy.'

She raised an eyebrow. 'You think he is CIA?'

'Well he certainly wasn't representing the DAR[2].'

'Sam did not mention the Americans had somebody at the meeting,' she mused, swivelling on her chair, and staring out of the window as if searching for the moon, but it had been swallowed by the clouds again. 'I take it you think the CIA knows about Operation QS?' she asked eventually.

'Yeah, although Olsen was very guarded in his comments at the meeting. All he said was, and I quote: "They're gonna shaft us."'

'If the Americans know about the Iranian plan, they might have killed Soleimani because they thought he was plotting with Sabawi al-Barak to attack them too. Is that what you think?'

'That's what I think.'

'And Berry gave Soleimani's flight details to Olsen?'

'Yeah, but you make it sound as if Will slipped Olsen the information in a plain brown envelope, but it wasn't like that. He briefed us all at the same time.'

'Was that wise with an American present?'

'Berry had no reason not to brief him. After all the Yanks are supposed to be our allies.'

The D-G swivelled back to face me again. 'Only when it suits them,' she said with a frown.

'You noticed?'

'Of course. I remember the Falklands War.'

I drank the last of my Glenfiddich. I wondered if I could wangle another one. I turned my glass upside down and stood it on her desk to show it was empty.

Dame Alexandra pretended not to notice and instead said, 'Perhaps the Americans thought taking Soleimani out would wreck the Iranian plans.'

'If the Yanks believe that, they're naïve,' I replied as I turned my glass the right way up.

'Very naïve.'

'Don't they realise the Iranians will simply appoint someone to replace Soleimani and press on with their plans regardless?'

'They have already done that.'

'Really? That was quick. Do we know who it is?'

'Yes. Brigadier General Esmail Ghaani.'

'That makes sense. Ghaani was Soleimani's Number Two. But, how do you know all this?'

'Because the second message GCHQ intercepted went from Tehran to the Iraqi Ministry of Defence. It notified the Iraqis of General Ghaani's appointment and said a member of his staff was being sent to Baghdad for a meeting with Sabawi al-Barak.'

'Do we have a name for this envoy?'

'Yes. Brigadier Ali Khadem. Does that name mean anything to you?'

'No.'

She pulled a photograph from a file on her desk and handed it to me. 'That is Khadem.'

'Still means nothing.' I handed the photo back to her. 'However, if we did have any doubts about their intentions, sending Khadem to Baghdad confirms the Iranians are definitely working with the Iraqis.'

'I know, and that is very worrying. Ghaani's appointment is a clear indication, if one were needed, that the Iranian built Shiite axis poses a real problem.' She stared at me and I guessed what was coming. 'Steven, we need somebody to visit the region to find out more about what they are planning.'

'I suppose that somebody is me?'

'You did not need to be a member of Mensa[3] to work that out,' she said with a smile.

'Which is just as well.'

'Why?'

'Because if I was bright enough for Mensa, I wouldn't be sitting here contemplating a trip to some God forsaken country in the Middle East, where bad people are no doubt waiting to take pot shots at me. Instead, I'd have a proper job, and be earning a lot more than I get working for you.'

'Money isn't everything. Being employed by the SSA has other fringe benefits.'

'Like what?'

'For a start, the satisfaction of serving Queen and country.'

'I could do that by becoming a scout leader, and teach spotty kids to chant dib-dib-dib, dob-dob-dob. Anything else?'

'What about getting foreign travel at the Government's expense.'

'Are you taking the rise out of me, boss?'

'Why not, Steven? You do not have a monopoly on Mickey taking, and you know what they say: "If you cannot beat them, join them."'

'They might say that, but I don't,' I told her. 'I have a different maxim.'

'And what would that be?'

'If you can't beat them, cheat them.'

---

1   PMF: Popular Mobilization Forces.
2   DAR: Daughters of the American Revolution.
3   Mensa is a society for the top 2% of people in the world with an IQ score over 148.

6

Friday 3rd January 2020. Vauxhall Cross, London.

The headquarters of MI6 is located at 85 Albert Embankment, Vauxhall Cross. Officially known as the SIS[1] Building, it is an impressive modern ziggurat style building, perched on the south bank of the River Thames in Central London, just a few hundred yards east of Vauxhall Bridge.

The SIS Building is well protected, with reinforced concrete walls, triple glazed windows and two moats. It is a large building with a total of 60 separate roof areas; seven underground levels, the lowest of which has a connecting corridor that runs under the Thames all the way to the Foreign and Commonwealth Office in Whitehall; and eleven floors above ground.

The management offices are on the eighth floor, overlooking Vauxhall Pleasure Gardens, and the room into which I was shown had a smart white plaque on the outside of its door that read: Senior Operational Manager – Europe and Asia.

James Bannerman was standing behind a battered mahogany desk positioned in front of a wide, green-tinted window. He was a big man, with a plump face that wore a permanent sheen of perspiration, and a huge belly that forced him to wear loafers because he found it impossible to tie the laces of the brogues that otherwise would have been his preference.

We shook hands and Bannerman invited me to take a seat, then sat down in his chair, which let out a loud squeal of protest. I really felt for that chair.

I looked out of the window. Although it was well past nine o'clock in the morning, the sky was full of unshed rain and the vehicles in the rush-hour traffic heading along the Embankment had their sidelights on. The small white lights twinkled in the gloom like stars in some murky terrestrial universe.

On the wallpaper next to the window was a large dark-brown water-stain. It was round with eight thin spurs running out from its centre. I pointed at the stain as I sat down opposite Bannerman. 'That looks like a giant squashed spider,' I said.

He looked at the stain. 'We have a leak.'

'That's the problem with flat roofs.'

'The roof isn't the problem, it's the wall.' He stared at the stain thoughtfully. 'Did you know that Legoland[2] was hit by a rocket about twenty years ago?'

I nodded. I remembered the incident well. The SIS Building was attacked by members of the Real IRA, who launched a Russian-built RPG-22 missile from Vauxhall Park.

'The missile hit the window, dislodged the frame and caused a hairline crack in the wall.'

Now I saw that one of the spider's legs reached to the very edge of the window-frame and was much thicker than the rest.

'Why hasn't the crack been repaired?'

'That's a sore point,' he moaned.

'Why?'

'The Works Department sent workmen round on a number of occasions to try and repair the damage, but none of their attempts were successful and eventually they gave up.'

'How difficult can it be to repair a bloody crack?'

He shrugged. 'That's exactly what I asked the last bloke who turned up.'

'What did he say?'

'Let's just say he wasn't happy and went away in a huff, which is probably why the Works Department hasn't sent anybody round since.' He pointed at the stain. 'As you can see, water still seeps through the wall when it rains, particularly if the wind is blowing from the southwest.'

We both stared at the wall in silence for a few seconds.

'You're right,' he said eventually. 'It does look like a squashed spider.'

'I've seen worse examples of urban art,' I said.

Bannerman turned to face me again and smiled. 'So, what do you want, Steve? I don't suppose you came here to look at my wallpaper.'

'I need your help, Jimmy.'

'What sort of help?' he asked warily.

'I need to know what intelligence assets you have in Iraq.'

'You know better than to ask me to reveal that sort of classified information.'

'I thought we were on the same side.'

'Tell that to my boss. Desmond is already hacked off because the PM asked the SSA to head up Operation QS.'

'Don't blame us. We didn't go touting for the gig.'

'I'm sure you didn't, but that won't make Desmond any happier if he finds out I've been sharing classified information with you.'

'Come on, Jimmy. That makes no sense. At our meeting on New Year's Eve you gave us chapter and verse about your Iranian January 16th cell, including the code names of your agents. Wasn't that classified information?'

'Yes, and I got a right bollocking from Desmond when he

found out what Will and I did. He'll go ape-shit if he finds out I've given you information about our agents in Iraq as well.'

I shook my head in frustration. 'Look, Jimmy. I'm not asking for the names and addresses of your agents, who they've been shagging, or what colour socks they wear, I just want a feel for how many you have available in Iraq. What's the big deal?'

He considered this for a few moments then asked, 'Why do you need the information?'

I did not answer, instead I asked my own question: 'Did you hear that Qasem Soleimani was dead?'

'Yes. Why do you ask?'

'Because it's our belief the Yanks suspect the Iranians are targeting them and took out Soleimani to discourage them.'

'They're bonkers if they think killing him is going to deter Ali Khamenei,' Bannerman said with a despairing shake of his head. 'In fact, he's already promoted General Esmail Ghaani to replace Soleimani.'

'I know.'

'And do you know also that Ghaani is sending somebody to Baghdad to meet with Sabawi al-Barak?' he asked.

'Yeah. We get reports from GCHQ too. The envoy's name is Brigadier Ali Khadem.'

Bannerman nodded and looked at me thoughtfully. 'So what has this to do with our Iraqi assets, Steve.'

'Because I'm flying out to Baghdad tomorrow to find out what the Iraqis and the Iranians are up to.'

'And?'

'And I wondered if you have anyone on the ground who could provide reliable backup if I need it. Do you?'

'You'll have plenty of backup, Steve, because last month

three hundred members of the 1ˢᵗ Battalion Irish Guards were deployed in Baghdad as part of the UK's training mission, and there is another company flying out tomorrow,' he explained, neatly side-stepping my question.

'I know all about the Micks,' I said. 'I read the same briefing note as you. In fact, I'm hitching a lift on one of the C-130 Hercules aircraft taking them to Iraq, and I'll be bunking down in their officers' quarters.'

'So what's the problem, Steve? You'll have over four hundred soldiers watching your back.'

'I know that. In fact, I've already arranged for the Micks to give me an armed escort while I'm in country. But that's not the sort of backup I'm talking about, Jimmy.' I looked at him steadily for a few moments. I noticed that perspiration from his face was now dripping down onto the collar of his shirt.

'You want more?' The big man shifted uncomfortably in his chair as he spoke.

'Yeah, in addition to the military backup, I need intelligence support too. Preferably somebody local, with their ear to the ground, who can provide me with information. Do you have anybody suitable?'

Bannerman tugged thoughtfully on his heavy jowls, but said nothing.

'What's the problem, Jimmy? Don't you trust me?' I prompted.

'Of course, I trust you, Steve. It's just a difficult question to answer?'

'A difficult question? Come on, Jimmy. It's hardly University Challenge. Do you have people or not?'

'Of course we do, however, the level of our intelligence assets in Iraq is currently fluid.'

'By fluid, do you mean they're running away?'

This brought a smile from the MI6 man. 'Yes, in a manner of speaking. We have lost a lot of agents recently and currently our active assets are limited,' Bannerman admitted quietly.

'How limited is limited?' I was beginning to understand his evasiveness. He was embarrassed.

'Unfortunately, we have only a very small network left in Baghdad and to be honest, what agents we do have are...' he paused as if searching for the right word. '...unreliable,' he finished eventually.

'So basically you have a non-functioning network?'

'That's not how I would describe it,' he protested weakly.

'Of course you wouldn't. So is there nobody in country who can help me?'

Bannerman hesitated for a few seconds. I could see he was torn. He took a paper tissue from a box on his desk and wiped his face with it. 'There is one guy who would have been perfect,' he offered.

'One guy is better than none. Who is he?'

'He worked as an interpreter for the Army and doubled as one of our agents. He has a number of useful contacts in the community and we used to get a regular supply of good stuff from him, but the information completely dried up.'

'Why?'

'Immigration Service box-tickers screwed us.'

'How come?'

'Our guy became very worried about his family being targeted by radical Islamists because he worked for the British Army.'

'I don't blame him. I'd feel the same if I was in his position.'
I was beginning to understand what had happened. 'I take it
he applied for permission to move his family to the UK?'

'Yes.'

'Once again I don't blame him. It makes sense for him to
get his family out of Iraq while he still can.'

'It makes sense to him, you and me, Steve, but unfortunately,
the jobsworths in the Home Office take a different view. The
problem with the Immigration Service is it's driven by statistics
and targets. Every application they refuse, reduces the overall
immigration total and increases their success rate.'

'I take it from what you're saying, your guy's application
was refused?'

'Yes.'

'Whoever made that decision is an idiot,' I said.

'I think that's insulting idiots.'

'So what happened to him, Jimmy?'

'As you can imagine, he was pretty hacked off and refuses
to pass any more information to us until his application for
indefinite leave to remain in the UK is approved.'

'Didn't you put pressure on the Home Office to reverse the
decision?'

'Of course I did, but they wouldn't listen, which is a great
shame because the interpreter's cousin is Sabawi al-Barak's
chauffeur.'

My ears pricked up at that news. 'Was the cousin working
for you too?'

'Not directly, but for the right price he used to pass over to
our guy a lot of information about his boss, but that too has
dried up.'

'This interpreter sounds like just the person I need. Can you arrange a meeting with him and his cousin.'

'I can try, but he's unlikely to agree unless he gets permission to come to the UK.'

'In that case we'll have to get him his permit.'

'Good luck with that, Steve. I told you the Immigration Service won't listen to reason.'

'What about your boss? Couldn't he lobby the Permanent Secretary at the Home Office to talk some sense into the IS?'

'I asked Desmond to do that, but he refused to get involved.'

'Why?'

'Because he didn't want to upset Sir Philip.'

'Why would a bit of discreet lobbying upset him?'

'Desmond thinks Sir Philip might take any complaints about the Immigration Service as a criticism of him personally.'

'That's nonsense.'

'Don't tell me, tell Desmond.'

'I might well do.'

He smiled. 'I believe you might, but it won't make any difference. Desmond won't do anything because he doesn't want to be seen to rock the boat.'

'Sometimes rocking the boat is the only way to get it out of the shallows.'

'Desmond wouldn't see it that way. Sir Philip is the last person he would want to upset at the moment.'

'Why?'

'Because he's an important member of the Civil Service Appointments Board.'

'What's that got to do with anything?'

'Apparently Sir Alex is leaving later this year.'

'And?'

'And Desmond is on manoeuvres.'

'Dessie wants to become your new Chief?'

'Yes.'

'So once again ambition trumps doing the right thing?'

'Yes, and it's very frustrating.'

'Tell me about it,' I said, thinking about Sam Brewer's own promotion ambitions. 'Look, I'd still like to meet your guy. Can you give me his details?'

'Of course.'

I smiled. 'What happened to not being able to share classified information with me?'

He grinned. 'That's not an issue in this case, because technically the interpreter no longer works for us. However, be warned, the only way you'll get any information out of him, or his cousin, is by waving an ILR[3] permit in front of his nose when you meet him.'

'I'll take my chances with that. I'm one of life's optimists. Just contact him and tell him he'll get his permit. I'll do the rest.'

'Okay. I'll get you his file. It will provide you with all the information you need.' Bannerman picked up his phone and punched in a number. 'Hi, Jen. Please can you pop downstairs to Records and get me a copy of the Fraser Goran file. Yes, straight away.' He put the phone down. 'It won't be long,' he assured me.

'Thanks.'

We sat in silence for a few moments. I stared out of the window and watched as a train pulled out from Vauxhall station and slowly headed up the line towards Waterloo.

It was Bannerman who eventually broke the silence. 'By the

way, I've heard back from Luigi Campisi.'

'What did he find out?'

'Well, first off he confirmed Soleimani's visit to Venice, where he stayed in the Hotel Danieli.'

'Very nice. How the other half live, eh? What else?'

'Whilst Soleimani was in Italy he had at least one meeting with Guiseppe Navarra.'

'Did he by God? And how did Luigi discover that little nugget?'

'It seems that one of his informers works on the front desk at the Danieli and was asked to arrange transport for Soleimani.'

'Where to?'

'Treviso.'

'Does Luigi have any idea why Soleimani and Navarra met?'

'No, all his contact told him was that the taxi's destination was the Mancini Polo Club.'

'Why did they meet at a polo club?' I wondered out loud.

It was not really a question to Bannerman, but he answered anyway. 'I asked Luigi that and he told me it's probably because Navarra owns the Mancini.'

There was a tap on the door.

'Come in,' he said.

The door opened and a middle-aged woman waddled in carrying a thin buff folder. She was not as fat as Bannerman, but it was a close-run thing and in a pie eating contest she would have been a worthy opponent. She handed him the folder.

'Thanks, Jen,' Bannerman said. The woman smiled at him and left without saying a word. 'Jennifer is my secretary. She doesn't say much, but she's damned efficient.'

'Perhaps she could give my secretary a few tips about efficiency,' I said.

He laughed and handed me the folder.

I opened the file and discovered a small head and shoulders photograph of a serious looking man, who I estimated was in his early thirties. There was also a single A4 sheet of paper. It contained the man's personal details, including his date of birth. I was right about his age, he was born in June 1987, which made him thirty-two.

'Fraser is an unusual name for an Iraqi,' I said.

Bannerman pointed at the sheet of paper. 'If you read on, you'll see Goran has an unusual background. His mother's maiden name was Kathleen McNeil, who named him after his Scottish maternal grandfather.'

I quickly read Goran's short biography. 'It says here his father was an Iraqi citizen who met Kathleen McNeil at Edinburgh Medical School, where they both trained as doctors.'

'Yes.'

'But they didn't stay in Scotland?'

'No. As soon as they qualified, they married and returned to Baghdad. That's where Fraser Goran was born.'

'The report says that Goran's parents are dead. What happened to them?'

'They were murdered by Sunni extremists about nine years ago.'

'Was it a political assassination?'

He shook his head. 'Neither of them had any interest in politics. They were just doctors who wanted to make sick people well.'

'So what was the motive?'

'The Islamic extremists in Iraq don't need a motive. It was enough that Adnan was a Kurd and Kathleen was a Christian.'

'Or a translator working for the British Army.'

'Exactly. Which is why Goran is desperate to get out.'

'Okay. I'll see what I can do,' I assured him as I got to my feet and picked up the file. 'Meanwhile, I'll get out of your hair.'

'I'll see you out,' Bannerman said as he followed me to the door.

As we travelled down in the lift to the heavily guarded reception area on the ground floor, we chatted about nothing very important, which was just as well, because part of my mind was already trying to work out what purpose Soleimani might have had to visit a polo club in northern Italy to meet with a leading member of the Venetian Mafia.

Two different polo clubs had been drawn to my attention within a few days of each other. Was it a coincidence, or was there a connection? I guessed the latter, but had no idea what it might be.

1   SIS: Secret Intelligence Service.
2   Legoland is the nickname given to the SIS building by some of those who work there.
3   ILR: Indefinite leave to remain permit that gives holders the right to reside in the UK.

7

Friday 3rd January 2020. St James's, London.

When we reached St James's Street my taxi driver pulled up at the entrance to the shopping precinct. As I was paying my fare, the dark rainclouds that had been waiting impatiently to relieve themselves onto London's pavements, finally ran out of patience and began sprinkling gently on my head.

I stuffed the Goran file inside my jacket and made a dash for the jewellery shop. By the time I arrived, the rain was hammering down in earnest. The duty security guard saw me coming and opened the door before I arrived.

'Thanks, Ken,' I said as I walked in.

'My pleasure, guvnor. It's not the best day to be hanging about outside.'

'You can say that again.'

'I'd rather not. The only time I repeat things is when I've eaten a curry.' He gave a theatrical rub of his stomach and grimaced as if in pain. 'They always give me farts hot enough to strip paint from the walls.'

'So why do you eat them?'

'Because I love Vindaloos. The hotter the better.'

'Have you ever thought perhaps that's why you have a problem with piles, Ken?'

'Wow! Now why didn't my quack twig that?'

'Have you ever told him about your addiction to hot curries?'

'Not on your Nelly, guvnor. I'm frightened he'd tell me to

stop eating them.' He laughed to show he was joking. Kenneth Paine was one of life's jokers, which is why I liked him.

'Morning, Mr S,' Colin Plum said as I passed his counter.

'Morning, Plummy.'

'Don't believe a word Kenny tells you.' He nodded towards the security guard, who had returned to his post watching the door. "e's almost as much of a wind-up merchant as what you are.'

Paine heard this comment. 'I ain't gonna deny it, Plummy,' he called out. 'In fact, me and Mr Statton are taking part as a tag-team in this year's All-England-Wind-Up Competition. Ain't that right, guvnor?'

'That's right, Ken.'

'I ain't never 'eard of no wind-up competition,' Plum said suspiciously. 'Where's it 'eld then?'

'Grimsby Auditorium,' I replied as I used my pin number to open the security door.

'Why Grimsby?' Plum asked.

'Because that's where all the red herrings come from,' I said.

As I went through the door, I heard the two men laughing behind me, although I suspected Plum was just following Ken Paine's lead, and had no idea why they were laughing. He was not the sharpest chisel in the toolbox.

I headed for Dame Alexandra's office, where I found her secretary tapping away on her computer keyboard. 'Morning, Rachel,' I said.

She looked up. 'Morning, Steve.'

'Is the boss in?' I batted back the warm smile she gave me.

'Yes, I'll see if she's free.' She got up from her desk and knocked on the door that divided her office from that of the

D-G. She opened the door and stepped inside. A few seconds later she was back. 'She will see you now, Steve. However, she has a meeting at the Cabinet Office in twenty minutes, so try not to keep her too long and whatever you do, please don't upset her.'

'Do I ever?'

'Yes, given half a chance.'

I grinned at her.

'It's not funny, Steve. I know it amuses you to pull Dame Alexandra's leg, but it really annoys her.'

'Does it really?'

'Yes, and she takes it out on me when she's cross at you.'

'In that case, my beautiful child, I promise to be a good boy today.'

'I am not a child,' she scolded. 'And don't call me beautiful, it's sexist and that makes *me* cross.'

'That's why I do it, Rachel. You look irresistible when you get angry.'

'You really are incorrigible,' she said with a glare that was softened by sparkling eyes and the smile that once again twitched at her lips.

I blew her a kiss and went to the D-G's office. 'Morning, boss,' I said as I strolled in without knocking.

Dame Alexandra glanced up at her ornate wall-clock. 'It is almost noon, Steven.'

'Well spotted. Which means it is still morning.'

'That's not what I meant. I was pointing out how late you are arriving in the office. So, what time do you call this?'

'I call it almost lunchtime.'

This brought a scowl from her.

'Anyway,' I went on, 'how do you know I haven't been in my office since eight o'clock?'

'Because you are never in the office that early,' she responded tartly.

'That's true,' I conceded. 'I have always had trouble getting up in the morning.'

'You should try cutting back on the alcohol,' she said, no doubt thinking about the way I got stuck into her Glenfiddich the night before.

'That's cruel.'

'Cruelty is just a state of mind,' she said, slipping into her Rupert Disraeli-Astor mode.

'Is accusing me of being a drunken layabout just a state of mind?'

'I never did that,' she insisted.

'No, but it was what you were inferring.' I sat down on a chair in front of her desk. 'As it happens, I was at Legoland by half past nine this morning,' I added proudly.

'Why were you there?'

'Checking out a squashed spider.'

She frowned. 'What on earth are you talking about?'

'It doesn't matter.'

'It does matter, and I wish you would not talk in riddles.'

'I was there for a meeting with Bannerman.' I explained about Jimmy's water-stained wallpaper.

'I sometimes worry about you, Steven,' she said when I had finished.

'You're not alone. I worry about myself sometimes.'

She gave a resigned sigh. 'So, what did you see Bannerman about?'

'I hoped Six might have some reliable contacts I can use when I go to Iraq, but apparently their intelligence network exists in name only. However, he did give me the details of somebody who might be able to help.' I took the buff folder from under my jacket and offered it to her.

She shook her head. 'Just tell me what's in it.'

So I explained about Fraser Goran and his circumstances. 'I'm hoping to tap him up for local information.'

'I see. So, what do you want me to do?'

'It would be helpful if you could use your influence to get Goran's application for ILR approved.'

'That might be difficult.'

'Really, and there was me thinking it would be easy for you. Isn't the Home Sec a friend of yours?'

'Yes, she is, but it is not that simple, Steven. The new Government, of which she is a member, pledged to clamp down on immigration and she is under pressure to deliver on that promise.'

'Of course she is, but have you seen the number of migrants who are crossing the Channel in small boats every week? Scores of them. What's one more family in the grand scheme of things?'

'I'll see what I can do, but there might be some resistance from the Home Sec's officials.'

'Well tell your friend to point out to her damned officials that all those migrants crossing the Channel are illegals and should be sent straight back, whereas Goran not only put his life on the line for our country, but also tried to do the right thing by following the correct procedure. If his application is turned down, it will send out entirely the wrong message and encourage more people to risk their lives trying to get here in rubber dinghies. Is that what those bloody bureaucrats want?'

'Okay, okay, get off your high-horse, Steven. I said I would see what I could do, and I will. However, even if I succeed, it is highly unlikely I'll be able to get the paperwork before you fly out to Baghdad, if that's what you are after.'

'No, it's not what I'm after. I don't expect miracles, boss, even from you. All I want is an agreement in principle that Goran and his family will be able to come to this country.'

She sighed heavily. 'Very well, I will make sure Goran gets his papers, even if I have to speak to the PM himself.' She looked up at her wall-clock again and jumped to her feet. 'I have a meeting with the Cabinet Secretary,' she explained as she took an overcoat off the coat stand. 'I must fly!'

I made a show of looking around her office. 'Where's your broomstick parked?'

'Get out of here!' she shouted.

8

Friday 3rd January 2020. St James's, London.

My boss thought it was a good idea for our new team member to gain experience by shadowing me. I argued vehemently against this, but she insisted.

To make matters worse, in Dame Alexandra's eyes, shadowing me meant Harriet Barratt should be at my side every minute of the working day, sharing an office with me, and being involved with everything I did, including field work.

In my eyes, this meant my assistant would be following me round like an over-enthusiastic, wet-behind-the-ears beginner, getting in my way, and seriously restricting my ability to do my job properly.

I tried pointing out to Dame Alexandra that there was not enough room for two people in my office, which was only marginally larger than the average bathroom. It was smaller even than the adjoining office occupied by my secretary, Marion Dudley.

In the hope of adding at least the sliver of a silver lining to the dark cloud now hanging over me, I suggested my enlarged team move - lock, stock, and barrel - to one of the larger suites of offices on the top floor. She rejected this out of hand, and instead decided Harriet should share with my secretary.

Marion was not happy with this arrangement, so it came as no surprise when I sensed a strained atmosphere in the office she was being forced to share with our new team member.

Marion had managed to organise their two desks so they were as far apart as possible, with her desk close to the outer door, through which I now entered, and Harriet's on the opposite side of the room, next to the door to my office.

My cheerful 'Good afternoon,' when I reached my secretary's desk, provoked no reaction. I stopped and looked down at her. 'I'm sorry, Marion, I didn't realise you were training to be a nun.'

Marion looked up from the travel brochure she was reading. I noticed it was similar to the unsolicited one I received on New Year's Eve. She frowned. 'What do you mean?' she asked with a distracted flick of her long black hair.

'I thought maybe you had sworn a vow of silence.'

'I was busy,' she said sullenly.

'So I see.'

She pursed her full lips briefly and then said, 'I meant I was busy looking for a cut price holiday and before you ask, I'm at lunch.' She pointed at a half-eaten sandwich on her desk.

'I thought you usually took your lunch break at one o'clock?'

'She wanted to go at that time.' Marion glanced at Harriet who was typing away at her computer, pretending not to be listening to our conversation, and wearing the enigmatic smile that seemed to be her default expression.

'Couldn't you both go at the same time?'

'I would sooner not, thank you very much,' Marion said coolly. 'The tearoom gets awfully crowded at this time of day.'

'But you're not in the tearoom, you're sitting at your desk.'

'That's not the point.'

'So, what is the point, Marion?'

'Ask her!' Her frown had darkened into a scowl, which

slipped like an angry mask over her naturally pretty face.

I gave up. I knew from experience there was no point pressing her any further. Instead, I walked over to Harriet's desk. She looked up and raised an eyebrow without allowing her half-smile to waver. I indicated with a sideways movement of my head that she should come with me to my office. She stood up and followed me, before closing the door behind her.

'Take a seat.' I sat down myself and laid the Goran file on my desk. 'So, what's the problem?' I asked when she was sitting opposite me.

'I don't think Marion likes me.' She said, still smiling gently.

'Why's that?'

'You tell me. You saw her attitude.'

For some reason I felt an irrational need to defend my secretary, who was actually one of the moodiest and irritating people I knew. 'You have to understand Marion has worked here for two years and has got used to having the office all to herself.'

'Our fight had nothing to do with the office.'

'You had a fight? Not fisticuffs I hope?'

She laughed. 'Of course not. Just a little verbal spat. Handbags at ten paces, as they say on the soccer pitch.'

'What was this little spat about?'

'Marion was being a bitch.'

'In what way?'

She shrugged. 'We were chatting normally and then she turned just like that.' She clicked her fingers. 'It started when she asked me where I lived. I told her Stattons Green. She looked down her nose and said "oh".'

'Oh?'

'Yes, she made it sound as if I was living on a Gypsy site.'

'What did you say?'

'I asked her where she lived and she said a luxury apartment in Knightsbridge.'

'Knightsbridge? Are you sure?'

'That's what she said.'

'That's odd. I thought she had a bedsit near King's Cross Station.'

'Yes, she told me about her bedsit, but apparently she moved out of it last year.'

I was surprised at this news, particularly the location of Marion's new home. 'Apartments of any description in Knightsbridge don't come cheap, let alone luxury ones,' I pointed out.

'I know.'

'How can she afford to rent somewhere like that on her salary?'

'She doesn't have to pay rent. Apparently, the apartment is owned by what she called her "sugar daddy".'

'I take it we're not talking here about her father buying her bags of Tate and Lyle?'

'No,' she said with a laugh. 'She was talking about her boyfriend, who she openly admitted is a married man. Apparently he lets her stay in the apartment free of charge, so he can see her whenever he wants.'

'I assume you mean sleeping with her whenever he wants.'

'I don't think there's much sleeping involved.'

'And Marion told you all this?'

'Oh, yes. In fact, she sounded quite proud of being a kept woman.'

'How did you react? Did you criticise her?'

'Certainly not. How she lives her life is none of my business. However, I obviously didn't react the way she wanted because that's when she turned nasty.'

'In what way?'

'She said, "I don't suppose you even have a boyfriend", in a really bitchy tone. I told her I didn't, which is the truth by the way. She then asked me if it was because I was a lesbian. Well, that really got my back up and I had a go at her.'

'What did you say?'

'Mind your own bloody business.'

'I'm sorry, I didn't mean to pry.'

'No, that's what I told Marion.'

'I know. I was just being facetious.'

'Oh! I see.'

'So, what was her response to being told that?'

'Well, she made matters worse by accusing me of having a relationship with Dame Alexandra, who she called "that old dyke".'

'What did you say to that?'

'I told her I would much prefer an old dyke, to a young tart who opens her legs for a man in exchange for a month's rent.'

'Ouch! You don't pull any punches, do you?'

'I can stand up for myself when it's necessary, and on this occasion I deemed it necessary.'

'You don't have to apologise.'

'I didn't realise I was apologising.'

'It sounded like an apology to me.'

She gave me one of her raised eyebrows. 'Why would I have to apologise to you?' She asked deadpan.

'That's not what I meant.'

'I know. I was just being facetious.' She grinned.

'Touché!' I said.

'So, what do you think?' she asked.

'I think you and I are going to get along just fine.'

'Me too,' she agreed, then changed the subject. 'So what did you see Dame Alexandra about?'

'News travels fast in this building.'

'Not really, I just happened to speak to Rachel.'

'Which Rachel?' I queried.

'Dame Alex's secretary. I rang whilst you were in with her.'

'You know the boss's secretary?'

'Oh yes. I've known her some time,' she replied, but did not expand. 'You didn't answer my question. Why did you see Dame Alex?'

'I wanted to discuss my trip to Iraq. I'm flying out tomorrow to see if I can find out what's going on in the region and Jimmy Bannerman is arranging for me to meet this guy,' I tapped the file.

'I don't have X-ray eyes. What's his name?'

I told her and then quickly briefed her on my meetings with both Bannerman and the D-G.

'And you think this Fraser Goran can help you?'

I shrugged. 'I hope so.'

'Am I coming to Iraq with you?'

I shook my head.

'But I'm supposed to be shadowing you.'

'I know, but on this occasion it isn't possible.'

'Is it because Iraq is dangerous? If so, you don't have to worry about me. I'm a big girl now.'

'Iraq is certainly a very dangerous place, particularly where

I'm going, but that's not the reason you can't come with me.'

'Why then?'

'It's because there are no spare seats on the military aircraft.' She accepted this lie without argument, but did not look happy about my decision.

'Okay, but be warned, I won't accept that excuse again. Next time you have an overseas assignment I'll expect to come with you.'

'It's a deal,' I agreed, confident I could come up with a different excuse, if and when necessary. 'Now, whilst I'm away I have a job for you.'

News of a task seemed to perk her up 'What is it?'

I stood up and recovered my briefcase from the top drawer of my filing cabinet, where it had been deposited three days before. I returned to my desk, opened the briefcase, and took the envelope and tweezers from it. I then used the tweezers to carefully pull the newspaper page from the envelope and unfold it. I showed Harriet the article about the stolen horse.

She was about to pick up the newspaper when I stopped her just in time. I held up the tweezers. 'Why do you think I used these?'

At first she looked at me blankly until finally the penny dropped. 'So as not to put your fingerprints on the paper?'

'Well, I wasn't using them to practice my chop-stick technique.'

'Sorry,' she said as her cheeks went pink with embarrassment.

'Don't worry, there's no harm done, but just read the high-lighted article without touching the paper.'

'So what do you want me to do?' she asked when she finished reading the article.

'I want you to find out more about the story. Start by contacting the local police in Surrey to see what they can tell you about the missing horse. They might have information they didn't reveal to the newspaper. Then check out the Grange Polo Club and see what you can find out about its management.'

'Okay, I'll get straight onto it.'

'Good, but first I want you to get the newspaper back into the envelope using these.' I handed the tweezers to her. 'Then pop down to our laboratory, which is next to the wine-cellar, and ask Annie Francis to dust the newspaper for fingerprints.'

'What about the envelope?'

I shook my head. 'Not worth it, too many people will have handled it, including the postman and me.'

I watched as she deftly folded the newspaper with the twee-zers. She was much quicker than me. I suppose it was a woman thing. Within seconds the cutting was back inside the envelope. She headed for the door, but stopped before she reached it. She turned round. 'I *am* sorry, Steve. I'll try not to make any silly mistakes like that again.'

'You don't need to apologise, Harriet. Just put it down to the learning process and remember two very important things.'

'What are they?'

'Firstly, a field agent who makes a mistake, can very quickly end up as a dead field agent.'

'I understand.' She considered me solemnly. 'You mentioned two important things. What's the second one to remember?'

'It's that everybody makes mistakes, but they can be forgiven. However, what is unforgiveable is when people don't learn from those mistakes.'

'Don't worry, I'll learn,' she assured me as she turned and

pulled open the door.

I believed her. 'Oh, and Harriet,' I called her back. 'Thinking about the envelope again, ask Annie to steam open its flap and carry out a DNA test on the glued section.'

'Will do,' she said.

As soon as Harriet left my office, closing the door behind her, I picked up my phone and called the Briggens Factory.

This was the nickname given to the SSA's small in-house document section, and took its name from Briggens House, which was used as the base for the British forgery team that was recruited during the Second World War.

Carl Pulsac ran the section with a small team of expert forgers, and, like his wartime counterparts, he could produce everything from a well-used Israeli passport to a Kazakhstani 10,000 tenge note.

I just hoped Pulsac knew what an indefinite leave to remain permit looked like, because I had no idea.

9

Tuesday 7th January 2020: Fallujah, Iraq.

The Iraqi city of Fallujah is bordered in the west by the Euphrates River and in the east by Freeway 1, a four-lane motorway that runs from the country's southern border with Kuwait, to its western border with Jordan. On the outskirts of the city this major motorway interchanges with Highway 10, which is the old road from Baghdad to Ramadi.

Fallujah is known as the City of Mosques, because of the 200 masjids that can be found there. As we drove off Highway 10 and made our way along a series of residential streets, I could see a host of minarets and towers dotted across the sprawling city, rising high over the low, typically Middle Eastern, mud brick homes.

Many of the sand-coloured buildings still bore battle scars from 2016, when Iraqi forces used mortar shells to liberate the city from the control of ISIL[1].

Four years later and Fallujah was still a very dangerous place in which to live, work and play. In fact, for a city with so many mosques, it was an unholy hellhole.

The city was home to a mainly Sunni community, with several militant militia groups waging a guerrilla war against those supporters of the Shia dominated government who remained.

Strangers were not welcome in Fallujah, particularly visitors who were not Iraqis - whatever their religion - and outsiders were wise to not visit unless they had an armed escort. That is why I was now travelling through the eastern suburbs of the city in the cab of a Foxhound armoured vehicle, accompanied by a section of Irish Guards, who were dressed in combat uniforms and carried reassuringly lethal looking L85A3 assault rifles.

Iraq in January is cold, bloody cold, so I wore a pair of fleece-lined trousers, a thick denim shirt, my old M4 Russian winter jacket, and a pair of hiking boots. Tucked into the inside pocket of my jacket was Fraser Goran's file and my Glock 17. The pistol was not as large as an assault rifle, but it could be just as lethal and felt just as reassuring.

'This is it, Sarge,' I told the Micks' section leader, who was driving the Foxhound. I pointed to a house at the end of the road, just behind the Hussein Bin Ali Mosque.

The sergeant parked so the rear of the armoured car was level with the front door of the house, then jumped down from the cab. Seconds later I heard the doors of the Foxhound clang open. My army escort clambered out and I watched out of the side window as they deployed in a well-practiced defensive formation in front of the house.

When the section leader gave me an all-clear thumbs up, I climbed down from the cab and walked quickly between the two rows of soldiers to the house. I knocked on the front door, which was opened immediately by Fraser Goran. He was expecting me.

'Welcome to my home, Mr Statton. I hope you had a safe journey from Baghdad,' the interpreter said in flawless English as he shook my hand. Goran had a firm, dry grip, which I liked. He had piercing blue eyes and was almost a foot taller than most Iraqi men, whose average height is an inch or two over five feet. He probably inherited both those characteristics from his mother's side of the family.

'Very safe. As you can see, I was well protected.' I nodded towards my Irish Guard escort.

'You are very lucky. Many of my countrymen have not been so fortunate.' He invited me into his house with a wave of his hand.

I stepped inside and Goran closed the door behind us. He led me down a dark corridor to a room containing a simple wooden table surrounded by half a dozen chairs.

The only other furniture in the room was a glass fronted bookcase and a much smaller table, standing against a side wall, which was covered by an intricately embroidered lace runner. On the table stood an ornate orthodox cross, a battered bible, two small candles and a string of prayer beads. Hanging on the wall above the table was a painting of Jesus standing with his arms outstretched, inviting into his arms those who need his help.

As we entered the room, a woman wearing a black hijab shepherded a small boy and girl out of a side door. The little girl stopped at the door and looked back at me with wide brown eyes. She smiled shyly before the woman, who I assumed was her mother, took her hand and eased her out of the door after her brother. The woman gave an apologetic shrug then followed the children silently out of the door.

'Please take a seat, Mr Statton,' Goran said.

Already sitting on one of the chairs at the table was a skinny man with a well-groomed short beard, who wore a Ralph Lauren shirt, opened at the neck to reveal a chunky gold necklace; and Ray-Ban sunglasses pushed on top of his head, where they lay across his slicked-back hair like an Alice band.

'This my cousin, Jamal Abbas,' Goran introduced the skinny man. 'He works for the Government.'

I offered my hand to Abbas, but he looked away and pretended not to see it.

Goran said something to him quietly in Kurdish. I had no idea what he said, but whatever it was, changed his cousin's mind for him. He shook my hand with a sullen expression on his face. Unlike Goran's handshake, Abbas' grip was the limp, damp type that makes you want to wipe your hand afterwards. He said nothing and looked away again.

'Was that your children I saw just now?' I asked Goran, pointing towards the side door.

'Yes.'

'Your daughter is very pretty.'

'Yes, she takes after her mother,' he said proudly.

'Was that your wife with the children?'

'Yes. Why do you ask?'

'Because I was surprised she was wearing a hijab.' I took out Goran's file and put in on the table. 'Your file says you are both Christian.' I tapped the buff folder.

'Yes, as you can see for yourself.' He pointed towards the painting of Jesus.

'Was that your mother's influence?'

Goran shook his head. 'No. Although my mother was a practicing Catholic, she never tried to influence me, nor did my father. Indeed, from an early age they told me it was my decision which religion I followed, if any.'

'And you chose Christianity?'

'Yes, but I was never as devout as my mother.'

'What about your wife? Does she come from a Christian

family?' I asked the question because there are very few Christians living in Iraq, and most of those that remain tend to live in Kurdish controlled areas.

'No, she was raised as a Muslim and it was only when we married that she converted to Christianity, which, by the way, was very much her decision and not mine. In fact, I tried to dissuade her.'

'Why did you do that?'

'Because her life will be in real danger if the militant Islamists who murdered my parents discover she has abandoned their religion.'

'I thought apostasy was legal in Iraq.'

'In theory. Although our constitution recognises Islam as Iraq's official religion, it also guarantees religious freedom for the followers of other faiths. The Government does its best to uphold that guarantee, but some Islamist fanatics, particularly the Sunni extremists who hold sway here in Fallujah, ignore the constitution and persecute Moslems who convert to another religion. That is why I want to keep my wife's conversion to Christianity a secret.'

'I understand.'

'I appreciate your understanding, Mr Statton, but under-standing sadly does not help our situation,' Goran said softly. There was no recrimination in his voice, but his torment was clear. 'My wife hates being forced to dress like a loyal Islamic wife, just to hide her Christianity. So, what would make me even more appreciative, is if you have brought with you a docu-ment permitting us to live in England. Do you have such a permit?'

It was mid-afternoon and the sun was slowly sinking in

the western sky, sending rays through the room's single large window, washing us in a warm yellow glow across.

Across the road I could hear the muezzin calling worshippers to prayer from his position high up on the minaret of the Hussein Bin Ali Mosque.

I was about to open my folder when the door opened, and Goran's wife came back into the room carrying a tray on which was a pot of steaming coffee, cups, cream, and sugar. She put the tray on the table and poured strong, dark coffee into three cups.

'This is my wife, Kathleen.'

'Wasn't that your mother's name?'

'Yes. My wife was given the name Karimah when she was born, but, in honour of my mother, she changed it when she was christened.'

Kathleen Goran passed one of the cups to me and then laid her hand gently on her husband's shoulder, in a gesture of affection that no Moslem woman would ever dare show in front of other men.

She looked at me expectantly and showed no sign she intended to leave the room, so I opened the folder and took out an oblong of paper.

'You asked me a question earlier,' I said.

'Yes,' Goran replied.

I slid the document across the table to him. 'That is my answer.'

He picked up the paper and stared at it intently. He looked up, smiled, and passed the document to his wife, who almost snatched it from his hand.

'Family, Goran,' she read aloud, tracing the words with her

finger as she spoke. 'Indefinite leave to remain.' She looked at her husband with tears in her eyes. 'We are going to England, Fraser,' she whispered before turning to Goran's cousin. 'Look, Jamal,' she said, excitedly showing him the permit.

Abbas nodded, but only gave the document a cursory glance and the sullen look on his face deepened noticeably.

'Thank you for keeping your word and arranging our permit, Mr Statton,' Goran said with a smile. 'Now, it is my turn to keep my word. When we spoke on the phone you mentioned something about needing information. How can I help you?'

'It's actually your cousin who might be able to help me, that's why I asked you to invite him to this meeting.'

'How can Jamal help you?'

'I understand he's a driver for Sabawi al-Barak.'

Abbas answered for himself. 'I am not a driver,' he snapped. 'I am the chauffeur to Mr al-Barak.'

To me they were the same thing, but I let it go. Obviously the difference was important to him. 'I have been informed that Brigadier Ali Khadem visited Baghdad to meet your boss. Is that true?'

Abbas hesitated for a few moments and then said, 'This is so.'

'Have you any idea what that meeting was about?' I asked.

'Yes,' was all he said.

'Are you able to tell me what it was?' The man's attitude was beginning to irritate me, but I forced myself to keep my voice neutral.

'That depends.'

'On what?'

'On how badly you want the information.'

'Are you going to tell me or not?' I asked, finally letting my feelings show. The Gorans looked very uncomfortable during this exchange, but neither said anything.

'As I said, Mr Statton. That depends on how badly you want to know why Brigadier Khadem visited Iraq.' Abbas paused and then added: 'You are an intelligent man. I am sure you can work out what I want.'

He was right. It was easy. I knew exactly what he wanted and had come prepared. 'How much do you want for the information?'

'I appreciate straight talking, Mr Statton,' Abbas said and then gave a brief insolent smile that was just wide enough to show me a set of nicotine-stained teeth.

'That's just as well. Because with me it's either straight talking, or no talking. So, I'll ask you again. How much?'

Abbas shrugged and still refused to make eye contact with me. 'You must understand that passing on such sensitive information is very risky and would lead to much trouble for me if I was caught.'

'I believe you have taken such risks before, have you not?'

'That is so, but only because your colleagues in MI6 always made those risks worthwhile.'

'How much?' I repeated.

'MI6 were always very generous.'

'How generous?'

'One thousand US dollars paid into my Swiss bank account.'

'Such an amount is not a problem.'

This seemed to perk him up and he actually looked at me, but only long enough to say: 'Excellent, then we have a deal, Mr Statton. Yes?'

'Possibly, but first I would like a flavour of what I'm buying.'

'That is reasonable,' he agreed.

'I know. So, what do you have?'

'For the past two days, Mr al-Barak and Brigadier Khadem have been out of the country.'

'Do you know where?'

'Of course. I drove them there and back.'

I waited expectantly, but Abbas did not elaborate, he simply stared at his fingernails. I got the message. I took out my iPhone and logged into the special SSA bank account to which I had access.

'What's your bank swift code and account number?' I asked.

He looked up and gave me the details.

It took me only seconds to arrange for the money to be transferred to his account. 'Done.'

Abbas took out his own phone and tapped in his password. Twenty seconds later he looked up and gave me another of his insolent smiles. 'The money has arrived,' he confirmed, but offered no thanks.

'So, talk. Where did you take your passengers?'

'Afghanistan.'

'You drove them from Iraq to Afghanistan?' I asked doubtfully.

'Yes.'

'That's not possible. It's at least a thirty-six-hour journey there, and the same back.'

'Not if you use a transport aircraft,' he retorted smugly.

'You flew to Afghanistan?'

'Yes, I drove Mr al-Barak and Brigadier Khadem to Baghdad Airport, where our car was loaded onto a Hercules C-130. It then took just under three hours to fly to Kabul. We returned the same way when their business was concluded.'

'I didn't know the Iraqis had C-130s.'

'The Hercules did not belong to my country. We cannot afford such expensive aircraft. Brigadier Khadem arranged for us to borrow one from the Iranian Air Force.'

'But why didn't your boss and Khadem just fly to Afghanistan in a passenger plane, and then pick up a car and driver at Kabul airport?'

'Mr al-Barak has a very special car. It is armour-plated with bullet-proof glass windows. He is always at risk of potential attacks so insists on using the car wherever he goes,' he explained, then added proudly: 'And when he is in his car, he trusts no other chauffeur but me to drive him.'

'So, where did you drive al-Barak's very special car when you arrived in Afghanistan?'

'To Charikar.'

I nodded. The town was about 30 miles due north of Kabul. 'What were they doing in Charikar?'

'They were visiting a farmer.'

'Do you know the farmer's name?'

'Of course, I made a note of it.' Abbas pulled a small notebook from his pocket, opened it, and flicked through the pages. He found what he was looking for. 'His name was Jalaluddin Haqqani.'

'Do you know why they visited this farmer?' I did not mention I knew of Haqqani's involvement in the production of heroin.

'Yes. Mr al-Barak and the brigadier stayed overnight with Mr Haqqani, and the next day I drove all three to a Buzkashi[2] match in Baghlan. Whilst at the match they had a meeting with a horse breeder called,' Abbas referred to his notebook again, 'Azad Nuristani.'

I took a pen from my pocket and made a note of the name on the inside cover of the folder and that of Haqqani.

'Has al-Barak met this Nuristani before?'

Abbas shrugged. 'That I cannot say. All I know is that I have never driven him to meet the man before.'

'Then how do you know his name?'

'Because Mr Nuristani's car was parked next to me at the Buzkashi match. His chauffeur told me.'

This puzzled me. 'You spoke with the driver?'

'Yes.'

'Was he an Iraqi?'

'No, Afghan.'

'Then how did you communicate? Do you speak Pashto?'

'No, a little Dari, but not enough to hold a proper conversation. We spoke in English.'

'The driver spoke English?'

'Yes, with an American accent.'

This was an interesting development. 'Did you get his name?'

'Of course,' he looked at his notebook again. 'It was Yamin Abdullah.'

I opened the folder again and added the driver's name to the other two. Whoever Azad Nuristani was, he must be somebody of substance to have his own chauffeur.

'Did this Abdullah tell you anything about his boss?'

'Not much, he just told me Mr Nuristani breeds horses that are used for Buzkashi. It is a business that has brought him much wealth.'

'I see. Did the driver have any idea why Nuristani was meeting with al-Barak and Khadem?'

'No, only that their visit to the Buzkashi match was arranged over two weeks ago.'

I considered this news. It meant al-Barak's visit to Afghanistan was arranged before Qasem Soleimani was killed, which suggested to me that the visit was organised at their meeting in Tehran.

'Do you have anything else for me?'

'Yes. A photograph of Abdullah and Mr Nuristani.' He pulled his iPhone from his pocket and showed me the photograph.

'How…?' I started but he pre-empted my question.

'I took the photo when they were not looking. Do not be alarmed, they did not notice.'

'Can you Airdrop me a copy?'

'Of course.'

I took my iPhone out and set it to receive the photograph.

Abbas punched a couple of keys on his own phone. 'It should be there now.'

I checked and found the photo had arrived. It showed two men, one was short and wore traditional Afghan clothes, including a lungee, who was just about to climb into the back of a Mercedes car. The second was a much taller and bigger man, with wide shoulders and a bushy beard. He was wearing a tight chauffeur's uniform, which accentuated his muscular frame, and was holding the car door open for his boss.

'Thanks. Do you have anything else for me?'

He shook his head and stood up. 'I must go,' he said as he put the notebook back in his pocket. He did not offer me his hand, which was no loss to me.

'I would very much like more information on Nuristani and

his driver if you can get hold of it,' I told him.

'I'll see what I can find out. For the same fee, of course.'

'Of course.'

'I'm sorry about my cousin,' Fraser Goran apologised when Abbas had left the room. 'Jamal can be difficult when he is unhappy.'

'Why is he unhappy?'

It was his wife who answered. 'Because we are going to England and leaving him behind,' she said sadly.

'You mean he wanted to come with you?'

'Yes, but that was not possible,' Goran explained. 'As you know, it was difficult enough getting permission for my direct family to seek refuge in your country. If we had added my cousin to our application I think it would have been turned down flat. Is that not so?'

'Yes,' I replied honestly.

'So how quickly can you get us out, Mr Statton?' Kathleen Goran asked quietly, still clutching the permit to her bosom as if worried I would snatch it back.

'I'm not sure,' I replied as I got to my feet and picked up the file. 'But I promise it will be as soon as possible, Mrs Goran.'

'Thank you, Mr Statton. I know you won't let us down,' the woman said with tears of joy in her eyes and a grateful smile on her lips.

I smiled back and prayed her faith in me was not misplaced.

'I'll show you out,' Fraser Goran said and walked me to the front door where we said our goodbyes.

As the Foxhound headed back to the army base, I sent Harriet an email and attached the photograph of Nuristani and Abdullah. I was not confident I would get much more information from Abbas, so I asked her to find out what she could about the two men.

For the rest of the journey I sat looking out of the armoured vehicle's window at the war-scarred buildings and thought about the promise I had just made to Goran's wife. I just hoped Dame Alexandra had managed to persuade the Home Office to issue an official ILR permit to replace the forgery that was currently being held close to Kathleen Goran's heart.

I thought also about something else that was puzzling me.

'Have you served in Afghanistan, Sarge,' I asked the driver.

'Yes, sir. I had three tours of duty there.'

'So, you know the country pretty well?'

'Too bloody well, sir. I lost some good friends in that shithole, begging your pardon for my language, sir.'

'You're pardoned. Do you know what Buzkashi is?'

'Yes, sir. It's really big in Afghanistan. It's their national sport and attracts thousands of people to the matches.'

'But what the hell is it?'

The sergeant explained how the game was played and then paused as he gave a long blast on the Foxhound's horn to warn off a group of children who were kicking a football round in the road. As one, the boys gave us the finger. The sergeant returned the gesture and then added: 'Basically, Buzkashi is just a barbaric form of polo, sir.'

That's exactly what it sounded like to me, and it worried the hell out of me. In my book, it was one polo connected coincidence too many.

1   ISIL: Islamic State of Iraq and the Levant.
2   Buzkashi, which literally means "goat pulling" in Persian, is a Central Asian sport in which horse-mounted players attempt to lift from the ground a goat or calf carcass and place it in a goal area.

10

Thursday morning was wet and windy and when I arrived in my secretary's office, water was dripping from my raincoat and the lenses of my spectacles had steamed up. It felt as if I was looking through the window of a sauna. Despite my poor visibility, I could see the chair behind Marion's desk was empty.

'Good morning, Steve,' Harriet said cheerfully from behind her own desk, where she was tapping away on her computer keyboard.

I removed my spectacles and took a tissue from the box standing on Marion's desk. I wiped the lenses dry and put my glasses back on. I could see Harriet now. As usual she looked immaculate. 'Why aren't you wet?' I asked.

'Because it wasn't raining when I came in.'

'But it's been raining for over an hour. What time did you get in?'

'Half past seven.'

'Why so early?'

'I wanted to get the report finished for you.'

'Which report?'

'My report into the missing horse.'

I had forgotten the newspaper article I gave her to research while I was in Iraq. 'Good work. I was about to ask you about that,' I lied, then added hurriedly: 'Where's Marion?'

'She rang in sick.'

'What's wrong with her?'

'She fell down the steps leading to her flat last night and had to go to hospital. She was in the A&E Department until the early hours of this morning.'

'Was she badly injured?'

'She broke a couple of fingers and bruised her face badly, but she's back home now.'

'When will she be back?'

'She's not sure. She's been signed off for a week, but it could be longer. She can't use a keyboard with broken fingers.'

'I suppose not. So now you have the office to yourself,' I stated the obvious.

'Yeah.'

'You must be delighted about that.'

'Why?'

'Because the last time I was here the pair of you were at loggerheads.'

'Oh, that was nothing.'

'It didn't sound like nothing. I thought World War Three was about to break out.'

She laughed. 'You do exaggerate, Steve. Don't worry, Marion and I are cool.'

'Cool is it? So when was the Armistice declared?'

'Monday morning.'

'What happened?'

'I apologised, she apologised, and then we kissed and made up.' She smiled. 'Not literally, of course.'

'Of course not.'

'I thought I might get Marion a Get-Well-Soon card and send it from both of us. What do you think?'

'That's a good idea.'

'In that case I'll pop out at lunchtime and get one. If I post it first class straight away, with a bit of luck she'll get it in the morning.'

'Okay, but I'll pay.' I took a ten-pound note from my wallet and handed it to her. 'Do you know her new address?'

'No, only that it's somewhere in Knightsbridge.'

'So where will you send the card?'

'I'll get her address from the HR Department.' The printer on her desk suddenly sprang into life and seconds later two sheets of A4 paper slid silently from its front chute. Harriet passed them to me. 'My report.'

I laid the sheets on her desk without looking at them, then went behind Marion's desk, wheeled her chair out and positioned it in front of Harriet.

'Did you find out anything about the photograph I sent you from Iraq?' I asked as I sat down.

'Yes. I got Six to run it through their database and they came up with a match straight away.'

'That was quick.'

'It was easy really because the Six database utilises the same NeoFace Live Facial Recognition technology as the Metropolitan Police.'

'Bully for Six.'

'You sound envious.'

'I am. That NEC software costs an arm and a leg. We never get such largesse showered on us. We're lucky to get a finger or a toe. The bean counters in the Cabinet Office complain if we order too many paper clips.'

'We don't have paper clips in the office. We use staples.'

'Exactly. That's because they're cheaper.'

She laughed. 'You really are an awful liar, Steve.'

'I know. So when did you become an expert on face recognition technology?'

'A very helpful young Six analyst called Darryl told me all about it.'

'So what did he come up with?'

'Darryl is a girl,' she said as she pulled a photograph from her desk drawer and handed it to me.

I looked at the head and shoulders photograph and recognised the man immediately. 'That's Yamin Abdullah.'

She shook her head. 'No, that's Sean MacDonald.'

'MacDonald, huh? Is he CIA?'

'No, he's tagged as a Canadian Security Intelligence Service agent. What made you think he was a Yank?'

I told her about meeting Goran and my conversation with his cousin, who told me Azad Nuristani's chauffeur had an American accent.

'I don't blame Abbas thinking that. It's easy to mistake a Canadian for somebody from south of the 49th parallel.'

'You'd best not tell a Canadian that.' I slipped the photo of MacDonald into my pocket. 'Good work, by the way,' I told her and picked up the report.

She looked at me expectantly.

I glanced at the first page. 'It's very professionally set out.'

'Thank you.'

'No doubt it's up to the high standard expected by FCO mandarins.'

She viewed me with suspicious eyes. 'Where's this leading? You don't seem entirely happy with my work?'

'I'm sure your work is fine.'

'But?'

I smiled. 'But I prefer verbal reports.'

'Oh.' She looked crestfallen.

'Don't take it to heart. Your report will make an excellent addition to the Section's file on horse rustling.' I handed the two sheets of paper back to her.

'Okay, where will I find the file?'

'There isn't a file at the moment, but I'm sure you can open a new one.'

She shook her head ruefully and put the report in her desk drawer.

'Now, what did you find out about the missing horse?' I asked.

She shrugged. 'Not much.'

'I'll be the judge of that. Tell me what you know, and let me decide.'

'Well the horse definitely came from Italy, as was stated in the newspaper article.'

'How can you be so sure?'

'Because I managed to track down the import document used to get the horse into the UK and it provided some other interesting information that wasn't mentioned in the article.'

'Which was?'

'The Italian horse dealer who sold the horse lives in Venice.' She gave me another expectant look.

'I don't want to rain on your parade, but that's hardly a surprise given that Venice is in Italy. It would have been more of a shock if you'd discovered he lived in Timbuktu.'

'But didn't you say Soleimani visited Venice a couple of days before he died?'

'Yeah.'

'Well don't you think that's significant?'

'Maybe,' I said cautiously. I was giving nothing away.

'Only "maybe"?'

I shrugged.

'But you said Soleimani had at least one meeting with the Mafia guy at the Mancini Polo Club in Treviso,' she pointed out.

I nodded. Despite my earlier reaction, I had already made that link.

'And polo clubs keep horses,' she persisted.

'They do.'

'Of course, it could just be a coincidence.'

'Yes,' I agreed, although I was certain it was no coincidence.

Harriet gave me a look that told me she thought the same. She was smart that girl. Very smart. 'I've never heard of Treviso,' she said. 'Where is it?'

'About Forty kilometres north of Venice,' I said.

'Some distance then?'

'Distance is only relative to the time it takes to travel from point A to point B. For instance, you can get from Venice to Treviso by road quicker than you can get from Whitehall to Stattons Green, which is only half the distance.'

'I see what you mean,' she said with a laugh. 'Getting out of Central London is a nightmare at any time of the day.'

I mulled over what she had told me. 'Do you know the name of this Italian horse dealer?'

'Yes, it was on the import document. His name is Mario Tafuri.'

'What about his address?'

'He lives in Calle del Paradiso.'

'You sound very knowledgeable. Have you ever been to Venice?'

She shook her head. 'No, the name was on the document and it stuck in my mind because it sounded so romantic.' She gave me a wistful look. 'What about you? Have you been to Venice?'

'Yeah.'

'I bet it's lovely.'

'That's not how I would describe it.'

'Why not? I thought it had lots of historic buildings, interesting shops, good food, wonderful wine, and canals full of gondolas.'

'Don't be misled by all the promotional guff pumped out by travel agents. The buildings are run down, the shops all stock the same tourist tat, the food is indifferent, the wine is expensive, the canals stink, and what you pay to ride in a gondola would feed the average Italian family for a week.'

'They told me you were a cynic and its true.'

'Cynicism is just a state of mind.'

She looked puzzled. 'What does that mean?'

'I have no idea. Ask your mate Dame Alexandra. It's what she told me. Now, did you find out anything else of interest?'

Harriet nodded and, as her head moved, hair fell across her face in a blonde cascade. She pushed it back behind her ears in an automatic, casual movement that made her look even younger. 'Yes, for a start the Grange didn't lose out financially, because they were insured against the loss, or death of the horse whilst in transit. I contacted the insurance company and they told me the settlement amount was over one hundred thousand pounds.'

'How did you find out the name of their insurance company? Did you contact the Grange?'

'No, Surrey Police gave me the information. I guessed the insurers wouldn't pay anything out without first investigating the claim and to do that they would have contacted the police. I was right.'

'And how did you get the insurance company to provide you with the information? What about the Data Protection Act?'

She smiled. 'I told them I was Detective Inspector Barratt from Scotland Yard following up on the case.'

'And they believed you?'

'Yes.'

'I'm surprised. You could have been anybody ringing them.'

'I didn't ring them. I visited their office in the City and showed them my Met Police warrant card.'

'I didn't know you had a warrant card.'

'I don't. It's a forgery.'

'That's my trick.'

'I know, and a good trick it is too. It works a treat.'

'Where did you get it done?'

'The Briggens Factory.'

'You found Pulsac?'

'Yeah. You seem surprised.'

'I am. We don't go out of our way to publicise the services Carl offers. How did you find out about him?'

'I asked Rachel Frewin where I could get a warrant card made and she told me about the Briggens Factory. Did I do wrong to involve her?' She looked worried.

'No, far from it. It showed initiative. You were right to ask Rachel because she knows everything about everything in the department. I'm impressed, well done.'

'Thank you,' she gave me an appreciative smile.

'Did the insurance company come up with anything else of interest?'

'Oh, yes.'

'What?'

'It seems this was not the first theft of a horse on route to the Grange. Two more horses have been stolen in the last few months in similar circumstances.'

'Did the insurance company stump up for all three losses?'

'Yes.'

'I bet they weren't happy about that.'

'No, but they made themselves slightly happier by bumping up the Grange's insurance premium.'

'How do you know that?'

'Because Judy told me.'

'Who the hell is Judy?'

'The girl I spoke to at the insurance company. When I got her talking she wouldn't stop. She told me everything I wanted to know and even more that I didn't.'

'So, since her company settled the claims, I assume none of the horses has ever been traced?'

'No, they simply disappeared from the face of the earth.'

I thought about that for a few moments. Instinct told me this information was relevant, but it did not tell me how or why. 'Do you have anything else for me?'

'Yes. I've left the best till last.'

'I hope you're right,' I said, then realised that I sounded like

131

an ungrateful curmudgeon, but she did not take umbrage. I was to find out this was one of her strengths.

'I've done some research into the Grange Polo Club.'

'And what did you find?'

'Quite a bit. It's a private members' club situated on the outskirts of a small village in the middle of Surrey Hills, where the annual membership fees would pay my mortgage for a year. However, you can't just join the club, you have to be invited by two existing members to submit an application.'

'So, it's a posh club, for posh people, in a posh part of Surrey.'

'Not everyone involved with the club is posh,' she said with a knowing smile.

'Go on,' I prompted her.

'I ran a check at Companies House. The club is a limited company with only five directors, all of whom have lengthy entries in Who's Who. One is a Member of Parliament, two are major players in the City of London, one is a Russian oligarch who made his money in oil exploration, and the final director is a minor member of the Royal Family.'

'You mean they are posh and influential people?'

'Yes, and apparently highly respectable.'

'So, what's so interesting about them?'

'Nothing, and that's the point.'

'You've lost me.'

'I think most of the directors are there as a cover.'

'Go on.'

'Well, I checked also people linked to the company with a significant controlling interest. There are three shareholders, two of whom own fifteen percent of the shares each. One of them is the MP and the other is the Russian. The rest of the shares are owned by a single person.' She paused and looked at me in a way that expected me to guess the person's identity.

'Give me a clue.'

'He lives in Routh Road.'

'That's not much of a clue. I've never heard of it.'

'It's ranked at number one in the thirty most expensive roads in Wandsworth.'

'That's probably why I don't know it. So, who is this mystery man?'

'Tommy Cassidy.'

'You mean the Balham Butcher?'

'The very same, and he lives in a house worth over four-million pounds.'

I found this hard to believe. 'Are you sure? Perhaps, it's a different Tommy Cassidy. There might be two people of the same name,' I suggested.

'That's what I thought. In fact, in a city the size of London, it's highly likely. So, I staked out the house and it's definitely our Mr Cassidy. He turned up driving a Bentley and I recognised him immediately. He lives there with his wife Rita.'

'How do you know that?'

'Because I checked the electoral register for the area and the only people listed at that address are Thomas and Rita Cassidy.'

'Okay, if you're right, it raises a couple of questions.'

'Which are?'

'First. How does a common thug like Cassidy get to be involved with an exclusive polo club?'

'That's not a question to which I have an answer, boss. However, I do think that somehow he's using a respectable board of directors to hide his involvement.'

'Right. I think we need to do some more digging and I know where to start. What are you doing this evening?'

She shook her head. 'I have nothing planned.'

'Do you fancy going for a drink after work?'

'Is that an invitation?'

'Well I can't order you to join me.'

'There's no need for that. Do you have somewhere in mind?'

'Yeah. It's a pub I know in Poplar.'

'Will I like it?'

'Probably not. It's a bit of a dive.'

'That's not a problem. I went to a few dives when I was at university. Where shall we meet?'

'Where's good for you?'

'I need to go home first.'

'Of course you do. You're a woman.'

'That's not exactly politically correct,' she said with a grin.

'I'm delighted about that. It makes my day whenever I upset the PC woke mob.'

'You really are an awful tease, Steve.'

'So why do you have to go home if not to change your clothes, put on fresh makeup, and sort out your hair?'

'Are you saying I need to do that?'

'Nope. If you go to the pub just as you are, you'll probably be the smartest person there.'

'Thanks for the compliment, but I really do have to go home, because I have a new fridge being delivered at six o'clock and I need to let the delivery guys in. Can we meet at about 7 o'clock'

'Let's make it eight. I've never known a delivery turn up on time.'

'Okay. That's cool. I'll be catching a train from Arnos Grove.

Can you pick me up at Hyde Park underground station?'

'No problem.' I stood up, leaving a wet patch on the carpet in front of Harriet's desk.

'Before you go. What was your second question?' she asked.

'I just wondered where Cassidy got the money to buy shares in the Grange Polo Club and a property worth four mill?'

'Perhaps his butchery empire is doing well, or perhaps he won the lottery.'

'He would have to sell a lot of bloody pork chops to make that sort of money, and I can't imagine Cassidy buying a lottery ticket. He doesn't believe in games of chance.'

'Last week you said he was a clever thug. Perhaps he's even cleverer than you gave him credit for.'

I was beginning to think she was right. Maybe I had underestimated Cassidy and that worried me. Underestimating your enemy always puts you at a disadvantage.

'One thing you can be sure of is that Cassidy's money came from some sort of criminal activity,' I said. 'We just need to find out what that activity is.' I went into my office, took off my raincoat and picked up my phone. The D-G's secretary answered. 'Morning, Rachel. Is the boss in?'

'Is that you, Steve?'

'Yeah, unless aliens have taken over my body.'

She laughed. 'I didn't recognise your voice. You sound husky.'

'All this rain has probably made my voice box go rusty. Is the boss in?'

'No, she's at the Cabinet Office.'

'When are you expecting her back? I need to talk to her.'

'Not until late morning, but then she is having lunch with her husband. It's their wedding anniversary today. I've set aside a couple of hours in her diary for that, so could we say four o'clock?'

'That will do nicely. Thank you. By the way, Rachel, you have a husky voice too. It makes you sound very appealing.'

'You are being sexist again,' she scolded.

'I know, but you love it.'

Rachel giggled and ended the call.

11

Dame Alexandra was sitting at her desk sorting through paperwork when I entered her office. A frown had ploughed a deep furrow into her usually smooth forehead and she looked like a woman who wanted to be somewhere else.

As she worked she put some of the documents in a neat pile on her desk, the rest she put into the waste bin that stood at her side.

'Did you enjoy your celebratory lunch with Angus?' I asked as I settled into a chair opposite her.

She looked up briefly. 'There wasn't much to celebrate, Steven,' she said before returning to the paperwork.

'Wasn't it your wedding anniversary today?'

'Yes, but do you know how long we've been married?'

'No. How long?'

'Forty-two years,' she replied with a barely concealed sigh. She looked up again. 'The truth is that when you've been married that long, anniversary celebrations become less important. They are nice, but not exactly special. Today's lunch was such an occasion.' She sounded deflated.

'Are you okay, boss?'

She smiled, but did not put much enthusiasm into it and it soon disappeared. 'Not really, Steven.'

'What's the problem?'

She did not answer immediately, she just picked up a Home

Office briefing note and stared at it. 'Do you know what I'm doing?' she asked eventually as she put the briefing note on the pile of documents.

'It looks like you're shuffling papers.'

That brought another brief smile to her lips. 'Almost right. I'm sorting through my paperwork to dispose of any that needs no action.' She pointed at the waste bin. 'The rest is going to Samuel,' she nodded at the little mound of documents on her desk.

'That's a relief. At least you're not dumping it in my In Tray.'

'That's because you're not going to be the Acting Director-General.'

'And Sam is?'

'Yes.'

'I see. So what's happened to prompt that?'

'This morning I had a meeting with the Cabinet Secretary.'

'I know, your secretary told me.'

'It was a long and very polite meeting.'

'Oh! One of those meetings.'

'Yes. Apparently a complaint has been made about me.'

'What sort of complaint?'

'It's a human resource issue.'

'Human Resources?' I snorted in disgust. 'Whatever happened to the poor old workers? Humans of the world unite, doesn't have the same ring to it.'

'The world is changing, Steven.'

'Tell me about it. I can't keep up,' I moaned and watched as she carried on sorting papers. 'So who complained about you?'

'Sir Mark didn't say.'

'How serious is this complaint?'

'Let's just say that Sir Mark made clear he had no option

other than to hold an internal inquiry.'

'An internal inquiry? So, it's not serious then.'

'It's not something to joke about, Steven.'

'Come on, boss. A Civil Service internal inquiry isn't exactly the Spanish Inquisition.'

'Maybe not, but it does mean I am being placed on gardening leave pending the outcome of that inquiry.'

'And Sam will be in charge while you're pruning your roses?'

'I don't have roses, I hate them, but yes, Sam will be in charge whilst I am away.'

'Wonderful. I need a drink.' I eyed the globe hopefully.

'It's a little early in the day, don't you think?' she said primly.

'My old granddad used to say that if the sun's almost down, it's early enough.' I pointed out of the window where the dusk of late afternoon was fast turning into the darkness of evening.

She gave another audible sigh then said, 'Very well. Help yourself.'

'So what was this complaint?' I poured myself a large scotch, but I did not ask her if she wanted a drink. I knew the answer would be no. 'Who have you upset?'

'I have upset nobody,' she insisted frostily. 'The complaint was about the circumstances surrounding my recruitment of Harriet Barratt.'

'So, what would those circumstances be then?' I sat back down.

'I know what you are thinking, Steven. I have heard the rumours about me having a lesbian affair with Miss Barratt...' She paused and stared at me as if challenging me to deny the allegation. I said nothing and she went on: '...so I would like to explain about my relationship with Angus.'

'You don't have to explain to me, boss.'

'But I do.'

'Why?'

'Because I trust you.'

'Well, that's a relief. I'd hate to think you doubted me. But knowing you trust me doesn't explain why you feel the need to tell me about Angus?'

'It's because I need you to know the truth about our marriage, for a number of reasons.' She picked up yet another document and stared at it, but I could see she was not reading it. She was just going through the motions. Eventually the document went into the waste bin. I hoped it was not important.

'Okay. Go ahead. I'm listening.'

'Thank you,' she said and then paused again, as if collecting her thoughts. 'Look, Steven. Celebrating the anniversary of my marriage might have become slightly less important, but I still love Angus very much, mentally, and physically.' She looked at me to ensure I understood what she was saying. I did, but she chose to emphasise the point anyway. 'I can assure you, I am happily heterosexual, Steven, and, as far as I know, so is Miss Barratt.'

'I don't need your assurances, boss. It makes no difference to me what your sexuality is, and it should make no difference to the Cab Sec.'

'It doesn't, and as it happens Sir Mark knows I'm not gay,' she said cryptically, but gave no explanation about the circumstances surrounding her suspension, instead she changed the subject. 'Now you asked to see me.'

'Yes, I wanted to brief you about a couple of things. The first is on some research work that the happily heterosexual Miss Barratt has been doing.' I went on to tell her about the missing

140

horses and everything that Harriet had discovered about them.

'And you think the disappearance of these horses has something to do with Operation QS.'

I shrugged. 'I have no proof there is a link between the two, but gut instinct tells me there is some sort of connection.'

'How can you get that proof?'

'I have a hunch that Mario Tafuri is the key and I think we should track him down.'

'It is certainly worth a try.' She paused and looked at me thoughtfully. 'In fact, I think you should go to Venice as soon as possible, Steven.'

'I'm happy to do that, except for one minor problem.'

'What is that?'

'I have no idea what Tafuri looks like. All I currently have is his name and address.'

'Perhaps I can help with that. Luigi Campisi and his wife are friends of mine. I'm sure Luigi will have contacts in the Guardia di Finanza[1]. I'll ask him to make some discreet enquiries and email you a photograph of Tafuri.'

'Thanks, boss. That would be very helpful. I'd hate to put the screws on the wrong man.'

She looked at me with narrowed eyes. 'I hope we're not talking thumb screws here, Steven?'

'It was just a figure of speech.'

'So, no actual torture will be involved?'

'Do you doubt me?'

'Sometimes.'

'That hurts.'

She stared at me and then said, 'I just don't want things to get messy.'

'What do you mean by messy?'

'You know exactly what I mean. I do *not* want you taking any action that could embarrass the Government in any way.'

'I'll do my best to protect our political masters.'

She looked at me doubtfully. 'I am not sure doing your best will be good enough?' She made this statement into a question.

'Who can tell? It depends how co-operative Tafuri wants to be. If he doesn't play ball, I might have to resort to using a little threat.'

'What sort of threat?'

'I don't know, something like telling him that unless he tells me what I want to know, I'll cut off his nose and ears.'

'Are you serious?'

'Of course, I'm serious.' I finished off the rest of my scotch in one gulp before placing my empty glass carefully on her desk. 'Look, I don't like violence any more than you do, but sometimes it's necessary,' I told her quietly and then asked, 'You've never been a field agent, have you, boss?'

She shook her head silently.

'Well, being out in the field is no place to be squeamish. Not if you want to stay alive.'

'So are you telling me you might need to use violence?'

'Of course. That's what you pay me for.'

She could not argue with that, so said, 'In that case, I think you should travel under an assumed name. We wouldn't want to create a diplomatic incident and upset our Italian allies, would we?'

'Wouldn't we?'

'No.'

I laughed mirthlessly. 'Come on, boss. What you really mean

is that if I'm caught you want to be able to deny all knowledge of me.'

'That's not what I mean,' she said in a tone that was supposed to convince me of her sincerity, but did no such thing. 'I just don't want the Government to be compromised in any way.'

'Don't worry. I know the rules of the game. If the assignment goes tits up, you'll hang me out to dry.'

'I wouldn't do that, Steven.'

'Of course, you would.'

'You really are cynical.'

'I've already pleaded guilty to that charge on numerous occasions. But it's my cynicism, combined with a violent streak, that keeps me alive and well.'

'Well, on this occasion, your cynicism is unnecessary because I'm telling the truth. However...'

I interrupted her before she could finish her sentence. 'Why does the word however always make me feel uneasy?'

She ignored my protest, instead she repeated: 'However, I still think it would be safer all round if you went undercover.'

'I see, and exactly which cover do you have in mind?'

'I'll leave the details up to you. I'm sure you can think of a good reason for visiting Venice.'

'I'll need back-up.'

'Of course, take Miss Barratt with you.'

'That's not the sort of back-up I had in mind,' I said unhappily. 'I had in mind somebody slightly more experienced. Perhaps Alan Brown.'

'Alan Brown is off sick. He has caught some sort of virus that's affecting his lungs. Anyway, Miss Barratt needs to gain some field experience as part of her training.'

'Having her tag along might make finding a believable cover more difficult,' I complained.

'Nonsense, you can pose as a couple of tourists.'

'There aren't any tourists in Venice at this time of year,' I protested, still not happy about having Harriet tag along. If Tafuri was involved with the Mafia, as I suspected, then I was going to have to watch my back. I did not relish having to watch the girl's back at the same time.

'Don't be difficult, Steven. There are tourists in Venice all year round, particularly the Chinese.'

'In that case we'll stand out like a couple of sore thumbs. Wouldn't it be better to postpone my visit until Alan Brown is better.'

'Certainly not. We have no way of knowing how long that will be. The last I heard Brown was struggling to breathe and on a ventilator in Guys Hospital. He could be out of circulation for weeks and we cannot wait that long. Anyway, taking Miss Barratt with you to Venice, was not a request, it was an order,' she insisted in a voice that did not broach further dissent.

I knew when I was beaten. 'All right, I'll take her.'

'Thank you, Steven.'

'That's okay, I'll organise something. However, in return, I'd like to know what the circumstances were surrounding her recruitment that led to your suspension.'

She thought about that for a few moments, then said, 'Very well. The complaint is that I used my position to ensure Harriet's transfer and enhance her career prospects.'

'I think I can guess why somebody might think you would do that.'

'The rumours about me having an affair with her?'

'Yeah.'

'That well might be the case. However, the Cabinet Secretary would never take disciplinary action on the basis of a rumour.'

'So why has Sir Mark taken action?'

'Because he knows that Harriet is my niece.'

'Your niece?'

'Well, to be honest, she is more like a daughter to me. Her mother was my younger sister. She and Harriet's father were killed in a car crash when my niece was ten years old. She came to live with Angus and me and we brought her up as one of our own children.'

I remembered the way she kept touching Harriet on the arm at the meeting. The more I thought about their interplay, the more it looked like the affectionate action of a doting mother, rather than the caress of a lover.

Then I realised the only reason I assumed Dame Alexandra was a lesbian, was because Sam Brewer had suggested it. This made me wonder whether he was the one who had started the rumours about the D-G and had somehow instigated the complaint about her.

'It doesn't look good, boss. I can see why some people might be shouting nepotism.'

'I know, Steven. However, let me be very clear. Harriett got her promotion on merit and the decision to transfer her was taken not by me, but Sir Mark, following a recommendation from the Permanent Secretary at the Foreign and Commonwealth Office.'

'But surely that puts you in the clear.'

'Let's just say that I am confident the Cabinet Office inquiry will exonerate me.'

'So why go through the farce of a full-blown inquiry?'

'You need to understand the way these things work, Steven. Sir Mark wants to avoid any suggestion of a cover-up. He not only wants to do the right thing, but he wants to be seen doing the right thing.'

'You don't think there's another reason for his action, do you?'

'No.'

'Let's hope you're right.'

'I am,' she said confidently as she picked up the papers from her desk and handed them to me. 'Please take these along to Samuel's office. Tell him I will ring later to bring him up to speed about what you have told me, and what action we have decided. Now, was there anything else?'

'Yeah, there was one other thing. I was going to brief you about my trip to Iraq, but perhaps I should brief Sam instead.'

'My gardening leave does not start until midnight tomorrow, Steven. Which means I am still Director-General until then, and still in charge. So, you tell me all about it, and I will brief Samuel when I ring him,' she said this in a steely voice that left no room for argument.

So, I told her about my meeting with Fraser Goran and his cousin.

'Can we trust the information this Abbas fellow gave you about al-Barak's visit to Afghanistan?'

I shrugged. 'I spoke to Jimmy Bannerman and he confirmed Abbas has been supplying stuff to Six for years. There's no suggestion any of the information he supplied was dodgy.'

'So, what does it all mean?'

'I'm not sure. However, I think al-Barak's visit was connected with Operation QS. My suspicion is that somehow there is a link between the Buzkashi ponies bred in Afghanistan, the stolen horses, and the polo clubs in Surrey and Venice.'

She nodded. 'I agree. Which makes your visit to Italy even more important, Steven. For a start, we need to find out why Soleimani met Navarra.'

'Yeah,' I replied simply.

'Do you have anything else?'

I took the photograph of Sean MacDonald from my pocket and slid it across the desk to her and explained what it was.

'So Nuristani's driver and this MacDonald are the same man?' she asked after she had studied the photo.

'Yeah.'

'And he is a CSIS[2] agent?'

'That's what Six reckon but it would be great to know for sure.'

'That is something else with which I might be able to help you.'

'In what way?'

'I happen to know the Deputy Director Operations of CSIS. His name is Lloyd Harper.'

'Is there any important and influential person in the world you don't know, boss?'

She looked up at the ceiling with a thoughtful expression on her face. 'Well, I have never met Stevo Pendarovski.'

'Who's he?'

'The President of North Macedonia,' she replied straight faced.

'Are you serious?'

'About what? Whether he is a president, or that I have never met him?'

'Both.'

'Both are true, but it was meant to be a joke, Steven.'

This was a light-hearted side of the D-G I had not seen before. 'That's what threw me. I didn't realise you had a sense of humour. I like it.'

'Thanks.'

'So, how do you know Harper?'

'Angus worked with Lloyd a few years back and our two families became quite friendly. We have kept in touch over the years. You know, Christmas and birthday cards and things like that. In addition, our two agencies have worked together a few times on matters of mutual interest, so I have dealt with him on a professional level too.'

'If MacDonald is a CSIS agent, I would dearly love to know what the hell he's doing in Baghlan masquerading as a chauffeur. Do you think Harper will tell you what's going on?'

'I am not sure. It depends on the sensitivity of MacDonald's operation. I'll ring Lloyd and see what he has to say. If I get any information, I'll pass it on to Samuel and he can brief you. Now, is there anything else?'

'Yes. The Goran family.'

'What about them?'

'What's happening about their application for an ILR permit?'

'Oh, didn't I mention that?'

'Not that I recall.'

'That was very remiss of me. I wanted you to know straight away.'

'Know what? Is there a problem?'

'A small one.'

'How small,' I asked suspiciously. 'Is the Home Office still playing silly buggers?'

'No, they approved their application this morning.'

'That's good news. So, what's the problem?'

'You told me you wanted them brought out of Iraq as soon as possible,' she said glumly.

'Yes.'

'Well, that proved to be a problem. We could not get them on a scheduled flight until the end of next week.'

I frowned. I was conscious the Gorans were now in real danger. As soon as word got out that they had entertained somebody from the British Army in their home, they would be targeted by the extremists.

Dame Alexandra saw the look on my face. 'Don't worry. The problem has been sorted. I have arranged for the Gorans to travel to the UK by MOD transport on Sunday. They will then stay in our safe house until permanent accommodation can be found for them.'

For once I was temporarily lost for words. 'Thank you, boss,' is all I could manage.

She smiled. 'That is quite all right. I am sorry I teased you.'

I smiled back at her. 'No problem. I've done my share of teasing in this room. As my old battalion sergeant-major used to say: If you can't stand the heat…'

'Get out of the kitchen?' she anticipated the rest.

'No, don't light a fire in the first place.'

That made her laugh. I stood up and made my way to the door, but she stopped me as I opened it.

'Steven.'

'Yes, boss?'

'I suggest you book a flight to Venice that leaves London before midnight tomorrow night.'

I understood her reasoning. 'Don't worry. I'll get the travel-office onto it after I've dropped this paperwork off to Sam.'

'I think that would be very wise,' she said and then added: 'Oh, and, Steven, I would be grateful if you would keep in touch with me whilst I am on gardening leave. You have my home number. Ring me at any time.'

When I arrived at Sam's office, I found he was out. I left the documents, and Dame Alexandra's message, with his secretary and headed back to my own office.

I rang the travel-office. After a few moans about the short notice I was giving him, the clerk agreed to book two return flights to Venice and arrange for me to pick the tickets up at the British Airways desk at Gatwick.

Next, I contacted Carl Pulsac. I needed new identities for two people, and he was just the man to deliver them quickly. After I came off the phone, I sat for a while thinking about the recent meeting with my boss.

Dame Alexandra appeared confident the Cabinet Office internal inquiry would find her innocent, and I thought she was probably right.

However, I sensed there was more to her being placed on gardening leave than she was admitting and I resolved to arrange a meeting with her when I got back from Venice.

One way or another, I was determined to get more information out of her.

1   *Guardia di Finanza* is an Italian law enforcement agency dealing with financial crimes.
2   CSIS: Canadian Security Intelligence Agency.

12

Thursday 9ᵗʰ January 2020: Poplar, London.

The Cardigan and Balaclava is a run-down public house, in an equally run-down part of Poplar. The pub has been serving beer to the local community for a hundred and fifty years and its shabby furniture and sawdust covered floor suggested it had changed little since opening its doors for the first time.

Over the past century and a half the walls and ceiling of the pub had been stained dark brown by tobacco smoked by generations of local customers. As we walked into the public bar the smell of freshly smoked cigarettes filled the air.

There was a handful of people sitting at scruffy tables, and a couple of drinkers were settled at the bar, looking as if they had been there since the 1854 Charge of the Light Brigade ended in such ignominious failure.

Harriet wrinkled her nose in disgust and complained in a whisper: 'Somebody's been smoking.'

'You don't say,' I muttered quietly.

'I do say and I'm not happy. I thought smoking in pubs was banned,' she hissed quietly.

'It is.'

'But that's definitely new smoke I can smell,' she protested, still keeping her voice low.

'Well don't have a go at me. I don't smoke.'

'I know that, but one of the guys in this bar has been smoking.'

'No doubt.'

'But aren't they worried about breaking the law?'

I gave a quiet chuckle. 'Breaking the law comes naturally to the Cardy's regulars.'

'What about the police? Don't they monitor what goes on in pubs?'

'The local police community team does visit occasionally, particularly on Friday nights, but they're more interested in catching drug dealers.'

'I can understand that is a priority for the police, but what happens if they do see somebody smoking? Do they take action?'

'Of course, but being caught breaking the law is an occupational hazard for people like those guys.' I nodded towards the two drinkers standing at the bar. 'Anyway, the worst a smoker can expect is a thirty-quid fixed penalty fine. To them that's the equivalent to a slap on the wrist, compared to the ten year stretch they can expect for aggravated burglary.'

'What about customers who don't smoke? Don't they have the right to be protected?'

'Can you see a queue of people lining up to complain?'

She shook her head in disgust. 'You were right, this pub really is a dive. So, where's your nark[1]?'

'Follow me.' I led her through an open door on our left. 'That's him over there.' I pointed to a table in a dark corner of the saloon bar. We headed that way.

Reggie Moore was a fanatical West Ham United supporter, who was first taken to watch a football match at Upton Park when he was just nine years old, by his equally Hammers mad father.

Reggie's passion for the West Ham stayed with him until he met an untimely death, at the age of fifty-three, when he broke his neck falling off the roof of St Dunstan and All Saints Church in Stepney from which he was stripping lead for sale on the black market.

Reggie was so devoted to the Hammers that he named his only son after his football idol, Bobby Moore, who was renowned for his athleticism and clean-cut image.

The Bobby Moore who sat at the table in front of us now, was an overweight, grubby looking parody of the super-fit central defender who led England to World Cup success in 1966.

Moore was sitting on his own, staring moodily into a glass. He was dressed in a baggy grey tracksuit, the top of which was unzipped to reveal a stained tee-shirt, so tight it showed in sharp relief his heavy man-boobs and the double roll of fat that encircled his waist.

The fat man looked up as I pulled out one of the three empty chairs at his table.

'Mr Statton! As I live and breathe!'

Harriet pulled out another seat and we both sat down. 'Can we join you, Humpy?' I asked.

'Looks like you've already done that,' Moore pointed out grumpily.

'What sort of welcome is that?' I asked.

He raised his hand in an apologetic gesture. 'Sorry, guvnor. I didn't mean to be rude. It's just that I have a few things on my mind, and I was happy just sitting here on my own watching the world go by.'

'There's not much activity to watch going by in here tonight,'

I said indicating the almost empty room.'

He shrugged. 'Thursdays are always quiet in the Cardy,' he said, which did not really address my point. 'So what brings you to the East End, Mr Statton?'

'We just popped in for a quiet drink.'

'In that case I don't mind if I do.' He finished off the drink he had been nursing and pushed his empty glass towards me. 'Mine's a bourbon on the rocks.'

Harriet stood up on cue. 'I'll get them.'

I took a £20 note from my wallet and handed it to her. 'The first round's on me.'

'In that case, I'll have a double,' Moore said, sounding much more cheerful now.

Harriet looked at me and raised an eyebrow. I nodded my assent.

'What are you having?' she asked me.

'A glass of Shiraz.'

She nodded and picked up Moore's glass.

'Who's the bird?' the fat man asked sotto voce as Harriet was about to go out the door to the public bar.

'My assistant.'

'Nice tits.' Although Moore lowered his voice further to make this observation, he spoke loudly enough for Harriet to hear. She looked over her shoulder, but he was too busy ogling her body to notice the glare on her face.

I chose to ignore his crass remark and instead asked, 'So, when did you get out, Humpy?'

'Last week,' he said, finally dragging his eyes away from Harriet, who by now was ordering our drinks from the shaven headed barman. 'I'm grateful for what you done for me, Mr

154

Statton. If you hadn't put in a good word for me, I'd have probably been banged up in Pentonville again.

'So, where did you end up?'

'Standford Hill on the Isle of Sheppey. It's in Kent.'

'I know where the Isle of Sheppey is, Humpy. I've been there. It's full of caravans, amusement arcades and sheep.'

'And fat people with tattoos,' Moore added.

'Most of whom come from London,' I pointed out.

'Yeah, and so are most of the inmates of the three prisons on the Island.'

'It must have felt like home from home. I expect there were a few old lags in Standford Hill you knew from previous stretches.'

'Nah, I didn't know nobody. Most of the other geezers were black or Asian, and I don't like mixing with them bastards.'

'But at least Standford Hill is an open prison,' I pointed out.

'That's true, but times have changed and doing bird ain't the doddle it used to be, even in a Cat D.'

'That's your own fault, Humpy. Nobody forced you to sell dodgy number plates online.'

'That was a mistake, which I very much regret.'

'Don't make me laugh. Your only regret is that you got caught. Anyway, compared to Pentonville, Standford Hill must have been like Butlins on sea.'

'Give over, guv. I missed my home comforts and in winter Sheppey is bleak, depressing, and bleeding cold. It weren't no fun I can tell you.'

'Prison is not meant to be fun, Humpy,' I said as Harriet returned with a tray of drinks.

'Bleeding cold,' Moore repeated, openly staring at Harriet's breasts as she leaned over to put the tray in the middle of the table.

'Of course it's cold. That's why all the farm animals on Sheppey wear sheepskin coats.'

'Very funny, guvnor.'

I took a sip of my Shiraz. It tasted stale and I guessed the bottle it came from had been open some time. Not much wine is sold in the Cardy.

'So, what's your name, darling?' Moore took his Jack Daniels from the tray.

'Harriet. What's yours?'

'Bobby,' he said and then took a sip of his drink. 'Bobby Moore, like the footballer. Geddit?'

'Did you play football?'

'Nah, I hate it. It's a game for fairies and foreigners. Why d'you ask.'

'It's just your hairstyle. It's really cool. It reminds me of a nineteen-eighties footballer.' Harriet kept a straight face as she delivered this obvious insult.

It was not obvious to Moore, who smiled with pleasure, showing a set of discoloured teeth that had not seen a tooth-brush for many years. He ran his fingers through his long, mullet style, dyed black hair. 'I like to keep myself looking smart.'

Somehow Harriet managed to sip her white wine without choking.

'I suppose you missed out on all the local gossip, while you were banged up, Humpy?' I asked.

'Far from it. I learn more about what's going on in the Smoke when I'm inside, than when I'm out.'

This was a typical Bobby Moore exaggeration, and contradicted his earlier claim that he did not mix with the other inmates. The truth was, home or away, he knew everybody who was involved in London's criminal underworld and what they were up to. What made him different from the other old lags in the East End, was he was willing to share that information with me for a price.

'So, what is going on?'

'It's carnage out there,' he replied with a roll of his eyes.

'That's a bit melodramatic, Humpy.'

'I'm not exaggerating, guvnor. There's a turf war to end all wars taking place as we speak. The manor ain't seen nothing like it since the Krays was put away.'

'Who's the war between?'

Before answering, Moore finished off his drink in one gulp, then pointed at my glass, which was still half full. 'I'd treat you to another one, but I'm boracic², he said mournfully.

'How much do you need?' I asked.

'A monkey.'

'Five hundred pounds to buy a round of drinks! This joint must be more expensive than it looks.' I took a brown envelope from the inside pocket of my jacket and slid it across the table to him. 'There's a ton in there, Humpy. Look upon it as a down payment. If I'm happy with your information, there's another ton in my pocket for you.'

'Okay, it's a deal.' The envelope disappeared into his pocket. 'But you cover my round for me.'

'Harriet, can you get Mr Moore another double bourbon on the rocks and another wine for yourself.' I reached for my wallet.

'Don't worry, boss. I still have the change from the last round.' Harriet stood up and tapped her pocket and made coins jingle. 'What about you? Do you want a top up?'

'No, I'm driving. I'll make this one last.'

Harriet picked up Moore's glass and headed for the bar.

'So, who's the turf war between?' I asked.

With my money safely in his pocket Moore was happy to answer my question. 'Who ain't it between?'

'I don't know, that's why I'm asking you.'

'Well, the Somalis are fighting the Nigerians and both of them are trying to muscle in on the Afro-Caribbean SW9 gang, who have a longstanding feud with the SW11 boys. Then there's the Yids, who will fight anybody and everybody for a slice of the action.'

'What are they fighting over this time?'

'The county lines drugs trade,' he replied as Harriet returned. 'Thanks, darling,' he said as she put his drink on the table in front of him.

Harriet bristled at Moore's familiarity and was about to say something when she saw the look I gave her. She gave a little shrug and kept her thoughts to herself.

I gave her no chance to change her mind. 'Humpy was just telling me about the gangland war that's raging in London,' I explained quickly.

'That's a war I know nothing about. It must have passed Stattons Green by.'

'Is that where you live?' Moore asked.

'Yes.'

'That's Yid country.'

'Really?'

'Yeah. I suppose you support Spurs.'

'No, I'm a Chelsea fan,' she insisted coldly. 'And, as it happens, I'm not Jewish. I'm a Rastafarian.'

'I thought Rastafarians was black?'

'Not all of them.'

'Bob Marley was a Rasta, and he was black.'

'I'm not Bob Marley.'

'Can we get back to the matter in hand?' I said. 'We were talking about county lines.'

'County lines? Isn't that where London gangs recruit vulnerable youngsters to distribute drugs across rural areas and small towns, using mobile phone lines to control their network of runners?' Harriet asked.

'Yeah, but it's not just happening in London,' I replied. 'Gangs in most of our big cities have climbed on the county lines bandwagon. It's a rapidly growing business.'

'And there's loads of dosh to be made,' Moore chipped in. 'Particularly in the wholesale supply of the drugs to county lines gangs.'

'So what's causing the conflict?' I asked. 'Surely there's enough money for everybody.'

'There's never enough money for some people. That's why the turf war started.'

'Why?' Harriet asked.

'Because one of the county lines gangs is greedy and ambitious. They would like to take over the trade of the wholesale distributors they currently buy their supplies from, but to do that they need to be bigger. So they tried to nick trade from one of their rivals, who didn't take the incursion into their area lying down. They fought back.'

'Are none of the gangs big enough to take on the wholesalers?' she asked.

Moore shrugged. 'Not yet.'

'Why's that?'

'Because the current wholesale distributors are backed by very powerful international organisations. For instance, the world's cocaine trade is controlled by the Colombian drugs barons, who use their friends in the American Mafia to distribute it to North America and Europe, including here in London. You don't mess with those Mafia boys.'

'What about heroin? Who controls that trade?' I asked. I knew the answer, but I wanted Harriet to learn more about the drugs trade from the horse's mouth, so to speak.

'The manufacture of H is controlled by Central Asian warlords, particularly Afghans,' Moore answered.

'Including the Taliban,' I added.

'Yeah, and they use the Italian Mafia to handle the distribution of their drugs across Europe.'

'How does the Mafia get the drugs into the UK?' Harriet asked. It was a good question.

'They've tried lots of different ways, darling,' Moore explained. He was enjoying lecturing my new assistant and being the centre of attention. 'They've set up several different supply-lines over the years, each of which was eventually sussed out by the Old Bill[3] and closed down.'

'But the traffickers don't give up,' I explained. 'As soon as one supply line is discovered, the Mafia dreams up new, more novel ways of getting drugs to their wholesale distributor in our country. It's a constant game of cat and mouse.'

'So who is the heroin wholesaler in the UK?'

'Whoever happens to be the Mr Big at the time,' Moore replied. 'The head-honcho changes from time to time. One guy builds up an empire large enough to be trusted and supported by the Mafia, and then is taken down by a rival, who then builds up his own empire, before being taken down by his rival, and so the cycle goes on.'

'Who is the current Mr Big?' I asked.

Moore looked furtively at the smoke blackened wall behind him, but it was not eavesdropping. 'Tommy Cassidy,' he whispered.

Harriet glanced at me, but my expression warned her to say nothing.

'You mean the Balham Butcher?' I asked.

'You know him?'

'Yeah, but I haven't heard much about him recently,' I lied.

'I ain't surprised. Tommy's gone up in the world. He ain't seen around this neck of the woods much these days, not since he bought a posh house in Wimbledon.' He took a sip of his bourbon. 'But because a geezer is rich enough to have a posh house don't make him a better person. A sadist is still a bleeding sadist, and a nutter is still a bleeding nutter.'

'Which one of those is Cassidy?' Harriet asked.

'Both, darling, and he's been like that since he opened his first butcher's shop in Balham High Street, all them years ago.'

'I take it you don't like Cassidy?'

Moore shook his head. 'Nah. Not since the bastard done the dirty on my sister.'

'I didn't know you had a sister, Humpy,' I said. 'You've never mentioned her before.'

'That's because it upsets me to talk about Janet.' For once

he sounded genuinely upset. I almost felt sorry for him, but resisted the temptation.

'What happened?' I asked.

Moore did not reply immediately, instead he took another sip of his bourbon before saying: 'Jan met Tommy Cassidy when she was only sixteen. He likes his girls young.'

'Why's that?' Harriet asked.

'Because they are easier to dominate and control,' Moore replied.

'Does Cassidy still have girlfriends?' I asked.

'Yeah.'

'But isn't he married?' Harriet asked.

'Yeah, to Rita. They've been married for years, long before Tommy met Janet.' Moore explained, then added: 'Rita's Big Liam Murphy's daughter.'

'Who is Liam Murphy?' Harriet asked.

'He's head of a notorious Irish travelling family based in South London,' I explained.

'Big Liam's a real hard-nut,' Moore added.

'If Cassidy is married, why does he go with other women?'

'Some men are like that, darling, and in Cassidy's case, he has certain needs that Rita can't satisfy.'

'What sort of needs?'

'He's a bit of a perve, for a start he likes to watch his women have sex with other geezers,' Moore replied, relating this fact with some relish. 'But Rita won't stand for any of that sort of nonsense, and Tommy knows if he ever asked her to do it, she'd tell her old man, and Big Liam is one of the only people in London who truly frightens him.'

'Are you saying that Cassidy went with your sister because

she'd do the things he wanted?' Harriet asked.

'Yeah. Of course, Janet didn't know what the bastard was like when she first met him, and she only found out he was married to Rita much later, by which time she didn't care.'

'Why was that?'

'Because she was greedy. Cassidy gave her everything she wanted. She had use of his apartment in Knightsbridge, a fancy car, designer clothes, and expensive jewellery. I tried to warn her what the bastard was like, but she wouldn't listen. She was as happy as a pig in shit. The problem was that she soon found out shit can be very messy.'

'So what happened to your sister?' I asked.

'Jan was a good-looking girl and one of Cassidy's mates fancied her like mad. Somehow Tommy got her to agree to give his friend what he wanted.' He paused and imitated a sexual movement with his fingers. 'Of course, Tommy expected a favour from his mate in return, which he got. He also insisted on watching his mate screw my sister.'

'That's disgusting.' Harriet spoke in a controlled, neutral voice, but I could tell she was shocked.

'You ain't heard nothing yet, darling. It gets worse,' Moore said. '

'What could be worse than that?'

'For starters, Jan told me she actually enjoyed having sex with another bloke and didn't mind Tommy watching.'

'Oh,' Harriet said simply.

'Yeah. Oh. And that was the start of the slippery slope, because when Cassidy realised how Jan felt, he arranged for another of his mates to have sex with her and soon he was pimping her out to all his friends.'

'How could he do such a thing?' Harriet asked.

'Because he takes after his mum.'

'What do you mean?'

He took another sip of his drink and then explained: 'When Tommy was a kid his mum used to take him to Clapham Common with her to keep watch while she sorted out her clients in the bushes.'

'You mean she was a prostitute?' she asked.

He nodded. 'Yeah, Mary Cassidy used to give blowjobs for a bob and would drop her knickers for half-a-crown. She even gave a tanner discount if a punter introduced her to one of his friends.'

'So, who was Cassidy watching out for, his father?' Harriet asked.

Moore sniggered. 'Don't make me laugh, darling. Cassidy never had no dad, not one he knew anyway. Nah, he was looking out for anybody who got too close to the bushes and discovered what was going on.'

'What happened if somebody did get too close?'

'Tommy warned them off. Nobody argued with him, because even at thirteen he was a big lad.'

'You used the past tense when describing your sister,' I said.

'Yeah. Jan's dead,' Moore said mournfully.

'Oh, my God. How dreadful. What happened?' Harriet asked.

'Cassidy did for her, good and proper.'

'How?'

'Eventually, watching her be screwed by another man wasn't exciting enough for him. He got bored and wanted more excitement. So, one day he tried to persuade her to take part in group sex with a bunch of his mates.'

'That's terrible,' Harriet whispered. 'Did she agree?'

'Nah, despite Jan's love of sex, that was a step too far, even for her.'

'She refused?'

'Yeah.'

'What happened?' I asked.

'What do you think happened? What always happens when somebody crosses Tommy Cassidy. He beat her up, stuck a syringe full of heroin in her arm and then let his mates take turns to screw her.' Moore paused and stared off into the distance. He shook his head slowly and then continued with his story. 'Jan was completely traumatised by the experience and never fully recovered. She became a heroin junkie and died of an overdose when she was nineteen.'

'That's terrible,' Harriet repeated.

'Yeah, Cassidy is terrible all right. But he has form. My sister wasn't his first victim, and she ain't gonna be the last. The bastard has had loads of tarts since Jan. He uses them and then discards them like used tissues. As I said before, he likes his birds young and usually gets rid of them by the time they reach their mid-twenties.'

'Why do his victims put up with him?' she asked.

'Because geezers like Cassidy have a fatal attraction for a certain type of vulnerable woman. People like Janet. He told her he'd leave his wife and marry her, but of course he never done that. The bastard just used her, dumped her, and moved on to somebody new, leaving her to top herself.'

I could see that Harriet was moved by Moore's story and viewed him with sympathetic eyes, but her mood changed when he reverted to type with his next words.

'You'd better hold onto your knickers if ever you meet Cassidy, darling,' he told her with a lick of his thick lips, before adding: 'He'd love to get his hands on your gorgeous young body.'

I stood up and stared down at Moore. 'Do you know what you are, Humpy?'

'What's that?'

'You're no better than those guys who abused your sister.'

He look shocked. 'Don't say that, Mr Statton.'

'Just think about it,' I told him, but saw from his face that he had no idea what I was talking about. I shook my head in despair. 'Come on, we're on our way,' I signalled for Harriet to follow me.

'What about my other ton?'

I took another brown envelope from my pocket and tossed it to him. I hated the fat slug, but a deal is a deal and the information he had given me was worth a couple of hundred pounds.

'There's more where that came from if you can come up with any additional information about Cassidy's involvement in the drugs trade,' I told him as we prepared to leave the table.

'Will do, guvnor,' he said and then turned to Harriet. 'Oh, and by the way, darling. The only reason I didn't give you a slap for taking the piss out of me all evening is because you work for Mr Statton.'

Harriet turned and faced him with a superior smile on her face. 'That's quite all right, Fatso, because the only reason I didn't tear off your balls for making objectionable sexist remarks about me all evening is because I work for Mr Statton.'

We started to leave the lounge bar when she stopped and

turned to face Moore. 'Oh, and by the way, Fatso,' she pointed at his chest. 'Nice tits.'

'Are you really a Chelsea fan?' I asked as we walked to my car.

She laughed. 'No, I hate football, which is about the only thing I have in common with that idiot.' She indicated the pub with her head. 'Talking of which, why were you calling him Humpy? Is it because he looks like Humpty Dumpty?'

I laughed. 'No, when Moore was younger he made a reasonable living performing an Engelbert Humperdinck tribute act.'

'Who's he?'

I explained how in the 1960s an unsuccessful pop singer from Leicestershire, by the name of Gerry Dorsey, metamorphosised into a huge international singing sensation, after he took the name of the German composer who wrote the opera Hansel and Gretel, and used it as his new stage name.

'I hate opera almost as much as I do football, but if Engelbert Humperdinck looked anything like Fatso, I think I'd have preferred Hansel and Gretel,' she said with a laugh.

'Moore hasn't always been that overweight. Believe it or not, when he was younger he was actually quite trim,' I said as we reached my car. 'Now, on a different subject, did you send Marion a Get-Well card?' I started the engine and pulled out of the side road in which I had parked and into the flow of late-night traffic that was heading west on the A13.

'I was going to mention that. It's all a bit odd really. When I checked with HR, the only address they had on file for Marion was her apartment in King's Cross.'

'There's nothing odd about that. Marion only moved last year and HR probably haven't had time to update their records yet.'

'I take it you're being sarcastic?'

'A gold star for observation. Now explain why you think there's anything odd about civil service incompetence.'

'That's not what I thought was odd.'

'So what was odd?'

'Well, when I found out HR didn't have Marion's new address on file, I popped round to her old apartment to see the current tenants. I thought they might have a forwarding address for her.'

'And did they?'

'No. They told me they've never heard of Marion Dudley.'

'Perhaps somebody else took over from Marion and the people you saw took over from them.'

'No. The current residents have lived in that apartment for almost ten years.'

'Perhaps you had the wrong apartment.'

'That's what I thought, so I spent the afternoon checking electoral registers and Marion wasn't listed in King's Cross or Knightsbridge.'

I thought about this as I turned into Commercial Street and headed towards Shoreditch. 'Perhaps she doesn't believe in voting,' I suggested eventually.

'That's true, but she would still have to register for council tax.'

'I suppose you're going to tell me she wasn't registered for that either?'

'Right. I checked with both local authorities and they had no record of her. As far as they are concerned Marion Dudley doesn't exist.'

'But what about our internal records. A security check would have been carried out on her when she was employed. That's a pre-requisite for everybody getting a job with the department, whoever you are. Even the cleaners have their background checked.'

'I thought of that as well. I had a look in Marion's file and found her application form. The home address she gave was the apartment in King's Cross I visited this afternoon. The security vetting form contained the same information, but there was a note attached to it, asking for the address be checked out. However, the security form had no final clearance stamp, so it looks as if no check ever took place.'

'Did you contact the Cabinet Office[4] Personnel Vetting Section?'

'Yes, but the guy I spoke to said he could offer no explanation other than that "the request must have fallen through a crack in the system"!'

'There are far too many cracks in their bloody system.'

'Has it happened before?' she asked.

'Yes, but it's difficult to know exactly how many times because we have little control over the accuracy of their checks.'

'With such inefficiency, no wonder there are so many government leaks. What on earth am I letting myself in for?'

'Come on, Harriet. I can't imagine the Foreign and Commonwealth Office is any more efficient than the Cabinet Office.'

She laughed. 'Didn't you know? The FCO thinks it runs the Cabinet Office!'

'So, it's your fault?'

'Not anymore. I no longer work for the FCO. I work for you.'

'In that case it's still your fault.'

'How do you work that one out?'

'It's called strategic apportioning of blame.'

She laughed again and then we lapsed into companionable silence until we reached the A4, and I pulled into the bus stop next to the underpass that leads to Hyde Park Corner tube station.

'So, how did you manage to get hold of Marion's file? Personnel files are carefully controlled in line with the Data Protection Act.'

'I'm not sure I should tell you.'

'I don't care how you got the file. I am just interested.'

She hesitated and then admitted: 'OK. I went to school with somebody who works in Central Records, but I don't want to get her into trouble. You won't report her, will you, Steve?'

'That would be difficult because you haven't told me her name.'

'I know, but I'm sure you could find out if you tried.'

I had no answer to that because she was right. 'Don't worry, I won't do that. Now what are your plans for tomorrow?'

'I thought I'd do some more digging into Cassidy's background.'

'You won't have time for that, I'll get the police onto it.'

'Why? Have you got something else for me?'

'Yes. I need you to pack an overnight bag.'

'A bag? Am I going somewhere?'

'Yes. We have a flight to catch.'

'What flight? Where to?'

'Venice.'

'Is this another of your jokes, boss?'

'No joke, we're going to find Mario Tafuri and have a quiet word with him.'

She looked at me in disbelief. 'Are you serious?'

'Yeah.'

She grinned. 'That's fantastic! At last I get to visit Venice.'

'Our flight is at two o'clock in the afternoon, so we need to be at Gatwick Airport by midday. I suggest we meet at Victoria Station at eleven and catch the Gatwick Express.'

'I won't be late. I'll pack a bag and dig out my passport as soon as I get home tonight.'

'You won't need your passport.'

'Why not?'

'Because we're travelling to Venice under assumed names. I'll have new passports with me when we meet tomorrow.'

'How did you get another passport for me?'

'Easy. The same place you got your dodgy warrant card.'

'The Briggens Factory?'

'Yeah.'

'What's my cover name going to be?'

'Harriet Thorvik.'

'Nice name. What about you?'

'Steven Thorvik.'

She studied me carefully for several seconds and then asked, 'Why have we got the same surname?'

'Because our cover story is that we're newlyweds on honeymoon in Venice.'

'Newlyweds?'

'Don't worry. I don't plan to elope with you.'

'I'm not worried.'

'So why did you go white?'

'Don't exaggerate. I didn't go white. I was just surprised, that's all. Surprised and excited.' She looked out of the window thoughtfully and then turned to me.

'You have a question?'

'Two.'

'Go ahead.'

'Why did you choose the name Thorvik?'

'It's my mum's name.'

'You mean her maiden name?'

'Yeah, although she insisted on keeping her name when she married my dad, so she's still Joan Thorvik. Why do you ask?'

'I was just interested. It's an unusual name.'

'My maternal grandfather was Norwegian,' I explained. I could have added that my mum was born in South Africa to a Scottish mother, went to school in Cape Town, spoke five languages and worked in the Ministry of Defence before joining DFCO, where she met my dad, but I left that for another day. 'So, what was your second question?'

'Where are we staying in Venice?'

'I'll leave it up to you.'

'Are you sure?'

'I'm sure. Choose a hotel and book us in.'

She thought about that for a while and then said, 'If we're supposed to be married, I'd better book us into the same room.'

'Yes, but book a room with twin beds.'

'Of course. Any preference for location?'

'Somewhere central.'

'Okay.'

'And not too expensive, or the Cabinet Office bean counters will have a fit.'

She gently touched my arm. 'Thanks for keeping your word, Steve.'

'What about?'

'Taking me on your next overseas assignment.'

'It's not a problem, however, it wasn't my idea.'

'Whose idea was it then?'

'Your aunt.'

'My aunt?'

'Yeah. Your aunt the Director-General.'

'Oh. You know?'

'Yeah.'

'How did you find out?'

'Not from you.'

She looked down at her hands and found something on the back of her left hand, which she suddenly needed to scratch with the nail of her right forefinger. 'I'm sorry about that,' she said eventually. 'I did feel bad about keeping my relationship with Auntie Xandra from you, but she thought it best if we kept it a secret.'

'Well it's no longer a secret.'

'Who told you?'

'She did. This afternoon.'

She sat in silence and found another invisible mark on her hand to scratch. On the A4 a short convoy of taxis drove past the bus stop. They were heading west, no doubt taking their fares home from the theatre, or dinner.

'Why did Auntie Xandra tell you?'

'You don't know?'

'Know what?'

'Your aunt has been suspended.'

'Suspended?' She sounded dumbfounded.

'Yeah. As of tomorrow night she's being placed on gardening leave pending an internal inquiry into allegations she arranged for your transfer to the department because of your relationship.'

'That's total bollocks!' she swore angrily. 'I was appointed on merit and my transfer was actually recommended by my boss at the FCO.'

'I know, your aunt told me.'

'Do you believe her?'

'Of course, but it's not me holding the Inquiry.'

'What are we going to do?'

'We're going to get on with our assignment.'

'But what about Auntie Xandra?' She looked at me with tears in her eyes. 'I love her so much. I want to help her. What can I do?'

'You can start by acting like the professional you need to be if you want to succeed in this job. That means setting aside your personal feelings and look at Dame Alexandra, not as your aunt, but as the Director-General.'

'That's easy for you to say, she's not your aunt.'

'No, she's my boss and your boss too. That counts for something.'

'But…'

'No buts, Harriet. I can assure you your aunt would be very disappointed if you let your emotions cloud your judgement. So, we're going to leave her to sort out the problem for herself.' I took her hand and squeezed it. 'Look, don't worry, Harriet, your aunt's one of the cleverest people I know, and I have every faith in her ability to see off the bastards who are after her blood.'

She squeezed my hand back and smiled bravely. 'Thank you,' she said as she wiped her eyes with the cuff of her coat. 'Okay, I'll see you tomorrow at Victoria Station.' With that she got out of the car and walked quickly to the underpass and disappeared down the steps.

I eventually arrived home at just before midnight. As I walked through my front door the telephone on the hall table rang. I hesitated before answering it. I'm like that with late night calls. They rarely bode well. The telephone persisted and wore down my resistance. I picked it up.

'Yes?' I said shortly.

'Is that Steve Statton?'

'I hope so, or else I'm likely to be arrested for breaking and entering.'

'I don't have time for jokes, Mr Statton. What I have to say is very important.' The caller was a woman, although her voice was muffled, as if she was talking through a folded handkerchief. Surprisingly, old tricks like that still work.

'In that case say it quickly and then I can go to bed. I'm tired.'

'I thought you might like to know that somebody went to Central Records today and requested a classified personnel file.' The woman was whispering now, and it was difficult to hear her properly.

'Whose file?'

'Yours.'

'Who requested my file?'

'Gerald Draper.'

'Are you sure? He's from MI5. What would they want with my file?' I was not expecting an answer from the mystery woman, because she had already rung off. I was talking to myself.

I took off my coat and headed for the lounge where I poured myself two fingers of malt whisky. I slumped in an armchair and took a generous sip. It tasted a whole lot better than the indifferent red wine served up at the Cardigan and Balaclava.

I mulled over the events of the day, which had ended with more questions than answers. Those questions worried me.

The first was something Bobby Moore had said and had slipped into the subconscious vault located in that part of my brain in which were tucked away snippets of potentially useful information.

I knew it was stored in one of the vault's safety deposit boxes, but I had not yet found the key to open the right box. I sensed the information was important, but the question was, how and why?

Next there was the late-night phone call. The thought that MI5 had requested my file was worrying enough, but worse was that I had no idea why they wanted it. I decided to ring Joe Onura first thing in the morning to see if I could find out.

But the call raised another two questions. The first was who was the caller? I knew it was a female, but that was about it. The second question was more worrying. How did she know my home phone number?

1   A nark is a police informer.
2   Boracic lint, is cockney rhyming slang for skint, which is another word for being broke.
3   Old Bill is slang for the police.
4   Because the Special Security Agency is only a small Government intelligence department, it subcontracts out its new personnel vetting to the much better resourced Cabinet Office.

13

Friday 10th January 2020: St James, London.

There was still no sign of Marion when I arrived in my office the next day, which meant I had the whole place to myself to make a succession of phone calls. First, I rang Carl Pulsac to find out if my forged passports were ready.

'What time is it?' Carl asked with a hint of irritation in his voice.

'Five past nine,' I replied.

'What time did I say your documents would be ready by?'

'Half past nine.'

'Exactly, and that is when they will be ready,' he said tetchily.

'Sorry, Carl. I wasn't doubting your ability to deliver on time. I was only checking because I know how busy you are.'

'That's because Briggens is seriously understaffed,' he moaned.

'I know that, which is why I was very grateful when you agreed to do this rush job for me.'

This seemed to mollify him. 'It's not a problem, Mr S. You know I'm always happy to help you out.'

'Thanks. I owe you one.'

'In that case, please can you have a word with Dame Alex and get me another pair of hands?'

'I'll do my best, but knowing the boss I can't be certain of success.' I failed to mention that by the time I got around to talking to the D-G, she was unlikely to be in a position to agree any request.

'I understand, Mr S. I learnt during my time in the Blues and Royals that the only certainty in life, is there are no certainties in life.'

'Very profound, Carl, but I must go. I'll pick up the passports on my way to the airport.' I put down the phone before he could launch into one of his well-rehearsed homilies about his service in the Royal Horse Guards.

My next call was to Joe Onura.

'Morning, Steve. What can I do for you?'.

'I need some information.'

'Information about what?' he asked cautiously.

'About what you're up to.'

'I don't know what you're talking about. I'm not up to anything.'

'I wasn't talking about you personally, more Box 500[1] generally.'

'I'm not with you, Steve.'

'Come on, Joe. Yesterday Gerry Draper requested my personnel file from Central Records. He works in your team, so don't insult my intelligence by pretending you don't know what I'm talking about.'

He did not reply, but his silence spoke volumes.

'How long have we known each other, Joe?' I asked quietly.

'A long time,' he replied.

'Back to our army days.'

'Twenty years.'

'At least. And we've been friends for all that time, haven't we?'

'Yes.'

'And how often do we see each other socially?'

'At least once a month.'

'Exactly, and we've had some great times together over the years, haven't we?'

'You're not being very subtle, Steve.'

'In what way?'

'Using our friendship against me.'

'Is that what I was doing?'

He laughed mirthlessly.

'Look, Joe. I'm not asking you to reveal any state secrets. I just want to know why Five is so interested in my file.'

'We aren't interested in your file,' he whispered. 'It was another agency.'

'Which agency?'

'Come on, Steve. I've told you more than I should. If my boss found out I was talking to you I could lose my job.'

'That's nonsense. Talking to a friend is hardly a sackable offence.'

'Don't you believe it. As far as my boss is concerned, you're not a friend, you're somebody who's employed by a rival security agency.'

'Rivals? For God's sake, Joe, we're on the same side.'

'The same side certainly, but with different rules, different secrets, different ways of doing things and different bosses. In Five my boss likes us to keep our cards close to our chest.'

'Bosses can be such a trial,' I agreed.

'Particularly my boss,' he said with feeling. 'He doesn't like me and has been looking for an excuse to get rid of me.'

'Look, Joe, I don't want to get you into trouble, but if somebody is interested in my file, they must have a reason and it's hardly likely to be because they want to check whether I'm suitable to join their club, is it?'

'No.'

'So I need to find out what that reason is, Joe. Which is why I need your help.'

'Please, Steve, you're putting me in an impossible position. I'd really like to help you, but I can't risk losing my job. I have to pay for my mum's care home, and I can only just afford the monthly fees as it is.'

'I know, Joe. You told me. By the way, how is your mum?'

'She's struggling with her arthritis, but her mind's as sharp as ever.' He paused and then added: 'She always asks after you, Steve.'

'That's nice. Give her my love when next you see her.'

'I will,' he promised and then lapsed into silence again. 'I'd really like to help you,' he repeated eventually. 'You know that.'

'I know, Joe,' I said gently.

'I often think about our time in the army.'

'Me too. We had some good times.'

'And bad.'

'I remember them well.'

'I'll always be grateful for the way you stood up for me when I was receiving all that racist abuse from some of our supposed brothers-in-arms.'

'That's what friends are for Joe. They help each other.'

'You're doing it again, Steve.'

I said nothing.

'Okay, what I will say is that your file was requested by somebody who wears a button-down shirt and whistles Yankee Doodle when he pees.'

'An American?'

'To paraphrase Frank Underwood in *House of Cards*, You

180

might suggest that, but I couldn't possibly comment,' he whispered, then rang off.

'Thanks,' I said into the silent phone. If an American agency had asked for my file, my money was on the CIA. I knew Draper had once been seconded to the Firm. My guess was that whilst at Langley he worked with Troy Olsen. I wondered if Draper was still working with the American, but I put that thought aside for another day.

Next, I rang Jane Manning to ask her if she could find out more information about Tommy Cassidy.

'What do you want to know?'

'Anything of interest. The names of his associates and friends; what recent crimes he's suspected of being involved in; what properties he owns; the state of his business finances, that sort of thing.'

'Is that all?'

'No, it would also help to know who he's currently shagging, other than his wife, of course.'

'You don't want much, do you?'

'You did say you wanted to take Cassidy down, Jane.'

'Is getting you this information going to help put him away?'

'There are no guarantees, but I'll do my best.'

'Your best is good enough for me, Steve. I'll see what I can find out.' With that she hung up.

As I was replacing the receiver the phone rang. It was Harriet.

'Morning, boss. Will it be okay if I meet you at Gatwick?'

'No problem. Wait for me at the BA information desk. Our tickets will be waiting for us there. But why the change of plan?'

'Uncle Angus has a meeting in East Grinstead this afternoon and he offered to drop me off at the airport first.'

'That's nice of him.'

'I think he wants to talk to me about Auntie Xandra. He knows I'm upset about what happened to her.' She went quiet, but I sensed she had more to say. I was right.

'I feel so guilty,' she went on.

'What do you feel guilty about?'

'Her suspension is all my fault.'

'That's nonsense, Harriet. You're definitely not to blame.'

'That's nice of you to say so, Steve, but if I hadn't applied for a job in the SSA, none of this would have happened.'

'Don't you believe it. There are people out to get your aunt, and if you weren't around, they'd have found another excuse to force her out of her job.'

'I don't understand.'

'It's political. Your aunt has made some influential enemies in the civil service hierarchy. They think she's too robust, too bloody minded, too independent, and too conservative.' I made this nonsense up as I spoke, but it sounded plausible to me. I hoped Harriet thought so too.

'But we have a Conservative government.'

'Tell that to the civil service mandarins who think they're the real government. They all come from the same liberal mould. They believe Laissez Faire is better than discipline; prevarication is better than action; and a fudge is better than a clear decision. Independently minded people like your aunt are an anathema to their creed. They think she is a loose cannon.'

'Is it really like that, or are you exaggerating?'

'I don't do exaggeration, Harriet,' I lied.

'Will her enemies succeed?'

'I hope not. However, I think your aunt is also being hung

out to dry by some very ambitious people, who are pushing their own agendas.' This at least was true.

Just then, Sam Brewer came into my office. Talk about coincidence.

'Like whom?' Harriet asked.

'Sam Brewer…' I said and then paused before adding: '… has just walked into my office. We'll talk about it later. I'll have to go now.'

'Okay, I understand. See you at the airport.'

'Don't be late,' I said and put the phone down. 'What can I do for you, Sam?'

'Just thought I'd touch base with you.'

'That's very thoughtful of you. Which particular base did you want to help me touch?'

He smiled. 'Well, there were a couple of things.'

'I'm all ears,' I looked at my watch, 'but only for a few minutes, because I'm on a tight schedule.'

'Okay, the first thing is your trip to Iraq. You spoke to Dame Alexandra about it yesterday.'

'That's right. She told me she would brief you.'

'Which she did and asked me to tell you she spoke to the Deputy Director Operations of CSIS about their agent, Sean MacDonald, and he is going to get back to us with an answer as soon as possible.'

'Don't hold your breath, the Canadians are not renowned for their speed. What was the other thing?'

'I assume you've heard the news about Dame Alexandra?'

'Yeah. She's been knifed in the back as I forecast.'

'I think that's an extremely jaundiced interpretation of events.'

'Jaundice is my middle name.'

'Setting aside your cynicism, do you at least accept the reality that the boss has been suspended?'

'What option do I have? Fact is fact.'

'Exactly. The Queen is dead. Long live the King.'

'I assume you're hoping the crown will be placed on your head?'

'Well, as it happens, I have been asked to take over as Acting D-G.'

'All Hail Caesar!' I raised my arm in a Roman salute.

He frowned. 'Are you mocking me?'

'Would I do that?'

He did not respond to my rhetorical question, instead he forced a smile and said, 'If you can resist the temptation to be flippant for ten seconds, I want to ask you something.'

'I'll do my best. Go ahead.'

'Okay. I would like your assurance that you'll be doing nothing to rock the boat during my tenure.'

'I've always given the captain of this boat my full support.'

'You're very wise.'

'I sometimes wonder about that.'

Sam did not try to reassure me, instead he said, 'Of course, I'm only Acting D-G and, as I told you before, your endorsement will be invaluable when I go for the post on a permanent basis.'

'I'll think about it.'

'Take all the time you like. Just as long as you end up making the right decision.'

'I always make the right decision,' I insisted, ignoring his ill-disguised threat. 'Now, was there anything else?'

'Yes. I want you to abort your proposed trip to Venice.'

'Why would I do that?'

'Because in my view the trip is a waste of time and money.'

'That's debateable.'

'My decision is not open for debate. I don't want you galivanting round Venice with Harriet Barratt.'

'Don't worry. I don't propose to galivant with anybody, anywhere.'

'You're not listening to me, Steve. I said I want you to cancel your trip.' He smiled at me again as he spoke, but it was a crocodile smile.

'No, Sam. It's you who's not listening to me. Harriet and I are booked on a flight to Venice this afternoon and we'll be on it.'

'Are you disobeying an order?' he asked, whilst maintaining the insincere smile they teach at the Civil Service Management College.

'No. I'm obeying an order. It was given to me by Dame Alexandra.'

At last his smile disappeared to be replaced by a glower. I had hit him where it hurt. 'I'm not sure I like your attitude, Steve.'

'You're not alone, Sam. Every boss I've ever worked for had the same problem, but they all learned to put up with it.'

'Well, I intend to be different, and it starts right now. I have given you a direct order. Are you going to abandon your trip to Venice or not?'

'That would be the not option.'

'Is that your final word?'

'Absolutely, and if you don't like it, I suggest you take it up with Dame Alexandra, who, unless I'm mistaken, is still the

D-G, and remains in charge of DFCO until her gardening leave starts at midnight tonight.'

By now Sam's face was scarlet with rage and frustration. He knew when he was beaten. Without another word, he got to his feet and stormed out of my office wearing a dark scowl.

I followed shortly after. Unlike, Sam, I was smiling.

14

Friday 10ᵗʰ January 2020: Gatwick Airport.

Gatwick Airport's departure area was bustling and noisy, but what's new? Harriet was standing near the information desk with a rucksack over her shoulder. Her blonde hair was tied up in a ponytail and she was wearing tight denim jeans, trainers, and a tracksuit top, unzipped to reveal a white tee-shirt that showed off her curves. She looked very young and very attractive.

'Why are you staring at me?' she asked.

'Was I?'

'Yes.'

'If you say so. I thought I was just looking at you.'

'Is there something wrong with me?'

'I don't know. I'm not a doctor.'

'I meant is there something wrong with what I'm wearing.' She looked down at her clothes.

'I'm sure the Italians will think you look sensational.'

'But what about you? What do you think?'

'Me? I think the Italians have impeccable taste.'

'I assume that was some sort of compliment,' she paused and looked at me suspiciously, 'but I'm waiting for the putdown punchline.'

'No punchline.'

'Thanks.' She rewarded me with a warm smile.

'Have you collected the tickets?' I nodded towards the B A desk.

'Yes, I have them here.' She pulled them out of her tracksuit pocket and showed them to me. 'Did you know we were flying first-class?'

'Yeah.'

'How did you wangle that? I thought the Cabinet Office was monitoring our budget.'

'It is, but one of the guys in the Travel Section emailed me to tell me these were the only seats they could get at such short notice. I told him to go ahead.'

'I'm not complaining.'

'Perhaps not. But the bean counters will have a touch of the vapours when they see the cost.'

She handed me my ticket and waved hers in my face. 'It seems I'm now officially Mrs Harriet Thorvik,' she said with a grin.

'Not quite.' I took her new passport out of my jacket pocket and handed it to her. 'But you are now.'

PART TWO

THE PAWNS

From the poverty shacks,
he looks from the cracks to the tracks
And the hoofbeats pound in his brain
And he's taught how to walk in a pack
Shoot in the back
With his fist in a clinch
To hang and to lynch
To hide 'neath the hood
To kill with no pain
Like a dog on a chain
He ain't got no name
But it ain't him to blame
He's only a pawn in their game

Bob Dylan

15

Friday 10th January 2020: Venice, Italy.

There is a lot of water in Venice, but on the day we arrived in Italy there was more than usual. Much more.

Water fell from the heavens in a steady torrent, as Indra, Thor, Zeus, and their cohort of storm gods, united to show us mere mortals their power over nature.

Rain pounded against the roof of the Alilaguna Blue Line waterbus in a staccato drumbeat, before streaming down its side into the lagoon.

The waterbus heaved and rolled as it ploughed through the choppy waters under the leaden sky of a rain-soaked January day, which was even greyer by the time the afternoon stepped aside to make way for an equally rain-soaked January evening.

We were travelling from Marco Polo Airport to San Zaccaria, which was the closest waterbus terminal to our hotel, but the first stop on our journey was Murano. As we approached the island, I could see a dozen Chinese tourists huddled in a shelter. Several were clutching carrier bags containing gifts from one or other of Murano's glass factories.

As the new passengers clambered aboard the bus, one or two of them wore unhappy expressions. I was not sure whether this was because of the driving rain, or because their fellow tourists had informed them they could have bought their glass ornaments for half the price in one of the souvenir shops dotted around the Piazza San Marco. If it was the latter, I understood their sour looks. Nobody likes to be ripped off.

Our journey from the airport took an hour and twenty-four minutes. It was dark and still raining when we alighted at the San Zaccaria jetty.

I was wearing a wax jacket, so was protected from much of the heavy drizzle, but Harriet's only protection was her open tracksuit top and tee-shirt. I did offer her my jacket, but she refused.

Luckily, the Hotel Commercio E Pellegrino was only a few minutes' walk away from the waterfront, located just off the Riva degli Schiavoni, on the Calle de le Rasse, which was little more than a wide alley separating our hotel from the far grander Hotel Danieli opposite.

The latter hotel dominates the Venetian Lagoon and enjoys fantastic views of the Grand Canal and the Venetian islands. It overlooks the Doge's Palace and is close to Ponte Dei Sospiri and the Piazza San Marco.

The Danieli actually comprises of three palaces. Palazzo Dandolo gives its structure a Venetian Gothic style and was once home to the Dandolo family; Palazzo Casa Nuova, was originally the city's treasury; and Palazzo Danieli Excelsior features guestrooms on its upper floors, with balconies that overlook the lagoon.

The luxury hotel houses a collection of precious art and antiques that form an important part of the city's history, and its facilities include a cocktail bar and two first-class restaurants, including the world-famous rooftop Terrazza Danieli.

With such a rich heritage the hotel is very special, so it is hardly surprising that in the past two hundred years its guests have included such famous people as Charles Dickens, Steven Britten, Leonard Bernstein, Harrison Ford, and Steven

Spielberg. It is very exclusive and very expensive.

As we headed up Calle de Le Rasse, Harriet pointed at the Hotel Danieli. 'I was tempted to book us in there,' she said as she wiped rain from her face with an already wet tissue.

'Are you serious? Sam would have a heart attack if we had stayed there.'

'I know. That's why I was tempted,' she said with a wicked gleam in her eyes as we stepped finally into the sanctuary of the Hotel Commercio E Pellegrino, which was neither exclusive nor expensive.

The hotel certainly had nothing that was likely to attract Hollywood "A" Listers. However, it would keep Sam and his bean-counter friends happy. They thought economy standard accommodation was good enough for the likes of Harriet and me.

The lobby was just large enough for a narrow reception desk, and a wooden display stand full of tourist brochures that stood next to the entrance to a small dining room.

On the wall next to the entrance was a notice, printed in Italian, French, German, Japanese and English, advising guests the only meal served was breakfast. If we wanted an evening meal, we would have to brave the rain again and go find a restaurant.

There was a male receptionist standing behind the desk smoking a cigarette. We must have looked like Brits because he greeted us in English. 'Good evening,' he said to Harriet's rain-soaked tee-shirt.

'We have a reservation in the name of Thorvik,' I said.

The receptionist reluctantly turned his attention from Harriet's chest and looked down at the visitors book laying open on the desk in front of him. 'Would that be Mr and Mrs Steven Thorvik?'

'Are you expecting any other Thorviks?' I asked.

'No sir.'

'Then it must be us.'

'Of course, sir,' the receptionist said coldly as he deftly slid a form towards me, 'Please fill this in,' he ordered and then went back to studying Harriet, who had started browsing through the tourist leaflets displayed in a rack next to the desk.

I wrote Steven and Harriet Thorvik in the space for guest names, before adding the false address in Whitstable that Carl Pulsac had created for us. I have no idea why he chose that Kent town. Perhaps he has a thing about oysters.

When I had finished, I passed the form back to the receptionist, who handed me a key and directed us to a small lift, which he said would take us to the top floor, where our room was located. There was no porter, and the receptionist did not offer to help us with our luggage, but this was no big deal. We had travelled light.

When we reached our room, I unlocked the door and pushed it open. The room was tiny and had a side window, against which the driving rain was beating a drum rhythm that would have been a credit to Ginger Baker[1].

'Ginger Baker would be proud of that rhythm,' I said, nodding towards the window.

Harriet looked at me blankly. 'What are you talking about?'

'The rain tapping on the window.'

'I got that, but who's Ginger Baker?'

'He was a drummer.'

'I've never heard of him.'

'He was big back in the Sixties and Seventies. My dad was a fan.'

'Was? Is your dad dead?'

'No, but Ginger Baker is. He died last October.'

There was a double bed in the room, with a small table on either side; a single easy chair; and a wardrobe with a long mirror inset into its front. There was a sliding door set into one wall. It was open and through it I could see a small bathroom and toilet. Next to the wardrobe was a wooden stand on which was a potted plant. Its brown tinged leaves were drooping and looked in need of a good drink. I felt the same way.

'I thought I told you to book twin beds,' I said as I slipped off my wax jacket and hung it on a hook behind the door.

'You did, but I decided it might look odd asking for twin beds when we're supposed to be a married couple, so I booked a double bed.'

'That makes sense. However, it does put us in a somewhat difficult position.' I opened the wardrobe and found some spare bedding. I pulled a blanket out and threw it over the easy chair. 'Don't worry. I'll sleep there.'

'I'm not worried. I knew we'd be able to sort something out. But that chair doesn't look very comfortable. I don't mind sleeping on the floor, or there's always the bath.'

There was a window opposite the bathroom door. I walked over and looked out onto a very wet Calle de Le Rasse. A man and a woman hurried past with a shared raincoat over their heads. They headed towards a brightly lit door, situated a hundred yards or so up the narrow alley. As they approached, a waiter appeared in the doorway carrying an umbrella. He stepped out to meet them and guided them towards his establishment.

'Are you hungry?' I pulled the curtains closed.

'I'm famished,' she said.

'Me too. Let's go eat. There's a restaurant a bit further up the alley. We can sort out the sleeping arrangements when we get back.'

'OK. I'll just dry my hair.'

'It's still raining. It will only get wet again.'

'There are umbrellas in the lobby. Didn't you notice?' She went into the bathroom, took a towel from the rail, and started rubbing her head with it.

'No. I was too busy checking out the layout of the lobby and restaurant.'

'So you wouldn't have noticed the sign on the umbrella stand which said they were for the use of hotel residents.'

'You might want to get out of your wet clothes too,' I suggested.

'I'm going to,' she said as she came back into the bedroom running her fingers through her tousled hair. She quickly stripped off her jeans, tracksuit top and tee-shirt, then returned to the bathroom wearing just her underwear and draped her wet clothes over the heated towel-rail.

She came back and took another pair of jeans and a jumper from her rucksack. She laid them on the bed, then stood facing me with her legs apart and one hand on her hip. 'Are you going to change?' she asked, pointing with her spare hand at my wet trousers.

For some reason I hesitated, perhaps it was because I was trying not to stare at her bare legs and was finding this very difficult.

'Don't be shy. You don't have anything I haven't seen before.

I've seen lots of half-naked men on the beach.' She saw me looking at her. 'And you've probably seen lots of women wearing bikinis. So what's the big deal?'

I couldn't fault her logic. I took off my trousers and went into the bathroom to put them over the heated rail next to hers. Very cosy. By the time I returned she was fully dressed again.

It did not take me long to find a pair of dry trousers in my bag and slip them on. As we left the bedroom, I took a small leaf from the potted plant and wedged it in the gap between jamb and door.

I locked the door, and we made our way to the small lift. When we reached reception, we found there was only one umbrella left in the stand. Thankfully, it was large enough for both of us to shelter under.

I held the umbrella as we made our way up Calle de le Rasse towards the restaurant. Harriet insisted on holding my arm. 'We're supposed to be a married couple, so we'd better behave like one.'

'You obviously know nothing about married couples. In my experience, getting up close and personal is the last thing they want.'

'You're just old and cynical.' She squeezed my arm tighter.

'Guilty as charge, M'lud.'

'M'lud? I'm not a man.'

'I noticed,' I said and she giggled.

By the time we finished our meal of over-priced pizza and greasy French fries, washed down by an indifferent Barolo red wine, the rain had stopped, and we were able to stroll back to our hotel, still arm in arm, in companionable silence.

There was nobody in the lobby when we arrived, so I

deposited the umbrella in the stand and retrieved our key from behind the empty reception desk, where it hung on a hook along with several others.

When we reached our room, I opened the door carefully, but the leaf I had left between door and jamb was already lying on the stained hall carpet. Somebody had been in our room.

'Perhaps it was the maid,' Harriet suggested.

'If it was a maid, she hasn't done her job properly because the bed clothes haven't been turned down.'

We checked our bags.

'My iPad is still here.' Harriet showed me the device in its bright-pink leather case. She looked relieved.

Nothing was missing from either bag, but perhaps that was because, apart from Harriet's iPad, we had left nothing in the room worth stealing. We had taken to dinner with us our money, passports, mobile phones, and my Glock 17 revolver, which was still tucked into the waistband of my trousers and was concealed under my jumper.

'What do you think?'

I shrugged. 'Perhaps somebody was just being nosey.'

'It was the receptionist,' she declared emphatically.

'What makes you say that?'

'Well it was obviously somebody with access to our room key.'

'Anyone could have taken our key from behind the reception desk without being seen. We did.'

'That's true,' she said as she took her mobile phone from the back pocket of her jeans, 'but the receptionist did look shifty.' She pointed her phone at me. 'Smile.'

I twitched my lips.

'What was that supposed to be?'

'A smile.'

'It wasn't much of one.'

'It's the best I can do right now.'

'Misery guts.'

'So, what made you think the receptionist looked shifty?' I asked as the phone's flash lit up the room.

'I noticed he didn't look at you while you were talking to him.'

'That's because he was too busy judging the wet tee-shirt contest.'

'What do you mean?'

'He couldn't take his eyes off you.'

'I didn't notice.'

'Trust me, our Italian friend has the hots for you.'

'That's ridiculous. I looked an absolute mess.'

'A mess wearing a wet tee-shirt.'

'Oh, I see. That's what you meant by the tee-shirt contest.'

'Which you won hands down.'

'Is that meant to be a compliment.'

'I told you the Italians have good taste.'

'Thank you,' she said with a smile.

'Mind you, there were no other contestants,' I added.

She gave me the finger, but smiled to show she knew I was joking. She showed me the photo she had taken.

'I have red eyes. I look like a demon.'

'Too much wine,' she laid her phone on the bedside table. She started to undress and when she was down to her bra and panties again, she went into the bathroom. I heard water splashing in the sink and then the sound of her cleaning her teeth.

'Your turn,' she said when she came back five minutes later.

I stripped down to my underpants and headed off to the bathroom with my toiletry bag. When I had finished, I returned to the bedroom to find that Harriet had taken the spare blanket off the chair and spread it across the bed.

She peeked out from beneath the covers. 'Come and join me.'

'Are you sure?'

'Yeah. I can't let you sleep in the chair; it's far too cold to sleep on the floor; and the tap in the bath is dripping. This bed is big enough for both of us. You can take that side.'

'I'm not sure this is a good idea,' I said as I took a couple of hesitant steps towards the bed.

'Don't be silly. It will be warmer with two of us in the bed.'

I was cold and did not need telling twice. I slipped under the covers, making sure there was plenty of space between our two bodies. I turned off the bedside light and lay on my back, looking up at the ceiling. I thought about how we would tackle Mario Tafuri when we visited him the next day.

'Are you still awake,' Harriet whispered.

'Yeah.'

'You're very quiet.'

'I'm thinking.'

'I'm cold.'

'Do you want another blanket?'

'No, I want a hug.'

'A hug?'

'Yes. Being cuddled helps me get to sleep.'

I stretched out my left arm to allow her to snuggle against me. As she pressed her body against mine, I realised she had taken off her bra and panties. If that was a surprise, what happened next was even more unexpected. She started stroking my chest, then took my right hand and guided it towards her breast. She pressed my hand against her nipple. It was hard with her arousal.

She ran her fingers gently down the length of my torso until they reached the waistband of my underpants. Slowly she pulled them down until we were both naked, then she rolled over and lay on top of me.

'I'm not sure this is a good idea,' I repeated.

'Why not?' she smiled down at me impishly.

'I don't think our boss would approve.'

'You'd be surprised, Auntie Xandra is very broad minded.'

'I was thinking more of Sam. He wouldn't like it.'

'That's okay because he's never going to be offered it. I don't fancy him.'

'I meant he doesn't like staff fraternising.'

'In that case he's an old fuddy-duddy. Anyone would think we're still living in the eighteen-hundreds.'

'As it happens, in the nineteenth-century, a lot of older men had young lovers. Many of them were scullery maids.'

'There you go. I'll be your scullery maid.' She started kissing me on the chest, then edged up my body until she was kissing me on the lips. I went to kiss her back, but she pulled her face away briefly. 'Be gentle with me, Steve,' she whispered.

So, I was very gentle with her and when we were both spent, we just lay there, me on my back and her lying on top of me.

'That was fantastic,' she said quietly. 'It's been a long time since I've had sex with a man.'

'Why's that?'

'Not for the reason you think.'

'What do I think?'

She rolled off me and snuggled against my side again. 'I think you've been listening to the rumours about me being a lesbian?'

'You know about them?'

'Of course.'

'Don't you mind?'

'What's to mind? I don't care what people think. I actually played along with the rumours and kept them guessing, because my sex life is my own business.'

'Of course it is.'

'Why did you say it like that?'

'Like what?'

'Like you want to know about my sex life, but are pretending you're not interested.'

'Is that what I was doing?'

'Yes, but I don't mind talking about it with you.'

'I feel privileged.'

'Not privileged, just special. Ask me anything.'

'Is that an order?'

'Yes.'

'Okay. Do you have a boyfriend?'

'No, in fact I've been celibate since uni.'

'What changed at university?'

'I had a really bad experience,' she said this in a small voice.

I hugged her gently. 'I'm sorry to hear that. Do you want to tell me about it?'

'Yes.'

'You don't have to say anything if it upsets you.'

'I want to tell you,' she insisted.

'I'm listening.'

'I went out with loads of boys when I was at school. However, by the time I went to uni, I realised I preferred older men.'

'Lucky me.' I said, provoking a light punch to my chest. 'Go on. What happened?'

'I had an affair with one of my tutors. He was a married man.'

'You wouldn't be the first student to do that.'

'He was okay to start with, but then he started wanting increasingly rough sex. I went along with him for a while, but then he started biting and pinching me. It turned him on, but it didn't do the same for me.'

'So why did you put up with it?'

'I didn't. I ditched him.'

'What did he do?' I guessed there was more.

'He wasn't happy and one night he came to my lodgings, when my housemates were out. He said he wanted us to get back together. When I refused, he lost his temper and attacked me. He beat me up and then raped me. I think that's why I got so upset when Bobby Moore told us what happened to his sister. I know how I feels to be raped, and she had to put up with far worse than me.'

'Did you report the attack?'

She shook her head. 'The tutor had been at the university for many years and was well respected. I didn't think anybody would believe me.'

She fell silent, but I did not push her and eventually she started talking again: 'But the experience put me off men and I haven't been with another one until tonight.'

'Why now and why me?'

'Because you're different. You made me realise not all men are the same. Some can be incredibly gentle, as you just proved.'

'I'm pleased you're satisfied. Now go to sleep. I want to make an early start tomorrow.'

'Who said I was satisfied?' she giggled.

'Go to sleep, Harriet.'

'So, no more sex then?'

'Go to sleep, Harriet,' I repeated.

She hugged me tighter. 'OK. You're the boss.'

We lay in silence for a while, until I felt her slipping towards sleep. I listened to her breathing deepen and, as sleep finally took her, she started snoring lightly, giving out little squeaks like a dormouse in distress.

I closed my eyes and tried to sleep, but my mind kept going back to the leaf lying on the bedroom carpet. Like Harriet, I was convinced the receptionist had been snooping round our bedroom, but had no idea why. That bugged me.

1   Ginger Baker was the drummer of a 1960's rock band named Cream, the other two members of which were Jack Bruce and Eric Clapton.

16

Saturday 11th January 2020: Venice, Italy.

Mario Tafuri lived in a shuttered building that was situated just off the Riva del Vin, which is a street that runs along the north bank of Venice's winding Grand Canal.

The rain clouds had been blown off to the west by a bitter easterly wind and were dumping their load on an unsuspecting Verona. Now there was a bright blue sky above us, but little of the sunshine filtered down into the dark, narrow alley that was Calle del Paradiso.

There was a winter chill to the air, but it didn't bother us. I was wearing my waxed jacket and Harriet had swapped her tracksuit top for a heavy jumper and anorak. We had walked quickly, but it still took us ten minutes to cover the distance between the hotel and our destination.

About two thirds of the way along Calle del Paradiso was a café, and we sat now at an outside table in the weak sun, drinking coffees and planning our next move.

'So which is Tafuri's place?' Harriet asked.

'See that narrow side-turning on the right?'

She nodded.

'Look past it and his building is about twenty yards further along. It's the one with the large red wheelie-bin outside.'

'I see it,' she said and looked thoughtfully down the narrow backstreet. 'Do you think he's at home?'

'Your guess is as good as mine.' I sipped some of my latte,

which had been quickly cooled by the chilly air and was now only lukewarm.

She stiffened. 'Is that him?' she hissed and raised her cup in an effort to hide the lower half of her face, which was a pointless exercise because it barely covered her chin.

A tall man came out of Tafuri's building and stopped next to the wheelie-bin. He wore a sheepskin coat, leather cap and ankle boots, into which were tucked a pair of black trousers. He had long, greasy hair, which hung down to his shoulders, and a thin, cruel looking face, with a long chin, on which grew a wispy goatee beard.

The man glanced towards the café, but if he noticed us sitting outside he must have assumed we were just two tourists enjoying a morning coffee in the winter sun, because he showed no interest in us.

The man turned his back on us and walked quickly down Calle del Paradiso towards the Grand Canal. When he reached the end of the alley he turned left and disappeared round the corner.

'Was that Tafuri?' she asked again.

I shook my head. 'No, but I've seen his face somewhere before.'

'Who is he?'

'I don't know. I can't even remember where I saw him.'

'In that case, how do you know he's not our guy?'

'Because Luigi Campisi sent me a photograph of Tafuri this morning.' I took out my phone and showed her.

'Well, that definitely wasn't the guy we just saw.'

'Very observant of you.'

'So, what are we going to do, now?'

'I want you to do something for me,' I replied.

'What?' she asked cautiously.

'Most of these buildings have an entrance at the back. I want you to go down there,' I pointed to the side-turning. 'A short distance down you will find a service passage on your left. I want you to locate the backdoor to Tafuri's place.'

'How will I know it's Tafuri's backdoor?'

'It will be about twenty paces along the passage.'

'Of course, I should have thought of that,' she said. Her cheeks had turned pink, perhaps from an embarrassed blush, on the other hand it might just have been the effect of the cold breeze that was blowing up Calle del Paradiso with increasing gusto. 'So, what do you want me to do when I get there?'

'Just wait outside and keep your eyes open. If you see anything suspicious, ring me immediately.'

'Okay, I'm on my way.' She got to her feet then paused. 'What are you going to do?'

'I'm going to use the front door.'

'How are you going to get in?'

'I have a hunch the door will be open.'

'What if it's not?'

'Don't worry, I'll find a way to get in.'

'I take it you intend to take Tafuri by surprise?'

'That's the plan.'

A worried frown flitted across her face. 'But what if he's armed?'

'I expect he will be, but so am I.' I opened the front of my waxed jacket and showed her the Glock tucked into the waistband of my trousers.

'Knowing you have a gun doesn't make me feel any better.'

'Maybe not, but it makes me feel much better.'

She touched my arm. 'I have a really bad feeling about this.'

'Don't be so dramatic.'

'I'm not. I just have a premonition that somebody is going to die.'

'Don't worry. It won't be me,' I assured her, hoping I was not being over-confident. 'Now go.'

'Okay, but be careful, Steve.'

'Being careful is how I've managed to stay alive so long.'

Harriet looked at me sceptically but headed for the side-turning without another word.

I waited until she was out of sight, then made my way to the front of Tafuri's building, where I found a solid wooden shutter protecting the entrance. However, the shutter proved no bar to entry because it had been levered open, leaving the internal padlocked hasp and staple dangling in the air, suspended from its wooden frame by one remaining screw.

The forced entry came as no surprise to me. When I saw the guy in the leather cap emerge from the building earlier, something about his demeanour made me suspect he was not an invited guest. But if he had to break in, did that mean that Tafuri was not at home?

I pushed the shutter gently and it swung open silently on well-oiled hinges to reveal a paint flecked door behind. I turned the handle and found the door was unlocked. Again I was not surprised.

I stepped into a dark lobby, from which a hallway led into the interior. I stood for a few seconds and cocked an ear. The building was silent, except for the sound of water dripping somewhere in the distance.

I made my way cautiously down the hallway, passing a flight of stairs and several doors, until I reached an open door to a large storeroom in which were stacked a number of wine boxes. I did not count the boxes, but whoever owned them was not going to run out of booze any time soon. The sound of the dripping water was louder now.

At the end of the storeroom was a back door, which I hoped Harriet was monitoring from outside. I considered opening the door to check she was in position, but resisted the temptation. If she was doing the job properly, she would not be visible anyway.

Against the right-hand wall of the store was an ancient metal sink, half full of water, into which more was dripping from a tap. There were a dozen wine bottles in the sink, some of which had their labels soaked off. I walked over and turned off the tap. The dripping stopped.

On either side of the sink was a stainless steel workbench. The right-hand bench was loaded with bottles labelled as French vin rouge, and the one on the left contained about a dozen bottles from which the label had already been removed.

At the end of this bench was a labelling machine which was loaded with a roll of labels for Grand Cru Saint-Émilion. It did not take a rocket scientist to work out what was going on. Tafuri was passing off cheap red plonk as expensive Bordeaux estate wine.

There was nothing else of interest in the storeroom, so I headed back up the hallway. I stopped at the first door and slowly pushed it open. The room was full of cartons. I opened several of the cartons and found they contained souvenirs, each with a label declaring they came from Venice. It was cheap tat, but no doubt the tourists loved it.

I closed the door and checked out the rest of the rooms. There was no sign of Mario Tafuri, but each room contained more cartons of tourist bait. Apparently the horse dealer had more than one side-line.

When I reached the staircase, I heard a noise on a floor above. I slipped off my shoes and placed them on the bottom step. I took my mobile phone out of my pocket and turned it off. I didn't want it ringing at the wrong time.

I drew my Glock 17, then, still shoeless, I made my way silently up to the first floor, where I found a passageway lined with doors leading to more storerooms and a couple of deserted offices. Once again, Tafuri was nowhere to be seen.

I made my way up to the second floor where I found a similar door-lined passageway. One of the doors was slightly ajar and I heard voices coming from behind it. I gently pushed it open with the barrel of my pistol and stepped inside.

I found myself in a study. On my right, the wall was lined with shelves on which were displayed some expensive hardback books and a number of ancient pottery artefacts. There was nobody in the room, but on a table standing against the left-hand wall was a radio on which a man and woman were arguing heatedly in Italian.

Next to the radio was a handful of grey folders, which had been taken from a low, two-drawer, filing cabinet that stood next to the table. I knew this because the top drawer was half open and was full of similar grey folders. I turned off the radio and picked up the folders from the table. They were all empty.

Set into the wall opposite the door was a small fireplace, complete with an ornate, wrought-iron fireside set, containing a poker, brush, and tongs. There were fresh ashes in the grate.

Using the poker I raked through the layer of charred papers, some of which were still smoking, and discovered a document that was only half burnt. I retrieved the paper and found it was an invoice with the Mancini Polo Club logo at its head. It was addressed to Mario Tafuri and was made out for the sale of a horse, but where the price should have been, there was just scorched paper.

I folded the damaged invoice carefully, put it in the pocket of my waxed jacket and went to investigate the rest of the apartment. There was still no sign of Mario Tafuri.

I left the apartment and headed for the stairs and was about to make my way down when I heard footsteps below. With my Glock back in my hand, I went down the stairs, carefully keeping one foot at either end of each step to reduce the risk of them creaking. When I reached the first floor, I heard a door open and close on the ground floor.

I went down the last flight and almost tripped over my shoes, which I had forgotten were on the bottom step, but quickly regained my balance. I put on my shoes and made my way down the hallway. The first door I came to was ajar and I could hear somebody rummaging around inside.

I slammed open the door with my shoulder and leapt into the room with my Glock raised to meet any challenge. It was pointing at Harriet, who stood with one hand inside an open carton, looking at me with wide, frightened eyes.

I lowered my weapon. 'What the hell are you doing?'

'I was looking for you.' She sounded shaken.

'Well you won't find me in that box.'

'I know, I just wondered what it contained.'

'And what does it contain?'

'Souvenirs.' She held up a small plastic gondola.

'Very tasteful.'

'It's cheap crap.' She threw the gondola back in the carton.

'I was being sarcastic.'

'I know that. I'm not stupid,' she insisted petulantly.

'I thought I told you stay outside and keep watch?'

'Don't glare at me like that,' she snapped. 'You did *not* tell me to stay outside. You told me to check out the back door, keep my eyes open and telephone you if I saw anything.'

'Well?'

'I did as I was told and I tried to ring you, but you didn't answer.'

That's when I remembered I had turned off my mobile phone. 'I could have shot you,' I said grumpily as I returned my pistol to its holster. I pulled out my mobile phone and switched it back on.

'You turned your phone off?' she asked incredulously.

I explained why and then asked, 'So, why did you try to ring me? Did you find something?'

'Yeah. A body.'

'Where is this body?'

'It's outside.' She walked out into the hallway. 'Come on, I'll show you.' She led me through the main storeroom to the backdoor, pulled it open and stepped outside, where it was spitting with rain. I followed her and found myself in a tiny, enclosed garden.

'Over there.' She pointed towards a small, ramshackle shed that stood next to the back wall of the building. 'I was going to hide inside the shed so I could view the back door without being seen. That's when I discovered the body.'

'How did you get in the backdoor?' I asked, pointing at the door we had just come through.

'It was unlocked.'

I walked over to the shed and opened its door. Amazingly it did not fall off its hinges. I stepped inside closely followed by Harriet. The rain had increased in intensity and was hammering against the corrugated iron roof in a cacophony of sound.

The body of a man was sprawled across a pile of sacks. Over his head was a hessian bag with a small hole in it, just where his skull met the top of his neck. There was a black powder mark round the bullet hole, from which a thin trickle of sticky blood had seeped.

'I'm going to roll him over,' I told her, raising my voice to be heard above the rain. I pointed at the powder mark. 'Although that hole is only small, it's likely the bullet has torn away half of his head. So, if you don't like looking at blood you'd best go outside.'

'I'll be okay,' she mumbled weakly.

I glanced at her and saw her cheeks had lost their pink colour. Her face was now a pasty white. She was obviously distressed and just putting on a show of bravery, but I let her stay anyway. Distressed or not, if she was going to make it as an intelligence agent she had to learn the realities of the job. It was not all loose women, fast cars, and shaken-not-stirred cocktails.

I pulled on a pair of gloves and rolled the body onto its back and found the front of the hessian bag was soaked in blood. I was not surprised. The blood was fresh, and had not yet stuck to the dead man's face, so as I tugged the bag, it slipped off easily to reveal a bald head.

As I expected, the bullet had ripped away the top half of the dead man's head, including his forehead, but there was enough left of his face for me to identify him from his photograph. It was Mario Tafuri.

The shed door opened and closed, but I did not bother looking up. I knew it was Harriet leaving.

I searched through the pockets of the dead man's blood-stained jacket and found his wallet. Inside there were four 500 Euro notes, three credit cards, a driving licence in the name of Tafuri, a membership card for the Mancini Polo Club, an out-of-date EuroJackpot lottery ticket, and a photograph of a grey-haired woman, wearing a black dress and head scarf, who I guessed was his mother.

I slipped the wallet in my pocket with the half-burnt invoice. When the body was eventually discovered, no doubt the police would be looking for a motive. Robbery was as good as any.

By the time I left the shed, the heavy rain had eased and had turned into a fine drizzle. Harriet was leaning against a wall with her eyes closed and droplets of rain glistened on her eyelashes like tiny diamonds. Her face was still pale and she was taking deep breaths.

'Are you all right?'

She did not reply immediately, she stood sucking in air like somebody who has just been rescued from drowning. Eventually she managed to get herself under control. 'Yeah, I'm cool now.'

'I'm proud of you. At least you didn't puke.'

'I almost did,' she admitted. She finally opened her eyes. 'How can you look at that sort of thing without feeling sick?'

'I don't like the sight of blood any more than you, but

sometimes it come with the job.'

'Will I ever get used to seeing it?'

'Eventually.'

'Like you have?'

'Yeah,' I said, but this was a lie. I will never get used to the sight of a blood stained dead body.

'Do you remember when you did that presentation to us just before you joined the department?' I asked Harriet later.

We were sitting outside a café in St Mark's Square. Harriet was sipping an Aperol spritz through a straw and I was drinking a Peroni beer straight from the bottle. It was mid-afternoon and the rain clouds had disappeared to be replaced by another clear blue sky. Although we were bathed in warm winter sunshine, there was still a chill in the air.

'You mean the day you were late arriving for the meeting?' There was a mischievous glint in her eye as she spoke. She had recovered much of her colour and with it her usual poise.

I ignored the barb. 'You showed us a photograph of a group of men with Qasem Soleimani just before he was killed.'

'Yes.'

'Do you still have access to the FCO file the photo was in?'

'Yes.'

'In that case can you dig it out when we get back to London?'

'I can do it now if you like,' she said with a smile.

'How?'

'Because it's filed in the cloud and I can access it on my tablet.' She pointed at the iPad that was on the table in front of her.

'Which cloud?'

She laughed. 'Do you really not know what I'm talking

about, or are you pretending to be a Luddite?'

'I have really no idea what you're talking about.'

'The cloud is a metaphor for the Internet.'

'Then why not call it the Internet?'

'Because it's not quite the same thing. Basically, cloud computing is just a method of storing and accessing data over the Internet, instead of wasting memory space on your computer's hard drive. Do you know what a hard drive is?'

'Of course.'

'Well that's a start.'

'Don't be so patronising.'

'You can talk. Pot and kettle spring to mind.'

I ignored this comment. 'So, let me get this straight, the file with the group photograph is up in the clouds somewhere?' I looked up at the clear sky. 'So where is it?'

She looked at me suspiciously. 'Are you being serious?'

'What do you think?'

'I think you know more about cloud computing than you're admitting. Is that true?'

'One of my instructors in the Army once told me it's an advantage if your opponent thinks you're stupid, but the tactic only works as long as you don't prove them right.'

She laughed. 'I knew you were winding me up,' she said as she typed in her password. It took her only seconds to find the photo. 'Here it is.' She showed me her screen.

I studied the photograph, then tapped the screen. 'That's him.' I pointed at one of the tall men who was standing behind Guiseppe Navarra.

'Who?' She stared at the photo.

'The guy we saw coming out of Tafuri's place.'

She stared intently at the screen then nodded. 'You're right. I recognise him now. Do you think he murdered Tafuri?'

'That's exactly what I think.'

'What makes you so sure?'

'Gut instinct and some circumstantial evidence. Think about it. Tafuri sold a horse to the Grange Polo Club, which is owned by Tommy Cassidy. Tafuri bought a horse from the Mancini Polo Club, which…'

'How do you know that?' she interjected.

I pulled out of my pocket the invoice I found in Tafuri's fire grate and showed it to her.

'Perhaps it's just a coincidence,' she said.

'There are too many bloody coincidences for my liking. For instance, as I was about to say before you interrupted me, the Mancini Polo Club is owned by Guiseppe Navarra, and its where Navarra met Qasem Soleimani. In addition, we have a photograph,' I tapped her iPad, 'in which we have Cassidy, Navarra, Soleimani, and a character who just happened to emerge from the house of a horse dealer linked with both polo clubs, and who we found dead shortly afterwards.'

She looked at me thoughtfully. 'So Navarra had Tafuri killed?'

'That's what it looks like.'

'So what are we going to do?'

'For a start I want you to run a check on our leather cap wearing friend and try to find out everything you can about him.'

'You think he was a Mafia hitman?'

'Yeah.'

'Okay. I'll get onto it when we get back to London.' She

studied the photograph on her iPad again. 'So why did Navarra have the horse dealer killed?'

'I suspect he thought Tafuri might give us information that incriminated him in some way. Which is why Navarra got his hitman to destroy any documents linking Tafuri with the Mancini Polo Club.'

'What is the significance of such a link?'

'I'm not sure. See what you can find out about the horses Navarra sold Tafuri, including where they came from.'

'Okay. I'll see what I can dig up.' She looked up at me with a frown on her face and said, 'Look, I get that for some reason Navarra wanted to destroy any evidence that might link him to the horse dealer, but what I don't understand is how he knew we were in Venice to meet Tafuri in the first place. Any ideas?'

'Only one.'

'Which is?'

'He must have been tipped off.'

'By whom?'

I shook my head. This was a question I had asked myself, but had been unable to answer.

17

Monday 13th January 2020: London.

The earliest flight from Venice was Monday morning and we eventually arrived back at Gatwick early in the afternoon. By the time we got out of the airport and caught the train to London, we did not reach Victoria Station until just after 2pm.

'Are you sure you don't want me to come into work this afternoon?' Harriet asked as we walked down the steps to the underground station.

'I'm sure.'

'I feel guilty.'

'Why?'

'Because you have to go into the office.'

'That's only because I have a meeting with Sam at four o'clock. Anyway, it's halfway through the afternoon already, so you might as well take some time off. You've earned it.'

'Thanks, that's great! I need to wash my hair and have a bath.' She twisted round and planted a passionate kiss on my lips. 'By the way thanks for fraternising with me,' she whispered in a husky voice as she pulled away. 'I'm still tingling.' With that she threw her rucksack across her shoulder, made her way through the barrier, and went down the escalator to the Victoria Line platform.

I headed for the District Line and caught an underground train to Hammersmith, where my car was parked. Half an hour later I was in Shepherd's Bush and drew up outside my apartment building.

I took my bag from the back seat and locked my car. As I headed towards the building's front door a British Gas van turned into my street and parked in front of my car. A man wearing blue overalls got out and opened the van's back doors.

Doris Warren, who lived in one of the ground floor apartments, and was our block's resident busy-body, opened the front door just as I reached it. No doubt she had been watching from her window.

'I missed you over the weekend, Mr Statton,' she said without preamble. 'Have you been away on one of your trips again?'

'Nowhere exciting, Doris,' I replied, then quickly changed the subject. 'I wonder what he wants?' I nodded towards the British Gas engineer who had taken a metal toolbox from his van and was closing the back doors.

'There's a gas leak,' Doris said in a matter of fact tone. 'I reported it to the Gas Board. I think it's coming from your flat.'

'Thanks, Doris. I'd better check it out then.' I eased past her and headed for the stairs.

'I wouldn't strike no matches,' she called after me. 'Better safe than sorry. Hey?'

'Thanks for the warning, Doris. I'll take care not to light a cigarette.'

'I didn't know you smoked, Mr Statton.' She sounded put out I had kept this a secret from her.

I looked back over my shoulder and saw that the gas engineer had arrived at the front door.

'Somebody reported a gas leak here,' he told Doris. He had a Scottish accent that was as thick as porridge. 'It's somewhere on the first floor, ye ken.'

'It's in his flat,' Doris pointed at me as I started up the stairs.

'Now, don't you forget, Mr Statton. No smoking.'

'She's right. I would nae light up if I were you,' the engineer warned as he followed me up the stairs.

'I don't smoke.'

'I thought the old biddy said you did.'

'She gets confused.' I tapped my temple.

When we reached the door to my apartment, the engineer stopped. 'Is this your place?'

'Yeah.'

He sniffed the air round the edge of my door. 'Och, the smell's definitely coming from here, so it is.'

I unlocked my front door, using three different security keys.

The engineer watched me push open the reinforced door. 'It's like Fort Knox. What d'ye keep in yon apartment, mate? Bullion?'

'Sadly not. The only gold any burglar will find is on the top of a milk bottle in my fridge.'

'What gas appliances d'ye have?' the engineer asked as he followed me into my hallway.

'A fire in the lounge, and a combi boiler and stove in the kitchen.'

The engineer opened the lounge door, walked in, and sniffed loudly again. 'It's nae the fire,' he said with certainty as I followed him into the room. 'But I think ye'd better open yon windows while I go check out the combi and stove. Where's the kitchen?'

I pointed out of the door. 'Down the end of the hallway and it's the door on the right,' I told him and then went to open the lounge windows.

I heard the engineer's footsteps as he walked down the

parquet floored hall and the sound of the kitchen door opening. A few minutes later the footsteps came back down the hall and he walked into the lounge carrying something in his hand.

'It's the stove, so it is.'

'Are you sure?'

'Och aye. I've checked it with this.' He showed me an instrument he held in his hand. It was a shiny black gadget with a large dial on its face. It meant nothing to me, but he seemed quite proud of it.

'What's wrong with it?'

'It's a problem with the hose, sure enough. I'll have to turn the gas off. Where's your meter?'

'In a cupboard in the downstairs lobby.'

'I might have a new hose in ma van. I'll check.' He went out and stomped noisily down the stairs.

I made my way through to the bedroom and dumped my bag on the bed. I looked out of the window and saw the engineer rooting round in the back of his van, but when he emerged he was empty handed. I swore to myself and guessed what was coming.

I heard the engineer come back up the stairs. I met him in the hallway.

He shook his head. 'I've nae hoses in ma van,' he said. 'I'll have to go back to the depot and get one, so I will.'

'Where's your depot?'

'Kew Bridge.'

I looked at my watch. It was 3.10pm. It would take the engineer at least twenty minutes to reach his depot and the same again to get back, add time to get a connector from the stores and it was likely to be at least an hour before he returned. 'I have a meeting in my office at four o'clock,' I explained.

'D'ye want me to come back tomorrow?'

'No. I'll leave my door keys downstairs with my neighbour. She'll let you in and then lock up after you.'

'That's grand. I'll leave ma toolbox in yon kitchen if that's okay with ye.'

It was very much all right with me. It meant he would have to come back and wouldn't leave me without gas overnight.

He must have read my mind. 'Don't worry. I'll turn the gas back on once I've fitted the new hose, so I will,' he said as we walked down the stairs together. 'And I'll check out the stove before I leave.'

'Thanks,' I said. When we reached the front door I took a ten pound note out of my wallet and handed it to him. 'Buy yourself a drink.'

He looked down at the tenner. 'Och, you're a belter, sir, so ye are,' he said and flashed me his first smile of the day. 'There's a chill to the air and a wee dram will go down a treat, so it will.'

Doris was more than happy to take charge of my door keys. It was not the first time I had asked for her help in this way, and her face flushed with pleasure as she assumed this responsibility.

'I'll keep my eye on him for you, Mr Statton.'

'Thanks, Doris, but I'm sure he's perfectly trustworthy.'

'I'm not so sure. I don't trust those Jocks.'

I didn't bother to ask her why; I knew all about Doris's prejudices and I didn't want to trigger one of her lengthy rants about our Scottish cousins. 'Don't worry, there's nothing worth nicking in my flat.'

'What about them records what you play all the time?' she asked in a tone that suggested she did not approve of my taste in music.

'I don't suppose he'd be interested in my Moody Blues collection. He looked more like a Proclaimers man to me.' I could see she had no idea who I was talking about, but I didn't enlighten her. 'Must dash,' I said and headed for my car.

'Don't worry,' she shouted after me. 'I'll keep my eye on him anyway.'

I slid into the driver's seat and started the engine. I glanced at my watch. It was going to be tight getting to Whitehall by 4pm, but life is too short to worry about being a few minutes late.

As it was, I made good time. The traffic was light, and I got all the way along Cromwell Road without much hindrance. I only had to stop briefly in Brompton Road when I hit a red traffic light outside Harrods, where a window dresser, wearing a pink top and black ski-pants, was putting the finishing touches to one of the store's fashion displays. It looked like a parody of changing the guard at Buckingham Palace.

At each end of the display was a wooden sentry box. Standing in front of each box was a mannequin dressed as a guardsman, wearing a tall bearskin cap. Between the two guardsmen were several female mannequins, dressed in a variety of scanty underwear. I was unsure as to the significance of the scene, but I guessed it was designed to sell bras rather than bearskin caps.

The window dresser was struggling to get an imitation rifle to stay on the shoulder of the left hand guardsman, but it kept sliding off. I never found out whether she succeeded in her task because the traffic lights changed to green.

The rest of my journey went without incident and I reached the car park at just before four o'clock. A few minutes later I walked into Rachel Frewin's office.

It had not taken Sam long to move into the office vacated by the suspended Dame Alexandra, but the transition was not going as smoothly as he might have hoped. His new secretary was not happy.

'Good afternoon, Rachel.'

'Is it?'

'Obviously not. What's the problem?'

'It's him,' she said disdainfully, nodding towards the adjoining door. 'He's only been in the office a day and he's already changed the way we operate.'

'Everybody likes things done their way,' I said gently.

'I suppose,' she conceded, 'but I hate change for changes sake.' She did not elaborate on the changes to which she took exception. I was grateful for that. I did not really want to hear about her problems because I had more than enough of my own.

'I miss Dame Alex. She was a real lady.'

'And, of course, your new boss isn't even a pretend lady.'

'Don't be silly, Steve,' she said with a reluctant smile. 'You know what I mean. Dame Alex knows how to treat people properly.'

'It's called breeding.'

'And another thing,' she began, but I interrupted her.

'Can I go in?'

'Yes, he was expecting you ten minutes ago.'

'I know, but I didn't want to raise his expectations. If I'd been punctual your boss would want it all the time.'

'You keep calling him my boss, Steve, but he's not, he's only Acting Director-General,' she emphasised as I made my way towards the adjoining door and opened it. 'Dame Alex is still my boss!' she added loudly as I entered the D-G's office.

Sam must have heard Rachel, but did not react, instead he looked up impassively from watering the red prize azalea he had brought from his old office, and which now took pride of place on the ultra-modern glass coffee table that he had brought with him also.

'How was your trip to Venice?' he asked pleasantly, his anger at my insubordination last week seemingly forgotten. He waved me towards a chair.

Although it was January, the winter sun was streaming through the window and had made the office warm. Sam had removed his jacket and was wearing a blue striped shirt and a pair of wide braces.

'You look like Gordon Gekko,' I told him as I settled into my seat.

'Who's Gordon Gekko when he's at home?' He sat down behind his desk. 'I've never heard of him.'

I told him.

'You think I look like a corporate raider?'

I could tell from his expression that he could not make up his mind whether to be insulted or flattered.

'An *amoral* Wall Street corporate raider,' I added to help him decide.

This made him cross. 'I am not amoral,' he insisted hotly.

'Don't take it personally. It was only a film.'

'So, remind me. Who was this Gekko fellow?'

'He was the anti-hero.'

'And you think I look like him?'

'Yeah, he was played by Steven Douglas.'

'Steven Douglas? Isn't he the good looking actor all the women lust after?'

'I wouldn't know. I'm not a woman.'

'Nor me. It's just what I heard.' He straightened a notebook on his desk and made sure the accompanying pencil was properly lined up with it. 'Do I really look like Steven Douglas?' he asked eventually.

I studied him carefully and frowned. 'Well, not physically, or facially, and to be honest, your hair is a different colour. However, you are wearing a similar shirt and braces.'

He stared at me. 'Are you taking the rise out of me, Statton?'

'Guilty as charged. But I can't help myself. You make it so easy for me.'

He glared at me. 'Do I really have to put up with your nonsense?'

'Yeah. I'm afraid it comes with the privilege of being my boss.'

'You really do push your luck sometimes.'

'Maybe, but unfortunately it rarely does me any good. Which is why they welcome me with open arms at my local bookies.'

He sighed and shook his head. 'So, what happened in Venice. How did you get on with the guy you were going to see?' He opened his notebook and looked down at it. 'This Mario Turfio chappie?'

'Tafuri,' I corrected him.

He tapped his notebook. 'No, I wrote down Turfio,' he insisted.

'That doesn't make it any less wrong. His name was definitely Tafuri.'

'Whatever,' he said with an irritable shrug. 'What happened when you met him?'

'I didn't meet him.'

'Why not?'

'Because it looks as if he pushed his luck too far and it ran out.'

'What do you mean?'

'I mean he's dead.' I explained what had happened in Venice and what we had discovered, ending with finding Tafuri's body.

'Do you really think he was murdered by a Mafia hitman?'

'It seems the only plausible explanation.'

'I see, and his death is somehow tied in with Operation QS?'

'That's what I think.'

He picked up his pencil and wrote something in his notebook. If my assessment was wrong, he would probably use it in evidence against me.

'Do you have much on at the moment?' he asked.

'Lots. Currently all my time is being taken up with this operation, and a load of documents have turned up on my desk, most of which look remarkably like the paperwork from Dame Alexandra that I delivered to your office last week.'

'I hate paperwork. I thought you might like to help with it.'

'Well, you thought wrong.'

'Well pass it onto that gorgeous secretary of yours to deal with.'

'I don't suppose my secretary is feeling particularly gorgeous at the moment.'

'Why's that?'

'Because she had an accident. She's off work and I'm not sure when she'll be back.' I decided not to mention the mystery surrounding Marion's actual whereabouts. I was clinging to the hope there was a simple explanation for her address not being on file.

'Well, never mind the paperwork, that can wait. I have another job for you. How would you like a trip to Suffield?'

'Norfolk in January is not an inviting prospect?'

'I'm talking about Suffield in Alberta, Canada.'

'You mean BATUS1[1]?'

'Yes.'

This did not sound good. 'When?' I asked.

'Tomorrow. I've booked you on a flight to Calgary.'

'You must be joking. Have you any idea how cold Alberta is at this time of year? It's worse than Norfolk, and that's saying something.'

'Just pack some thermal underwear and you'll be fine. Don't worry.'

'If you don't mind, I'll carry on worrying about catching frostbite, thank you very much.'

'Don't be such a wimp.'

'I like being a wimp.'

'Your old unit is currently based at BATUS,' he said this as if it would make me feel better. It did no such thing.

'Which unit? The Intelligence Corps, or the Royal Tank Regiment?'

'The Tankies.'

'Are you sure?'

'Positive,' he said, and then added: 'You look surprised.'

'I am. Our tank regiments usually undertake live-fire exercises at BATUS between May and October.'

'This is an exception to that rule. It seems the Canadians are undertaking an Arctic warfare exercise and they asked the Ministry of Defence for some tank support. The Chief of Staff decided to send the Tankies. Perhaps you'll bump into some of your old comrades.'

'I doubt it. I was only with the regiment for a couple of years back in the late Nineties, before I transferred to the Intelligence Corps. Since then a lot of the people I served with have been made redundant, particularly the better paid, long serving guys.'

'Why did you transfer?'

'Have you ever been inside a tank?'

'No,' he admitted.

'Try it sometime and then you'll understand. They're hot, smelly, and bloody uncomfortable.'

'I'll pass, thank you. By the way, you will be staying in the British Officers' mess at BATUS.'

'Are you coming to Canada with me?'

'No. The Prime Minister has asked me to attend the World Cybersecurity Conference in New York,' he answered smugly.

'What about Harriet?'

'Miss Barratt will not be going with you,' he replied frostily.

'I thought she was supposed to be shadowing me?' I was not really fussed whether Harriet joined me or not, but I wanted to make a point.

'That was when she was a member of your team, but that is no longer the case.'

'What do you mean?'

'Miss Barratt will no longer be working with you.'

'And why's that?'

'Because she was only assigned temporarily to the Ops Section until another post was found for her.'

'And?'

'And I have found her a post.'

'How convenient!'

He ignored my sarcasm. 'She is being transferred to the Research Section, where she'll be filling in for Debbie Hart, who is on maternity leave.'

I could see from his tone that there was no point questioning the decision. Sam Brewer was laying down a marker: he was now in charge.

'Okay, so why exactly am I going to Canada?'

'I received a call from Lloyd Harper,' he replied and then paused.

'I'm sure chatting to Harper must have been very exhilarating for you, but it doesn't answer my question.'

'If you can curb your impatience for a few moments longer you'll get your answer,' he said with a pompous smile. He was enjoying himself. 'Lloyd told me CSIS has uncovered a plot to smuggle high grade heroin into North America from Afghanistan.'

'A drugs ring?'

'Yes, and I have agreed that you will liaise with a couple of his agents so you can exchange information with them.'

'How much information?'

'I will leave that to your discretion. No doubt, you will want to discover as much as possible about their operation, whilst at the same time telling them as little as possible about ours.'

'No doubt I will. So, why's the meeting taking place at BATUS and not Ogilvie Road[2]?'

'I don't know,' he admitted, and I guessed he had forgotten to ask Harper that question. 'All I know is you are to meet Lloyd's guys at the base,' he went on hurriedly. 'I'm sure they will brief you fully then.'

'Let's hope you're right. Is there anything else I should know?'

'Yes. It seems the Americans asked Lloyd if they could send somebody to the meeting and he agreed.'

'I hope they don't send some gung-ho joker who thinks Uncle Sam rules the world.'

'Why not?'

'Because the CSIS already believes the CIA thinks they're amateurs. The Canadian agents won't be impressed if Langley send somebody who patronises them.' I stood up to leave.

'I'm sure you'll be able to use our special relationship with both America and Canada to smooth any ruffled feathers.'

I did not want to shatter Sam's illusions, so I left his office without another word. However, if he thought Britain still had any real influence over either country, he was even more naïve than I thought.

'Evening, Mr S,' Colin Plum said when I stepped through the security door into the jewellery shop. 'Off 'ome are we?'

'I don't know about you, but I'm having an early night.'

'I don't blame you. I suppose you'll be 'aving to pack for your trip.'

'What trip?'

'Your trip to Canada.' He winked and tapped the side of his nose. 'But don't worry if it's supposed to be a secret, Mr S. I won't say nuffink.'

I silently cursed the lax security in the department, but did not respond. However, my face must have shown my concern, because Plum quickly repeated his assurance.

"onestly, guv. Your secret's right safe with me. On me muvver's life.'

'I thought your mother was dead.'

'She is. She's been gone for nigh on ten years now, God bless 'er,' he said without showing any outward sign of remorse.

'So, who told you about my trip?' I asked. There seemed little point in denying the truth.

'It don't matter who tipped me off. Let's just say I know everything what goes on in this place.'

'Lucky you. I wish I did,' I moaned and headed for the door.

1   BATUS: British Army Training Unit Suffield.
2   1941 Ogilvie Road, Gloucester, Ottawa is the address of the CSIS headquarters.

18

Monday 13th January 2020: London.

When I arrived back in Shepherd's Bush the British Gas van had disappeared and there was a parking space right outside my apartment. This was a result. At that time of day in my neighbourhood, parking spaces were like gold dust.

I entered the building and turned on the downstairs' hall light. I knocked on Doris Warren's front door, but there was no response. I knocked again, but again there was no answer. That's when I remembered that Tuesday was her bingo night down at the local community centre. Retrieving the spare keys I gave her would have to wait until the next day.

I made my way up the stairs to my apartment. I could no longer smell gas, just food cooking. It had the aroma of an Italian sauce of some kind. I guessed it was coming from the flat opposite mine, into which a young couple had moved a couple of weeks before.

They seemed to live well. Unlike me they did not rely on a diet of tinned food and TV meals, instead they cooked proper dinners. Suddenly I realised I was hungry and tried to remember what food I had in my cupboard and fridge. Probably not much.

I paused when I reached my front door. I always make sure the coast is clear before entering my flat. It was part of my training. However, my recent experience in Venice made me even more cautious, because the Mafia's influence extended to London.

I looked back down the stairwell, but there was no sign of anybody on the ground floor, let alone somebody wearing a leather cap.

I checked my door, but found no sign of a forced entry. Satisfied, I unlocked the door and pushed it open. The hallway inside was dark and quiet. I stepped inside and flicked on the light.

Suddenly there was a noise from the direction of my kitchen. It sounded like metal tapping against wood. I crept up the hallway and pressed my ear against the door. I could hear somebody whispering.

I pulled my Glock 17 from its holster and cocked it. Silently I twisted the door handle and pushed the door open gently. Holding my weapon in the classic shooter's stance, I edged into the brightly lit kitchen. I was prepared for any eventuality, except the scene with which I was confronted.

Harriet was standing at the central work island cutting up a French-stick on a wooden chopping board and putting chunks of bread in a round wicker basket. She was singing quietly to herself. She looked up and smiled.

'Don't just stand there pointing that thing at me, open the wine.' She pointed at a bottle of red with the bread knife. 'I would have done it myself, but I couldn't find a corkscrew.'

'What are you doing?' I re-holstered my pistol.

'Performing a post-mortem on a baguette.'

'Very funny.'

'What do you think I'm doing? I'm cooking.'

Now I saw she had already laid the kitchen table for two and realised the smell of Italian herbs was coming from a saucepan on my stove.

'It's spaghetti Bolognese,' she explained.

'I didn't know I had spaghetti in my cupboard.'

'You didn't. In fact, you don't have much of anything worth eating in your flat. I went to the local supermarket and bought everything I needed.'

I picked up the bottle and saw it was a South African Shiraz. 'A good choice.'

'I do my best.'

I retrieved a corkscrew from the back of the utensil drawer where it was kept. I showed it to her and raised an eyebrow.

'I did a man search,' she said with a grin. 'I didn't have time to look properly because I was worried the spaghetti would stick.'

'How did you get in?' I asked as I opened the wine and sniffed the cork. 'Did Doris let you in?'

'Who's Doris?'

'She lives downstairs.'

'So why does she have the keys to your apartment?' She eyed me suspiciously.

'So she could let in a British Gas engineer for me.'

'Oh, that would be the guy who was just leaving when I arrived. He said he'd repaired your cooker.'

'I see. Did he leave my spare keys with you?'

'Yup.'

'What just like that?'

'I told him I was your girlfriend, but he didn't seem fussed either way.'

'Did he have anything else to say for himself?'

'No. He just wanted to get away as soon as possible.'

That did not surprise me. He probably wanted to get down the pub and spend the tenner I gave him.

'I put your keys in the desk drawer in the hall.'

I took one of the glasses from the table, poured some red wine into it and handed it to her.

'Thanks.' She passed me the basket of bread. 'Take that to the table and sit down while I dish up.'

I did not argue. I sat down and I poured myself a glass of wine.

She brought a plate over to the table and put it in front of me. It was piled high with steaming spaghetti that had been stewed in a rich Bolognese sauce, some of which sat in pools on my plate. It smelt wonderful.

Harriet had bought some Parmesan cheese and grated it into a dish. I sprinkled a couple of heaped table spoonfuls over my dinner. I took a chunk of the French bread from the basket and dunked it in the Bolognese sauce. It tasted delicious.

'Where did you learn to cook spaghetti Bolognese this way?' I asked as I spun some pasta on my fork and put it in my mouth.

'Auntie Xandra's mum taught me. She's from Italy. Do you like it?'

'No, it's horrible.'

'Then why are you wolfing it down like you haven't eaten in a year?'

'Because I'm hungry.'

'You beast! What do you really think?'

'I thinks it's the best spag-bog I've ever eaten.'

'Really?'

'Really.'

She smiled happily and got stuck into her own meal. 'How did your meeting with Brewer go?' she asked eventually. 'What

236

did he have to say?'

'He told me you were being transferred. I assume you've been told?'

'Yeah, there was a letter waiting for me when I got home today.' Her smile had disappeared.

'Sam didn't waste any time, did he? He only took over on Saturday.'

'He's a vindictive little twat,' she said with feeling. 'He's only moving me out of Ops as a way of getting at Auntie Xandra.,

I did not argue with her. She was probably right.

'So, what else did you discuss?' she asked.

'I have to go to Canada.'

'I know. Auntie Xandra told me all about your trip to BATUS.'

'You saw her?'

'No, I rang her to find out how she was.'

'How is she?'

'She said she was okay, but I could tell she was not herself.' She picked up her wine glass and looked at the deep red liquid thoughtfully.

Momentarily I wondered how Dame Alexandra had found out about my trip, despite being at home suspended. Either somebody in the department told her, or she had spoken with Lloyd Harper.

Harriet finished off her wine with one long swig then asked, 'So, you're flying out tomorrow evening?'

'Yeah, but I'll be in the office in the morning. I need to sort a few things out before I leave.' I poured her another glass and topped up my own. 'How much do I owe you for the food and wine?' I asked, changing the subject.

'Nothing. It's my treat.'

'Nonsense. I want to pay.'

'But I enjoyed cooking for you.'

'That's not the point.'

'Okay. If you want to give me something in return. Let me stay the night with you.'

'I don't have a spare bedroom.'

'That doesn't matter. I'm happy to share your bed. I enjoyed doing it in Venice and I want to do it again.'

'It?'

'Yeah. It.' She gave me a suggestive wink.

'Are you sure?'

'I'm very sure. Look at it this way. If I stay the night, it will save me going back to an empty apartment?'

'Well we can't have that, can we?' I tried not to smile. 'All right, you can stay the night.'

Harriet jumped to her feet and gave me a big hug. 'Can we go to bed soon?' she whispered in my ear.

'What's that perfume you're wearing?'

'Decadent. Which is exactly how I feel. Sitting looking at you was enough to make me horny.'

'You really are a brazen little hussy.'

'Take me to bed and I'll show you how brazen.'

'Okay, but answer me one question first,' I said.

'What's that?'

'How did you know where I live?'

'That's easy. I got it from HR.'

'HR gave you my address?'

'Yeah, I told them I wanted to send you a birthday card.'

'But my birthday isn't until June.'

'HR obviously don't know that because they didn't argue.'

'I give up on those numpties,' I said with a resigned shake of my head.

'Forget them.' She took my hand and pulled me to my feet. 'Just take me to bed and treat me like a hussy.'

So, we went to bed and I didn't get to sleep until the early hours of Tuesday morning.

19

Tuesday 14th January 2020: Canadian Forces Base, Suffield, Alberta, Canada

When my plane landed in Calgary the hands on my watch indicated it was 8.17pm local time, on 14th January.

I have never been able to sleep when travelling by plane - no matter how long the journey - and my eyes were heavy when I trudged slowly down the aircraft stairs and stepped onto Canadian soil.

By the time I had retrieved my bag from the luggage carousel, and gone through the immigration process, the digital clock on the wall next to the green Nothing To Declare sign in the customs area showed the time in Alberta was 21:30 hrs.

Although it was difficult for my eyes to argue with the clock, my mind refused to accept this reality because my body thought it was still in London, where the time was already 4am on Wednesday 15th, and most people were still tucked up in bed, sound asleep.

My tired body envied them.

I passed through a set of automatic sliding doors and stepped out into the arrivals hall, where I found a couple of dozen people standing on the other side of a rope barrier. Some of them were holding up signs, each with a name written on it. One of the names was mine.

I went over and introduced myself to the driver who would be taking me to the Canadian Forces Base in Suffield. He was tall, black, muscular and wore army fatigues with the three stripes of a sergeant on a tab hanging in the centre of his chest. On his beret was a Royal Canadian Regiment badge.

The sergeant gave me a brief smile, and an even briefer salute, then relieved me of my heavy rucksack and threw it effortlessly over his shoulder. 'Please follow me, sir, your transport is close by,' he said in a velvet-smooth deep voice.

My driver was not exaggerating. An old Khaki coloured Land Rover Defender 90, flying a red and gold coloured pennant, and with a single black maple leaf stencilled on each door, was parked alongside the covered walkway just outside the sliding doors to the arrivals hall.

I was pleased we did not have far to walk because the jeans, shirt, and light jacket I wore for comfort on the plane, did not offer much protection from the falling snow that had already turned the Land Rover's roof white.

The sergeant stowed away my rucksack in the back of the Defender and pulled out a Canadian Army issue parka. 'Our base Quartermaster thought you might need this, sir.' He handed the khaki-coloured coat to me along with a smile.

'Your QM was right,' I told him as I took the proffered parka.

My driver opened the passenger door for me, and I climbed onto the seat. It was cold inside the Land Rover, so I gratefully pulled on the heavy parka and snuggled down.

'I didn't realise the Canadian Army used Landys.'

'We don't have many. I usually drive a Mercedes G Wagon, but it's in the workshop being serviced at the moment,' the sergeant explained as he settled into the driver's seat. 'However, we trialled Land Rovers a while back and we still have a small fleet of them on the base. This baby was all I could get my hands on today.'

I shivered. 'It's like a fridge on wheels.'

'Don't worry, sir. The heater will soon kick in.' The driver started up the engine.

'How long is the journey going to take?'

'Just over three hours,' he replied and switched on his wipers to clear the snow from his windscreen and then added: 'If you don't mind me saying so, sir, you look pretty pooped.'

'I haven't had much sleep in the last couple of days,' I said and immediately thought of Harriet, who was an energetic and demanding lover.

'No shit? In that case I'd grab some shuteye if I were you.'

He did not have to tell me twice. I closed my eyes and slept until I was woken up by my shoulder being gently shaken.

'We're almost there, sir.'

I looked out of the window. On our left we were passing a brick walled structure on which a plaque read:

Canadian Forces Base Suffield

Base des Forces Canadiennes

There was a tall flagpole on either side of the structure, one flying the Canadian flag and the other the Union flag of the United Kingdom. Both flags were flapping wildly, as if urging reluctant troops into battle.

Black clouds had dumped a thick layer of snow on the ground in front of the wall and were now scudding across the sky, blotting out the light from the moon, which occasionally managed to show us its frowning face. The clouds were driven by a brisk wind that blew up the highway, whipping some of the snow back up into the air from where it had only recently fallen.

We turned off the highway onto a slip road that led into the base, and stopped at a red and white painted manual raise barrier arm that blocked the road. A soldier came out of the guard booth with a carbine over his shoulder and walked up to the driver's door.

The sergeant wound down his window and showed his identity card. The guard gave the card a cursory glance and then craned his neck to look at me.

'He's a British Veep,' my driver told the guard, who accepted this explanation without comment. The guard raised the barrier arm and waved us through into the camp. He seemed keen to get us out of the way quickly so that he could get back to the warmth of his booth. Who could blame him?

The joint Canadian and British military base was home to a cluster of buildings. Some were brick built, but most were made from corrugated iron and looked like aircraft hangers. These were garages and workshops where tanks and other vehicles were serviced and stored.

We drew up outside a long brick built building with a flat roof, which looked like a prison block. It must have felt like that to those military personnel who were forced to stay in the camp throughout the winter.

'This is the British officers' quarters, sir,' the sergeant explained, as he opened the driver's door and got out of the Land Rover. I was still too tired to tell him I knew this because I had been to the base before.

The soldier did not seem worried about the cold that slapped us round the face once we were out of the warm cab. He retrieved my bag and I followed him towards the building.

In the entrance stood a tall, slim man dressed in the evening dress uniform of the US Marines. His chest was decorated with two rows of medal ribbons, above which was pinned the eagle insignia of a colonel.

'I'll take that, soldier,' the officer said, taking my bag from the driver.

'Sir!' The sergeant sprang to attention and saluted smartly. Then he turned on his heel and disappeared out of the door with the hint of a smirk on his face.

'You're up late, Troy,' I said.

'I've been to dinner in the officers' mess,' Olsen explained.

'Complete with plenty of booze I see.'

'What makes you say that?'

'Your face is flushed, your speech is slightly slurred, and you have a couple of red wine spots on your dress shirt.'

Olsen looked down at the front of his shirt and then laughed out loud, filling the air with alcohol fumes. 'You'd make a good Sherlock Holmes, Stevie,' he said when he finished chortling.

'Not me. I don't smoke a pipe and I can't stand the sound of the violin.' I responded. 'So, I was right about there being plenty of booze?'

'Yeah and it's still flowing.'

'So why aren't you in there flowing with it?'

'Because I wanted to welcome you to the base personally.'

'I'm deeply touched and can't thank you enough.'

My sarcasm was lost on Olsen. 'It was my pleasure, pal,' he said and then paused for effect. 'Although it might have been different if the mess hadn't just run out of Jack Daniels.' He offered me a lopsided grin.

'You look smart.' I pointed at his dark blue evening coat. 'I hope they're not expecting me to dress like that for dinner.'

'No, but they won't let you in the mess wearing those,' he pointed at my jeans and trainers. 'Did you bring a uniform?'

'Of course, but only my old combat uniform.'

'That's cool. You won't need anything fancy. They don't usually wear Number Ones to dinner, but tonight was a special occasion. It was a farewell banquet for Chas Mitchell. Do you know him?'

I shook my head.

'Colonel Charles Mitchell is in charge of BATUS,' he told me, as if he expected the explanation to jog my memory.

'The name still means nothing to me,' I said. 'So, why the banquet? Is Charlie Boy retiring?'

'No, he's been transferred to the British Training Unit in Kenya.'

'I bet he's happy about that. It's a hell of a lot warmer in Nanyuki than it is here in Ralston. So, how come you were invited to his leaving do?'

'Chas and I got to know each other during the Gulf War and have been buddies ever since.'

'Are you telling me that you came all the way from London for a bloody booze-up?'

He smiled. 'Nope. The timing of Chas's farewell party was coincidental. I'm here for the same reason as you.' He headed towards an internal door and indicated that I should follow him.

'And what reason would that be?'

'We're gonna be briefed about a drug smuggling ring the Canucks have uncovered in Afghanistan. Didn't Langley tell you guys I was coming?'

I shrugged. 'We were told the Firm was sending somebody, but they didn't say who.'

'Well Bishop[1] sent me. Is that a problem?'

'Of course not. I'm just surprised you need a briefing.'

'How so?'

'Because I heard you guys were working with the Canadians on the Afghan operation, so I thought you'd be up to speed with what's happening.'

'Dream on, pal, dream on. I probably know less than you about what's going on.'

'How come?'

'Because the Firm's tie up with the Canucks is being handled out of Langley. As you know, I've been based in London for some time and have been out of the loop.'

'So why did Bishop bring you all the way from London, rather than use somebody based Stateside?'

'Your guess is as good as mine. I just do as I'm told. Anyway, you came all the way from London.'

'That's because we don't have an office in North America and, like you, I do as I'm told.' I was not at all taken in by his story. Olsen might think I am stupid, but I knew he was not.

'I suppose the bottom line is you and I are only pieces in a geopolitical chess game being played by our masters,' he said sounding as if he had rehearsed this line many times before.

'Yeah, we're the poor bloody pawns.' I played along with his charade.

'Damn right!' he snapped as he led me down a corridor. 'But let me tell you something, Stevie. This pawn's had enough, and it's gonna bite back.'

'Pawns don't have teeth,' I pointed out gently.

This provoked a mirthless grin. 'Maybe not, pal, but some-day soon I'm gonna pull down their pants and stick their king where the sun don't shine.'

He glared at me, daring me to argue with him. I was not taken in by his confected anger and I chose not to rise to the bait. From what little I already knew of the American agent he was not one of life's natural rebels. If you cut him in half, he would have the word Establishment running through him like a stick of seaside rock.

He stopped and opened a door. 'This is our room.'

'Our room?' I queried as I looked through the door. It was a very small room.

'Yeah, you're bunking down with me.'

'I thought these rooms were reserved for us Brits. How come a Yank spook was allowed into our club?'

'I can be very persuasive. Howdya think I managed to get you a rack in this joint,' he said with a grin. 'So, Major Statton, do you have a problem with our temporary sleeping arrangements?'

'Not at all, as long as you don't mind having a limey as a roommate.'

'I had no choice, pal,' he said with another grin. 'All the other rooms are taken. It was either this or sling a hammock in one of the hangers.'

I pointed at his uniform. 'So, how come you're dressed as a Jarhead[2]?'

'I'm still an honorary colonel and a uniform goes a long way on a military base. The enlisted ranks are always suspicious of civilians, particularly spooks.'

I followed him into the room, which consisted of two tiny sleeping areas, separated by a clear plastic curtain decorated with faded blue dolphins.

Olsen had already appropriated the left-hand cubicle and he dumped my bag on the right-hand bed to emphasise the point.

'The head[3] is through there.' He pointed at a door set into the opposite wall.

I opened the door and saw a shower with a matching dolphin curtain, a sink with a mirror above it, and a stained metal toilet. They were better facilities than you find in a prison cell, but only by a toilet seat.

'Do you know where the CSIS guys are staying?' I asked as I pulled my bag from the bed and stowed it in a rickety wooden cupboard.

'No idea.' Olsen replied as he stripped off his uniform and headed for the bathroom. 'Don't know about you, bud, but I'm gonna clean up and hit the sack.'

I stretched out on my bed to wait for him. 'I won't be long behind you,' I said with a yawn. I was wrong. By the time my new roommate came out of the bathroom, I was already asleep. He did not wake me.

---

1   Vaughn Bishop was Deputy Director of the CIA from August 2018 until January 2021.
2   Jarhead: slang name for a US marine.
3   Head: naval name for a toilet.

20

Wednesday 15th January 2020: Canadian Forces Base, Suffield, Alberta, Canada

Olsen and I had breakfast in the British officers' mess. It was a wood-panelled room, with a thick carpet and plush curtains, which seemed out of place in the functional military-style building in which it was located.

At one end of the mess was a pool table, a few low armchairs, and a long coffee table on which was an untidy stack of newspapers and magazines.

On the wall behind the pool table was a dartboard cabinet, the open doors of which were lined with blackboards showing, written in white chalk, the scores from the most recent game of 301 played there. It looked as if somebody had been badly beaten.

At the other end of the room was a long dining table, surrounded by chairs, and a sturdy oak sideboard on top of which were displayed a range of cereals and metal lidded serving dishes containing hot food, to which Olsen helped himself to a double helping.

I was still suffering the after-effects of jetlag, so restricted myself to a bowl of cornflakes, a couple of slices of toast, and several cups of strong, black coffee.

When we had finished, we left the mess and walked the short distance to the Canadian Forces administration building, in which our meeting with the CSIS agents was being held.

The previous night's clouds had been replaced by a clear, cobalt-blue sky, in which the sun was just creeping above the roof of the neighbouring garage. However, what warmth the sun offered was never going to be enough to melt the snow that fell during the night, not least because it was immediately nullified by a bitterly-cold northerly wind.

Olsen and I both wore camouflage combat uniforms, which included thermal vests and thick woollen jumpers, and we were grateful for the protection they offered from the biting cold air.

The American wore a US Marines' utility peaked cap, and I wore the black beret of the Royal Tank Regiment, complete with a silver badge depicting a laurel wreath enclosing a stylised tank, and topped with a crown.

Our meeting was in a room at the end of the main corridor. As we walked up the corridor, we passed the open door of what looked like a conference room, in which I could see two long tables, each with several swivel chairs alongside. On top of each table stood a number of computers and telephones. These tables were facing a wall on which were fixed two giant screens.

There were no lights on in the room, except a flashing screen saver on one computer monitor, which no doubt an operator had forgotten to switch off.

In a corner of the room I could see two desks. These too had chairs alongside them and each displayed a computer and phone.

'Looks like an operations room,' I said.

'Or a telephone call centre,' the rangy Texan suggested.

'I don't think so, they're all based in Mumbai these days.'

When we reached the meeting room, the two Canadian agents were waiting for us. They were sitting at a table, but stood up when we entered the room.

One was a scruffy young man with long, greasy, black hair tied back in a ponytail. He wore a University of Ottawa sweatshirt and denim jeans. Despite affecting a wispy goatee beard, he looked young enough still to be at school. He introduced himself as Lenny Bruce and then yawned loudly behind his hand before apologising for this rudeness.

His colleague introduced herself too. Geneviève Le Strange also had long hair, but hers was light brown, stylishly cut in layers and lay across her shoulders. She was dressed smartly in a body-hugging silk top and tight denim jeans, which were tucked into the tops of a pair of silver cowboy boots. Geneviève did not yawn, nor did she look like a schoolgirl.

Olsen and I introduced ourselves.

'It's a pleasure to meet you, Major Statton.' The woman took my proffered hand in a firm grip and shook it. She studied me with shrewd, vivid-blue eyes, the liveliness of which was not dimmed by the dark shadows of tiredness under them.

'Since we'll be working together, Geneviève, let's make it Steve.'

'I'm cool with that, but if we're gonna keep it informal, Genny is just fine with me.' She had a wide mouth and a set of perfect white teeth, which were revealed when she smiled. I soon found out they were on show a lot.

She turned to shake the American's hand. 'And it's good to meet you also, Colonel Olsen.'

'The pleasure is all mine, ma'am,' he told her with old fashioned Southern charm that could have graced the set of *Gone With The Wind* and he held onto her hand longer than was strictly necessary. 'And Geneviève is a real pretty name,' he continued to ham up, 'but like my limey friend says, if we're gonna work together, let's drop the starchy stuff. So, I'll call you Genny and y'all can call me Troy.' He nodded at Bruce to include him in his remark.

'It's a deal,' she agreed with another smile, before resuming her seat next to her colleague.

Olsen and I sat opposite them.

'You look rough, kid,' Olsen told Bruce without preamble.

'That's what twenty-hour days do for you, sir,' the young man replied. 'Ain't that right, boss?' he directed this question at his colleague.

'Yeah. Long days and short nights lead to dreadful sights,' she agreed, reciting it like a well-rehearsed rhyme. She turned to me and explained: 'Lenny and I have spent the last few days setting up an operations room as part of the mission we're working on. It's been a pretty exhausting time for us both.'

'What exactly are you working on?' I asked.

'Have you ever heard of Buzkashi?'

'Yeah.' I said and told her what I had found out about the sport during my recent trip to Iraq.

'Our current mission is code named Project Buzkashi,' she explained when I finished talking. 'My boss told me to brief you about it, but he didn't tell me how much you guys already knew. He just sent me in blind.'

'I know the feeling,' I said.

'I'm pleased I'm not alone,' she said with a smile. 'Point is, I don't want to waste time telling you something you already know. For instance, how familiar are you with the drugs trade in Afghanistan?'

'Well, I know drugs are being smuggled into North America from Afghanistan. I know you have an agent operating undercover in the country investigating the drugs ring. I know he uses the name of Yamin Abdullah, and I know he works as a chauffeur for a horse breeder called Azad Nuristani.'

Geneviève raised an eyebrow in surprise. 'You know about Abdullah?'

'Yeah, and I know also that his real name is Sean MacDonald.'

'Anything else?'

I shook my head. 'No,' I lied. I did know more, but I was not inclined to reveal that to her yet.

Geneviève stared at me silently for a few moments. 'How did you find out about Sean?' she asked eventually.

I explained about the photograph of Abdullah we obtained and how Harriet Barratt was able to trace him through the MI6 database. 'But it shouldn't come as a surprise to you that I know MacDonald's name.'

'Why not?'

'Because last week my boss had a conversation with Lloyd Harper during which they discussed MacDonald.'

'I see. Just one more thing Lloyd forgot to mention to me,' she moaned and then quickly changed the subject before being sucked into the quicksand of disloyalty. 'So, this Harriet is your assistant?'

'She was.'

'Why the past tense? Has she left the Agency?'

'No, she's been transferred to another section.'

'You sound disappointed.'

'Yeah. People of Harriet's calibre are difficult to find.'

'That's for sure. You find somebody with half a brain, get them used to your way of working, and then they get promoted.

Take Lenny, he's leaving my team soon to head up the SIS IT Department.'

'So now I have only half a brain?' Bruce protested with a grin to show he was only joking.

Geneviève laughed and it fluttered lightly round the room like a butterfly searching for nectar. It was a nice sound. 'Far from it. Indeed, sometimes I think you were gifted two brains.' She turned to me. 'We're gonna miss Lenny. What he doesn't know about hardware and software could be written on the back of a postage stamp.'

'I'm the reverse,' I told her and was rewarded by the butterfly fluttering again.

'What about you, Troy? How much do you know?'

'I'm the same as you, Genny. My boss has kept me pretty much in the dark on this one. I only know what the Brits told me and that ain't much. In fact, I'd never heard of Buzkashi until you mentioned it.'

'In that case, perhaps I should start by telling you exactly what Sean MacDonald has discovered in Afghanistan.' She turned to me again. 'As you rightly said, Sean is working for Azad Nuristani, who breeds and sells horses that are used in Buzkashi matches.'

'So are these Buzkashi horses like polo ponies?' Olsen asked.

'Yes,' Geneviève confirmed. 'In fact, some of Nuristani's horses are sold to a polo club in Italy.'

'The Mancini Polo Club,' Bruce chipped in. 'Which we believe is owned by the Italian Mafia.'

'Sean found out the Buzkashi horses are transported by road to Italy in horseboxes,' the woman went on. 'He discovered also that the horses go there via a poppy farm in Charikar, which is owned by one of the leaders of the Taliban.'

'His name is Jalaluddin Haqqani,' Bruce added.

I knew some of this, but again kept my mouth shut.

'A poppy farm?' Olsen murmured thoughtfully.

'I know what you're thinking, Troy, and you're right,' Geneviève said.

'Drug trafficking?'

'Yes. Haqqani has on his farm a sophisticated processing plant that converts opium into morphine and then into heroin. Sean thinks bags of the finished product are loaded into hidden compartments in the chassis of the horseboxes and then transported along the Balkan Route[1], before being smuggled into Italy via the Durres to Ancona ferry.'

'I've been on that ferry,' Olsen said. 'The journey takes over eighteen hours. Why not use one of the shorter routes, like Vlora to Brindisi?'

'That's easy to explain,' Geneviève said. 'The smugglers are relatively safe during their journey from Afghanistan to Albania, and even whilst on the ferry. However, as soon as the horseboxes reach Italy, they are at risk of being stopped by an overzealous cop. The shorter the road journey, the lower the risk.'

I could see understanding dawn on Olsen's face, but Geneviève did not seem to notice because she carried on with her explanation.

'The distance from Ancona to the Treviso, is only three hundred and sixty kilometres, and takes around three and a half hours, so, using the Durres ferry reduces the risk considerably.'

'That makes sense,' Olsen conceded. 'So what happens to the horseboxes when they reach Treviso?'

'They are delivered to the Mancini Polo Club, where the heroin is unloaded and distributed by the Mafia using their drugs network, which stretches across Western Europe,' Geneviève answered.

'How does the Mafia get the horse from Italy into North America?' Olsen asked.

'Don't you know?' Geneviève asked.

He looked surprised. 'Should I know?'

She smiled. 'Yes, because that particular drug route was uncovered by your CIA agents based in Rome only last month.'

Olsen closed his eyes and shook his head in disbelief. 'Why am I not surprised?'

'You weren't told?'

'No, Langley must have forgotten me when they sent out the memo,' he replied in a tight voice. 'So what's the story?'

'The story is that the drugs are shipped to Canada, via Greenland. A small private jet is loaded with packages of heroin at Marco Polo airport in Venice, and is then flown to Nuuk Airport, where it's refuelled before heading for Calgary International.'

'If that's the case, why's your operations room being set up here?' I asked. 'Why not Calgary?'

'Because the drugs never reach Calgary,' Geneviève explained. 'As the plane descends on its approach to the airport, it lands discreetly on an isolated landing strip out on the prairie. Once the drugs are off loaded they are taken south to Montana by road.'

'And nobody notices all this happening?' I asked.

'No, the plane lands, the drugs are unloaded, and the plane takes off again within minutes. It all happens so quickly the air traffic controllers don't have time to notice the plane has disappeared momentarily, because they are concentrating on the more important airliner traffic.'

'So, the landing strip is somewhere out on the Suffield Block?' I asked, pointing out of the window.'

'Yes,' she replied. 'In fact it's only about a hundred and thirty kilometres[2] north of this base.'

I was not surprised at her use of the word "only" to describe a distance roughly the same as from London to Southampton. The province of Alberta, where BATUS is located, occupies an area of 660,000 square kilometres[3]. In the grand scheme of things, the landing strip was on the base's doorstep.

'It's in a place called Albert Springs,' she went on, 'which until the Second World War was a prosperous farming community, but a succession of droughts has turned it into a ghost town. All it consists of these days is a few derelict farmhouses and outbuildings.'

I nodded. I knew that area quite well. 'I assume you have the landing strip under observation?'

'Yeah, we're using a drone to keep tabs on what's happening,' Lenny Bruce answered, making a rare contribution to the conversation.

'Is that your operations room next door?' Olsen asked.

Bruce laughed. 'No, sir. Sadly we have nothing as grand. That's the operations centre for the Canadian Forces division that's currently undertaking Arctic warfare exercises out on the Block. Desk geeks direct the battle by monitoring information provided by the Fire Control Battlefield Information System.' He turned to me and pointed at the cap badge on the beret that lay on the table in front of me. 'You probably know there's a battle group from your regiment taking part in the exercise.'

'Yeah. I assume we're the enemy.'

'Only for the purposes of the exercise, I assure you,' Geneviève interjected quickly, showing her teeth again.

'That's a relief,' I said. 'I'd hate to fall out with our Commonwealth cousins.'

'Never.'

'How are my guys doing? Are they acquitting themselves well?'

'They sure as hell are. I was chatting to the CF Commander, who told me your Royal Tank Regiment crews are awesome. Apparently they're giving his guys a real lesson in tank warfare in Arctic conditions.'

A door opened and closed at the other end of the building. We lapsed into silence as we heard footsteps coming down the corridor. However, the footsteps didn't reach our room and soon we heard the murmur of voices coming from the room next door.

Olsen broke the silence: 'I bet your boys ain't happy having a bunch of limeys running rings round them,' he said to Geneviève.

'The very opposite,' the Canadian agent insisted. 'Our tank commanders take a very pragmatic view of the exercises. They don't see themselves as being in competition with our British allies, but partners working together for the common good. In fact, our guys are very happy with the lessons they are being taught, and the Brits are very modest about their technical and professional superiority.' She gave Olsen time to let her words sink in before adding quietly: 'They don't patronise us like some nations I could mention.'

The putdown was less than subtle, but if Olsen noticed the implied criticism of his countrymen, he did not respond.

Instead he said to Bruce: 'I was involved in the battlefield control ops during the first Gulf War. I'd sure like to see what the set-up is like next door. What about it, kid?'

'Good idea!' the youngster said enthusiastically. 'As it happens, I was able to commandeer a desk next door, which we're using as a back-up to our Ops Room. We can sit there and watch.' Bruce gave his boss an enquiring look.

'No problem,' she said. 'We're pretty well finished here anyway.'

Bruce eased himself to his feet. 'Come on then, Colonel. It sounds like the Ops Team has started arriving.' He nodded in the direction of the room next door from where we heard somebody sneeze. 'They'll be preparing for today's battle soon. While we watch them I can explain about the equipment they are using.'

'So where exactly is your Ops Room?' I asked Geneviève when the two men had left the room.

'We've installed a portable building in woodland between Alice Springs and a little place called Bindloss.'

'When do Troy and I get to see it?'

'Very soon. We've been tipped off by the CIA resident agent in Rome that a shipment of drugs is due to leave Venice tomorrow.'

'Any idea when it will arrive?'

'Not really. The CIA agent will send us a message first thing in the morning to confirm the plane has taken off. It should take around seven hours to reach Greenland. Once the plane has refuelled, we can expect it to land here plus or minus six hours after that. But the actual timings will depend on the wind.'

'So sometime tomorrow evening?'

'That's what we're working towards.'

'Are you ready for it?'

'We will be. Lenny is going up to Bindloss later today to prepare the Ops Room for action, and he'll stay there overnight. As soon as we receive the flight confirmation from Rome tomorrow we'll join Lenny in Bindloss, and ensure the backup forces are in position and ready for action.'

'Backup forces?'

'Yeah. The Canadian Special Operations Regiment are assisting us with a platoon of soldiers and the RCMP[4] are sending a dozen cops from K Division as cover. In addition, your Tank Regiment is providing a section of troopers to make up the numbers.'

'How many smugglers are you expecting to be on the plane?'

'Just the pilot.'

'Do you think forty or so guys will be enough?' I asked drily.

'I hope so,' she said, missing the irony in my voice. 'I'm sure they'll all be heavily armed.' She opened the laptop that was positioned on the table in front of her. 'There's something I want to show you.' She pointed at a flat screen that was fixed to the wall opposite us and yawned loudly. 'Sorry,' she apologised, tapping away on the keys of her computer. 'I'm whacked.'

'Are you staying on the base?' I asked as the screen lit up.

'No, we're booked into a hotel in Medicine Hat.' She punched some more keys and an aerial photograph of the Suffield Block appeared on the screen. 'With Lenny staying up at Bindloss, there will be little more I can do today, so with a bit of luck I'll be able to eat dinner at a reasonable time and get an early night.'

She hit another key and the photo zoomed in until a more detailed view of the snow-covered prairie came into sharp relief.

She stood up and walked over to the screen. 'This is the landing strip,' she pointed at a straight brown slash in the otherwise pure white landscape, 'and this building is where the smugglers store their equipment and aviation fuel,' she pointed at what looked like a dilapidated barn, before returning to her seat.

She punched her keyboard again and the photograph zoomed out slightly, taking in more of the area adjacent to the landing strip. Due east was a splash of green. This time she used the screen cursor to point to it. 'That's the wood where our ops room is located.'

We sat looking at the photograph in silence.

'So where can you get a decent meal in Medicine Hat?' I asked eventually.

'Are you fishing?' she asked.

'Depends on whether you like fishermen.'

'I like fishermen.'

'In that case, I'm fishing.'

'There's a great steakhouse. They use local beef and it's so fresh their T-bone steaks start mooing if you don't eat them quickly enough.'

'Sounds perfect. Mind if I join you for a meal?'

'I'd be delighted.'

'Want me to pick you up?'

'Do you have transport?'

'I'm sure I can sort something out. The camp commander is a friend of Troy, and he's loaned us a Land Rover.'

She smiled. 'Snap! Colonel Mitchell has loaned me one also.'

'Do you share the Landy with your sidekick?'

'No, Lenny is a two-wheel freak. He rode his HD^5 from Edmonton, and will be using it to get to Bindloss.'

'Rather him than me. It's too cold for four wheels, let alone two. So, what time do you want me to pick you up?'

'How does seven-thirty suit you?'

'Suits me just fine. Where's your hotel?'

She didn't answer immediately, instead she scrolled down the photograph until an area south of the CF base could be seen. Using the cursor, she pointed at the length of a road that had been exposed. 'That's the Trans-Canada Way, which links Suffield to Medicine Hat,' the cursor stopped and hovered over an oblong shaped building, 'and that's our hotel. It's the Hampton Inn. You can't miss it.'

'I'll find it,' I promised.

'Okay, I'll meet you in the hotel lobby,' she closed down her laptop and stood up. 'Come on, we'd better go rescue your colleague. Lenny loves a captive audience and he'll keep Troy there for hours if we're not careful. In addition, Lenny needs to get himself sorted before his trip up north this afternoon.'

'Lead the way. Troy and I need to make a move anyway. We have an appointment with a Challenger Two tank.'

We went next door where we found the pair had migrated from Bruce's commandeered desk and were now sitting alongside one of the Ops Room staff, watching his computer screen intently.

'Come on, Colonel Olsen, our big boy's toy is waiting.' I said.

The American got to his feet.

'I understand you're going for a ride in a Challenger Two,' Bruce said without looking away from the operator's screen.

'That's right,' I replied.

'That's so cool, man.'

'I wish that were true, because it's bloody hot inside a tank, even in this weather.'

Geneviève escorted us out.

'That's one bright kid you have there,' Olsen told Geneviève when we were in the corridor and out of Lenny's earshot.

'I know, trouble is other people know it as well, which is why I'm losing him.'

We reached the outer door where she shook Olsen's hand. 'I won't come out, it's too damn cold.'

'See you later, Steve,' she said as she shook my hand, then headed back down the corridor.

'What's happening later?' Olsen queried.

'We're having dinner together.'

'Wow! Do I smell romance in the air?'

'It's only dinner,' I insisted as we headed towards our loaned Land Rover. 'We're not getting married.'

He grinned. 'So, where are you meeting?' he asked as we reached the Land Rover.

'Medicine Hat. Any chance I can borrow this?' I tapped the vehicle's bonnet with my hand.

'No problem, bud.' He unlocked the driver's door and climbed in. 'I wasn't planning on going anywhere special tonight. I promised Chas a game of pool in the mess, and I thought after that I might hit the sack early.'

I joined him in the cab just as he started the engine. 'I'll try not to disturb you if I'm late back.'

'That's if you make it back.' He winked at me.

'Just drive,' I said.

---

1   The Balkan Route runs through Iran, Iraq, Turkey, Bulgaria and Albania.
2   About 80 miles.
3   About 231,616 square miles.
4   RCMP: Royal Canadian Mounted Police.
5   HD: Harley Davidson

21

Wednesday 15th January 2020: Rattlesnake Camp, Suffield Block, Alberta, Canada

The Royal Tank Regiment usually uses Salisbury Plain, in Wiltshire, to undertake the training needed to ensure its warfare readiness is maintained, and the area in which they undertake their exercises is spread across 150 square miles.

However, although Salisbury Plain is suitable for most of the regiment's training needs, more dangerous exercises, such as those involving the firing of live ammunition, need somewhere much larger and more remote. The Suffield Block is an ideal place.

Located in the Alberta section of the Canadian prairies, it has more than enough space. The battlefield training ground consists of over 1000 square miles of undulating barren scrubland on which little grows except brown grass.

That's where we were now.

We were on our way to join Badger Squadron of the Royal Tank Regiment, which was taking on the role of the enemy in another day-long Arctic warfare exercise being undertaken by C Squadron of the Royal Canadian Dragoons Regiment.

Between them, the two squadrons would be represented on the battlefield by 21 Canadian Leopard 2 tanks and 15 British Challenger 2 Main Battle Tanks. In addition, both sides in the exercise were supported by a couple of armoured personnel carriers and several other military vehicles.

The squadrons were based in a makeshift battlefield camp deep in the Great Plains. That's where Troy and I were heading in our borrowed Land Rover Defender.

We were travelling along a wide tarmacked road, which ran through the Suffield Block, from the Canadian Forces Base in the south, to the far north-east corner of Cypress County.

Olsen was uncharacteristically silent as he concentrated on his driving, or perhaps he just did not want to talk. So, I sat and stared out of the window.

The landscape was blanketed in snow and looked deserted. In vain I scanned the plains for signs of life. I knew they were populated by scattered herds of deer, but none were visible that day. This endless view of nothingness did not become any more interesting when we turned off the road and made our way along a narrower track.

Our journey took an hour and a half, but it seemed longer. Much longer.

When we were within a couple of hundred yards of our destination, the gates to the camp compound swung open and a column of Challenger 2 MBTs rumbled out and headed along the track towards us.

Olsen slowed down and pulled off the track onto the snow-covered verge to give the column a wide berth. We sat and watched as the tanks trundled past us. I counted twelve.

The first tank in the leading troop was flying a green, red, and brown pennant, in the middle of which was a bright yellow triangle containing the black head of a badger on a white background. The tank commander was standing with the top half of his body out of the turret. He looked down at us and waved amiably.

Once the tanks were safely behind us, Olsen drove back onto the track and headed towards the gates. There was a high wooden fence surrounding the camp and somebody had hung a large handmade sign on it adjacent to the gates.

WELCOME TO RATTLESNAKE CAMP.

'What's with the name, Stevie?' Olsen asked, pointing at the sign.

'The clue is in the skull and crossbones.'

'You mean there are rattlers in the camp?'

'That's what I mean.'

'God dammit. That's all I need,' he grumbled as we drew up at the gate to the camp. A guard carrying a carbine approached the Land Rover. He leaned down and stared through Olsen's window.

The guard recognised the American's colonel insignia and immediately straightened his back. He waved us through the gate without further question.

'I hate those mothers,' Olsen mumbled as we drove into the camp.

'You hate guards?'

'Hell no. I hate snakes.'

'Don't worry. Rattlesnakes are not aggressive. They only attack humans if they are threatened.'

'Has anyone told the frigging snakes that?'

I laughed. 'You'll be okay. You're going to be stuck inside a Challenger Two for most of the day.'

'Is that supposed to make me feel better?'

'It should do. As far as I know snakes haven't yet perfected the art of climbing up the side of a two-point-five-metre-high tank, not even prairie rattlers.'

'There's always a first for everything,' Olsen said miserably.

'You'll be quite safe,' I assured him.

'That's what JFK's[1] security detail told him back in 1963, when he climbed into his open-top Lincoln Continental for a drive through Dallas,' he said sourly as we drove into the compound.

We found ourselves in a vast area containing a collection of corrugated hangers, tents, and porta-cabins. It was a hive of activity.

At the far end of the compound stood a row of Leopard 2 tanks surrounded by Canadian Armed Forces personnel, who were milling round in organised activity. Some were mechanics undertaking last minute checks, while others were tank crew members, some of whom were already clambering into the tanks.

Over to our right, in another part of the compound, were parked a couple of armoured personnel carriers, a few jeeps and a gigantic low loader, on the back of which was a tank with a damaged caterpillar track.

Much closer to us, parked along the left-hand fence, stood a troop of Challenger 2 MBTs. There were a dozen or so soldiers preparing the three tanks. They all wore the black coveralls that were unique to the Royal Tank Regiment.

'That's our man,' Olsen pointed towards a man who was

standing outside one of the porta-cabins. Hanging from a front button of his black coveralls was a tab displaying the three pips of an army captain.

'He looks very young,' I said.

'Either that or we're getting old, bud.'

'How do you know it's him?'

'Because he's the spitting image of his old man.' Olsen was referring to the BATUS Camp Commander, whose friendship he had used to wangle us an outing in one of the Challenger 2 tanks.

The captain waved when he saw us and indicated we should park alongside the porta-cabin.

One of the soldiers who was standing with the Challenger 2s, watched us park then headed our way.

We got out of the Land Rover and the young officer stepped forward to shake Olsen's hand. He introduced himself, tapping the white name badge sewn on the breast pocket of his coveralls as he spoke. It read simply: MITCHELL. 'Ignore the name badge, most people call me Mitch.'

Up close he looked even younger.

'I've heard a lot about you from my dad, Colonel.'

'I'm retired, son. Let's keep it friendly, huh? Troy will do.'

Mitchell nodded his agreement, then turned to shake my hand. 'And you must be Major Statton.'

'I'm retired too, Mitch. I'm Steve.'

Mitchell smiled his gratitude. 'Dad told me you guys want to take a ride with my team today.'

'Yeah,' Olsen said. 'We had nothing much planned for today and we didn't want to waste our time kicking our heels back at the base.'

'Are you here for tomorrow's action up north?' the youngster asked.

Olsen looked at me and raised an eyebrow. 'You know about that?' he asked softly before I could warn him to say nothing.

Mitchell shrugged. 'I don't know all the details, but I heard something about an ambush being set up at a landing strip near Bindloss. Apparently some of our guys are involved.'

'So what's happening today,' I interjected before Olsen could say anything else.

Mitchell explained the day's battle plan. 'We're currently on a winning streak. Five days on the trot we've been declared the winners and I'm determined to make it a double hat-trick.'

The trooper who had been with the MBTs arrived at our side. He wore the three stripes of sergeant. 'We're ready to move out now, skipper,' he said to Mitchell, then remembering Olsen and I were there, he turned to us and gave a perfunctory salute. 'Sirs.'

'Okay, Chalky,' Mitchell said. 'We'll be right over.'

The sergeant flipped another salute and headed back to the tanks.

'Sergeant White's my number two,' Mitchell explained as he turned to Olsen. 'You'll be riding with him today, Troy.'

'How many guys crew a Challenger?' Olsen asked.

'Four,' I answered for Mitchell. I thought it was time to remind them I used to be an officer in the Royal Tank Regiment. 'There's a commander, driver, gunner and an operator, who amongst other tasks, loads the gun.'

'So how many seats does the tank have?'

'Four,' Mitchell answered with a wry smile.

'Jeez. So where am I gonna sit?' the Texan asked him.

'That's easy,' Mitchell assured him. 'Two of my guys have gone down with a bug and are on the sick list today. One of them is Sergeant White's gunner and you'll be taking his place.'

'I hope you're not expecting me to fire the damn gun,' Olsen protested. 'I've never even been in a tank before.'

Mitchell shook his head and smiled. 'Don't worry. Chalky will be able to handle the gun as well as command the tank. You'll just be watching.'

'What about me?' I asked.

'You'll be riding shotgun for me. You'll be my operator. Have you ever loaded before?'

'Yeah, but a long time ago and only on a Challenger One.'

'Don't worry. The loading procedure is the same in both tanks. Now, I think we need to get going. The Dragoons are about to leave.' He pointed to the other end of the compound where the CAF mechanics had all disappeared and the final crew members were climbing into their tanks. 'I want to link up with the rest of Badger Squadron before our Canadian cousins arrive on the battlefield.'

We headed over to the MBTs and Mitchell helped me clamber up to the turret, where I climbed into the operator's hatch and stood so I was half in and half out of the tank.

Mitchell slipped into the commander's hatch on my right and handed me a set of headphones with a trailing jack-plug, which I plugged into its socket. His voice immediately came through the headphones. 'Can you hear me, Steve?'

I gave him the thumbs up.

'Okay, let's go!' He held his right arm in the air and gave the signal to move off.

Our big 62 tonnes tank surged forward with a clatter as

its tracks gripped the asphalt surface. We headed out of the compound and half an hour later we joined the rest of Badger Squadron. We took up our designated position on the battle-field, with the other two tanks in our troop on either side of us.

'Time to batten down the hatches,' Mitchell said and disap-peared inside the turret.

I lowered myself into the seat on which I had been standing and pulled the hatch closed behind me. I looked around the cramped space in which the operator worked.

On my right was the main shell loading mechanism, which I was delighted to see was almost identical to the delivery system in Challenger 1. Both tanks used a three-part ammunition, which consisted of an armament projectile, a bag charge and a vent tube that activated the charge electronically. It would be my job to load the shell's components.

I looked up to where Mitchell was sitting next to a mini-computer and LCD display. This was the tank's Battlefield Information Control System.

'What happens next?' I asked.

'We're just waiting for the Ops Room back at base to send through target co-ordinates, which will be automatically fed into the FCC[2].'

'How many…' I began, but Mitchell held up a hand to cut me off.

'Here we go guys.' He gave me the thumbs up. 'Solly, have you got the target in your sights?' Mitchell asked the gunner.

'On target!'

'Over to you, Ops. Time to show us what you can do.'

It took several seconds to realise Mitchell was talking to me.

'Come on, Steve, we're waiting for you!' he scolded.

I quickly loaded a shell into the gun and then completed the process of setting the charge. 'Loaded!' I shouted.

'Fire!' Mitchell ordered and that was the start of a very hot and noisy couple of hours on the battlefield.

'It was no joke in that tin can,' Olsen moaned as we drove back to the CFG base after saying our goodbyes to Mitchell and his team at the end of the exercise. 'I sweated like a goddam pig.'

'It's hotter than that in the summer.'

'Are you kidding me? How could it be any worse than what we've just been through? I feel like I've pissed myself.' He pointed at a large wet patch on the crutch of his trousers. 'And what about that goddam noise. My head feels like somebody used it as a punchbag.'

'Welcome to the world of tank warfare.'

'You mean it's like that all the time?'

'All the time.'

He shook his head. 'I feel for those poor bastards stuck inside that mother for hours on end.'

'Not just hours, sometimes days when they're on active duty.'

'Jeez! How do those guys cope?'

'The same way that submariners cope when they're under water in confined quarters for 3 months at a stretch. They get used to it after a while.'

We lapsed into silence. Olsen stared straight ahead, as if he was deep in thought. He looked troubled, but I had no idea why.

I checked my mobile phone for messages, without much expectation of success. I had not seen a single mobile phone mast during my time in the Suffield Block, so was not surprised when I found I had no signal.

I put my phone away and spent my time looking out at the barren countryside, as the weak pale sun slipped down the sky with increasing speed, as if in a hurry to bury itself in the blanket of snow that covered the Canadian prairie.

As I watched the endless flow of the white nothingness through which we were travelling, I mulled over in my mind some of the things that worried me about Operation QS. One was Olsen.

'So, what's troubling you, Troy?' I asked eventually.

'What do you mean?' he asked.

'You usually suffer from Texan verbal diarrhoea, but you haven't said anything for the last half an hour.'

He glanced across at me. He looked uncomfortable, but maybe that was because he still had a damp groin. 'You don't say.' He glanced at me as he spoke and I felt the Land Rover swerve slightly towards the snow laden verge.

'Keep your eyes on the road!'

'Don't worry,' he replied, switching his attention back to the track. 'I'm chilled, man.'

'You will be if we end up in a snow drift. Because, if the Landy has to be dug out, it won't be me out there shovelling the white stuff.'

I thought I detected a fleeting smile on his face, but I could have been mistaken because the rapidly approaching dusk had turned the inside of the vehicle as dark as a sepulchre.

'So, what *is* your problem?'

He lapsed into silence again, but after a few minutes thought he said, 'I'm going to be straight you, Stevie.'

'Thanks for the advance warning, because hearing somebody tell the truth could be a shock to my system.'

'You really are a cynic.'

'What do you expect? I've spent most of my working life being fed a diet of half-truths and downright lies, but go ahead, hit me with whatever it is you want to say and I'll take my chances on having an adverse reaction.'

He was silent for another couple of minutes and then said, 'I'm worried.'

'You're not alone. I'm always worried about something or other. So, what in particular are you worried about?'

'I have a bad feeling about Operation QS.'

'Why?'

'I think it might be compromised.'

'What makes you think that?'

'Do you know about the January 16th cell MI6 is running in Eye-ran?'

'Yeah. You and I were at the same briefing, Troy.'

'So we were. Well, do you remember we were told a member of the cell was picked up and executed?'

'Cuckoo?'

'That's the guy.'

'What about him?'

He hesitated and started tapping out a short tattoo on the steering wheel with the thumb of each hand. 'We're also running a cell in Eye-ran,' he said eventually.

'By we, I assume you mean the CIA?'

'Yeah.' The steering wheel tattoo started again. I waited for it to stop.

'I'm listening,' I said when his fingers finally stopped their tapping.

'The two networks built up a close working relationship.'

'How wonderful.'

'There's nothing wrong with co-operation,' he said defensively.

'I didn't say there was.'

'Our two outfits work well together, don't we?'

'Sometimes.'

Olsen glanced at me through the gloom, as if deciding whether to take umbrage. He must have decided against, because he looked away and returned his gaze to the road ahead. 'Anyway, one of the January 16th agents told the leader of our cell that Cuckoo was fingered by somebody in the British Secret Service. To be more specific...' He paused briefly to add emphasis to his words. I guessed where this was leading. '... your outfit.'

'DFCO?'

'You got it, brother.'

'Do you know who it is?'

'Not yet. There have been suspicions about a traitor for months, but we've only just started investigating in earnest because of the Jan 16th fiasco.'

'Are you investigating me, Troy? Is that what this is all about? Were you sent here to watch me?'

'No to all those questions.' He gave me one of those toothy, insincere smiles all Americans seem born with. If his smile was meant to convince me he was telling the truth, it failed miserably.

'In that case, why did you want to see my personnel record?'

His stitched-on smile slipped momentarily at that question. 'Who told you that?'

'Are you denying it?'

He lapsed into silence again. Either he was deciding whether to brazen it out, or I was wrong and he was not the Yankee-Doodle-Dandy whistler Joe Onura had told me about.

'Before you answer, Troy. Just remember that you should never try to con a conman.'

'Is that what you are? A conman?'

'Of course I am, and so are you. It's what keeps agents like us alive.'

'Point taken, bud. Okay, the truth is I wanted to check you out.'

'So, you asked your mate Draper to pull my file?'

'Yeah.'

'Why?'

'Gerald works in MI5 and has access to the files.'

'Don't play games, Troy. I meant why me?'

He shrugged. 'I asked Gerald for possible suspects in your outfit and he pointed the finger at you.'

'And you believed him?'

'Why not?'

'Because Draper is a dickhead and he doesn't like me.'

'You might be right, but I asked him because I thought he'd know you guys better than I do.'

'So, what did he tell you?'

'He said you were an insolent, argumentative, uncouth, cynical, bolshie, working-class oik.'

'He said that?'

'Yeah, and if the annual assessments in your personnel file are to be believed, he was bang on.'

'Nobody's perfect.'

'So Draper's description was accurate?'

'Absolutely and I wear it as a badge of honour.'

Olsen nodded his head at the windscreen sagely, but said nothing.

'But let me tell you something, Troy. I might be all of those things, but that doesn't make me a traitor.'

'I know.'

'You do?'

'Yeah.'

'Why's that?'

'Because your annual assessments said also that you were good at your job; utterly loyal to your country; have no skeletons in your cupboard; are low risk for both blackmail and bribery; and have a Top Secret Plus security clearance. In fact, overall you were scored as outstanding.'

'Sadly, that score isn't reflected in my salary.'

'But you have an unblemished record and that is beyond price.'

'Having an unblemished record doesn't pay my mortgage.'

'Maybe not, but it does mean you're less likely to betray your country.'

'It's reassuring to know you don't think I'm a traitor. I hardly know what to say.'

'Don't jump to conclusions,' Olsen said, either missing the sarcasm in my voice or choosing to ignore it. 'I didn't say you were in the clear.' He smiled again. 'But don't take it personally, Stevie. You're not the only person being investigated. There are other guys in your mob, and MI6, who are in the frame.'

'So, who authorised this little witch hunt of yours? In my experience, all governments hate washing their dirty linen in public, and our new administration is no exception. Letting the CIA run the nation's laundry is a sure-fire way of ensuring news of your investigation leaks out.'

'That's harsh.'

'Harsh but true,' I said and then asked another question before he could argue with me: 'So, who offered you the Queen's shilling, Troy?'

'It came from the very top.'

'The Prime Minister?'

'That's what your Intelligence and Home Security Minister inferred.'

'Benedict Fletcher?'

He glanced at me and raised an eyebrow. 'Do you think he was lying?'

I shook my head. 'No, and I'm not surprised Fletcher was being circumspect. The PM won't want his own fingerprints over the evidence if the Official Opposition get wind of CIA involvement in our internal affairs. If that happens, Fletcher will make a great sacrificial lamb.'

'The PM needn't worry. I'm being very discreet.'

I tried not to laugh at his naïvity, instead I asked, 'Has your very discreet investigation got anything to do with Dame Alexandra being put on gardening leave?'

'I can neither confirm nor deny that.'

'You sound like a bloody politician, Troy.'

'That's because I'm practicing.'

'What do you mean?'

'It's my intention to go into politics when I retire from the Firm.'

'Are you serious?'

'Yeah, I'm serious. I would much rather be somebody who

moves the pieces around on the chessboard of life, rather than one of the poor pawns who are first in line when the shit hits the fan.'

'At least a pawn can look himself in the mirror when he shaves in the morning. Very few politicians can do that without feeling guilty. But I suppose you could grow a beard.'

Olsen laughed. 'My old man had a beard.'

'Don't tell me he was a politician.'

'Yeah. He was a congressman. I suppose it's in the blood and why I've always had an interest in politics. I got a first-class honours degree in political science from Harvard.'

'I had no idea. But as I said before; nobody is perfect.'

'What about you? Do you have a degree?'

'Yeah.'

'Really? Which university did you attend? I don't remember seeing it in your file.'

'That's because it's not in my file.'

'Why not?'

'Because the British Civil Service doesn't recognise the first class degree in bolshiness I got from the University of Life.'

---

1   JFK: President John F Kennedy, who was assassinated in Dallas, Texas in November 1963.
2   FCC: Fire Control Computer

22

Wednesday 15th January 2020: Medicine Hat, Alberta, Canada

Traffic on the road to Medicine Hat was very light and I made good time in our borrowed military Land Rover. When I walked into the lobby of the Hampton Inn the digital clock behind the reception desk showed it was19:25.

My mobile phone vibrated. It was Geneviève. 'At last. I've been trying to get hold of you for ages. Where are you?'

'I've just arrived at your hotel. I expected you to be waiting in the lobby but I can't see you.'

'You won't I'm still in Ralston. That's why I'm ringing. I tried to contact you a couple of times this afternoon, but I didn't get an answer.'

'I was on the prairie all day, and there was no mobile phone signal.'

'Welcome to Alberta.'

'What did you want me for?'

'To tell you I couldn't make our date.'

'It's not a problem. These things happen.'

'I know, but I'm still sorry you had a wasted journey to Medicine Hat on such a cold night.'

'Don't worry about me. I'm wearing a nice warm parka, courtesy of the Canadian Army.'

'Me too. The Quartermaster issues them to visitors who forget to bring suitable outerwear.'

'I plead guilty to that charge,' I said.

'Me too,' she admitted with one of her lovely laughs.

'So why are you still at the base?' I asked.

'Because we had a problem. Lenny's DJI Smart Controller went kaput.'

'What the hell is a smart controller?'

'It's what Lenny uses to pilot his drone.'

'So it's important then?'

'Very which is why he rang me from Bindloss to ask if I could get hold of a replacement for him I eventually tracked one down to a computer shop in Brooks and drove over to pick it up but it wasn't as straight forward as you might think there was a multi-vehicle pile-up on the TC Highway and the road was closed while somebody was cut from their car then when I finally reached the city it took ages to find the computer shop which wasn't located where I thought it was so the round trip took me almost four hours all in all it has been a crap day because when I arrived back at the base I got Colonel Mitchell to arrange for a courier to pick up the Smart Controller and take it to Lenny that was ages ago but the courier hasn't arrived yet,' she said all this without pause.

'You sound fed up.'

'That's because I've no idea when I'll get back to Medicine Hat and I was looking forward to having a steak dinner with you.'

'If I come back to the base, can we eat there?'

'Yeah, but it probably won't be a T-bone.'

'I don't care, as long as it's food. I'm famished.'

'Tell you what. You come back here and I'll meet you in the Battlefield Op's Room. We can wander over to the officers' mess and see what's on offer there.'

'You're on. I'll be with you in about thirty minutes.'

'Okay, but don't break any speed limits. The police hereabouts are red hot when it comes to speeding. I think they must get commission on every ticket they write.'

'Don't worry, I'll slow down if I see a horse galloping up the freeway after me.'

She laughed again. 'Our Mounties drive cars these days.'

'Ford Mustangs I assume?'

'Very funny. Just get here as soon as you can.'

'I'm on my way.'

As I was leaving the hotel my phone rang again. It was Sam Brewer. 'How's Alberta?'

'Bloody cold. How's London?'

'I'm not in London. I'm in New York.'

'Of course you are.'

'At the World Cybersecurity Conference.'

'I know,' I said, although I had forgotten his trip to the US. 'How is it?'

'Like all the other security conferences I've ever attended; full of dull speakers with strange accents.'

'Sounds gripping stuff.'

'It's just one more cross I have to bear.'

'Don't expect me to feel sorry for you? I bet your accommodation is better than the tiny room I'm sharing with Troy Olsen. It has a faulty heating system and mould on the walls of what is laughingly described as a bathroom.'

'Well, I must admit my hotel room is rather nice,' he said, and I could visualise his smirk. 'In fact, I'm ringing you from it now.'

'What about the conference?'

'The evening session finished half an hour ago and I thought

I'd touch base before I have dinner. How are things going?'

I gave him a quick rundown on everything that had happened so far, including the planned CSIS operation being planned to ambush the gang that was waiting for the shipment of drugs the following day. However, I thought it best not to mention my upcoming dinner date with Geneviève Le Strange.

'Are you sure British soldiers are involved in the ambush?'

'Yup, about a dozen.'

'Who gave permission for that?' he asked sharply.

'I have no idea.'

'Didn't you ask?'

'As it happens I did, but all I got from the guys on the ground here, was it was an agreement made between the CSOR[1] and the MOD.'

'That is most irregular. I should have been notified,' he snapped.

'Well, don't have a go at me, Sam. If you're unhappy, you'd best take it up with the Chief of the General Staff[2].'

'That's exactly what I will do. I'll ring him straight away.'

'Good luck with that then.'

'Why?'

'Because it's the middle of the night in London.'

'Is it?'

'Yeah, it's almost 3am.'

'Oh! In that case I'll ring him first thing in the morning. Meanwhile, contact me and let me know how you get on tomorrow.'

With that he put down the phone, but not before I heard a woman's voice say: 'Come on, Tiger, get into bed. This gal is hungry for some loving.'

As I made my way out of the hotel, I wondered who the hungry gal was. It was certainly not Sam's wife inviting him to bed. Bessie Brewer was from Barnsley and did not have an American accent.

It had started snowing again, but the cab of the Land Rover was still warm, so I took off my parka, threw it on the passenger seat and eased myself behind the wheel.

The falling snow thickened as I drove out of Medicine Hat and headed up the highway towards Suffield. By the time I arrived at my destination I was driving through a full-scale blizzard, and visibility was down to only a few yards.

When I reached the entrance to the Canadian Forces Base, a Volvo V90 station wagon came out of the gate. I signalled my intention to turn left into the camp and expected the Volvo to stop, but it kept coming at speed onto the highway towards me.

I thumped my horn in warning and the driver finally saw me through the curtain of snow. I caught a glimpse of a man's startled white face before he slammed on his brakes. The station wagon skidded on the slippery surface and slewed across the road, missing my vehicle by only inches.

As the car cut across my line, I saw a man sitting in the passenger seat. It was only a quick glimpse, but was long enough for me to see he wore a leather cap over his long hair.

Just when I thought the Volvo was going to spin out of control, the driver slammed down on his accelerator and the heavy vehicle righted itself. As the car straightened up, and before it sped away up the highway towards Calgary, I managed to take a note of its Alberta registration number.

I stared thoughtfully at the Volvo's vanishing taillights and then drove into the camp. The security barrier was already raised and there was no sign of a guard. No doubt whoever was on duty had decided to stay inside his booth rather than face the howling blizzard and be blinded by snow.

I would have done the same in his position. Only lunatics like me, and the Volvo driver with whom I had almost collided, would be venturing out onto the roads that night, and who wants to confront a lunatic?

I drove through the checkpoint and quickly discovered the snow was falling onto a road surface that had already turned to ice.

It was like driving on a skating rink and suddenly my rear wheels slewed alarmingly to the left as they sought traction. I managed to get the Land Rover back under control and made my way at snail's pace to the admin building in which the Battlefield Ops Room had been set up.

When I arrived at my destination, I could just make out through the thick curtain of snow, a military Land Rover parked further along the road, several yards to the left of the building's entrance. I guessed this was the vehicle being used by Geneviève.

Because of the treacherous conditions, and to avoid any risk of sliding into Geneviève's Land Rover, I parked to the right of the entrance, well away from her vehicle.

Once parked, I took my parka from the passenger seat and pulled it on. I pushed open my door and was confronted immediately by the full force of the blizzard.

I clambered out and made my way through the driving snow towards the admin building, with my head lowered and my shoulders hunched, but this did little to protect me from the elements. By the time I reached the entrance my ears were ringing from the howling wind, and the lens of my spectacles were covered in a fine, white coating.

Despite being half-blinded, I managed to locate the door handle, twist it, and pulled open the door. It was a relief to step into the shelter of the building's entrance foyer.

I slipped out of my parka and hung it on one of the coat hooks that were attached to the wall adjacent to the door. I took a handkerchief from my jacket pocket and wiped the snow from my spectacles.

The foyer was in darkness, but I did not switch on the light because I sensed something was not right. If the military Land Rover parked outside belonged to Geneviève, where was she? She was expecting me, so if she was inside the building somewhere, why had she not left the foyer light on for me? On the other hand, if the vehicle was not Geneviève's, then whose was it?

I stood motionless and cocked my head, listening for any sound of life. I could hear nothing except the wind whistling through the eaves. The building itself was as silent as a tomb.

As I edged slowly up the corridor towards the Ops Room, I pulled my pistol from its holster. I held the weapon at my side in a loose grip, but not so relaxed I was ever at risk of dropping it.

A slither of light had escaped from beneath the Ops Room door and lay across the floor in a thin luminescent line. When I reached the door, I pressed my ear against one of its wooden panels. I could hear no movement in the room.

I pressed down on the lever-handle and pushed against the door. It swung open and a shaft of brilliant white light streamed into the corridor. I narrowed my eyes, to adjust them to the sudden brightness, and then stepped into the room, with my pistol raised to counter any attack. It was now gripped tightly in my hand.

There was no ambush. The room was deserted. However, the apparent absence of any threat did not lull me into a false sense of security, or tempt me into returning my pistol to its holster.

Apart from being unoccupied, at first glance the room looked no different to when I had visited it with Geneviève that morning. The two very long tables, each with four swivel chairs, four computers and four telephones, were still there, as were the two shorter desks in the corner. Fixed to the wall were the same two giant screens.

I walked over and stared down at the computer hardware that was sitting on the desk Lenny Bruce had commandeered. The PC was humming quietly, and the monitor showed a blue Dory swimming endlessly across the screen after an orange Nemo she would never catch.

I sat down to wait for Geneviève.

About twenty minutes later I heard the front door open. A gust of wind whistled down the corridor, blew through the open door of the Ops Room and fluttered the handful of A4 sheets of paper that lay on the corner of Lenny's desk. Then the front door slammed shut and the draught was cut off before any of the loose papers were blown to the floor.

I heard footsteps coming down the corridor towards the Ops Room and realised immediately the tread was too heavy to be that of Geneviève. I stood up and tip-toed quickly across the room and hid behind the open door.

I waited until the newcomer came into the Ops Room and then stepped silently out from behind the door. It was a man and I watched as he walked across the room and stood in front of Lenny's desk.

The man was wearing dirty caribou snow boots and an identical parka to the one I had left in the foyer, even down to the thick covering of snow on its shoulders and hood. One of the man's hands was thrust deep into the pocket of his parka and in the other he carried a heavy flashlight.

I kicked the door closed with a loud bang. The man spun round and pulled his hand out of his pocket. It was holding a Glock 19.

'Snap!' Troy Olsen said, staring at my Glock 17, which was pointing at his chest.

'Not exactly. Compared to mine, you're holding a peashooter.'

The Texan shrugged and put the pistol back in his pocket. 'Neither of us will be needing hardware. We're too late.'

I slipped my Glock into its holster. 'What do you mean?'

Olsen ignored my question, instead he asked, 'What the hell are you doing here, bud?'

'I'm supposed to be meeting Geneviève.'

'I know, but I thought you were meeting her in Medicine Hat?'

'There was a change of plan.' I explained about the phone call I received from Geneviève. 'Have you seen her?'

Again he ignored my question, instead he said quietly: 'I think you'd better come with me.'

I followed him out of the room and up the corridor.

'You might want to put your coat back on, Stevie,' he said, pointing at my parka, which was still dripping icy water onto the foyer floor. 'It's blowing a hoolie out there.'

I took my coat off the hook and put it on, then together

we stepped back out into the blizzard. The wind was howling across the parade ground. On its way, it picked up snow from the ground and threw it into the air, where it joined the flakes that were falling from the sky in an almost impenetrable blanket.

Olsen headed towards Geneviève's Land Rover. I followed him as he trudged through the snow and round to the far side of the vehicle. That's when I saw for the first time that the driver's door was open, and the car was slowly filling up with snow.

Slumped in the driver's seat was a figure covered from head to toe in a thin layer of snow, although some of the white covering on the Canadian Forces parka's hood was stained a deep red, where blood had seeped from a wide gash and turned into crimson ice.

'It's Genny,' Olsen shouted to be heard above the howling wind. 'I was heading to the mess to meet Mitch,' he said, pointing at the building on the other side of the road. 'I saw the Landy's door open and came to investigate.'

'How do you know it's her,' I shouted back.

'Look at her feet.'

I looked down and saw the glitter of Geneviève's distinctive silver cowboy boots. I was about to lean into the car, to check whether she was still alive, when Olsen stopped me.

'I've already phoned the cops. Their crime scene team will be along soon, and they won't be happy if you've touched the body.'

'How do you know she's dead?'

'She's dead all right.' He pointed at her head. 'That was done by a shotgun blast. You don't survive those.'

I knew he was right, but still hesitated, not willing to accept the truth.

'Come on. Let's talk inside. I can't hear myself speak out here.'

Olsen was right about that, not only was it difficult to talk, but my spectacles were once again covered in snow, blotting out the dreadful sight of Geneviève's shattered head. I followed him into the building without arguing.

'Who d'ya think killed her?' Olsen asked eventually.

We were standing side by side staring out of the foyer window at Geneviève's Land Rover. Somewhere in the distance I could hear a police siren. The level of its strident sound rose and fell as it battled to be heard above the wind, but it was definitely getting closer.

'I have my suspicions,' I said and explained about my near collision with the Volvo station wagon. 'I recognised the passenger.'

'Who was it?'

I told him about the murder of Mario Tafuri and the guy with long hair, wearing a leather cap, who came out of Tafuri's building.

'And you think he's a Mafia hitman?'

'Yeah.'

'How come?'

'Do you remember a guy called Guiseppe Navarra?'

'You mean the sottocapo you mentioned at that meeting we had in the House of Commons?'

'That's him.'

'So, what about him?'

'I think the hitman who killed Tafuri works for Navarra,' I said and told him about the photo that showed the killer standing behind the Mafia underboss.

'And you think he murdered Genny?'

I shrugged. 'Let's just say I'm certain he's the passenger in the Volvo I saw coming out of the base, and I don't believe in coincidences.'

Olsen looked thoughtful.

'So, what do you think?' I asked.

He did not answer immediately, he just stood staring out at the Land Rover. 'I think the guy you saw tonight is a Mafia hitman and he shot Genny,' he said eventually, although he sounded reluctant to admit I was right. 'Did you get the license plate number of the Volvo?'

'I did.' I told him the number and watched as he wrote it down on the back of his hand.

'I'll have the local cops check it out. Are you sure the car was heading towards Calgary?'

'Yeah. They were probably going to the airport, if so, the police should be able to trace them on the terminal's CCTV security cameras.'

'There's something I don't understand, Stevie.'

'What's that?'

'If it was a Mafia hit. Why whack Genny?'

'What makes you think she was the target?' I asked. I pointed at Geneviève's Land Rover and then in the other direction at the almost identical vehicle I had been driving. 'What do you see?'

Olsen made the connection straight away. 'You think the killer made a mistake and Genny wasn't the intended target?'

'It did cross my mind.'

He blew out his cheeks, then released the air with a loud popping sound. 'Perhaps it was me they were after,' he suggested.

'What makes you think that?' I asked quietly.

He shook his head slowly, as if he was trying to wake himself up from a bad dream. 'What would you say if I told you the brakes on my Beamer failed last week and I almost ended up in the River Thames?'

'I'd say you should use a different garage to service your car.'

'It was nothing to do with my last service. The brake pipe was disconnected from one of the rear wheel drums and all the fluid leaked out during my journey from home to my office.'

'Vibration could have caused the problem. It happens.'

'You don't think the Mafia sabotaged my Beamer do you?'

I shrugged.

'OK. In that case, tell me this,' he said, misreading my response. 'If I wasn't the Mafia's target, and nor was Genny, who does that leave?'

'Me.'

He nodded. 'I suppose that's possible, but d'ya wanna know what I think, Stevie?'

'I'm all ears.'

'I think we both could be on the Mafia hit list.'

'You're out of luck if you're expecting me to argue with you, Troy.'

'So you agree with me?' He looked at me with narrowed eyes as if I was deliberately hiding something from him.

'Do you want me to sign an affidavit to that effect?'

That seemed to satisfy him. 'In that case, the question boils down to who those Eyetie bastards want dead most, me or you?'

I took a coin from my pocket and tossed it in the air. When it landed in my right hand, I slapped it on the back of my left and said simply: 'Heads or tails?'

He gave me a begrudging smile. 'OK. I get your drift.'

'Of course, in addition to you and me, it's quite possible Geneviève was a target also,' I pointed out. 'They might just have got to her first.'

Troy looked away and went back to staring out of the window. 'Whether or not it was the Mafia who whacked Genny, she's still dead and you know what that means, Stevie?' he asked quietly.

'Tell me.'

'It means young Lenny will have to step up to the plate and take charge of tomorrow's operation.'

'I hope he's up to it.'

'He'll be fine. He's a good kid.' His words might have been meant to be reassuring, but to me he just sounded like somebody who was trying to convince himself.

'Will you break the news of her death to Lenny, or shall I?'

'I'll do it. I have his number on my cell phone. I'll ring him while I'm waiting for the police to arrive.'

'In that case I'll leave you to it. I need to contact my boss to let him know what's happened.' I left the foyer and was already searching for Sam Brewer's number on my mobile phone as I headed down the corridor towards the room where, earlier that day, I had met Geneviève Le Strange for the first time.

Now the Canadian agent was lying in a pool of freezing blood, on the front seat of a Land Rover, slowly being dressed in a shroud of snow. I felt guilty. I was sure it should have been me in the car, waiting for the crime scene team to arrive and officially pronounce me dead.

'I'm sorry but I'm not available right now,' my boss's voice-mail box told me. 'Please leave a message and I'll get back to you as soon as possible.'

I declined the offer. It was now gone 11pm in New York and Sam was probably tucked up in his hotel bed, perhaps with the woman who was hungry for loving. Whether or not my boss was alone under his duvet, he would not be responding to his messages any time before tomorrow morning. I decided to contact him again then.

I rang Harriet and only when her phone was trilling did I realise the time was only 6 am in London. I was about to ring off when she answered: 'Who is this?' She sounded remarkably wide awake.

'It's me, Steve.'

'Hi, Steve. What's it like in Canada?'

'Cold and miserable. What are you doing awake at this time of the morning?'

'Talking to you,' she said with a laugh.

'Very funny. You know what I mean. You don't strike me as being an early bird.'

'How would you know? You've only ever woken up with me twice, and both times it was following a night of energetic horizontal gymnastics. As it happens, I usually get up at six, o'clock on working days, so I've plenty of time to get ready. Now, what's happening in the land of the caribou?'

I gave her a potted version of everything that had happened, including Geneviève's murder.

'Oh, that poor woman. Why did they kill her?'

'I'm not sure it was intentional.'

'How could shooting somebody in the head with a shotgun

be unintentional?'

'I didn't mean it that way. It could have been a case of mistaken identity,' I said and explained why.

'So you think you were the real target?'

'It's possible,' I replied cautiously.

'Have you any idea who the killer is?'

'Yeah. Remember that guy we saw coming out of Mario Tafuri's warehouse.'

'Yeah, Angelo Salvatori. Did he murder her?'

'That's what I think, but how the hell do you know his name?'

'Because you asked me to check him out.'

'I know, but that was before your transfer to the Research Section.'

'So what? Where better to undertake research about a suspected mafia killer than in the Research Section?'

'Does anybody know you're helping me?'

'You mean Sam Brewer?'

'Yeah.'

'Well, I haven't actually posted a message on his Facebook page.'

'Very wise. Best he doesn't find out.'

'It's cool. I'm doing the research in my own time.'

'Just be careful. Sam can be a vindictive bastard.'

'Don't worry. I can take care of myself.'

'I dare say that's what Geneviève Le Strange thought.'

'You sound like my father.'

'Your father is dead,' I pointed out.

'That's true, but I'm sure he would have sounded just like you if he was still alive. Now, what did you want me for? I'm sure you didn't ring me just to get me out of bed.'

'No, I didn't. Do you remember the horsebox that was stolen from the service station on the M3?'

'Of course.'

'Have you any idea what happened to it?'

'No, but I can do some digging.'

'Don't worry, you have enough on your plate. Contact Jane Manning at Scotland Yard and ask her to get somebody to trace the horsebox for me.'

'Okay, but talking of Jane, she rang me yesterday evening.'

'What for?'

'She wants a meeting with you. She thought I still worked for you.'

'When does she want to meet?'

'As soon as possible.'

'Did she say what it's about?'

'No.'

'She probably wants to sell me tickets for the Yard's Annual Ball.'

'Ooh, I love balls,' she said and giggled suggestively.

'Behave yourself,' I told her sternly. 'It's too early in the morning for smutty talk.'

'Sorry, I couldn't help myself. So, when do you want the meeting?'

'I'm due back on Thursday morning, tell Jane I can come to her office in the afternoon. Hopefully, by then, she'll have some information about the horsebox.'

'Righto. I'll ring her when I get to the office. Was there anything else?'

'Yeah. Did you have any luck finding out about Mario Tafuri's business transactions?'

'Not yet. I'm still working on it. I'm also doing some research into polo horses generally. I'll put together a briefing note for you. Hopefully it will be ready when you get back.'

'Thanks. Now, what else did you find out about Salvatori?'

'Quite a bit. He was born in Sicily but grew up in New York and is now a naturalised American. He made his bones with the Colombo Mafia family and went on to become a leading capo.'

'Made his bones? Where did that come from? Have you been watching *The Godfather*?'

'No, but I did read the book as part of my English Literature degree course at university.'

'God help us. Whatever happened to Shakespeare and Dickens?'

'I read them as well,' she said with a laugh. 'Anyway, five years ago Salvatori was sent to work for the Mala del Brenta in Venice, to establish links between the two families.'

'How did you get all that information? I bet that wasn't in any book.'

'No, I spoke to Auntie Xandra, and she sent a copy of the photograph to Luigi Campisi. He identified Salvatori immediately and came up with all the information about his background.'

'Good work.'

'It was nothing,' she insisted, but there was a hint of pride in her voice. 'I'll see what more I can find out about him.'

'Okay, but remember what I told you about Sam.'

'I will.'

'Good and, Harriet, one more thing,'

'What's that?'

'I owe you a drink when I get back to Blighty.'

'I want more than a drink,' she said.

'All right, I'll throw in a nice dinner.'

'I was thinking of something more energetic.'

'We'll see.'

'Oh, you'll see a lot all right,' she said with another suggestive giggle and then hung up.

I returned to the front of the building and joined Olsen outside. He was watching the police crime scene investigator inspecting Geneviève's dead body. The area surrounding the Land Rover was now lit by portable halogen lights. It had stopped snowing, but the temperature had dropped further. Olsen was blowing on his hands to warm them up.

'What's the verdict?' I asked.

'The cop's just finishing up, but he's confirmed already that Genny was killed by two shots from a double-barrelled sawn-off shotgun. There wasn't much left of her face from the first shot and the second one blew away the left-hand side of her head. Mercifully, death would have been almost instantaneous.'

'Did he get a fix on the time of death?'

'He put it at about eight o'clock this evening.'

That fitted in with my near collision with the speeding Volvo station wagon as I arrived at the base. 'The killer's name is Angelo Salvatori,' I told him and then explained what Harriet had found out.

'Do you still think Salvatori made a mistake?'

'I don't know,' I admitted. 'But I keep asking myself why the Mafia would want Geneviève dead.'

'I've been thinking about that too. What if they thought killing her would force CSIS to abort their operation?' Olsen asked.

'I suppose anything is possible.'

'You don't sound convinced.'

'I'm not. I still think I was the target.'

'I get that, but let me be the Devil's Advocate.'

'I'm listening.'

'Okay. Why would the Mafia want you dead?'

'I think Navarra found out I visited Tafuri's place and decided I was getting too close for comfort.'

'So how come Salvatori mistook Genny for you?'

'Well, in addition to her driving an identical Landy to ours, she was wearing the same CF issue parka as me. If she had her hood up, he might not have seen her long hair.'

We stared over at where the police crime scene investigator was still examining the murder scene in the light from the work lights. He was kneeling on all fours carefully inspecting the ground next to the Land Rover. He was a big man wearing white coveralls, the hood of which was pulled up over his head making him look like a foraging polar bear.

'How long is Huggy Bear going to be?' I asked.

'No idea.'

As if he heard our conversation, the investigator eased himself slowly to his feet and padded over to join us, pulling off his latex gloves as he came. Now he was standing upright, he looked even larger and towered over us.

'So, what d'ya have for us, bud?' Olsen asked.

'Nothing conclusive.' It was the stock response of scenes of crime investigators the world over.

'What's your gut instinct,' I asked.

'This is Major Statton,' Olsen explained.

The cop looked down at me and held out a hand as a big as

a soup plate. We shook hands and I found he had an unusually gentle grip for such a big man.

'Good to meet you, Major,' he said in a voice that was as gentle as his grip. 'Sergeant Major Carsons,' he introduced himself. 'But I'm happy with Huggy.' He grinned at me through a bushy beard.

'Sorry about that,' I said.

'Not a problem, sir. I've been called worse things. But my given name is Richie.'

'Okay, Richie it is. I'm Steve.'

He grinned again. 'What do you want to know, Steve?'

'I'm not asking you to make a statement and sign it in blood, Richie. All I want to know, strictly off the record, is what you think happened here.'

'Okay. There were at least two people involved with the shooting. They followed the victim here and when she parked, they drew up alongside her. If you look carefully you can still see clearly the second car's tyre marks over there.' The cop pointed to where he had been kneeling in the snow next to the Land Rover. He had better eyesight than me because all I could see was snow.

'The guy with the shotgun jumped out of the passenger side of the Land Rover and pulled open the victim's door. Once again, if you look carefully you can see footprints in the snow leading to the car.' He pointed at the road again. 'The victim was startled when her door opened. She looked round to see who it was, and the killer shot her in the face. Bang! Then, as she slumped down, he emptied the second barrel into the side of her head. Bang!'

We stood in silence for a while as Olsen and I digested what the investigator had told us.

'Anything else, Richie?' I asked.

'It all would have happened in seconds. Once the killer shot the victim he jumped back into the car and the driver reversed, skidding as he did so, and then drove off at some speed up the road.'

'Thanks. I appreciate it.'

'Don't forget, that was all strictly off the record.'

'You have my word,' I assured him. We all shook hands and the big man trudged across the road to the police van parked there.

'If the cop was right and Genny did look round to see who opened her door, the killer would've known it wasn't you,' Olsen said. 'Which would send straight down the chute your theory her death was a mistake.'

'Not necessarily. Don't forget there was a blizzard blowing for most of the evening. Salvatori could have been blinded by the driving snow. I certainly was. Yes, he might have seen the flash of a white face as he pointed his weapon, but if he was convinced it was me in the Land Rover, he would have just pulled the trigger without checking who the face belonged to.'

'That makes sense,' he agreed, 'and when he fired again, what was left of Genny's face would have been obscured by her hood.'

We lapsed into silence again until he asked, 'So, what did Brewer have to say?'

'Nothing. He didn't answer his phone. I'll ring him in the morning. What about Bruce, how did he take the news of his boss's death?' I asked.

'He was pretty cut up about it. Seems Genny was like a mom to him. He idolised her.'

'Will he be able to handle the operation?'

'I think so. Lenny's a strong kid and he's determined to make the ambush a success, if only out of respect for her.' He stared silently out of the window for a few moments and then mumbled bitterly: 'Life's such a bitch.'

'Yeah, but being dead is worse.'

'That's for sure.'

'Let's go get drunk,' I suggested.

So that's what we did and eventually we fell into our beds in the early hours of Thursday morning.

---

1   CSOR: Canadian Special Operations Regiment.
2   The Chief of the General Staff is head of the British Army.

23

Thursday 16th January 2020: The Alberta Plains, Canada

Olsen woke me up at eight o'clock the next morning. Despite our heavy drinking session the night before, and only a few hours' sleep, we both felt fine. I suppose practice makes perfect.

'I've heard from Lenny,' he said.

'Is the plane on its way?'

'Yeah. It left Venice at fourteen hundred hours local time and is on its way to Greenland.'

'Do we have an ETA[1] yet?'

'Lenny reckons the plane will land in Nuuk around midday, but that's only an educated guess. It will depend on the wind direction. If there's a tailwind it could reach us at about eighteen hundred hours MST[2].'

I sat up and slid my legs out of bed. 'In that case we'd better get ourselves up to Bindloss as soon as possible and help Lenny get the reception party in position. But first I want to shower and ring my boss.'

'What about breakfast?'

'You go. I'll meet you in the Landy in an hour.'

'Okay.'

'Oh, and Troy,' I stopped him as he reached the door to our shared room. 'If you bring a crispy bacon sandwich with you, I promise not to complain about your crap driving.'

'It's a deal,' he said with a grin and headed for the officer's mess.

I had a shave and a lukewarm shower and got into my combats. Then I rang Sam. He was just about to go into the morning session of his conference and there was a hint of anger in his usually neutral voice.

I briefed him on the death of Geneviève Le Strange.

'When was she killed?' he asked, although I had only just told him.

'I told you. Last night.'

'Why didn't you ring me straight away?' he snapped.

'I did, but your phone was switched off.'

'You could have left a message.'

'What was the point? Talking to your mobile phone would have achieved nothing. I took the view that you were unlikely to pick up any messages until this morning, by which time I could speak to you in person. That's what I'm doing.'

'And you think the woman's killer was the same guy who murdered the horse dealer in Venice.' Sam had a masterly knack of quickly changing the subject when he knew he was in the wrong.

'Yeah. His name is Angelo Salvatori.'

'How do you know that?'

'Because I asked Harriet to check him out when we were in Venice.'

'Why didn't you tell me about Salvatori as soon as you found out?'

'That's what I'm doing now.'

'Now?'

'Yeah. I only found out last night?'

'Last night?' he asked suspiciously.

'Yeah, I rang her.'

'You rang her?'

'Why are you repeating everything I say?'

'Because I wasn't sure I was hearing you right.'

'I'll tell you what. To save time, perhaps I should repeat everything twice in future. Would that help? Would that help?'

'There is no need for sarcasm,' he said crossly. 'You had no right ringing Miss Barratt. She no longer works for you.'

'No, but she does work in DFCO's Research Section, which is where she undertook research into Mario Tafuri's killer for me. Isn't the role of the RS to research things?'

'I suppose so,' he conceded grudgingly. 'However, in future, before using personnel from outside your section, I would be grateful if you would clear it with me first. Is that understood?'

'Yes, sir.'

'Are you trying to provoke me, Steve?'

'No, sir. Cub's honour, sir.'

He fell silent as he decided whether to rise to my bait and have an argument. He decided to pass. 'So, what makes you think this Salvatori fellow was sent to kill you?'

I explained why.

'But isn't it possible Le Strange was the Mafia's target all along?'

'For what reason?'

'Because they thought her death will disrupt the CSIS operation to ambush the drug runners,' he repeated Olsen's theory.

'If that was the Mafia's intention, they're going to be disappointed.'

'Why's that? Surely the operation will be suspended?'

'No. The show goes on. Geneviève's colleague is taking control of the operation. Olsen and I are going up to the

Bindloss Command Centre to help him make the necessary preparations.'

'That's excellent news,' he said, although I could detect no noticeable enthusiasm in his voice. 'Let's hope it all goes according to plan.'

'Yeah, let's hope so.'

'Well good luck, keep me informed of progress,' he said.

'Of course,' I assured him.

'And without delay.'

'Of course,' I repeated.

'Christ! Is that the time? I must dash, I don't want to miss the first speech of the session it's being given by the Director of the CIA. Now, don't forget to let me know what's happening without delay,' he said in a rapid torrent of words before finishing the call abruptly.

'And goodbye to you too,' I said and went to join Olsen, who was waiting in the Land Rover. He already had the engine running and was talking on his mobile phone, but finished his conversation as I opened the door and slid onto the passenger seat. It was warm inside the vehicle, for which I was grateful.

'Your sandwich is in the glove compartment,' he said as he put the car into gear and drove towards the main gate.

I removed a white greaseproof bag from the glove compartment, pulled out the sandwich and took a generous bite from it.

'I was just talking to the local Mounties,' Olsen explained as we left the base and headed north on Highway 884.

'And?' I asked through a mouthful of bacon and bread.

'It was good and bad news. The good news was that they traced the Volvo station wagon. It was an Alamo hire car, and you were right, it was left at Calgary Airport.'

'What about the two guys in the car?'

'More good news. The cops checked both the CCTV cameras in the Alamo car park, and those inside the terminal. They found several good shots of the perps.'

'Were they able to identify them?'

'Yeah, and you were right also about the name of the passenger. It was Angelo Salvatori. His sidekick was a young Mafia hood called Joe Rossi. It seems the pair caught a flight to JFK Airport. As soon as they were identified, the Mounties contacted the NYPD[3].'

'Is Salvatori in custody?'

Olsen shook his head. 'That's the bad news. By the time the NYPD got its act together, and sent a couple of squad cars to JFK, Salvatori and Rossi were long gone.'

The American lapsed into one of his lengthy silences, so after a while I took the opportunity to take out my iPhone and check my emails, but I gave up after ten minutes, because my signal disappeared as we moved further away from the base.

An hour later we were driving east down Highway 555 when Olsen finally spoke again. 'We're now in Albert Springs.' On either side of the road was a scattering of ruined buildings. 'The landing strip is behind that barn over there.' He pointed towards a ramshackle building.

Olsen drove on, and a few minutes later we reached a wooded area. He pulled off the highway onto a heavily rutted track leading through the trees. Although the American slowed down, and dropped into second gear, our Land Rover still bounced around like a plastic duck on white water.

Eventually, we turned onto a second track, narrower than the first, but just as rutted. My body was beginning to feel like it had been trapped inside a tumble drier, so I was delighted when, five minutes later, we entered a glade, at one end of which stood a small, prefabricated building with camouflage netting draped over its roof.

Next to the building, a Harley Davidson motorcycle was parked under a long shelter, the canvas roof of which was camouflaged also. Olsen parked next to the Harley, and we got out. It was a blessed relief.

Lenny Bruce must have heard our approach, because he was already standing in the open doorway as we approached the cabin. He was still dressed in his U of O sweatshirt and denim trousers, but now he had a woollen Ottawa Senators beanie hat pulled down over his ears.

'You made good time,' he said in a voice flat enough to suggest he was only going through the motions of being polite.

'There wasn't a lot of traffic on the road,' Olsen responded.

'I'm sorry about your boss,' I told the youngster once we were inside the building.

'Words of sympathy won't bring her back,' Bruce snapped.

I said nothing. He was right.

'Sorry, man,' Bruce apologised, and his face flushed in embarrassment. 'That was rude of me.'

'It's not a problem. I understand how you feel. You must be pretty cut up about her death.'

'I am, but I shouldn't take my grief out on you. It wasn't your fault.'

I was not convinced his last comment was correct, but there seemed little point arguing with him. Again I said nothing.

'I'm sure Genny's death has hit you hard, kid,' Olsen said quietly. 'But when you're paddling round in a sewer chasing rats, some shit is likely to stick to your boots.'

'I know and so did Genny. She understood the dangers we face in our job. We both accepted that the threat of death is part and parcel of being a CSIS agent.'

'Don't worry, you're not alone,' I told him. 'It's the same for field agents the world over.'

'Yeah, we're just government pawns in a damned global chess game,' Olsen added, repeating one of his favourite analogies. 'But remember kid, we do what we do, not for our governments, but for our countries.'

'I get that, but it doesn't make it any easier when you lose one of your own.' Bruce gave a sad shake of his head. 'Problem is I'm just a computer wonk and I don't really enjoy field work,' he said with a sigh.

'Don't worry, Lenny, only lunatics *enjoy* field work,' I said.

'But it sometimes makes me feel like a coward,' Bruce insisted.

'We're all cowards at heart. The only difference between you and me, is that you're a sane coward,' I told him.

He tried to smile. 'I appreciate you're trying to make me feel better, sir, But the only way that will happen, is if you find the bastard who murdered Genny and put a bullet in his head.'

'I'll certainly do my best,' I assured him.

That perked Bruce up. 'Thank you.' This time he managed a grateful smile. He held wide his arms. 'So, welcome to the Project Buzkashi Ops Room, guys.'

I looked round the room. Hanging over a coat rack in one corner was a set of motorbike leathers, and on a table next to the rack was a red crash-helmet and an impressive looking, multi-rotor drone.

One wall of the room had been fitted with a long bench, on which was an assortment of electronic equipment, including computers and monitors. In front of the bench were a couple of office chairs, and above the bench were three large digital wall clocks, each with a handwritten sign underneath.

The first clock showed it was currently 20:07 in Venice and its sign read MARCO POLO. The middle clock was marked NUUK, and showed the time on the west coast of Greenland as 16:07. The last sign read CALGARY and its clock gave the local time as 12:07 MST.

I looked at my own wristwatch and found that the third clock was telling the truth.

'So, show us what you've got, kid,' Olsen said.

'Okay.' Bruce walked over to one of the computer monitors. 'Let's start with the incoming target. You've come at just the right time.' He pointed at the screen, which was mainly black, with luminous green lines separating it into vectors. There were also several white dots, of differing sizes, on the screen.

'This is the view of the skies over Greenland that is currently being seen by the controllers at the Reykjavik Air Traffic Control Centre, and this is the plane carrying the cargo of drugs.' He touched a tiny dot. 'It's on time and due to land at Nuuk Airport about now.'

'How come you have access to the Reykjavik traffic control system?' Olsen asked.

'Canada has a long standing and very cordial relationship with the Icelandic government,' Bruce explained with a wry smile.

'So, what happens next?' I asked.

'Nothing immediately, but when the target is a couple of hours from us, we'll call up the cavalry.'

'And when the troops arrive? What then?'

'We make sure they take up their positions as quickly as possible. Let me show you what's been planned.' He moved to another computer and brought up on its monitor a map of the Albert Springs area.

Several NATO military symbols had been superimposed on the map. One symbol was positioned in the woods in which we were located, close to its western boundary; a similar symbol was positioned on the other side of Highway 555, behind a building opposite the landing strip; and third was shown in another clump of trees south of the airstrip.

Bruce explained the symbols represented BV206S tracked personnel carriers, he also pointed out different symbols showing sections of CF Special Forces soldiers that would arrive in the vehicles.

Surrounding the landing strip itself, were symbols representing police officers from K Division and soldiers from the Royal Tank Regiment, who would be hiding a couple of hundred yards from the strip.

Olsen whistled softly. 'Wow. That's some fire power. When did they announce the start of World War Three?'

'I know it looks a bit like overkill,' Bruce said, almost apologetically, 'but Genny didn't want to take any chances. However, if she was still alive, I'm sure she wouldn't mind you suggesting changes.'

'Don't worry, I'm all for a gung-ho approach,' Olsen said.

Bruce gave me a questioning look.

'I'm with Troy.'

'That's cool,' Bruce said with a relieved smile.

'What's that?' I pointed to the end of the long table, where a third desk-top and its monitor sat. However, in addition to a standard keyboard, this computer also had a gadget attached to it.

'That's the smart controller for my drone. Come on, let me show you how it works.' He led us to the end of the table.

An A4 poster had been taped to the wall behind the computer monitor which showed an unusual design.

'What's with the picture?' Olsen asked.

'It's the all-seeing eye,' I told him.

'Otherwise known as the Eye of Providence,' Bruce added. 'It's why I call my drone EP,' he pointed at the multi-rotor drone in the corner. 'Isn't she a beauty?'

'It doesn't look very large,' I said.

'Size isn't everything,' Bruce said with a grin. 'Believe me, for her size, EP is the best surveillance and intelligence gathering drone in the world.'

'I believe you.'

'Would you like to see her in action?'

'You betcha!' Olsen said.

'Are you going to launch it now?' I asked.

'That won't be necessary,' Bruce replied as he bent down and switched on the computer. 'I sent her up earlier, to test my new controller, and I can show you the quality of the pictures taken by her camera.'

As he spoke a list of video files appeared on his monitor screen and he clicked on the bottom one. Immediately the list was replaced by an aerial view of trees.

'That's a shot taken almost immediately after I launched EP. She's hovering just above the spruce trees, close to the edge of the woods to the west of the ops room.'

The images were so good I could see individual needles on the sprigs. As we watched, the trees slipped away as Bruce piloted the drone out into open ground, quickly rising higher as it went. Soon it was flying over the landing strip, at one end of which could be seen a Ford Transit 250 van, next to which four figures were standing in a group.

Suddenly the camera zoomed in and I could see each figure in detail. They were all men, dressed in winter clothing and drinking from plastic cups. The camera zoomed in again until all that could be seen was a single plastic cup. I could see steam rising from what was plainly black coffee.

It was my turn to whistle softly.

'Good, huh?' Bruce said proudly.

'Yeah,' I agreed with a nod of approval. 'Who are those guys?'

'Mafia hoods from Hamilton.'

'They're a long way from home.'

'Yeah, we've had them under observation since they arrived in Alberta yesterday.'

'I assume they're here to meet the plane and take the drugs back to Ontario?'

'Yeah.'

'So why are they here so early?'

'They have to prepare the landing strip for the arrival of the plane. It will be dark when the plane lands, so the pilot will

313

need lights to see the runway.'

'Didn't those goons realise the drone was watching them?' I asked.

'Can you see any of them looking up?'

'No.'

'That's because EP was flying so high the guys on the ground couldn't see her, and the engines are so quiet they couldn't hear her.'

The camera zoomed back out and the image changed again. The landscape flashed across the screen as the drone headed at speed back to its base. Bruce turned off the video.

'Very impressive, but isn't there a risk the hoods will see the good guys getting into position?' Olsen asked.

Bruce shook his head. 'No, because once I call them up, the Special Forces and Tank Reg guys will travel up from Rattlesnake Camp in the Bee Vees. They will come across the prairie and it will be dark by the time they arrive. The Mounties are already in Albert Springs and know what to do, and where to go once I give the signal. Don't worry, they won't let us down. All those guys are good at their jobs.' He looked up at the clocks. 'Come on, let's see what progress the plane is making. It should be well on its way by now.' He walked back to the computer linked to the Reykjavik Control Centre.

Olsen and I followed him and watched as the young man touched the space bar on the keypad and the monitor lit up again. He stared at the screen and then swore. 'Shit!'

'What's the problem?' I asked.

'Shit three times over!' Bruce swore again, more vehemently.

'What is it?'

'It's the plane.'

'What about the plane?' It was Olsen who asked this time. 'It's heading in the wrong direction.'

'What do you mean?'

'I mean it ought to be on a south-westerly flight path towards Newfoundland, but it's currently heading east towards Iceland.'

'What are you saying?' Olsen asked.

'He's saying the pilot has aborted the mission and the plane is heading back to Italy,' I said.

'That's what it looks like,' Bruce agreed.

Olsen stared morosely at the screen. 'Perhaps the plane will turn around in a minute.'

'No way, Jose,' Bruce insisted. 'That plane is already halfway across Greenland. If the pilot turns back now and heads our way, he'd run out of fuel well before he reached us.'

Olsen looked at me. 'What the hell is happening?'

'It looks like the Mafia found out about the reception Lenny was planning for their pilot.'

'What a bitch!' Olsen hissed.

'But how did they find out?' Bruce asked.

'Somebody told them,' I said simply.

1   ETA: Estimated Time of Arrival.
2   MST: Canadian Mountain Standard Time.
3   NYPD: New York Police Department.

24

Thursday 21st January 2020: St James's, London

'So, somebody tipped off the Mafia?

We were sitting in Sam's office and his fan heater was pumping out hot air. The leaves on his prize azalea were starting to turn brown and the top of his coffee table was covered in shrivelled red petals.

I'm no expert, but it looked to me as if the azalea was on its way to flower heaven and would no longer be winning any prizes in the village garden show. However, Sam didn't appear to have noticed what was happening to his pride and joy.

'That's what I think,' I answered.

'Who was it?'

'Take your pick from a cast of thousands.'

'Don't exaggerate, Steve.'

'Okay, I might be guilty of a little hyperbole, but replace thousands with scores and you wouldn't be far from the truth.'

'How can that be? Our joint operation with CSIS was supposed to be a secret.'

'You must be joking.'

'What do you mean? Who else knew about the operation?'

'Where do I start? First there were all the people who took part in the joint Canadian and British Arctic war exercise. Our tank guys knew about the ambush up at Bindloss and it's not unknown for soldiers to blab when they've had a few drinks.'

'That was very bad security,' he said crossly and glared at me accusingly.

'Well don't blame me. Take it up with whichever MOD desk-jockey thought it was a good idea to let our tankies take part in the ambush.'

'And who was that?'

'How the hell would I know? That's what you were going to take up with the Chief of Staff. Have you contacted him yet?'

'No, I haven't found time.'

'Well when you find time, have a go at him, not me.'

'Don't worry, I'll do just that.'

'Of course you will.' My scepticism must have been obvious because he glared at me again. This did not stop me continuing my attack. 'So, what about the rest of the potential suspects? What are you going to do about them?'

'What other suspects?'

'Well there are the CF Special Forces who were due to take part in the Project Buzkashi ambush, they would have been briefed in advance. Then there is CSIS, the CIA, MI5, MI6, the Foreign and Commonwealth Office, the Cabinet Office, the Home Office, DFCO, and not forgetting Uncle Tom Cobley, of course.'

'Not DFCO,' he insisted sharply, ignoring my jibe about Tom Cobley. 'Nobody from my department would have leaked information to the Mafia.'

'How can you be so sure?'

'Because access to details of operations within the department is strictly on a need-to-know basis.'

That brought a hoarse laugh from me, which provoked another glare.

'What's so funny?'

'Because sometimes, Sam, I think you've just been teleported down to earth from a parallel universe. Let me explain how it really is; Colin Plum knew I was going to BATUS before I did and if he knew, everybody else in the building will have known.'

'Who is Colin Plum?'

'He's the bod downstairs in our pretend jewellery shop.'

'You mean the shop assistant?'

'The pretend shop assistant. Yeah, him. He's the department's resident blabbermouth.'

'How the hell did he find out?'

'He's probably been chatting to that skinny girl in the travel office with the tattoo of a zombie on her neck and a safety pin through each earlobe.'

'I can't say I've seen her.'

'You haven't missed much,' I told him. 'Anyway, it doesn't matter who told Plummy, the point is nothing in the department stays secret for long.'

'I'm shocked,' he said with a disbelieving shake of his head. 'I simply cannot believe such a culture of unforgiveable internal indiscipline could be allowed to fester, without action being taken to stamp it out,' he said in a burst of confected outrage that sounded to me like another nail in the coffin in which he was planning to bury Dame Alexandra's career.

'I'm shocked, you're shocked, Sam. After all, you were the Deputy Director-General during that time of unforgiveable internal indiscipline.'

'That's not fair, Steve. You know I've only been in the department for a few months,' he said defensively. 'But now I'm Director-General things are going to change.'

'Acting Director-General.'

He waved a hand to bat away my unwanted point.

I changed the subject. 'Did you hear anything from Marion Dudley while I was in Canada?'

'Marion who?' he queried and then it clicked. 'You mean your secretary?'

'Yeah. Did she ring in at all?'

He shook his head. 'I've heard nothing. Why do you ask?'

'Because I'm going to need help in my office until she comes back to work.'

'Why?'

'Why? Are you pulling my leg?' I could see he was serious. 'Okay, for a start I need help because I still have on my desk all that paperwork Dame Alexandra left for you.'

'I thought that would be finished by now.'

'Finished? Exactly when do you think I've had time to work on it? I haven't been in my office for longer than five minutes in the past week. Look, either you get me somebody to help with the paperwork, or it will be back on your desk first thing in the morning.'

'I'll see what I can do.'

'That's not good enough, Sam, I'm bloody serious. I need help.'

'I take it you have somebody mind?'

'Yeah. I want Harriet Barratt back.'

'That's not possible,' he snapped.

'Anything is possible when you're the Director-General.'

'Acting Director-General,' he said with a sadistic smile.

'Acting or not, you have the power to make it happen. You transferred her out of my section, and you can transfer her back.'

'But she is standing in for Debbie Hart.'

'Find somebody else to stand in.'

He stared at me. 'Why are you so keen to get Miss Barratt back with you? I can't believe it's because she's good at paperwork.'

'As it happens she's very good at paperwork. However, that's not the only reason I want her back.'

'So, what other reason do you have?'

'Because she's a damn fine intelligence officer.'

'But is she trustworthy?'

'What do you mean?'

'Well, it was you who pointed out it might be somebody in the department leaking to the Mafia.'

'And you pointed out it wasn't possible.'

'I've changed my mind. Perhaps it *was* one of our own. For instance, did Miss Barratt know why you went to Canada?'

'Yeah.'

'How did she find out? She's no longer in the Operations Section.'

'Dame Alexandra told her,' I replied, which was not the whole truth, but close enough.

'How did she know?'

'You'll have to ask her, but my guess is Lloyd Harper told her.'

He swivelled his seat and stared out of the window.

'What are you getting at, Sam?'

He swivelled back to look at me. 'Don't you see, Steve? What you have just told me, means that both Miss Barratt, or Dame Alexandra could be the mole.' Now there was an ugly glint in his eyes.

I said nothing. I guessed where the conversation was heading.

'And my money is on Dame Alexandra.'

'Dame Alex being a traitor is about as likely as the Chief Rabbi eating a bacon sarnie,' I said.

'Stranger things have happened, Steve.'

I shook my head. 'Not in my local synagogue.'

'Come on, think about it. Dame Alexandra has lots of contacts in Italy. Some of those contacts could have connections to the Mafia.' He sounded as if he was continuing to build a case against his predecessor.

'Do you have proof of that?' I asked in exasperation. 'If not, I wouldn't repeat the allegation outside these four walls, unless you have enough money in the bank to employ a top-class libel lawyer.'

'I was just speculating,' he said hurriedly. 'I'm only making the point that both Miss Barratt and Dame Alexandra could be considered suspects.'

'Every person who works in the department could be considered a suspect,' I agreed. 'But that doesn't make them guilty, and the same goes for Harriet and the D-G.'

'But you have to admit it's a possibility?'

I shrugged non-committally, but he took this as a sign of agreement.

'So, you agree one of them could have tipped of the Mafia?'

'I did not agree,' I insisted. 'Indeed, I think it's highly unlikely.'

'But not impossible?'

'Nothing is impossible,' I conceded.

'Exactly, and because there is a possibility Miss Barratt is the traitor, no matter how remote, I think it would be inappropriate for her to work in the Operations Section at this time.'

'Who are you trying to kid, Sam?' I stared at him, but he avoided my eyes. Instead he found something interesting about one of the stains on the top of his desk.

'I don't know what you mean,' he protested, rubbing the stain vigorously with the tip of his finger.

'I mean all that crap about Harriet Barratt and Dame Alexandra is just so much bullshit. This has nothing to do with them does it? It's just you trying to be macho.'

'I don't understand.' He still refused to look at me.

'In that case let me spell it out for you. You're refusing my request to have Harriett transferred back in order to assert your authority.'

'Is that what you think?'

'Yeah. In fact, I think it's why you moved her out in the first place. You were trying to prove a point. But you don't have anything to prove, Sam. Everybody accepts you're in charge. Just transfer her back. You know she's wasted where she is.'

'No, I've made up my mind. She must stay in the Research Section.'

'Is that your final word?'

'Yes,' he said, which was the cue for a lapse into strained silence.

'Did you enjoy your trip to New York,' I asked eventually.

Now he looked up, perhaps grateful to have moved onto a different subject. He even managed a smile as he answered: 'Very much so.'

'Did your wife enjoy it?'

The frown returned to his face. 'I didn't take my wife,' he said.

'Did you not?' I stared at him again.

'No,' he insisted, this time meeting my stare with defiant eyes.

'That's strange. I could have sworn I heard a woman's voice in the background when you rang me from your hotel bedroom.'

'There was no woman in my room. I think you're mistaken.'

'I'm not mistaken. My hearing is perfectly sound.'

He looked down at his hands and flexed his fingers as if making sure they still worked. 'So, what did you hear this phantom woman say?' he asked without looking up.

'She called you Tiger.'

'Tiger?' he asked, still checking out the flexibility of his fingers.

'Yeah, and she said something about being hungry, but it didn't sound like she was angling for a cheese sandwich.'

Sam said nothing, but the tops of his ears went red as he felt my eyes drill into the top of his head.

'Of course, it could be just a figment of my imagination, brought on by the stress of thinking about all that paperwork on my desk, with nobody to help me clear it. Now, if I had Miss Barratt working with me...' I left the rest of my sentence hanging in the air.

Now Sam looked up and stared silently back at me. He knew I had him over the proverbial barrel and he did not look happy. Finally, he said, 'Okay. I'll do a deal with you.'

'What sort of deal?' I asked cautiously.

'I'll transfer Miss Barratt back to your section, if you support my application for the D-G job.'

'Is that all you want?'

'It might not seem a big deal to you, but to me it is very

important. Having the support of senior staff in a department really does go down well with the Cabinet Appointments Board.'

'Okay,' I agreed.

'Thank you.' He opened a desk drawer and took out a sheet of paper. He slid it across to me. 'I've prepared this for you to sign.'

It was addressed "To whom it may concern", and was a short reference saying what a wonderful boss Sam would make. My name was printed at the end of the statement, with room for my signature above it.

He handed me a pen. 'Sign it.'

I signed the statement and stood up.

'Miss Barratt will be back at her desk in your office first thing in the morning,' he said with a satisfied smile.

I headed for the door with an uneasy feeling that somehow I had been outmanoeuvred.

'Oh, and Steve,' he said, stopping me in my tracks. 'You did hear the voice of a woman in my room. I was watching a movie on the television.'

That's when I realised Sam had indeed been one step ahead of me. Momentarily I was lost for words, then I pointed at the coffee table. 'Your prize azalea is dying,' was all I could think to say.

25

Thursday 16th January 2020: New Scotland Yard.

It was nearly four-thirty in the afternoon when Jane Manning showed me into her office on the top floor of New Scotland Yard. Through her window I could see the brightly lit London Eye on the other side of the Thames. Despite being mid-winter, the pods were still edging round at a leisurely half a mile per hour.

'I have a mug of tea on its way, would you like one?' Jane asked.

'I would prefer an injection of caffeine.'

'No problem.' She picked up the phone and spoke to her secretary. When she had ordered my coffee, she asked, 'How was your trip to Canada?'

'You know about that?'

'Yes, Sam told me.'

'Sam Brewer?'

'How many people called Sam do we know? Yes, it was your new boss.'

I almost laughed out loud. So much for Sam's indignation about the lack of security in the department. 'When did you speak to him?'

'It was the Monday before last. I rang your direct office phone and Sam answered. He told me about your trip and gave me Harriet's number. He told me to contact her to arrange a meeting with you.'

This information rang true and seemed to confirm that Sam had decided to transfer Harriet back to my section long before my meeting with him earlier that day. He really was a Machiavellian bastard.

There was a discreet knock on the door and a young woman came in carrying a tray containing two mugs and milk and sugar. She put the tray down on the corner of Jane's desk and then disappeared.

'Help yourself,' Jane said as she picked up her own mug of tea.

'Thanks.' I added milk and sugar to the mug of black coffee. 'So, what did you want to see me about?'

'A couple of things. The first is Tommy Cassidy.'

'What about him?'

'We have received a tip-off that he's involved in the wholesale drugs market.'

'You mean he's selling paracetamol to Boots?'

She laughed. 'No, illegal drugs. Apparently, he's supplying heroin to county lines gangs.'

'Has the tip-off been substantiated?' I asked, although I was inclined to believe her because the news fitted in with what Bobby Moore had told me.

She shook her head. 'Not yet. SC and O[1] have had somebody working undercover for a couple of months, but he hasn't come up with anything concrete yet. However, I do have something else about Cassidy in which you might be interested.'

'What is it?'

'Does the name Gwyneth Jones mean anything to you?'

I shook my head. 'Not a name that's crossed my radar. What about her?'

'Three days ago she was found unconscious in her apartment. She had been badly beaten and was suffering from a heroin overdose.'

I shrugged. 'So somebody beat up a junkie. It happens. Who was it? Her supplier?'

She shook her head. 'We're not even sure she was an addict, although that's what the first uniformed guys on the scene thought. However, when the SCO[2] started investigating he took a different view.'

'Why was that?'

'Well, for a start, none of the usual drug paraphernalia was found in the flat and there were no track lines visible anywhere on the girl's body.' She paused to sip her tea. 'Just a single puncture mark in the bend of her arm.'

'Perhaps it was a one-off hit. Were there any clues as to why she took the drugs?'

'Not really. However, she was found lying on her bed and there was clear evidence she had taken part in sexual activity with multiple partners on the day she was attacked.'

'What sort of evidence?'

'Forensic. Body fluids were found on her body and bedsheets, including what looks like semen.'

'Sounds like she was on the game.'

Jane shrugged. 'That's always a possibility.'

'You don't sound confident.'

'I'm not.'

'Why?'

'Well, in addition to heroin, traces of gamma-hydroxybu-tyrate[3] were found in her blood.'

'GHB? That's not usually the drug of choice for a brass[4].'

'Exactly. Mind you, that in itself doesn't rule out her being a prostitute.'

'If she was on the game, is there any clue to the identity of her punters[5]?'

She shook her head. 'Not yet, but DNA tests are currently being carried out on samples of the body fluids. The result of those tests might provide a clue to the identity of those mystery sexual partners.'

'It's a long shot, but perhaps you'll get lucky.'

'Police work is all about long shots and luck,' she replied with a resigned smile. 'In fact, it was luck that led to the girl being found in the first place.'

'How come?'

'Well, she was only discovered because water started dripping through the ceiling of the downstairs flat. When her neighbour went up to investigate the cause of the leak, he found the front door of the girl's apartment ajar.

'When the neighbour didn't get any response to his calls, he went into the flat and found the hall passage flooded. He discovered a tap in the side cloakroom had been left on and the basin was overflowing. That's when he became alarmed. He checked the rest of the flat and found the girl unconscious on the bed. She was naked and her face was covered in blood.

At first the neighbour thought she was dead, so he called us. He had the good sense not to touch anything, instead he left the flat and waited on the landing. When our guys arrived, they discovered the woman was still alive, so called an ambulance.

'Our biggest problem is that nobody seems to know much about Gwyneth Jones. Her neighbours say they saw her coming and going, but never actually spoke to her.'

'It's the Twenty-First Century Syndrome,' I said. 'Everybody's always in a rush and there's never time to get to know other people. So what happens now?'

'We're going to release a photograph of her to the news media. We'll leave out the juicy sexual bits, and just say she was attacked in her flat We'll ask anybody who recognises her to contact us. Hopefully a friend or relative will come forward and provide us with some information about her.'

'Has the girl not been interviewed yet?'

Jane shook her head. 'No, when she arrived at the hospital she was in a critical state, so doctors decided to protect her brain by putting her into a medically induced coma.'

'How long will she be in a coma?'

She shrugged. 'The doctors have no way of knowing. It could be days, or it could be weeks.'

I thought about that as I finished my coffee. 'Look, this is all very interesting, Jane,' I said eventually, 'but what relevance does it have to me?'

'The thing is, Gwyneth Jones doesn't own the flat in which she was attacked. She rents it.'

'Lots of people rent. Not everybody can afford to own their home, particularly in London.'

'I know, but it's the identity of the flat's owner who I thought might be of interest to you.'

'Who is it?'

'Tommy Cassidy.'

'You're right. I am interested,' I said and then instinctively asked, 'Out of interest, how much rent is the girl paying?'

'That's another odd thing,' Jane said. 'When we checked her bank account, there was no record of any rent payments being made to Cassidy.'

That's when my instinctive question was vindicated when I remembered my conversation with Bobby Moore. 'Perhaps she was paying him in kind,' I suggested and then told Jane what Moore told me about Cassidy and his sister.

'So, Moore alleges his sister was pumped full of heroin by Cassidy, who then beat her up and joined his friends in gang raping her.' She looked at me thoughtfully.

'Yeah.'

'It could just be a coincidence.'

'If the DNA test shows Cassidy was one of those who had sex with the girl, it would be beyond a coincidence.'

'That's true, but even if they did have sex, there's no way of proving it wasn't consensual.'

'Unless, of course, the girl recovers, confirms it wasn't consensual, and is willing to provide evidence against Cassidy.'

'That would be a perfect outcome,' Jane said, adding with feeling, 'I really want to nail that bastard, Steve.' Then she fell silent as she finished off her tea.

'Did Harriet talk to you about the horsebox that went missing on the M3?' I asked, breaking the silence.

'Yes and it didn't take us long to track it down.'

'You found it?'

'Yes, it was in the Met Police car compound in Charlton. Apparently, it was discovered dumped in a supermarket car park in the Old Kent Road.' She smiled. 'And before you ask, the horse wasn't in it.'

'Can you get the horsebox taken apart?'

'Of course, but what are we looking for?'

'Hidden compartments.'

She raised an eyebrow. 'You think the horsebox was used to smuggle stuff into the country?'

'Yeah, drugs,' I said and then, without mentioning Sean

MacDonald by name, I explained about CSIS having an agent in Afghanistan and his theory about heroin being smuggled into Italy inside horseboxes. 'If the Canadians are right, the Mafia could be using the same trick to smuggle drugs into the UK.'

'That's a very worrying development, Steve. Can you imagine how much heroin can be hidden in the chassis of a horsebox?'

'I don't need much imagination to work out that it will certainly be more than enough to supply Cassidy's county lines gangs for several months.'

'If you're right then it means Cassidy is working with the Mafia?'

I shrugged. 'Yeah, but I might be wrong. Hopefully we'll know more once the horsebox has been checked out.'

'I'll get somebody onto it straight away. Was there anything else?'

I shook my head.

'In that case I'll show you out.'

We stood up and Jane ushered me to the door. 'By the way,' she said as we stepped into the corridor leading to the lifts. 'The woman who tried to assassinate Benedict Fletcher has turned up at last.'

'Where?'

'She was found dead on Bermondsey Beach a few days ago.'

'How do you know it's her?'

'The body was dressed in the uniform of a House of Commons security guard and looked as if it had been in the water a couple of weeks.'

'That sounds about right. Her name was Asma Malik.' I said.

'Yes, that's what her name tab said,' Jane confirmed. 'However, we're not so sure.'

'What makes you say that?'

'Because when she applied for the job as a parliamentary guard she gave a Shipley address. I had West Yorkshire Police check it out to see if she had any friends or relatives in the area, but they drew a blank. Nobody had heard of an Asma Malik. My guys are trying to establish who she really is.'

'Let me know what they find out.'

With that we said our goodbyes and I headed home.

As I drove along the Embankment questions buzzed around inside my head like a swarm of invisible mosquitoes.

For instance, had Gwyneth Jones taken part in the multiple sexual activity willingly? Who had beaten her up and left her close to death? Was the heroin injected into her arm taken voluntarily, or had it been administered by force? Did the heroin come from Afghanistan? What was the involvement of Tommy Cassidy in what happened to Gwyneth Jones? And finally, there was one big fat king mosquito, which had nothing to do with the Gwyneth Jones.

Jane Manning told me that Sam Brewer answered my phone when she rang the first time. I found that very odd. The D-G's office was two floors above mine, so what was he doing in my office?

I could think of no good reason, which was particularly worrying.

1   SC&O. – Serious Crime and Operations.
2   SCO - Scene of Crime Officer.
3   Gamma-hydroxybutyrate is used illegally as an intoxicant and a date rape drug.
4   Brass – prostitute.
5   Punter – prostitute's client.

PART THREE

HORSE WITH NO NAME

I've been through the desert on a horse with no name
It felt good to be out of the rain
In the desert you can remember your name
'Cause there ain't no one for to give you no pain.

Dewey Bunnell

26

Friday 17ᵗʰ January 2020: St James's, London

'How did you arrange for my transfer?' Harriet asked when I arrived at the office the next day.

'I did a deal with the Devil.'

'You mean you sold your soul just to get me back in your office?'

'Yeah.'

'Is that because you missed me?'

'No, it's because I need somebody to sort out my paperwork and make me a cup of coffee.'

She pulled a face at me. 'Your paperwork is sorted and I'm already dealing with most of it.' She pointed at the pile of documents she was working on. 'However, there were a few reports I thought you might want to see, so I've put them on your desk for you to read.'

'Thanks. Now, what about the coffee?'

'I assume that means you want one now?'

'You assume right.'

'Okay, I'll get one for both of us and join you in your office. You can bring me up to date with everything that's happened.'

'Why are you sitting at Marion's desk?' I asked.

'Because it's bigger than mine. Look at it.' She pointed at the desk she had been using. 'In addition, I hated being tucked away in the corner. It felt like I was sitting on the naughty step.'

'That's probably your guilty conscience.'

'Thanks for the sympathy.'

'I like to please if I can.'

'You certainly did that when last we met.' She gave me a knowing wink. 'In fact, I can't wait for our next meeting.'

I had already decided it was best to keep a Chinese wall between our departmental and personal relationships, so I headed for my office without responding.

Ten minutes later Harriet arrived in my office carrying two steaming mugs of coffee. She put one in front of me and sat down in the chair in front of my desk. She held her mug in both her hands as if she was warming them.

'I'm sorry,' she said quietly.

'What for?'

'I shouldn't have said what I did out there. It was unprofessional.'

'I agree.'

'Oh!'

'What did you expect me to say?'

'I don't know. I suppose I thought you might patronise me, by telling me not to be so silly.'

'Instead I told the truth.'

'You did.'

'I thought it was best to be honest.'

'I appreciate your candour.'

'The thing is, Harriet, the only way we're going to make our relationship work, is by keeping business strictly separated from pleasure.'

'Does that mean you still want to give me pleasure?'

I raised an eyebrow at her.

'Oops! There I go again,' she said with an apologetic grimace.

'Sorry, you don't have to answer that question.'

'It's okay, I'll answer the question, but just this once. Yes, I still want to give you pleasure, but at the right time and in the right place.'

'That's cool. I can live with the right time and place, as long as it's worth waiting for.' She offered me her hand. 'Let's shake on it.'

So, we shook hands and I think that little, business-like gesture helped us both.

'What's all this about doing a deal with the Devil?' she asked. 'I take it you were referring to our new boss, hash-tag Acting Director-General, hash-tag Acting Arsehole.'

'I couldn't have put it better myself,' I replied and then went on to explain how I had endorsed Sam Brewer's application for the post of D-G.

'And you did that for me?'

'No, for both of us.'

'Well thank you anyway. I know how difficult signing that letter must have been for you. I'm really grateful you think so highly of me.'

'I wouldn't go that far,' I said, and this time she raised an eyebrow. I smiled. 'I'm joking, I think you're an extremely talented, efficient and trustworthy member of my team.'

'Currently, I'm the only member of your team,' she pointed out.

'That's true. However, that doesn't make you any less trustworthy, and that's just what I need right now.'

'You can trust me, Steve,' she said softly, before taking a sip of her coffee. 'So, tell me what's been going on.'

I briefed her on everything that had happened since my

return from Canada, including my meeting with Jane Manning.

'I bet it was Cassidy who beat up that poor girl,' she said. 'What happened to her is almost a carbon copy of what happened to Bobby Moore's sister.'

'That's what I told Jane. However, suspecting is one thing, proving it will be something else. Now, what do you have for me?'

She pointed at the handful of buff coloured folders that were stacked neatly in my In tray. 'The top one is the briefing note I prepared about the horses Mario Tafuri bought and sold.'

I took the file from the tray, laid it on the desk in front of me and opened it. I did not read the report it contained, instead I asked, 'Can you just run the important bits past me?'

'You're a nightmare,' she moaned, but gave me a resigned smile.

'Don't take it personally. I'm just allergic to written reports generally. It's something I inherited from my dad. He always used to say that departmental reports are full of bullshit, and long words that nobody uses in the real world. So, what did you discover?'

'Quite a lot. For starters I managed to find out more about the three horses that went missing on route to the Grange Polo Club.'

'How did you do that?'

'Is this some sort of test?'

'No, I'm genuinely interested.'

'Okay, I started by using the Grange's insurance paperwork and the import documents that were lodged with HMRC[1]. They show that all three horses were bought from Tafuri, which cannot be a coincidence.'

'I'd be amazed if it was. Good work.'

'Thanks, but finding that information was the easiest part. Establishing where those three horses originated was much more difficult.'

'Why was that?'

'Well, in Italy the sale of a horse has to be registered.'

'Surely that made your task easier.'

She shook her head. 'No, for some reason the tax authorities in Rome were not keen on sharing information with me.'

'But you found a way to get it?'

'Of course. I chatted up Luigi Campisi, who, by the way, is a darling of a man, and asked him if he could get hold of copies of the bills of sale for all Tafuri's business transactions in the past year.'

'And did he?'

'Yes, but I don't know how he managed it.'

'Because he's very resourceful.'

'As he proved, but how did he manage to persuade the tax authorities to hand over the information.'

'That's easy. He knew who to bribe.'

'Is that how it works in Italy?'

'That's how it works in most countries.'

'Even Britain?'

'Sometimes.'

'That's shocking.'

'You have a lot to learn, child. It's a dirty and corrupt world out there. Now, what about the horses?'

'I found the relevant bills of sale and they showed all three horses that were shipped to the Grange, were bought from the Mancini Polo Club.'

'But we already guessed that was the case,' I pointed out.

'I know. However, Luigi managed to go a step further. He also has a contact in the Italian Customs Department and discovered that those same horses were imported into Italy from Afghanistan.'

'I assume they were bought from Azad Nuristani.'

'How did you guess?' she asked with a pout.

'Not guesswork. I prefer to call it intuition.'

'Well, did your intuition tell you what they were described as on the documentation?'

'How about Buzkashi horses? Am I right?'

'Yeah, but how...?'

'It wasn't difficult to work out. That's the type of horse Nuristani breeds. Now, what other information was on the import documentation?'

'It gave the sex, height, weight, and colour of each horse. It also showed the horse's medical history.'

'All those details are requirements when importing animals from outside the European Union.'

'Yeah, and it's also a requirement when moving an animal from one EU member country to another. In fact, the only thing not included on the documents was the name of the horse.'

'Any idea why that should be?'

'Yeah, I wondered that myself, so I did a bit of research and found out that Buzkashi horses are rarely given names.'

I thought about that for a moment. 'I've been through the desert on a horse with no name, it felt good to be out of the rain,' I murmured.

'What?'

'Don't worry. It was just a line from a song that was popular long before you were born.'

'What made you think of that song?'

'Word association, I suppose. It was recorded by a group called America, which was banned by some radio stations in the US because they alleged the word horse was a reference to heroin.'

'Was it?'

'I have no idea. You'd have to ask the composer that question. So, did you find out any other interesting facts about the missing horses?'

'Well, for a start, I think I know why somebody might want to steal a Buzkashi horse.'

'I don't suppose it's because they want to take part in a pony club gymkhana?'

'Don't be silly. No, it's because some of them are worth a lot of money. Did you know that some of the best Buzkashi stallions are nineteen hands high, weigh six hundred kilos and are worth eighty thousand pounds?'

'No I didn't. That's some expensive horse meat.'

'Yes, and if you throw in the value of a horsebox, you're looking at over a hundred K. A good reason for the theft, don't you think?'

'No doubt about it. However, I don't think getting hold of the horse was the sole reason for stealing the horsebox.'

'But surely whoever stole the horses did it for money?'

'They did, but I suspect the value of the horse itself was irrelevant.'

'I don't understand.'

'It's simple. A Buzkashi stallion is worth far less than a

shipment of heroin.'

'So, you're still convinced the horsebox was used to smuggle drugs into Britain?'

'Yeah, and I'm hoping we'll find out more once the police have taken the box it apart.'

'If you're right, how much money are we talking about?'

'Well, for ease of calculation, let's assume you can somehow hide a hundred kilos of pure heroin in a horsebox. Once a cutting agent has been added, using a fifty-fifty percent ratio, each shipment would produce two hundred kilos of street strength drugs.'

'How much does heroin sell for?'

'The current street price in some parts of the country, such as London, is £100 pounds per gram.'

'Per gram?'

'Yeah.'

'Really? That much?'

'It varies, but you can use that as a rough price.'

She did the mental arithmetic. It did not take her long. 'It means a kilo of pure heroin has a street value of two hundred thousand pounds.'

'And a one hundred kilo shipment would be worth twenty million.'

'Jesus Christ, that's crazy. But it does explain something else that was puzzling me.'

'What?'

'Something about the stolen horses didn't make sense. One of the articles I read during my research said that Buzkashi riders prefer stallions, because they want mounts that are big and brave. It's why stallions are more valuable than mares.'

'I didn't know that, but it makes sense,' I said. 'So, what's puzzling?'

'Well, selling a stallion would have been worth more to Nuristani and Tafuri, so it seemed odd that all three of the horses stolen on route to the polo club were mares. Now I know the reason. The sex and value of the horses didn't matter.'

'I'm not so sure. I don't think value mattered, but sex did.'

'I don't get it,' she said with a frown.

'Look, I'm no expert, but think you'll find polo players prefer mares.'

'I still don't understand the significance.'

'Think about it. If the Mafia had shipped stallions to the UK, any smart person in the Border Force, who happened to know something about polo, might have asked why mares were not being supplied.'

'So it looks like the Mafia thought of everything,' she said glumly.

'I sincerely hope not, or we're stuffed.'

When Harriet had returned to her desk, I put her briefing note in my Out Tray and picked up another file from the In Tray.

The buff folder contained a classified report from GCHQ which set out details of unusual social-media activity in the Chinese city of Wuhan. Many of the posts claimed thousands of residents had become ill since the beginning of December and the local hospitals had already been overwhelmed. Some posts speculated there had been a leak of a deadly coronavirus from a laboratory at Wuhan's Institute of Virology.

There was speculation also that the illnesses were being caused by a virus similar to SARS, which, in 2003, swept across

China and then spread to 29 other countries. However, when confronted about the sudden outbreak, the Chinese authorities denied the illnesses were being caused by a SARS like virus, instead they insisted the increased incidence of pneumonia in Wuhan was normal at that time of year.

The report, which was a month old, went on to set out in detail the potential harm that could occur worldwide if nothing was done to stop the spread of the virus. I was just considering the scale of the deaths being predicted in the report if the Chinese were lying, and a virus pandemic was about to spread across the world, when my phone rang.

'Jane Manning is on the phone for you,' Harriet said.

'Okay, put her through.' I closed the GCHQ file and threw it in my Out tray, where it landed on top of Harriet's briefing note. 'Hello, Jane. What can I do for you?'

'It's what I can do for you.'

'That makes a nice change. What is it?'

'I have information.'

'Is it about the horsebox?'

'Yes, my guys took it apart and there's no sign of any compartments, hidden or otherwise.'

'What about other possible hiding places? For instance, did they check inside the spare wheel,' I asked, clutching at straws.

'My guys checked everywhere. They stripped that horsebox down to its chassis and took the tyre off every wheel. Take my word, there was nowhere in that horsebox where drugs could have been hidden.'

'So, there was no sign of drugs?'

'That's not what I said,' she said and I sensed her smile.

'You mean they did find drugs?'

'Yes, there was a small puddle of liquid on the wooden floor and tests showed it contained traces of heroin.'

'What sort of liquid?'

'Equine urine.'

'How do you know the urine was from a horse and not a human?'

'Because my guys had it chemically analysed.'

'So how did heroin get into horse piss?'

'I have no idea. Perhaps the drugs were stacked in the horse-box, and some seeped out of a bag.'

'Wouldn't it have been risky stacking bags of heroin openly in the horsebox? After all they could easily have been spotted by customs at Dover.'

'Border Force officers don't check every vehicle,' she pointed out. 'They only do random checks.'

'Yeah, I know, but the Mafia had millions of pounds at stake. Would they really have risked being one of the random vehicles checked?'

'I suppose not, but I can see no other explanation for the presence of heroin in the horsebox.'

'Is it possible it was left over from a previous shipment?'

'Very unlikely. The urine was relatively fresh.'

'Bugger,' I swore.

'Indeed. So, what are you going to do now?'

'That's a very good question, to which I have no immediate answer.'

'Let's hope you find one soon, Steve.'

'I'll do my best, Jane. Was there anything else?'

'Yes, I now have the results of the DNA tests taken on the body fluids found on Gwyneth Jones and her bedclothes.'

'Any matches?'

'Yes, two. One of them was Tommy Cassidy.'

This did not surprise me. 'Are you going to have him picked up?'

'Already done. He's in custody and being interviewed.'

'I suppose he's denying he had sex with the girl?'

'No, that would have been impossible, because of the DNA evidence.'

'So, he admitted it?'

'Yes, but he maintains it was consensual.'

'Did he say who the other guys were who had sex with her?'

'No. He claims the girl and he were alone in the flat when they had sex.'

'And I suppose the girl beat herself up?'

'He says the girl must have been assaulted after he left the flat.'

'That's bollocks.'

'Yes, as no doubt his victim will testify.'

'So, can you keep Cassidy in custody until the girl is out of her coma and can be interviewed?'

'That depends how long she takes to recover. The problem is that currently we have no evidence to link Cassidy with any crime. Which means we can't charge him, and we can't hold him any longer than twenty-four hours,' Jane explained this in a voice tinged with frustration, before adding: 'His tame mouthpiece is already screaming blue murder.'

'Who is it?'

'Solomon Wiess. Do you know him?'

'Yeah. Only the best for Tommy. Now you mentioned there were two DNA matches. Who was the other person?'

'Now that is really bizarre.'

'Why?'

'Because it belonged to Kevin Wilder.'

'Wilder? The guy that Cassidy murdered?'

'Yes.'

'How can that be? He died over ten years ago.'

'I can think of only one explanation.'

'Which is?'

'The DNA belonged to a member of Wilder's immediate family.'

'But his family were killed with him.'

'Not his daughter, Kylie.'

I had forgotten Wilder's daughter, now I could see where this was leading. 'So you think the second positive DNA sample belonged to Gwyneth Jones, who is really Kylie Wilder?'

'Yes.'

'Remind me how old she was when her family was murdered.'

'She was just nine years old,' she replied.

'And how old is Gwyneth Jones?'

'Late teens.'

'So the age would fit.'

'Yes, so would the change of name. After the killings, Kylie was placed on the Met Police's witness protection programme and sent to live with foster parents in Wales, where she was given a new name.'

'A Welsh name?' I suggested.

'That's my guess, which is why I have somebody checking back through the records to find out whether that name was Gwyneth Jones.'

'Okay, keep me in the loop.'

'Of course.'

'Have you had any response to the request for information you made to the news media?'

'Not yet, but we only circulated our press release this morning. I'm hoping something will be printed in tonight's London Evening Standard.'

'Thanks. Let me know if anybody comes forward.'

'Will do,' she promised, and with that was gone.

I put my own phone down and it rang again.

It was Harriet. 'Lucifer wants to see you.'

'Okay, tell him I'm on my way.'

---

1   HMRC – His Majesty's Revenue and Customs. The UK Tax Authority.

27

Friday 17ᵗʰ January 2020: St James's, London

'We have a problem,' Sam said when I sat down in front of his desk.

'Was that a royal we?'

'No, I meant you and me.'

'It's very kind of you to share the problem with me, Sam. However, I already have a lot on my plate, and I don't want to be greedy, so I'll let you keep whatever is worrying you all to yourself.'

'Very funny.'

'It was no joke. I really don't need another problem, I have enough of my own. However, you've piqued my interest, so tell me about your latest one.'

'It's Troy Olsen.'

'Why is he a problem?'

He answered my question with one of his own: 'What do you know about Olsen?'

'Not much. I know he's an ex-marine colonel, who currently works for the CIA.'

'That's what I thought too, but it seems our American friend has been secretly moonlighting.'

'Moonlighting? Don't tell me he's been pulling pints in a pub, or touting punters for a Soho strip joint?'

'No, he's been working for the Government.'

'That's strange, I always thought the CIA *was* a government agency.'

'I meant he's working for our Government, not the Americans.'

'Are you serious?'

'Very serious. Apparently a year ago Olsen was seconded to work in the Cabinet Office, where he heads up a very small, very discrete team that's investigating government leaks.'

This unexpected news explained something that had been puzzling me. I had been wondering why MI5 allowed a CIA agent to gain access to personnel files.

'Olsen did tell me he was looking into security leaks,' I admitted. 'But I assumed he was part of some joint exercise between the CIA and Five. So what's the problem? Is it because he's working for the Cabinet Office?'

'No. The last time I looked the Cabinet Secretary was on our side.'

'Sometimes I have my doubts about that,' I said.

That made him laugh out loud.

'So, what *is* the problem?'

'I had a telephone call from Sir Mark this morning. He rang in his capacity as the National Security Advisor.'

'Wow! The National Security Advisor! I hope you stood to attention when you were talking to him.'

Sam was not amused. He closed his eyes and let out a resigned sigh.

'So what did God want?' I asked.

'It seems Olsen has gone AWOL.'

'You mean he's disappeared?'

'Not exactly. He was expected in the office yesterday, but never turned up. A member of his team tried to contact him at home, but there was no answer. That's when the alarm was raised.'

'I bet they're crapping themselves in Downing Street.'

'They were at first, but not any longer because Olsen rang Sir Mark late last night.'

'So, he's not dead.'

'Not unless it was his ghost talking.'

'Does Sir Mark know where Olsen is?'

'Yes, he's shacked up in France.'

'Do we know why he did a runner?'

'He claims he's in danger.'

'What sort of danger?'

'He claims somebody is trying to kill him.'

'I know the feeling,' I said.

'Are you referring to what happened in Canada?'

'Yeah. I came close to being shot.'

'Don't you think you're being over dramatic?'

'That's easy for you to say. It wasn't your car that Geneviève Le Strange was murdered in.'

'It wasn't yours either.'

'No, but we were driving identical Land Rovers that night.'

'I thought you said there were loads of them on the base. The target could have been anyone, including her.'

I remembered what the CIA agent told me when we were in Canada. 'Actually, Olsen did claim he was the target, but what makes him think somebody is trying to kill him now?'

'Sir Mark didn't say.'

'Didn't you ask him.'

'No. I didn't think it was any of our business.'

'Fair enough, but if it's none of our business, why is it our problem?'

'Because the Prime Minister told Sir Mark he wants

somebody to meet with Olsen and persuade him to come home.'

'Can't Sir Mark do that?'

'No. Olsen insists he will meet only you. That's why it's our problem.'

'Why me?'

'He says you're the only person he can trust.'

'I'm flattered, but not persuaded.'

'Why?'

'Why? Because it's all very odd.'

'In what way?'

'Well, for a start. Why did Olsen choose France as a refuge?'

'That's something you'll have to ask him in person,' he said in a tone of voice that told me all I needed to know.

'I suppose you want me to meet Olsen?'

'No, the PM wants you to meet him.'

'In that case, how can I refuse?'

'You can't.'

'So where is Olsen?'

'I told you. He's in France.'

'I know that Sam, but France is a bloody big country. Can you be more specific?'

'He's based somewhere near Honfleur.'

'That's nowhere near specific enough. I can hardly go traipsing around the town, knocking on doors, and asking if they know the whereabouts of a paranoid American who has an over-inflated opinion of his own importance. They'd probably direct me to the White House.'

'Don't worry, you won't need to use any extra shoe leather. Olsen gave Sir Mark this telephone number.' He handed me a slip of paper. 'When you reach Honfleur, ring that number and Olsen will tell you where to meet him.'

I took the paper and put it in my pocket. 'I wonder if the Olsen business has anything to do with Operation QS,' I said.

'That's what I wondered too. Talking of which, what is the latest with the operation?' Sam asked.

'I visited Jane Manning yesterday and she told me the police have traced the missing horsebox. I asked her to get a team to tear it apart and check for hidden compartments, but they didn't discover any.'

He nodded sagely, as if he had guessed this would be the outcome.

'However, they did find traces of heroin, so it's clear that somehow the drugs are being smuggled into the country using horseboxes.' I went on to explain what Harriet had found out about how Buzkashi horses were being exported to the UK via Italy.

'Very interesting,' he said, but looked totally disinterested. 'Was there anything else?'

'Yeah. Manning also had some news about Tommy Cassidy,' I said and told him about the assault on the girl in a flat owned by Cassidy and how his DNA had been found on her sheets.

'And they think the girl is really Kevin Wilder's daughter?' Sam asked.

'They're checking, but that's what it looks like.'

'Well, let me know what they discover,' he said with a dismissive wave of his hand.

I took the hint and stood up. 'I'll see if I can get a flight for tomorrow.'

'The PM wants you to meet Olsen as soon as possible.

Preferably today.'

'I'm unlikely to get a flight at such short notice,' I pointed out.

'I know. That's why I've booked you on the Eurotunnel Shuttle service.' He handed me an envelope. 'That's your ticket. You need to be at the terminal by half past four. Don't be late checking in. The train won't wait for you.'

When I got back to Harriet's office, she was making herself a cup of tea. 'Do you want one?'

'I don't have time,' I said as I went through to my own office to get my overcoat and car keys. 'I'm popping home to collect a few things, and then I'll be driving down to Folkestone.'

I heard a clink as she put her mug down on her desk. 'Where are you off to now?'

'France,' I replied as I walked back out into her office, pulling on my coat. 'I'll ring you when I'm in the car. I'll brief you then.'

Harriet did not respond, instead she sat staring at her computer screen. 'I think you'd better look at this before you go,' she said quietly.

'What is it?'

'Come see.' She pointed at her screen. 'It's from the London Evening Standard news feed.'

I looked at her screen and saw the headline: DO YOU KNOW THIS WOMAN? POLICE PLEA FOR HELP.

It was a short article, which gave a brief account of the attack on Gwyneth Jones and asked for anybody who knew her to come forward. After I had read the article, Harriet scrolled down to reveal a head and shoulders photograph.

The photo looked as if it had been taken from a passport,

or a driving licence. It showed a woman's face, set in that stern way demanded by authorities the world over. It was a look that made the sitter difficult to age, but her unblemished skin, sparkling eyes, and a pert prettiness, betrayed the woman's youth.

'That's Marion,' Harriet said quietly.

'That's Marion,' I agreed.

'So her real name is Gwyneth Jones?'

I shook my head. 'No, it's more likely that her *real* name is Kylie Wilder.' I quickly repeated everything Jane Manning had told me.

She stared at me. 'Of course. Now it makes sense,' she whispered.

'What does?'

'Remember you asked for a DNA test to be carried out on the envelope in which the newspaper article about the missing horsebox arrived?'

'I do.'

'Well, I received the result today.'

'And?'

'The only DNA on the envelope belonged to Kevin Wilder.'

'Or, as we now know, Kylie Wilder.'

'Exactly. Which, if we're right about her real identity, means it was Marion who sent the article.'

'Looks like it,' I said as I headed for the door, conscious of the time it would take me to get home and then drive to the shuttle terminal in Folkestone.

'But why did she do that?' Harriet called after me.

'I have no idea,' I replied, 'but hopefully we'll be able to ask her by the time I get back from France. Meanwhile, please book a hotel for me in Honfleur. You can give me the details when I contact you.'

'Will do. Anything else?'

'Yes. Go to the hospital and make sure the police have put a guard on Marion. I don't want to give whoever attacked her, a second chance.'

'Let's hope I'm not too late.'

'Amen to that,' I said with some feeling.

28

Friday 17th January 2020: Honfleur, France

There are three Ibis hotels in Honfleur. Harriet had booked me into the one located on Cours Joan de Vienne. Like the other two, it was a budget hotel. Not that this worried me. I have modest needs. All I want is a clean bedroom, a working shower, and a decent breakfast.

The Ibis Honfleur ticked all three boxes. In addition, it had its own parking, which was a bonus tick in a town where few hotels boast a car park.

I checked into the hotel and then rang Olsen from my bedroom.

'Is that you, Stevie?' he asked cautiously, before I could speak.

'Yeah, but how did you know it was me?'

'Because I was expecting your call. I'm using a burner phone[1] I bought specially for you. Are you alone?' he asked.

'As far as I know,' I replied, 'although I haven't had time yet to check if there is anybody hiding in my wardrobe.'

'You don't have to take that attitude, Stevie,' he moaned grumpily.

'Sod attitude, Troy. You wanted to talk, so talk.'

'No. I'm saying nothing until we meet, hotel phones can be bugged.'

'You're getting paranoid in your old age, Troy.'

'Being paranoid is why I've reached the age I am.'

'So, where are you? Do you want me to come to you, or do

we meet here in my hotel?'

'You come to me, but not today.'

'When?'

'Tomorrow evening. When it's dark.'

'Okay, but you still haven't told me where to come.'

'Ring me again tomorrow afternoon and I'll let you have the address. Do you have sat-nav[2] in your car?'

'Yeah, but I never use it.'

'You'd better use it tomorrow, because you'll never find where I'm staying without it.'

'I don't need sat-nav, I can read a bloody map.'

'D'ya know what happened to the last person who told me that, pal?'

'No, but I'm sure you're going to tell me.'

'He was driving in Angola, got lost and drove into a mine-field.'

'Don't worry, Troy. I'm not planning on getting my car blown up anytime soon,' I replied. Little did I know what was round the corner.

29

Saturday 18ᵗʰ January 2020: Honfleur, France

'Do you have a pen and paper?' Olsen asked when I rang him the next day.

'Yeah, courtesy of the hotel,' I picked up the complimentary notepaper and cheap pen that had been left on my bedside table.

'Okay, write this down.'

As he spoke, I scribbled down the address and postcode he gave me.

'Where are you staying?' he asked.

'The Ibis Honfleur.'

'Is that the hotel opposite the Basin Carnet?'

'Yeah.'

'Which means you're on the Cours Joan de Vienne?'

'That's right.'

'In that case, it should take you only about twenty minutes to reach me. You'll find the house at the end of a track that leads off from the D-17 at a place called Le Val de l'Air. It's in a heavily wooded area. If you get lost ring me on this number again.'

'I won't get lost. What time do you want to meet.'

'Eighteen hundred hours. On the dot.'

'Don't worry, I'll be on time.'

'I hope so, because if you're early or late, I won't open the door.'

'I said I'll be on time.'

'You'd better be, bud, or you'll be talking to yourself,' he insisted. 'Oh, and come alone. If you have company, I won't open the door. Have you got that?'

'Don't treat me like an idiot, Troy.'

'I'm cool with that, bud, just as long as you don't act like one. See you later.' With that he was gone.

I left the hotel at five o'clock.

As a precaution, and despite my earlier conversation with Olsen, I put the postcode he gave me into my car's sat-nav. I drove south-east down Cours Joan de Vienne until I reached a roundabout and headed onto the Rue des Quatre Francs. Soon after that I joined the D579.

I drove on for about 9 kilometres. From time to time I glanced in my rear-view mirror to see if I was being followed. Every so often, cars drove up behind me, but when I slowed, they overtook me and disappeared into the distance.

Eventually I joined the D-17 and found myself driving through heavy woodland. I continued to glance regularly in my rear-view mirror, but saw no more headlights behind me. Twenty minutes after leaving the Ibis, I left the main road and made my way down a narrow track that led deep into the woods. A couple of minutes later I glanced at the sat-nav, which indicated I was only 250 metres away from my destination.

I was early, so I pulled into a narrow, muddy clearing on the edge of the trees, and turned off my engine. I sat in the dark and thought about my impending meeting with Olsen.

I had no idea what the American was up to, but whatever it was I would need to have my wits about me. Olsen was a consummate professional, as had been demonstrated by the way he had arranged for our meeting to take place when it was dark.

This was a smart move that meant I would not be able to

see him watching me, wherever he was, but he could see me approaching and check I was alone. He would also be able to see if I was being followed, because nobody would be able to drive a car down that track safely without using their headlights.

As it happens, I was both right and wrong, but how was I supposed to know that?

At two minutes to six I started the engine, switched on my headlights, and made my way the rest of the way down the winding track, until I reached a larger clearing, in the middle of which stood a small, rundown cottage.

I stopped and studied the building in the bright beams of my headlights. It looked derelict. It had a plain wooden front door, attached to which was a rusty, metal horseshoe that was being used as a knocker.

There was a single window, with dirty panes of glass, one of which looked as if it had been cracked by a pellet from an airgun. The window frame was warped and had been repaired with putty.

Hanging on the inside of the window was a pair of net curtains, which at one time were probably white, but were now a dirty-grey colour.

There were two windows on the upper floor, but these had been roughly boarded up with corrugated metal sheets. One side of the front wall was covered in ivy, which partly covered the top corner of the ground floor window, and at the other end of the building was a lean-to, half of which had collapsed strewing rubble across the ground.

I could see holes in the cottage's roof where tiles were missing, and the single chimney was several bricks short of a stack. It looked as if it might collapse at any time and add to the holes in the roof.

If it was not for the occasional wisp of smoke I saw coming from cracks in the cottage's chimney stack, I might have thought the building had been abandoned.

I turned off my headlights and got out of the car. I was about to reach into the car for my overcoat, when the front door of the cottage opened, and a figure appeared in the oblong of light that was revealed.

It was Olsen, and he was pointing a pistol at me. I decided my overcoat could wait. I slammed the car door closed, and headed towards the cottage.

'I thought you trusted me,' I said as he waved me through the open door with the tip of the pistol.

'I do trust you, bud,' he replied with a smile that lacked the strength to reach his watchful eyes, 'but not enough to let my guard down.' He closed the door behind me, then locked and bolted it.

'Are you carrying?' he asked.

In reply I unbuttoned my jacket, took my Glock from its holster, using only my finger and thumb, and showed it to him. There was no point lying because I knew Olsen would frisk me anyway. He did.

Olsen relieved me of my pistol and put it on a battered kitchen table that stood in the middle of the room. He laid his own Glock next to it and then patted me down to make sure I had no concealed weapons.

As I was being frisked, I looked round the dimly lit room. What light there was came from two oil lamps hanging from the low ceiling, and a fire that roared from a grate in the far corner and was clearly the only source of heating in the surprisingly warm room.

Standing on either side of the fireplace were two low armchairs, which had seen better days, and against one wall stood a tall Welsh dresser on which was piled an assortment of books, newspapers, and bric-a-brac.

The only other furniture in the room was a kitchen table and the four wooden chairs that stood round it. On one of the chairs sat a sprightly old man, holding an empty balloon glass, who watched with indifferent eyes as Olsen searched me. The old man seemed much more interested in the bottle of brandy, which stood in the middle of the table next to our pistols, along with two more glasses.

'Take a seat and help yourself to a drink,' Olsen said when he had finished frisking me.

'Thanks,' I said as I sat down opposite the old man, who watched closely as I poured myself a generous measure of brandy. He offered me his empty glass, into which I splashed some brandy, but he carried on holding out his glass, so I added another generous measure. This time he was satisfied.

Olsen sat down and introduced the old man: 'This is Daniel Schumann. He owns this place.' He poured himself a brandy as he spoke. 'This is the mensch I was telling you about, Uncle Danny.'

The old man looked at me suspiciously. 'Je déteste les Bosche,' he said and spat on the floor.

'Mr Statton is not German, Uncle Danny,' Olsen explained patiently, as if to a child. 'He's English.'

'Je déteste les Bosche,' the old man repeated, as if he had not heard.

'You must excuse my uncle,' Olsen said with a sigh. 'He had a hard time during the war.'

'Which war?' I asked.

'World War Two.'

I was surprised. 'He doesn't look old enough.'

'He's ninety-three.'

'He's worn well,' I said.

Olsen looked at his uncle and smiled fondly. 'We have good genes,' he said.

'How long has he lived here?' I asked.

'Since 1945, although as a child he came to the cottage often. It was owned by my grandparents, who used it as a summer hunting lodge.' He took a sip of brandy and wiped his mouth with the back of his hand.

'My grandfather was a wealthy merchant who had a large house in Neuilly-sur-Seine,' Olsen went on. 'However, in July 1942, during the Vélodrome d'Hiver Roundup, the family was arrested and sent to the Drancy internment camp, prior to their deportation to Auschwitz.'

'Je déteste les Bosche,' the old man hissed at this. 'Porcs fascist!' he added, before spitting on the floor again. He held out his glass and watched in silence as Olsen poured him another drink.

'My grandfather used the deeds to the family home in Neuilly-sur-Seine to bribe the local Gestapo commander to let Uncle Danny and his younger sister, my mom, stay in Drancy. Miraculously, they survived until the camp was liberated two years later.'

I did a quick calculation. 'So, he would have been about seventeen when he was freed.'

'That's right, and my mom was twelve.'

'Did they try to get their home back after the war?' I asked.

He shook his head. 'There's the real irony,' he said with a

wry smile. 'Paris suffered relatively little bomb damage during the war. However, in September 1944 the RAF bombed the western suburbs. Three hundred and ninety-five people were killed during that raid, including the Gestapo commander, who was in my granddad's old house when it was hit by a bomb and completely destroyed.'

'Je déteste les Bosche,' the old man repeated, bang on cue.

'The death of a Nazi sounds like poetic justice,' I said, 'just a shame about losing the house.'

'Yeah. But with the house in Neuilly-sur-Seine destroyed, my mum and Uncle Danny had to come here to live.' Olsen looked round the room. 'I'm sure it was a lot nicer back in those days.'

Daniel Schumann said nothing, he just continued to sip his brandy, but he did give a slight shrug of his shoulders. This suggested that he understood English, despite speaking only in French himself.

'My mom stayed here with Uncle Danny until she was eighteen,' Olsen went on. 'Then she went off to the Sorbonne University, where she met my old man, who came over to France from New York to study. They both graduated in nineteen-fifty-five, and my mom went home with my dad when he returned stateside.

'My dad went to work for the newly formed Chase Manhattan Bank, and my mom became a French teacher at a high school. They married four years later, and I was born seven years after that.' He smiled. 'They called me their miracle baby, because mom had several miscarriages before I was born, and they had given up hope of having a child.'

'Are your parents still alive?' I asked.

'No, my old man died of lung cancer ten years ago, probably as a result of the three packs of cigarettes he smoked every day, and my mom died in an auto crash a couple of years back.' He looked fondly at Schumann again. 'Uncle Danny is the only family I have left. That's why I came here when I needed a bolthole.'

'So why do you need a bolthole, Troy?'

'You know why, Stevie.'

'You still think somebody is trying to kill you?'

'I know they are.'

'Are you talking about the shooting at Batus?'

'Not only that, although I still believe it was me that was supposed to get whacked.'

'We went through that at the time, Troy.'

'Yeah, and I know you think you were the target, but there's something you're forgetting.'

'What am I forgetting?'

'You're forgetting that the Land Rover you were driving on the night Genny died was booked out in my name and only I had driven it up until that time. So, what d'ya think about that?'

'I think you're taking two and two and making four, just to make sure you get your sums right.'

'Okay what about the other times somebody tried to kill me?'

'Such as?'

'I told you the brake line on my auto was cut.'

'No, you told me the brake pipe was disconnected.'

'It's the same thing, pal,' Olsen snapped. He was starting to get angry now.

'No, it isn't, Troy. Cut and disconnect are two different verbs entirely. As I said at the time, vibration could have caused your brakes to fail.'

He shook his head to contradict me and then insisted, 'That's not all.'

'There's more?'

'Yeah, there's more. For instance, the day I got back from Canada somebody tried to push me under a tube train at Victoria station?'

'Now you're being melodramatic.'

'It's true. Somebody pushed me.'

'There's probably a simple explanation. Perhaps somebody was in a hurry to get home, they tripped over their feet on the platform and knocked you off balance.'

He looked at me incredulously. 'Do you really believe all that crap you're spouting?' He was leaning across the table towards me and was almost shouting.

Daniel Schumann sipped his brandy and looked at us in turn, like a spectator watching a tennis match. He said nothing and nor did I.

'Okay, what about this, you smart-ass Limey,' Olsen smacked his hand down on the table, just missing the two pistols that were still lying on the tabletop. 'When I got home that same night, somebody threw a Molotov cocktail through my bedroom window. What d'ya say to that?'

'Have you upset one of your neighbours?'

'Are you being serious?' His voice rose even higher as he gave a fair impression of John McEnroe. 'You think I'm making it all up, don't you?'

It was my turn to shake my head. 'No, I don't.'

'So, you believe me?'

'Yeah, I think somebody's been trying to kill you, Troy.'

He slumped back in his seat and puffed out his cheeks, then he said, 'Thanks, Stevie. That really means a lot to me, pal.'

'Have you any idea who might want you dead?'

'I have my suspicions. You know I've been investigating the intelligence leaks in your security services?'

I nodded.

'Well I think I was getting close to the source.'

'Close enough to give me a name?'

He did not answer and we sat in silence for a while, listening to the burning wood crackling in the hearth. I guessed he was deciding whether to tell me more. I decided to give him longer to make up his mind.

'I need a leak,' I said.

'The john's outside. Come on, I'll let you out.' He stood up, picked up his pistol from the table and led me over to the back door. He unlocked the door and pulled the heavy bolt across, then stepped aside with his gun raised and let me pass.

He watched as I made my way out into the dark yard. 'Knock three times when you want to get back in,' he called after me, before closing the door and locking it. He was taking no chances.

I looked around the yard and, with the help of an almost full moon, I saw a dilapidated wooden privy located about six foot from the back wall of the house. I made my way to it and opened the door.

I stepped inside and was immediately hit by the stench rising from the stained porcelain pedestal that was perched over what seemed to be little more than a hole in the ground.

I had just finished relieving myself when I heard the

rat-a-tat-tat sound of a machine gun close by. I pulled up my fly zip and automatically reached for my Glock, but my holster was empty. I swore as I remembered my pistol was on the kitchen table.

Suddenly, two explosions shattered what was left of the winter night's tranquillity, sending pieces of broken roof tiles clattering down round the wooden privy where I stood deciding my next move.

Eventually I stepped cautiously out of the toilet and was confronted by a scene of devastation. One side of the cottage had been completely demolished by the explosions and a massive hole had been blown in the roof. Ten-feet-high orange and yellow flames poured out of the hole, accompanied by swirling black smoke that drifted across the night sky like soot laden storm clouds, blotting out the moon and stars.

I could feel on my face the searing heat of the flames that soon engulfed the cottage, and could only imagine what the temperature must be inside the building. It did not take Troy's first-class honours degree for me to work out what had happened, just experience in guerrilla warfare.

I had that experience. Somebody had used a machine gun to shoot out the front window of the cottage and spray the room with bullets. The attacker had then thrown a concussion grenade into the room.

If Olsen and his uncle escaped the murderous hail of lead, they would have been killed by the devastating blast from the grenade.

Mercifully, death would have been instantaneous for the two men, because what happened next would have led to an even more horrible end.

To make doubly sure everyone inside the cottage was dead, the attacker had then thrown an incendiary grenade into the room.

The white phosphorous inside the grenade would have burnt at 2800 degree Celsius and created an inferno that was currently turning into a cinder anything and everything unfortunate enough to be inside the cottage.

All this went through my mind as I edged my way carefully round the side of the crippled cottage. When I arrived at the front it was just in time to see a tall figure clamber onto a motorcycle. Slung across his back was a machine gun.

The hungry flames that were noisily devouring Daniel Schumann's home had turned the night into day, lighting up the area around the cottage so that I could see the attacker clearly.

I recognised him immediately. It was Angelo Salvatori.

I cursed again, frustrated at not having a weapon to hand, because the Mafia assassin would have been a sitting duck. Instead, I could only watch as, with one smooth movement, Salvatori kick started the motorcycle, turned it round and headed up the track through the trees. The cycle's exhaust was barely audible, and I guessed it had been fitted with a silencer.

My car was where I had left it, but it too had been torched and was a blazing wreck. As I stared at my burning car through narrowed eyes I thought about what had just happened.

My first thought was that Salvatori had been sent to kill Olsen and thought my car belonged to him, but I soon dismissed that theory. If Olsen was the target, the Mafia must have had him under observation already, and would have known the car was not his. No, either I was the target, or we both were. If the latter, I had led Salvatori to the American.

But how did Salvatori find me? I was confident I would have spotted a motorcyclist if he had followed me from Honfleur, so I guessed he had fitted a tracking device to my car in the hotel car park so he could follow me without being seen.

Of course, I had no idea whether this is actually what happened, all I knew was that I was stranded, without a weapon, transport, or coat. I started walking up the track and it took me over an hour to reach the road, where I started thumbing a lift.

After several failed attempts, I eventually managed to flag down a battered Citroen Acadiane 2CV van, driven by a farmer whose breath smelled of garlic and alcohol, who offered me a lift into Honfleur, where he told me he was meeting a friend.

The farmer said very little during the journey; he was more interested in the open bottle of cheap red wine that was wedged between the front seats in easy reach of his right hand.

Every so often the farmer pulled the bottle out and raised it to his lips. Each time he tipped up the bottle and gulped down a mouthful of wine, the car began to drift over to the other side of the road, but luckily there was no other traffic about and he always managed to get us safely back on an even keel.

The journey to my hotel took less than fifteen minutes, which gave me enough time to wonder how Salvatori knew I was in France in the first place, but was not long enough to come up with an answer.

1   Burner phone: a cheap prepaid mobile phone that you can be discarded.
2   Satellite navigation.

30

Sunday 19ᵗʰ January 2020: Honfleur, France

The next morning, I got a taxi to Le Havre station, where I caught the 11:02 to Paris Gare St Lazarre. Three hours later I was sitting in the Eurostar departure lounge at Paris Gare du Nord, having lunch and waiting for the next train to London.

It would be a long wait, because the earliest train on which I could get a seat was the 17:13. I was just finishing a sorry excuse for a cheese and salad baguette when my mobile phone buzzed. It was Bobby Moore.

'Is that you, Mr Statton?'

'Yeah, it's me.'

'Can you talk?'

'I've been doing that, with varying degrees of success, since I was eighteen months old.'

'My, you are touchy today, guv.'

'Listen to me, Humpy. Last night I had my car torched, I was forced to walk miles in the freezing cold without an overcoat, and I only got two hours sleep. Now I'm sitting in a draughty railway station and have just been stiffed ten Euros for a luke-warm cup of coffee and a stale baguette filled with tasteless cheese and limp lettuce. How do you expect me to feel?'

'Pissed off, I suppose.'

'Bullseye. Now, what do you want?'

'Have you heard about Tommy Cassidy?'

'What about him?'

'He's been at it again. They found some bird in his flat, stoned out of her mind and with her head bashed in.'

'How do you know what happened?'

'My mate is one of the paramedics who went to pick the bird up from Cassidy's gaff. They're saying she was shagged by a dozen blokes and still had her legs wide open when they found her.'

'Is that what they say?'

'Yeah.'

'So why are you telling me?'

'Don't you see, guvnor. It's just like what happened to my sister.'

'What was the girl's name?' I asked, pleading ignorance.

'No idea. My mate didn't say.'

'So, is this why you rang me, Humpy?'

'Partly, Mr Statton, but the main reason is you asked me to find out what Cassidy was up to.'

'And what is he up to?'

'He's just received a shipment of heroin.'

'Has he?' I wondered whether this was connected to the horsebox Jane Manning's team had pulled apart. 'What do you mean by "just"? When did the shipment arrive?'

'A couple of days ago, guv.'

That ruled out the horsebox in which traces of heroin were found.

'The thing is, Mr Statton. I know where the horse is stored.'

That made me sit up straight on the hard departure lounge plastic chair. 'Where might that be, Humpy?' I asked quietly.

He lowered his voice in response. 'I want you to promise me something, guv.'

'That depends on what it is.' I tried to keep any irritation out of my voice.

'Promise not to tell anybody where the information come from. Okay?'

'I've told you before, Humpy. Anything you tell me is strictly between the two of us.'

'I know that, but…'

'But nothing,' I interrupted him. 'Look, do you want to tell me or not?'

'Course I do, guvnor.'

'In that case, stop messing about. Just tell me where the bloody heroin is being stored.'

'It's in an abattoir what Cassidy's got in Peckham.'

'Thanks, I'll check it out. If the info is pukka there will be another wedge coming your way.'

'Don't worry, its pukka all right, but I don't want no money, guv. This one's on me. It's for Janet. The only payment I want, is for you to take Cassidy down. I want the bastard to get what he deserves,' he lowered his voice further and was almost whispering now. 'I want Cassidy as dead as my kid sister.'

'You obviously didn't notice, Humpy, but Britain abolished the death penalty back in 1965.'

'Don't you worry, guvnor. You get the bastard banged up and I'll do the rest. There's more than one way to skin a rat.'

'I think you mean cat,' I said, but Moore had gone.

I sat staring into my coffee cup, wondering whether I could face drinking the remainder of the tepid liquid and mulling over the events of the last 24 hours. Finally, I made two decisions; I pushed the coffee away from me and took my mobile phone out of my pocket again. I punched in Harriet's number.

'Who is this?' she asked cautiously.

'It's me?'

'Steve? Is it really you?' She sounded surprised.

'Why are you surprised? I thought you had my number logged into your phone.'

'I do, but I was told you were dead.'

'Who told you that?'

'Sam Brewer.'

'When did you see him?'

'I haven't seen him. He rang me at home to break the news to me.'

'I bet he could barely hold back the tears.'

'Sometimes I think you take your cynicism too far, Steven.'

'Is that what you think?'

'Yes, as it happens Sam sounded really upset.'

'I bet he did.'

'You think he was acting?'

'Let's just say I heard he was in line for an Olivier Award this year.'

'Well I felt sorry for him.'

'What happened to hashtag Absolute Arsehole?'

'He's still an arsehole,' she said and gave a little laugh. 'But he sounded like a worried Absolute Arsehole.'

'Well, you can tell him not to worry. Like Twain said, reports of my death are greatly exaggerated.'

'That's a relief. I'd hate to be talking to a ghoulie,' she said with another laugh. 'So, what time do you arrive back in London?'

'My train is due to get into St Pancras International just after six. Why do you ask?'

'I was hoping to see you tonight.'

'Unfortunately that won't be possible. Something has cropped up that I must sort out this evening.'

'What's that?'

I told her about my conversation with Moore.

'An abattoir in Peckham seems a strange place for Cassidy to store drugs,' she said when I had finished. 'Are you sure Fatso has his facts right?'

'He's usually reliable, but there's always the possibility he's wrong this time. Which is why I'm going to check out the abattoir myself as soon as I get back to London.'

'Won't it be closed on a Sunday evening?'

'I'm counting on it.'

'Why?'

'Because it will mean there won't be as many people about.'

'But if Cassidy is storing heroin in the abattoir, won't he have men there to keep an eye on it?'

'I hope so.'

'That's very confusing. I don't understand why in one breath you say you don't want people around, and in the next that you want Cassidy's men there.'

'It's simple. If there are people inside the building, it's unlikely the burglar alarm will be switched on, which makes it easier for me to break in.'

'You're going to break in?'

'How else am I going to gain entry? I can hardly knock on the door and ask to be let in. Can I?'

'I suppose not,' she said, then went quiet.

'Are you still there?' I asked.

'Yes. I was thinking.'

'What about?'

'Why are you catching a train? I thought you drove to France.'

'I did, but somebody decided to torch my car.' I told her what had happened the previous night.

'Sam told me you and Troy were killed in a house fire, but he didn't mention Troy's uncle.'

'He probably doesn't have all the details. To be honest I'm surprised he knew as much as he did. The local municipal police in France are not renowned for speed, or accuracy.'

'So, how are you going to get to Peckham?'

'That's where you come in.'

'You want me to pick you up from the station?'

'No, I want you to go to the office and book out a pool car in my name. If the duty officer asks what I want the car for, say you don't know. I don't want anybody to know about my visit to the abattoir.'

'Okay.'

'Nobody, Harriet,' I emphasised. 'Don't even mention it to Sam should you happen to bump into him in St James'. Is that clear?'

'Very clear, but don't worry about Sam. I won't be bumping into him because he's in Cheltenham.'

'What's he doing in Cheltenham?'

'He has an early morning meeting at GCHQ tomorrow. He was on his way there when he rang me.'

'Okay, once you have the car, drive it to the NCP[1] car park in Judd Street, which is next to King's Cross Station. Park the car, lock it, and leave the key on top of the front offside wheel. Then text me the car's make, colour, registration number, and the floor on which it's parked.'

She was silent again.

'Have you got that, Harriet?'

'I think so,' she said hesitantly.

'You don't sound too sure.'

'Don't worry. I know what to do.'

'So why the hesitation?'

'Well there was one thing.'

'What is it?'

'Which is the offside wheel?'

'It's on the driver's side,' I told her with a laugh.

'Thanks. I always forget which is which.'

'Try not to forget this time'.

'I won't. I promise.'

'There's something else I'd like you to do for me.'

'What's that?'

'Find the address of Cassidy's abattoir and text me the details. It will be easy to locate. I don't suppose there's more than one slaughterhouse in Peckham.'

'No problem,' she said and then added. 'Steve, can I ask you something?'

'Of course. I'm in no rush.'

'Do you know who killed Troy and his uncle?'

'It was Angelo Salvatori.'

'Do you think Troy's death has something to do with Operation QS?'

'That's what it looks like.'

She went silent yet again.

'Are you still there?'

'Yes,' she said, 'I was just thinking. Why did the Mafia want

Troy dead? Are you sure you weren't Salvatori's target?'

'It's possible,' I admitted. 'However, Olsen was convinced somebody was trying to kill him.' I then repeated what the American had told me.

'So, Troy knew the identity of the traitor?'

'Who he thought was the traitor,' I corrected her.

'Did he tell you?

'No, but there might be a way to find out.'

'How?'

'By finding out whose was the last file Olsen booked out from Central Records. Can you have a word with your old school pal?'

'No problem. I'll get onto it in the morning.'

'Of course, it's possible Salvatori was sent to kill both Olsen and me.'

'You mean, like Sam told me happened?'

'Yeah,' I replied and for some reason the old quotation, 'Out of the mouth of babes, cometh truth and wisdom,' popped into my head.

She went quiet again and I could almost hear her mind working. Eventually she asked, 'If Troy was the target, how did the Mafia know where to find him?'

'Because unwittingly I led Salvatori to him,' I replied and explained my theory about a tracking device being fitted to my car.

'But surely if there was a tracker it would have been fitted when your car was parked outside your home or at the office?'

'Or at my hotel in France,' I pointed out.

'But if Salvatori fitted the device to your car in Honfleur, how did he know where you were staying? I was the one who booked your hotel and I told nobody except you.'

'He could have followed me from London.'

'What? And he just happened to have a place booked on the same shuttle as you?'

'Anything is possible. Salvatori could have made an inspired guess about my plans,' I replied, not believing a word of it.

Nor did Harriet. 'Don't take me for an idiot, Steve. Something about this whole business stinks.'

I did not argue with her, because she was right. In fact, a month old rotting fish smells better.

'Please be careful, Steve.'

'I will, I promise. Just make sure there's a car waiting for me when I get to the Judd Street car park.'

'Don't worry. It'll be there because I…' but she did not finish her sentence.

'Are you there, Harriet?' I asked, but this time there was no answer. I checked my mobile and discovered I had lost my signal. I hoped this was not a bad omen.

1   NCP: National Car Parks.

31

Sunday 19ᵗʰ January 2020: London, England

Unusually high pressure over Southern England had brought with it clear skies, which had led to temperatures in London plummeting below freezing. As I stepped out onto the pavement, and left behind the warmth of St Pancras International Station, the bitter night air hit my face and stung it like a slap across the cheek from an angry woman.

For the second evening running I cursed myself for leaving my overcoat in the burnt-out car in Honfleur. Now, as I walked to Judd Street, I pulled my suit jacket tighter, but this made no noticeable difference and by the time I arrived at my destination I was shivering.

Harriet had sent me a text with details of the pool car, and I soon found an old silver Toyota Prius, with the correct licence plate, on the ground floor of the almost empty NCP car park. It took me only seconds to retrieve the ignition key from the top of the front offside wheel.

As I slid onto the driver's seat my nose started dripping. Whoever had used the pool car last had left an almost full box of tissues in the otherwise empty glove compartment. I took a handful of tissues out, wiped my nose with one and stuffed the rest in my jacket pocket.

I started the car's engine and turned on the heater. It took a few minutes for the engine to warm up, but the fan was already pumping out hot air when I reached Tavistock Square. By the time I hit Euston Road I had warmed up a bit and stopped shivering, but my nose was still dripping.

I encountered very little traffic on my way home, and it took me only twenty minutes to reach my apartment. I unlocked the front door and found a handful of envelopes on the hall floor. I picked them up and threw them onto the hall table, where they joined the still unopened mail from Friday.

I turned on the light and made my way through to the bedroom, where the heady fragrance of Harriet's Decadent perfume still lingered in the air. It was certainly a better smell than natural gas.

I took off my suit, hung it in the wardrobe and pulled on a pair of denim jeans and a black bomber-jacket. On the floor of the wardrobe was a stack of shoeboxes. I pulled out the bottom box, put it on my bed and opened it. I took out a Glock and as I felt the cold grip of the pistol in my hand it triggered memories of where it came from.

The Glock was the same model as the one I lost in France, but this one had not been issued by the department's armourer. The weapon was unregistered. I took it from a member of an extreme Islamic State jihadist group, following a bloody water-front fight in Beirut, which ended with me having a dislocated shoulder, and my assailant, dead from a broken neck, floating face down in the sea off the coast of Lebanon.

I loaded the pistol, using bullets from a box also stored in the shoebox, and slipped it into my holster. Feeling the weight of the pistol under my armpit felt comforting. It was good to be armed again.

I slipped a set of lock-picks into one pocket of my bomber-jacket, put my mobile phone into the other pocket, along with some tissues, and headed for the door. My nose was still dripping, and I wondered if I had a cold coming.

It was still bitter outside and when I reached my car I found my windscreen was covered in frost. Once inside the car, I started the engine and wiped my steamed-up spectacles.

Now I could see, I put the address of Cassidy's abattoir into the car's sat-nav system. By the time I had done that, the heater had cleared the windscreen and I was able to set off for Peckham.

There was even less traffic on the roads than earlier in the evening, but it was still almost nine o'clock before I reached my destination.

The abattoir was situated on a rundown trading estate next to the main railway line that carries thousands of commuters from Kent to and from Victoria Station every day.

The estate had an ungated entrance and had seen better days. It was dimly lit by a number of lights attached to buildings that looked so dilapidated and rundown that at first I thought my sat-nav had directed me to the wrong place, but then I saw a grubby white sign on one of the largest buildings. The faded black letters on the sign read:

The London Abattoir & Meat Co. Ltd.
(Est 1973)
Tel: 01 795 7979

Next to the building was an area in which were parked a lorry with the picture of a cow painted on its side, a dirty white transit van, and two even dirtier cars that looked as if they belonged in a scrap yard.

As I drove along the service road in front of the building, my headlights lit up a row of grimy windows, on the inside of which were fitted equally dirty venetian blinds. I could see no movement to show I was being watched through the closed slats of the blinds, but that meant nothing.

There was a CCTV camera affixed to the front of the building and it was pointing at me. However, the camera remained as motionless as the venetian blinds, and did not follow my car as I drove past it. I hoped this was a sign the camera was not being manually operated or monitored, but decided to take no chances.

I drove to the end of the deserted estate where I did a three point turn and then drove back the way I came. I hoped that if anybody in the building was checking the CCTV, they would think I had driven into the estate by mistake.

Once I reached the main road, I drove along it for a couple of hundred yards and then parked in a side street. I locked my car door and walked back to the industrial estate. When I arrived, I drew my pistol and headed warily towards the abattoir, keeping to the deep shadows cast by light from the slowly waning moon.

I made my way silently across the parking area, checking each of the vehicles in turn as I passed them. There was nobody hiding in the vehicles, and judging by the amount of frost on their windscreens they had been parked next to the abattoir for some time.

When I reached the rear of the abattoir, the moon was hidden from view and I found myself in an area that was pitch black.

I took out my mobile phone, switched on the torch and used it to make my way along a narrow path running alongside the high wire fence that separated the industrial estate from the railway line.

I found a back entrance to the abattoir halfway along the path. I trained the torch on the door's lock and was pleased with what I found. It was an ancient two-lever mortice lock, which I guessed had been installed when the building was built. I said a silent prayer that nobody had thought to install security bolts on the inside of the door to supplement the lock.

I slipped my pistol back into its holster, took out my pouch of lock-picks and, after selecting the right tool, it took me under a minute to click the two levers open. When I turned the handle the door opened immediately and silently. There were no bolts. I suppose nobody expected any burglar worth his salt to break into an abattoir.

I returned the lock-pick back to its pouch and stepped into the building, where I found myself in a dark corridor. I stood silently for a few moments but could detect no sign of life. Using the phone's torch to find my way, I made my way cautiously up the corridor until I came to an opening on my right. It led to a large empty chamber. I walked in.

The tiled walls of the chamber were splattered with dried blood and, although the floor had been hosed down, there were still pools of congealed blood in the open drain that bisected the chamber. The smell of slaughtered animals hung heavily in the air, filling my nostrils with the stench of death.

However, after a quick look round it soon became obvious there was nowhere to hide drugs in the bare chamber. I left the slaughterhouse quickly and headed for a room on the opposite side of the corridor, sucking in mouthfuls of clean, fresh air as I walked.

This second chamber had been sub-divided into two smaller units, across the entrances of which were hung heavy-duty PVC strip curtains.

I pushed my way through the curtain of the first unit and found myself in a storage room, in the ceiling of which a chiller unit was pumping out ice-cold air.

Hanging from hooks connected to steel rails set into the ceiling, were three rows of sheep carcasses, from which the fleece, head and innards had been removed. I made my way down the length of the unit, walking between the first two rows, checking there was nothing hidden amongst the carcasses.

When I reached the back wall, I discovered a metal cabinet. I pulled open one of the double doors and looked inside. The cabinet contained a bucket, two well-used floor mops, a couple of dirty cloths, and a large container of cleaning fluid. There were no drugs.

I headed back towards the entrance, this time walking between the second and third rows, again checking between the carcasses. I found nothing untoward, so made my way to the second unit, which turned out to be another cold storage room.

This unit had two rows of beef carcasses hanging from the rails on its ceiling. I walked down between the two rows, once again checking as I went. There was nothing hidden amongst the carcasses and, just like next door, there was a cabinet at the end of the unit containing nothing more than cleaning materials.

I headed back towards the entrance, but when I got halfway down the narrow gap between the carcasses, I stopped and made my way back towards the cabinet. There was something odd about the last carcass in the right-hand row.

I inspected the carcass carefully and immediately realised that it looked different from all the other beef. For a start it was much lighter and leaner. I wondered why this should be, but no immediate answer sprang to mind so I headed back to the entrance again.

I went to push my way through the PVC curtain to get back out into the corridor, when I saw another door at the end of the cold storage unit, which I had not noticed before.

I went to the door, opened it, and stepped inside a small room containing several metal bins. I lifted the lid of the first bin and the smell of rotting meat filled my nostrils. I shone my torch into the bin and saw it was full of glistening animal entrails.

I guessed that all the bins would be full of similar offal, but I decided to check them anyway. I lifted the lids on all the bins and found the same pile of stinking entrails, except when I got to the last bin. Is that not always the way? Like the others, this bin contained offal, but in addition there was something else.

Lying on top of the pile of entrails was the head of a horse. It lay with one of its dark eyes staring up at me, as if accusing me of separating the head from its light, lean body, which I now realised was hanging, skinned, on a hook at the end of the row of beef carcasses I had just inspected. I replaced the lid of the bin, left the room, and closed the door.

Once back in the corridor I stood for a few minutes and thought about what I had found. It did not take me long to work out that I had just found the remains of the latest in a line of Buzkashi horses that had been shipped from Italy, before going missing.

What I did not know was why the mare had been slaughtered. I was just starting to develop a plausible theory when I noticed a glimmer of light at the other end of the corridor.

I pushed the theory to the back of my mind as I tip-toed silently down the corridor until I reached a T-junction with a second passage that ran parallel with the front of the building.

I peeped round the corner and saw to my right a thin shaft of light coming from the window of a room at the far end of the passage. Looking to my left I saw nothing but darkness. I took out my Glock and headed silently and cautiously towards the light.

When I reached the door I discovered its window was covered by a blind that was raised half an inch, allowing a sliver of light to escape from the room and pierce the darkness.

I peeked through the gap and saw three men in the room. Two were standing behind a stainless steel bench on which were a set of scales, an opened catering size bag of powdered milk, an empty mixing bowl, and a variety of utensils.

One of the men was black, with dreadlocks and a woollen Rasta hat knitted in alternative bands of green, yellow, red, and black wool. He was tall and heavily built, and when he picked up a small packet of white powder from the table, his hand looked too large for such a delicate task. He weighed the packet and put it into a large clear plastic container that was already almost full of similar packets.

Compared with the black man, his companion was tiny. He was white, with a shaved head, a gold stud in each ear and a mass of tattoos on both arms.

Tiny picked up from the bench an empty polythene bag and

raised it cautiously towards his face, holding it carefully between finger and thumb. No doubt the bag had once contained a kilo of pure heroin.

The third man was lounging in a battered armchair smoking a cigarette. He had sharp features and was watching his colleagues work with the cold, hard eyes of a sewer rat.

The man was wearing a white Ralph Lauren shirt, Hugo Boss trousers, and Gucci trainers. There was a Belstaff Outlaw 2.0 leather jacket thrown nonchalantly over the back of his chair. I had no idea how much Ratty paid for his designer clothes, or where he bought them, but I don't suppose they came from one of the many local charity shops.

When the empty bag was level with Tiny's chin Ratty slid from his seat like a king cobra unwinding and eased himself upright in one fluid movement. That's when I noticed the pistol poking out of the back waistband of his trousers.

I saw Ratty's mouth move, but could not hear what he was saying. Instead he stood there, with an angry look on his face, opening and closing his mouth like a goldfish in a bowl. Whatever he said, Tiny hastily dropped the polythene bag on the bench as if it had suddenly become red hot.

Ratty picked up the bag and examined it carefully. Seemingly satisfied it was empty, and none of the valuable merchandise had been pilfered by his two helpers, he smoothed it flat, then put it in on top of the small packets in the plastic box, pushed it down and snapped on a lid.

He took the box from the bench and walked over to a heavy metal door that was set into the wall. He took a key from his trouser pocket, unlocked the door, opened it, and stepped inside a vault.

Because of the position of the window I only had a restricted view and could see only half the vault through its open metal door. However, there was enough of a gap for me to see the vault was lined with shelves.

Ratty put the plastic container on one of the shelves, where it joined a row of similar boxes, then he bent down and took a kilo bag of heroin from the bottom shelf of a long, two-tier metal trolley. When Ratty came out of the vault, he was carrying the bag in both hands like a small white baby.

This was my opportunity. I silently eased the door lever down and was relieved to find that the door was not locked. I kicked the door open so hard it swung back fast on its hinges and smashed against the wall with a loud bang. The three men froze and stared at me with gaping mouths as I stepped into the room with my pistol pointing at them.

Ratty was the first to react. He dropped the bag of heroin on the floor and instinctively went for his pistol. However, before his hand even reached his hip the realisation showed on his face that he stood no chance of drawing his weapon before I shot him. Common sense took over from instinct. He first raised his hands briefly in submission, then dropped his arms to his side.

'Wise move,' I told him. 'You wouldn't want to ruin your fancy shirt by getting blood on it, would you? Now turn round and put your hands flat against the wall above your head.' Ratty hesitated, but then obeyed with another of his smooth, snakelike movements.

Without dropping my guard, I glanced quickly at the two men standing behind the bench, who were still staring at me open mouthed. It was clear they presented no immediate threat.

'You!' I nodded at Tiny. 'Take your mate's gun from his waistband.'

Tiny did not move. He looked at me blankly, as if I was talking in a foreign language.

'Now!' I shouted and pointed my pistol at him.

That woke him up. There's nothing like looking down the barrel of a Glock 17 to concentrate your mind. He scuttled from behind the bench and was about to reach for Ratty's gun when I stopped him.

'Stop! Not like that. Just use two fingers.' I watched as he obeyed my instruction. 'Okay, that's good. Now, place the gun on the floor and kick it towards me.'

Tiny did as he was told and pistol slid across the floor towards me. Still keeping the men covered with my Glock, I bent down and picked up Ratty's weapon with my left hand.

It was a Spanish made Star BM. The 9mm parabellum semi-automatic pistol was a cheap copy of the classic Colt M1911 and was the type of pistol often used by both sides during the Libyan Civil War.

After the defeat of Colonel Muammar Gaddafi, hundreds of weapons were smuggled out of the Middle East to raise funds to pay for the half-hearted insurgency campaign that Gaddafi loyalists were waging against the newly installed National Transitional Council.

The Star BM I now held in my hand certainly looked as if it might have come from a war zone. The matt coloured surfaces of the pistol's barrel and slide were badly pitted and discoloured, and the trigger guard was dented.

Black adhesive tape had been roughly wrapped round the butt to provide a better grip and was now badly fraying at the edges. However, despite the pistol looking old and battered, I was in no doubt the bullets stored in its magazine would be new and very lethal.

'Okay, my friend,' I said to Tiny. 'Here's what I want you to do now. I want you to go into the vault and load all the plastic boxes onto the trolley and bring them out here.'

Tiny glanced nervously at Ratty.

'Don't do it, Tony,' Ratty said in a threatening voice. 'Not unless you want your hands chopped off.'

Tiny, who was now Tony, looked at me in desperation with eyes that betrayed his fear.

I nodded at him. 'OK. Get back behind the bench, but no stupid moves, or I'll chop off more than your hands.'

Tony did not need telling twice. Slowly he edged crablike across the floor, where he joined his black companion behind the bench. I pointed my Glock at the two men and covered Ratty with his own pistol.

'Turn round,' I told him.

Ratty turned smoothly on the balls of his feet until he was facing me with his hands still in the air.

'Since you don't want your oppo to load up the trolley. I'll let you do it.'

'Bollocks to that,' Ratty said, giving me a look that could not quite make up its mind whether to express anger or defiance.

It made no difference to me either way. I smiled at him. 'Is that your final word?'

'You're full of shit, arsehole,' he said with a sneer.

'I'll take that as a yes, then,' I said as I pulled back the slide of the Star to load a bullet into the chamber. 'Okay, here's the deal. I'm going to start counting and if you're not heading towards the vault when I reach ten, I'll shoot off *your* bollocks.' I pointed the pistol at his groin. 'In fact, you'll be able to cover what's left of your wedding tackle with a postage stamp. Are you ready?'

Ratty said nothing.

'If you think I'm bluffing, let's see who really holds four aces in their hand. 'One, two, three, four…' I intoned quickly. To give the guy his due, he waited for me to reach five before he blinked. '…five…'

'All right, you bastard. I'll do it.'

'…six, seven, eight,' I went on, ignoring him.

'I said I'll do it,' Ratty screamed and strode over to the vault, taking care to keep his hands where I could see them.

'Hold it right there!' I shouted when he reached the vault. I had no way of knowing whether there were weapons stored inside. 'Before you go inside, open the door wide so I can see what you're doing.'

Ratty threw me another poisonous look, then angrily pulled open the metal door and let it clang against the wall. He stepped into the vault, and I watched as he took boxes of drugs from the shelf and loaded them onto the trolley. It took him only a few minutes to clear the shelf.

'Wheel it out and put it over there.' I nodded towards the bench. 'On the way, pick up the bag you dropped.'

He did as he was told and put the bag of heroin on the bottom shelf of the trolley with the bags that were already stored there, before parking it alongside the bench. He gave me a sullen look.

'Okay, back inside the vault.'

'Why?'

'Why do you think?'

'You're gonna lock me in.'

'Clever boy.'

'Well I ain't gonna do it.'

I smiled at him grimly. 'Oh, I think you will. Either that or you die where you're standing. It's your choice.'

Ratty stared at me and I could see he was trying to decide if I was serious about shooting him.

'I'm serious,' I told him quietly and pointed the Star at his head, 'and if you're wondering whether I've shot anybody before, the answer is yes. Many times.'

This made his mind up for him. He shrugged, sauntered over to the vault with a cocky sneer on his face and stepped inside.

I turned to Tony and his black colleague. 'Your turn. Go join your pal.'

The Rasta stared at the vault in horror. 'But we won't be able to breath, man,' he protested in a high-pitched voice that was at odds with his massive size. It was the first time he had spoken.

'If you don't bleat too much, there will be more than enough air in the vault to see you through until somebody lets you out in the morning.'

'What if you're wrong?'

'Then you'll probably suffocate, but if you expect me to feel sorry for you, think again. Now get in the bloody vault.'

Without another word the two men trooped miserably into the vault.

'You think you're clever,' Ratty shouted, 'but when my boss finds out what you've done, he's gonna cut you up into little pieces and feed you to his dogs.'

'He'll have to find me first,' I replied, before slamming the door shut and locking it. I smiled to myself because I had every intention of letting Cassidy find me.

I walked over and stared at the now fully ladened trolley. Looking at the hoard of white powder reminded me of the year I spent seconded to the Metropolitan Police drugs squad. I recalled the words of Bill Brown, the old-style copper who was given the task of bringing me up to speed with the trade in drugs.

'This is heroin, son,' Bill held up a small packet of white powder. 'Otherwise known on the streets as brown sugar, China white, scag, smack, or my own favourite name, Mexican horse.

'In its purest form, horse is a fine white powder. But by the time it hits the street – if you excuse the pun – it's more likely to be grey, brown, or black in colour. That colouring comes from additives which have been used to dilute it.'

'Why's it diluted,' I asked.

'You've got a lot to learn, haven't you, son. It's all about money. The thing is street heroin is never pure, it's always mixed with other stuff, like milk powder, castor sugar, or, more dangerously, strychnine. The dealers call it cutting the merchandise.

'The problem is that those additives never fully dissolve, and when they are injected into the body, they can clog the blood vessels that lead to the lungs, kidneys, or brain. This in turn can lead to infection or destruction of vital organs.

'In the case of strychnine, if too much is used to cut horse, it can kill a user, particularly if they are long term addicts with health problems.

'Users buying horse on the street, never know the actual strength of the drug in that particular packet. It means that users are constantly at risk of an overdose.

'Horse is very adaptable. It can be injected, smoked, or sniffed. The first time it's used, the drug creates a sensation of being high.

'A person can feel extroverted, able to communicate easily with others and may experience a sensation of heightened sexual performance. The problem is that wonderful feeling doesn't last for long.

'Of course, horse is highly addictive and withdrawal extremely painful. The drug quickly breaks down the immune system, finally leaving users sickly, extremely thin, bony and, ultimately dead.'

'Knowing all that, who on earth would want to even try heroin?' I asked when Bill had finished.

'An addict, son, that's who. Some kids get addicted to marijuana but then find they no longer get the same kick from taking it, so they look for something else that will give them the same high feeling. That's when they move to harder drugs like cocaine and heroin.' He sucked on his false teeth again. 'There are thousands of addicts and degenerates in our country, which is why the drugs trade is so lucrative.'

I thought of that conversation with Bill Brown as I calculated the amount of heroin stacked on the trolley. There were 45 kilo bags on the bottom shelf and 11 boxes on the top shelf, each containing 2 kilos of street strength drug. Assuming the latter was cut with 50% powdered milk, then it made a total of around 56 kilos of pure heroin.

I whistled softly as I wheeled the trolley out of the room. I was pushing a load of heroin, which, once it had been cut, had a street value of just over £11 million.

No wonder Cassidy can afford to live in a swanky house in

Wimbledon, I thought as I parked the trolley at the junction with the corridor that led to the back entrance.

I left the trolley and headed down the dark corridor, opening doors as I went. I was in the abattoir's administration area and I eventually found what I was looking for in a room that was directly adjacent to the front entrance lobby.

It was a small, oblong shaped room, with an internal window on my left that looked out into the darkened entrance lobby. There was an L shaped desk, with its shorter side under the internal window, and the longer side under the outside window. There was a swivel chair positioned in front of this longer side.

I made sure the blinds on the outside window were properly drawn and then turned on the lights so that I could see what I was doing. I sat down.

On the desk was a CCTV control box, with a flat-screen monitor perched on top of it. The box was humming and there was a green diode shining beside the On-Off switch. I switched on the monitor and a split screen with eight camera shots appeared.

All the shots, except two, showed dark areas in which it was difficult to see anything. The first of the two exceptions showed the entrance lobby, with a shaft of light coming from the room in which I was sitting. The second gave a view of the forecourt and service road in front of the abattoir and was lit by the security lights I saw earlier.

There was a date and time showing in the top left-hand corner of each shot and the camera's location in the top right. In addition to the two shots showing some light, the darkened images were for cameras sited outside - at the rear of the abattoir and at the side to cover the stock yard entrance - and at various locations inside the building, including the slaughter hall, the cold storage area, and the despatch bay.

Next to the control box was a CCTV keyboard and joystick. I tapped a key on the keyboard and immediately the picture being relayed by the forecourt camera filled the screen. I used the joystick to pan the camera and was pleased to see the estate was still deserted.

I pressed the reverse key and watched as the figures on the digital time counter in the corner of the screen rapidly ticked backwards. Suddenly the headlights of a reversing car appeared and then rapidly went out of shot.

I pressed the key and the moving video view, slowed down to normal speed and the image started to move forward. I tapped the key again and the car came back into shot, but this time in slow motion. A final tap and the image froze. I zoomed in and, despite the glare from the car's headlights, I was able to clearly see the registration number plate of my Toyota Prius.

Anybody checking the video would be able to see that number and I was confident Cassidy would find a way of identifying me, which is what I wanted. I had his heroin and now I wanted him.

I pressed the forward key and allowed the video recording of the forecourt to return to real-time mode. I pressed the multiple shot key, and the views from the other seven cameras appeared on the monitor screen again. Satisfied nobody would know I had used the CCTV video recorder I turned off the monitor.

I switched off the lights, left the room and returned to the drug ladened trolley. I wheeled it down the main corridor to the back door and out onto the pathway.

The moon had risen above the roof of the building and filled the area between the abattoir and railway line with a ghostly ethereal light. Now I was able to see the CCTV camera, which had been lost in dark shadow when I broke into the building.

I waved cheerily at the camera, before pushing the trolley round to the parking area, where I parked it in the shadows thrown by the vehicles. I hoped nobody would see it while I went to get my car.

I knew it was a risk, but it was less of one than wheeling the trolly up the main road, where I could be seen by any of the many drivers and pedestrians who were out and about that night.

It took me no longer than ten minutes to reach my car and drive it back to the trading estate. This time I did not drive past the front of the abattoir, instead, I drove straight to the parking area, where I reversed alongside the meat lorry.

The trolley was where I had left it. I loaded the plastic boxes of street strength heroin into the boot of my car and then piled the kilo bags of pure drug on top of them. A few minutes later I slammed the boot shut, jumped into the car, and pulled out of the estate.

I drove sedately, not wanting to attract the attention of any passing police car, whose occupants might be tempted to liven up a quiet Sunday evening by pulling me over on suspicion of whatever infringement they could dream up on the spur of the moment.

My forged warrant card would probably dissuade any over enthusiastic plod from searching the car, but I didn't want to take the chance. It would be just my luck the cops were bored enough to waste time checking my ID with Scotland Yard.

Justifying my impersonation of a police officer was not beyond the capabilities of a member of Her Majesty's Secret Service, however, explaining away a boot full of heroin might be more difficult.

On a corner of the next junction was a superstore. I pulled into its carpark and parked as far away from the entrance as possible. Being a Sunday night, the store was closed, however, its lights were on, and I could see a man stacking onto shelves merchandise he was taking from cardboard outer cartons that were piled on a cage trolley.

I took out my phone and rang Bobby Moore. 'Are you on your own, Humpy?' I asked when he answered my call.

'Nah. I've got a bird sitting on my lap and the bleeding Queen of Sheba is in bed waiting for me to go up and give her one.'

'I take it your feeble attempt at sarcasm means you're on your own and can talk?'

'Yeah. I'm at home and I'm all alone, but you caught me just in time, because I was about to pop round the Cardigan for a swift half.'

'Is that another joke, Humpy? I've never known you drink beer, let alone a half pint. It's always been large measures of bourdon for you, particularly when somebody else is buying.'

'You have me bang to rights there,' he agreed with a chuckle. 'So, what do you want to talk about?'

'I have a favour to ask.'

'Anything for you, Mr Statton. You know that. What is it?'

'Do you still have that lock-up in Bethnal Green?'

'Yeah, why?'

'What have you got in it?'

'A load of junk and a few hooky camcorders and sat-navs that fell off the back of a lorry. Why?'

'Can I use the lockup?'

'No problem, as long as you don't nick my gear.'

'I hate to tell you this, Humpy, but these days most people use their mobile phones to make videos and cars have sat-navs fitted as standard.'

'Not round here they don't, guvnor. They might start off having them, but most are nicked within the first week.'

'And how many of those stolen sat-navs end up in your lock-up?'

'I've no idea where my suppliers get their merchandise and I don't ask.'

'Of course not.'

'It's true,' he insisted plaintively.

'Don't worry, Humpy. I don't care where you get your hooky gear from, I won't steal any of it and I won't grass you up.'

'I know you won't, Mr Statton. I trust you.'

'Thanks for that reassurance. I'll be able to sleep easy tonight.'

'Now who's being sarky?'

I took that as a rhetorical question and ignored it, instead I asked, 'Look, can I use your bloody lock-up or not?'

'Of course, you can, guvnor.'

'Thank you.'

'What do you want to do about getting the key?'

'Take it to the pub with you. I'll meet you there and buy you a drink.'

'You're one in a million, Mr Statton. A real gent.'

'Don't be deceived by my table manners, Humpy. Just because I hold my knife and fork properly and can tell the difference between Saint-Émilion and Nuit-Saint-George, doesn't mean I've forgotten my working-class roots. I still know how to use a knuckle duster if somebody crosses me.'

'I won't cross you, guvnor. Honest,' Moore insisted hurriedly.

'Good. I'll see you in about half an hour.'

I put my phone away and sat staring at the supermarket. The shelf filler had emptied all the cardboard outer cartons, broken them down and stacked them neatly in the merchandise cage. He was now working his way through a second trolley.

As I watched him work, I mulled over my next move. I had somewhere to hide the heroin, now I had to get everything organised for when Cassidy came after me. My guess was I would not have long to wait.

I was right.

32

Sunday 19ᵗʰ January 2020: London, England

Bobby Moore's lock-up garage was situated underneath the railway arches, close to Bethnal Green Station. Back in the 1980s, when he took out a 99-year lease on the unit, the district was rundown, home to drug dealers and prostitutes, and ignored by the local police, who were bribed to turn a blind eye on any illegal activity.

It was an ideal base for Moore.

These days, one local estate agent described the area as a "prime addictive location, much sought after by the up-and-coming generation". Moore joked that this was just another way of saying it was still home to druggies and slags.

The lock-up's large double-doors were secured with a heavy chain, which was threaded through a sturdy hasp and staple. Linking the ends of the chain together was a heavy duty padlock it would take an industrial angle-grinder to cut off. Luckily for me, I had a key. I unlocked the padlock, removed the chain, and pulled open the doors.

The lock-up was massive, reflecting that before Moore took it over, two single units had been converted into one larger unit. I reversed the Prius inside the lock-up and found there was still plenty of room, despite the assortment of junk that was being stored in the unit.

There were three long bolts on the inside of the doors, which I slotted home with reassuring clunks. Satisfied I was now safe from any inquisitive visitors, I switched on the double row of fluorescent lights that hung from the ceiling on rusty metal chains.

On the left hand side of the lock-up were a couple of metal warehouse racking units. Most of the shelves contained what looked like second-hand bric-a-brac and other similar cheap junk. However, the top two shelves contained more expensive goods.

On one shelf was a row of camcorders and on the other a dozen or so satellite navigation systems. I could not tell whether any of these electrical goods were brand new, but none of them were in their display cartons, which spoke volumes about their origin.

Most of the wall opposite the racking was hidden behind a stack of old furniture, including two double-wardrobes, and larger pieces of household goods.

Two thirds of the way up the unit, a partition wall had been erected out of breezeblocks. It stretched from the right-hand wall, just beyond the pile of furniture, to the centre of the unit, and was about eight feet high. In front of the wall was an assortment of garden equipment, including a rusty petrol lawn-mower, from which engine-oil had leaked onto the concrete floor.

Sitting incongruously on top of the wall, was a row of identical china dolls, each dressed in a lavender and white polka dot dress, red pinafore, white ankle socks and black patent leather shoes. The dolls all had blonde hair, tied back with a matching lavender ribbon. As I walked towards the wall, the dolls stared down with wide, unseeing blue eyes and smiled at me in unison with red Cupid's bow lips.

Behind the breezeblock wall was a low workbench, across which were scattered various tools. Next to the bench, and leaning at an angle against the partition wall, was an aluminium stepladder.

In the back left-hand corner of the unit, next to the water stained rear wall, was a small, breezeblock built, doorless, toilet cubicle, complete with a stained pedestal, grimy sink and cracked wall mirror. Under the mirror was a shelf on which was an untidy stack of paper-towels and a half-full bottle of hand-wash.

On the outside wall of the toilet cubicle was a 1985 Pirelli calendar, showing a colour photograph of Iman Abdulmajid, slouched in a chair smoking a cigarette, with her long left leg almost horizontal, as if she had just kicked off the single black high heeled shoe that was lying on the floor in front of her.

Next to the calendar, three tea chests with **Indian & Ceylon Blended Tea** stamped in large black letters on their sides had been stacked against the cubicle wall. When I checked, I found the top two chests were empty, but the bottom one was full of straw.

As I stared at the tea chests I began to formulate an idea, but I soon lost my train of thought as exhaustion hit me like an Atlantic wave breaking over my head, stinging my eyes, and making it difficult to keep them open.

I decided it would be sensible to rest for a while before driving home. I switched off the lights and stretched out on the backseat of the car. I lay in the dark and tried to flesh out my plan, but within minutes I was fast asleep.

33

Monday 20th January 2020: London, England

When I woke up, winter daylight was creeping under the lock-up doors, but the light was weak and insipid, as if the sun was struggling to get out of bed after a boozy night on the tiles.

I checked my watch and found it was eight o'clock. I had slept for almost nine hours, and would probably have slept longer if the need to relieve myself had not forced my eyes open.

I put on the lights and used the toilet, before filling the sink with cold water and dunking my face in it to wash off any lingering tiredness, then I dried myself as best I could with paper towels. I looked in the mirror. I needed a shave badly, but that would have to wait.

I turned off the lights and cautiously unbolted the lock-up doors. I opened them just wide enough to let in slightly more light, and enable me to see what was going on outside.

The area surrounding the railway arches was deserted and there was no activity in the road outside any of the other units. I pushed open the doors fully, drove the car out, and closed them again. I put the chain through the hasp and secured it with the padlock.

I spent the next two hours shopping, taking care to spread my purchases across several different shops, ending up in a hardware store where I purchased a large, shrouded, hardened-steel padlock.

When I had finished my shopping, I returned to the lock-up,

satisfied I had not drawn attention to myself by buying unusual quantities of the same goods in any one shop.

The road, and the area outside the other units under the arches, was still deserted and I managed to get the car back inside the lock-up without being seen. I got to work on the next part of my plan.

My task took longer than anticipated, and it was late afternoon before I finished storing all the heroin away in the tea chests and covering it with straw. Confident the drugs were unlikely to be found any time soon, I drove out of the lock-up in the gathering gloom, once again unseen, but this time with an empty boot.

I secured the doors to the unit, using the chain and the newly purchased padlock, and headed to the office, safe in the knowledge that now not even Moore would be able to access the lock-up without an angle-grinder.

It was gone five when I reached the office, but Harriet was still at her desk. She shot to her feet when she saw me walk through the door. At first I thought she was going to run to hug me, but she pulled back when she remembered where we were.

'Where have you been, Steve?' she said quietly as she sat back down.

'You know where I've been.'

'I've missed you.'

'Don't be silly. I've only been away two days.'

'It seems longer,' she said simply.

'Why are you still here?'

'I'm waiting for a call from Judy.'

'Who's Judy?'

'My school pal from Central Records. I rang her this...' She was interrupted when her phone trilled. She sat back down at her desk and picked it up. 'Hi Judy,' she said. 'Did you find out anything? You did?' she listened for a few moments and then said, 'Thank you, no don't worry, it's not a problem. I understand. I promise nobody will know where the information came from. I appreciate your help. Listen, perhaps we can do lunch sometime. My treat. Yeah, of course. My lips are sealed.' With that she put down the phone.

'Well?'

'Judy apologised for the delay in contacting me,' she explained as she looked up at me. 'She wanted to get home before ringing me, because she was worried somebody in her office might overhear and find out she was passing information to me.'

'So, was she able to tell you whose file Olsen withdrew last before he was killed?'

'Yes,' she said in a distracted voice.

'Well whose was it?' I pressed her.

'Troy signed out two files at the same time.'

'And?' I asked, trying to keep out of my voice the impatience I felt.

'One was Gerald Draper's.'

'Draper?'

'Yes.'

This was a surprise, and my mind went into overdrive at this revelation. 'Why did Olsen feel the need to check Draper's file?' I spoke my thoughts out loud. 'I thought they were bosom buddies.'

'I don't know,' she said and then asked, 'Do you still think Troy was killed to shut him up before he revealed the identity of the traitor?' she asked with a worried look on her face.

'It's possible,' I said with a shrug.

'So Draper could be behind his death?'

'Or whoever the other file belonged to.'

She shook her head. 'I don't think so,' she said confidently.

'Why? Whose file was it?'

She did not answer immediately, but then said hesitantly: 'It was Auntie Xandra.' She looked up at me expectantly, as if waiting for a comment. I did not respond, and she did not push it, instead she said, 'I'm going to visit Marion in hospital this evening.'

'How is she?'

'She's still unconscious, but off the critical list. When I visited her on Saturday afternoon, her doctor said that they might bring her out from her induced coma today or tomorrow. Will you come with me?'

'Not tonight, but perhaps tomorrow.'

'Okay. How did you get on at Cassidy's abattoir?'

I told her what had happened the previous evening and her eyes widened when I related how I had taken the heroin from Ratty and his pals, and how I left them locked in the vault. I did not mention my subsequent conversation with Moore, nor my visit to his lock-up.

Her eyes widened even more when I told her how much I estimated the heroin to be worth.

'How much?'

'About eleven mill,' I repeated.

'Are you telling me that you have eleven million pounds worth of drugs in the boot of your car?'

'I did, but no longer.'

'Where are the drugs now?'

'It's best you don't know. What I'm doing is not strictly

legal.' This was not true, because as one of the security services, the SSA was able to operate outside most of the usual laws. However, it was the best excuse I could come up with on the spur of the moment for not telling her.

The truth was that the fewer people who knew where I had hidden the heroin, the lower the risk of discovery. But I should have known better than to think I could deceive her.

'That's bollocks,' she said bluntly. 'Be honest, it's because you don't trust me.'

'Not true,' I protested. 'I trust you explicitly.'

'So why won't you tell me?'

'Because if Cassidy, or his Mafia friends, suspect you might know the location of the heroin, they will pick you up and interrogate you.'

'I wouldn't tell them anything,' she insisted stubbornly.

'You might say that now, but I promise you'll feel differently when they start pulling out your fingernails and worse. Remember what happened to Humpy's sister and Marion? I don't want that happening to you.'

She stared at me. 'Thank you, Steve. That's the nicest thing you've ever said to me. Is that why you don't want to come to the hospital with me tonight? Are you worried they will spot me with you?'

'Partly, but there's another reason.'

'What's that?'

'I think Cassidy will come for me tonight.'

She looked confused. 'I don't understand. How does Cassidy know you have his drugs? Did the guys at the abattoir recognise you?'

'No, but I made sure that the CCTV camera recorded the

registration number of my car. No doubt Cassidy has access to the Driver and Vehicle Licensing Agency records.'

'But you were driving a pool car. Wouldn't it be registered to the Cabinet Office?'

'It would. So, if Cassidy does come for me tonight, it will prove he was tipped off by somebody who has access to the transport section's records that show the pool car was booked out in my name.'

'You mean Troy Olsen's traitor?'

'That's exactly what I mean.'

'You don't suspect Auntie Xandra do you, Steve?'

'In the words of Jacques Clouseau: "I suspect everyone, and I suspect no-one,"' I said in a phoney French accent of which Peter Sellers would have been proud.

'What about me? Do you suspect me?'

I shook my head. 'No. Olsen told me the Yanks have suspected for some months there was a mole in the department. You've only been with us since the beginning of the year. So, you're in the clear.'

'That's a relief. I just wish the same applied to Auntie Xandra.'

'So, do I. I would much prefer to bang-up somebody like Dickhead Draper.'

'I'd better go.' She stood up.

'Did you speak with Sam today?' I asked as I helped her on with her coat.

'Yes. He said he would ring you when his meeting finishes today.'

'Wonderful. I can't wait.'

'Don't be an old grouch. He sounded jolly pleased when I told him you were alive.'

'That's only because he wants me to carry on doing his paper-work.'

'That's strange,' she said as she picked up her handbag. 'I thought it was me who was doing his paperwork.'

'Under my supervision.'

'You must be joking? I must have been asleep when all that supervising was taking place.'

'I'm the one who's supposed to be sarcastic.'

'You haven't got a monopoly on it.' She reached out and squeezed my arm. 'I suppose seeing you later is out of the question?' she whispered.

'I'm afraid it is, but all being well, we should be okay for tomorrow night. We'll visit Marion at the hospital and then go for a meal somewhere.'

'What time?'

'I don't know. I'll ring and let you know.'

'I look forward to it.' She squeezed my arm again and was gone.

I went into my office and took off my shoulder holster. I put the Glock in my desk drawer and locked it. There was no point having the pistol if Cassidy or his lackeys came for me that evening, because I had no plans to use it.

However, I never like to be without a weapon for too long and knowing I could retrieve the Glock from my desk drawer the following morning was a comforting thought.

Of course, in an emergency, I also had the option of using Ratty's Star BM, which was now safely squirreled away in Moore's lock-up, but the battered old Spanish automatic was not my weapon of choice.

I was just about to leave the office when the phone rang. It was Sam.

'Thank God you're still alive,' he said, hiding his crocodile tears well. 'I was really worried about you. What the hell happened in France?'

I told him everything that I had been through in the last two days, including my visit to Cassidy's abattoir and what had occurred. I gave him the same version Harriet received, which excluded any mention of Moore's lock-up.

Unlike Harriet, he was not surprised when I told him my estimated value of the heroin, he already knew a gram of the drug was literally worth more than its weight in gold. However, he did ask the same question as her. 'So where are the drugs now?'

'Where are you ringing from?'

'My hotel in Cheltenham.'

'That's what I thought. I hope I haven't caught you watching television.'

'What do you mean?' he asked crossly, reverting to type.

'Nothing. It's just that I don't think it would be sensible revealing any sensitive information over an open line.'

'I suppose that's true,' he agreed reluctantly.

'When are you coming back?'

'Tomorrow. Probably late afternoon.'

'Okay, I'll brief you then.'

'What about...' he started, but I interrupted him.

'Must dash. I have a meeting with Jane Manning in ten minutes.' This was a lie, but what the hell. I was flying by the seat of my pants and there was already a chilly draught freezing my backside.

'Hang on!' he shouted.

Fat chance, I thought as I put down the phone.

34

Monday 20ᵗʰ January 2020: London, England

It was all so predictable.

They were waiting for me when I arrived home. I saw two of them sitting in a car on the other side of the road opposite my apartment. They were trying to look inconspicuous, but to my practiced eye they stuck out like a sore thumb.

I guessed the two men were not alone and that their back-up would be hiding somewhere close by, waiting to spring the trap.

Under any other circumstances the waiting men would not have seen my exhaust fumes for dust, but on this occasion I pretended not to notice them. I parked the Prius as close to my home as possible, locked it and walked nonchalantly towards my apartment building.

I saw the third man when I was about six feet from the entrance. He stepped out from the shadow cast by the high garden wall of the neighbouring building. I recognised him immediately. It was Ratty.

Out of the corner of my eye I saw Ratty's two colleagues get out of the car and circle round until they were behind me. Both those men were tall, wide, and tough looking. They were not guys to mess with.

'Stay just where you are,' Ratty said, pointing an automatic pistol at me. It was Star BM 9 mm parabellum, similar to the pistol that was hidden in Moore's lock-up. Cassidy must have bought a job-lot.

'I see your boss found you a new toy to play with.'

'Shut your mouth, arsehole,' Ratty said, sounding like a gangster from a Hollywood B movie.

I half raised both hands in a gesture of submission.

'Check him out,' Ratty told one of the heavies who were now standing close behind me.

'What happened to the other two Stooges?' I asked Ratty as his pal patted me down.

He frowned. 'What are you talking about?'

'Your mates from the other night. Little and Large.' He looked at me blankly. 'Don't worry, it was just an observation.'

'Well keep your fucking observations to yourself.'

'He ain't carrying, Vinny,' the heavy told Ratty.

'Where are your car keys?' Vinny asked.

I pointed to my jacket pocket and raised an eyebrow. Ratty nodded. I took out my car fob and handed it to him. In turn, he threw the fob to the heavy.

'Check the boot of his car, Deano.'

'Yes, Vinny.'

'Okay, over there,' Vinny told me, pointing to the car from which the two heavies had emerged. 'Help the bastard find his way to our car, Kev,' he told the second heavy, who grabbed me by the scruff of the neck.

I resisted the temptation to break Kevin's arm, instead I let him propel me across the road to the car. Vinny followed, standing to one side so that he could continue to cover me with this pistol.

Kevin opened the rear passenger door and bundled me onto the back seat. Vinny opened the other rear door and slid onto the seat next to me, still pointing the pistol at me.

Kevin went round the front of the car and opened the driver's door. He climbed behind the wheel, just as Deano opened the other door.

'The boot was empty, Vinny,' Deano said. He offered my car fob to Vinny, but I reached out and took it from him first.

Vinny jabbed the pistol into my side. 'What d'ya think you're doing?'

'Taking my key back,' I replied coolly as I put the fob in my jacket pocket. 'I think you'll find your boss will want me to have it.'

'I wouldn't bank on it. You ain't gonna need your car at the bottom of the Thames.' He scowled at me with hatred in his eyes.

'Let's wait and see what your boss has to say about that. I assume you're taking me to see him.'

'Just shut the fuck up, arsehole,' he said with another jab from his pistol.

I turned my head and stared into his eyes. 'Do that again, Vinny, and I'll take that gun from you and ram it up *your* arsehole.'

'You and whose army?' he sneered, but pulled the pistol away from my side.

'I don't need an army,' I assured him, before turning away and staring out of the window. As the car picked up speed I watched as the buildings in my road flashed by.

Vinny's face was reflected in the glass. He was staring straight ahead, and I could see he was struggling to contain his anger. I smiled to myself. It confirmed my hunch. Cassidy wanted me delivered to him unharmed. Whether he would feel the same once we met was debateable, because no doubt he was seriously pissed off with me.

Ten minutes later we went over Putney Bridge, and I thought they were taking me to Cassidy's home in Wimbledon. However, when we hit the A205 the driver turned left and headed east until we joined the A3, before carrying on in an easterly direction. I changed my mind and decided they were taking me to the abattoir in Peckham.

I was right. Twenty minutes later, we pulled into the car park of the London Abattoir & Meat Co. Ltd. and parked next to a silver Rolls-Royce. The two cars I had seen the previous day had gone, but the lorry and van were still parked in the same place.

'Out of the car,' Vinny said. He was about to prod me with the barrel of his pistol to emphasise his order, but I gave him a sharp look and he thought better of it. Instead, he added: 'Hurry up, arsehole. The boss is waiting for you.'

'I very much hope so, otherwise we've had a wasted journey,' I said as I got out of the car and followed Vinny to the front door of the building, with Deano and Kevin on either side of me. If they thought I was going to try and escape they were mistaken. I wanted to meet their boss.

We were greeted at the door by another of Cassidy's heavies. This one too had the build of a nightclub bouncer, with the cauliflower ears and flattened nose of a rugby prop forward.

'The boss is in his office, Vinny,' the bouncer said as he opened the door and let us into the foyer.

'Okay, this way.' Vinny led me out into the corridor, with my two shadows close behind. Tommy Cassidy's office was halfway along the corridor. Vinny knocked on the door and then pushed it open without waiting for an invitation.

Cassidy was sitting behind a desk, lounging in a large, plush executive chair, smoking a Montecristo cigar. I knew a great deal about him, but this was the first time I had seen him in person. However, none of the photographs of him I had seen did justice to the aura of menace he exuded, nor the malevolent power of his personality.

He stared at me and any complacency I might have felt about my dealings with him were quickly dispelled. He had the cold soulless eyes of a serial killer. Here was a man who would crush the life out of you without compunction or compassion.

Those eyes brought home the level of threat he posed to me, and why so many people were intimidated by him. But I was determined not to let him bully me. I smiled at him.

'Thanks for seeing me, Tommy,' I made it sound as if the meeting was my idea.

Cassidy did not respond, instead he took a nonchalant draw of his cigar and then blew smoke rings into the air. He took the cigar from his mouth with a ring-bedecked hand and studied the end of it, as if checking it was alight then he switched his gaze back to me. His eyes had narrowed and were still soulless.

He was immaculately dressed in a well-cut three-piece suit, crisp white shirt and a silk tie that was held in place with a gold pin topped by a large sparkling stone. It did not look like cubic zirconia to me.

Suddenly he sat up straight in his chair and shot his shirt cuffs to reveal diamond studded cuff links that matched his tie pin. He placed his cigar gently in a large cut glass ashtray that stood on his desk, then he leaned forward and glared at me. 'Where's my gear, Statton?' he growled.

'I'm impressed, Tommy. Whoever your snitch is must be a pretty important person to track me down so quickly. It usually takes days to get anything out of the Cabinet Office.'

'I don't need no snitch. The information came from friends.'

'Would that be the friends who eat lots of pasta and sing O Sole Mio?'

'What's it to you?'

'Just interested.'

'Well, I'm more interested in the merchandise you stole. Where is it?'

'Somewhere safe,' I replied.

My response seemed to enrage Cassidy, or perhaps it was the smile that accompanied it. He leapt to his feet and came striding round the desk to where I was standing surrounded by my three guards.

'Hold his arms,' he hissed angrily, his fleshy face flushed with anger as he towered over me.

Deano and Kevin grabbed one arm each and held me tightly. Vinny took a couple of steps to the right and was watching with an amused grin, which widened when he realised what Cassidy intended to do.

I realised too and tried to prepare myself against the blow I knew was on its way. I tightened my stomach muscles, but was much too slow, and a jagged pain tore through my lower abdomen as Cassidy's punch drove the breath from my body. I crumpled like a rag doll and would have slumped to the floor if the two big men had not been holding me upright.

'Where's my gear, Statton?' Cassidy asked again.

I was unable to answer straight away, instead, I struggled desperately to suck air back into my lungs and rise above the pain that was cramping my stomach.

Cassidy pushed his puce face closer to mine, sharing his bad breath with me. 'Where's my fucking merchandise?'

I tried to answer him but could manage only an incoherent mumble.

'Tell me where it is, turd, or I'll clock you again,' he hissed. As if to emphasise his point, he thrust his ring ladened fist in front of my streaming eyes, then took off my spectacles and threw them onto his desktop with a clatter. 'But this time it'll be your face I mess up,' he added.

'That wouldn't be a good idea, Tommy,' I finally gasped. 'Punch me again and you'll never see your drugs again.'

Now I had his attention. He took a couple of steps backwards and looked at me suspiciously.

'I think we should talk,' I managed to get out through gritted teeth. 'Can I sit down?'

Cassidy continued to look at me with suspicion for a few moments and then nodded his head slowly. 'Bring that chair over, Vinny,' he pointed at a hard-backed chair that stood against the far wall. He walked back behind his desk and sat down. 'Let him go, but stay close,' he told my guards.

Vinny fetched the chair and placed it in front of the desk. He was no longer grinning.

I gently probed my lower rib cage with the fingers of my right hand, but it did not feel as if any bones were broken. However, knowing that did not make my abdomen any less painful. I sat down in the chair and took another deep breath.

'So, are you going to tell me where my merchandise is?' Cassidy asked.

'Your drugs are safe.'

'Safe where?'

'Shepperton.'

Cassidy glanced at Vinny, who nodded and moved towards the door.

'I wouldn't let him do that,' I told Cassidy. 'Your drugs are currently with a friend of mine, on a boat in the middle of the River Thames.'

This news got his attention.

'If by some miracle your guys are able to find my friend's boat, he has instructions to drop all the drugs overboard if anybody gets within ten yards of the boat.'

'Leave it, Vinny,' Cassidy said. He picked up his cigar and lit it with a gold Dunhill lighter he took from his waistcoat pocket. Once he was satisfied the cigar was alight, he studied me carefully. 'I suppose you think you're clever, Statton.'

'No. If I was clever, I would have caught you before you raped that girl in her apartment.'

'It was my apartment and it wasn't rape. She was a whore and she got what she wanted.' He blew more smoke rings with his Montecristo cigar. 'So, what happens now?'

I took out my mobile phone and showed it to him. The digital time displayed on the screen showed it was 19:53. 'My friend is expecting me to ring him every hour on the hour. If I fail to contact him, he will ring me. If I don't answer, he has instructions to throw the drugs overboard.'

'I could take your phone from you and ring your friend myself,' Cassidy said.

'You could certainly try. However, you don't know my friend's number and my phone is a burner which has not yet been used to ring anybody, so you couldn't even try to guess his number.'

'I could force you to reveal his number.' Cassidy opened

his desk drawer and pulled out a long, thin knife, which he waved at me. It looked very sharp. 'I have ways of using this that would make you tell me everything.'

I shook my head and smiled at him again. 'I have been trained to resist torture.'

'Not the kind of torture I have in mind.'

I gave him what I hoped was a confident smile. 'There's no pain you could inflict on me that would break me down in under an hour,' I boasted, hoping it was true. 'By which time it would be too late because your merchandise will already have been dumped in the Thames.'

Cassidy puffed on his cigar and thought about that. He decided I was telling the truth. He put the knife back in the drawer. 'So, what do you want, Statton?'

'Five hundred thousand pounds.' Cassidy did not balk at this figure, but why would he? He knew how much the heroin was worth. 'In used notes,' I added.

He nodded. Suddenly he seemed relaxed and I guessed why.

My mobile phone vibrated. I took it out and checked the screen. It showed the time was now exactly 8 pm. I punched in my home number. 'All okay,' I said to my answerphone. 'I'll ring again in an hour.' I quickly deleted the number I had just called, ensuring Cassidy saw what I was doing, and put the phone back in my pocket. 'So, do we have a deal?' I asked him.

'Yeah. When and where do you want to meet?'

'Do you know the Knight Street multi-storey car park in Bermondsey?'

Cassidy nodded.

'I'll meet you on its roof tomorrow at midnight.'

'Why so late?' he asked suspiciously.

'What's the problem, Tommy? Worried about your beauty sleep?'

'No. I just wondered, that's all.'

I shrugged and explained: 'Okay. It's because at that time of day the roof car park will be deserted. We'll have the whole place to ourselves.'

He nodded his understanding.

'I will park on the right-hand side of the roof close to the exit ramp, with the bonnet of my car facing the wall, and my boot open so that you can see the drugs. You do the same, but park on the opposite side of the car park.'

Cassidy nodded again.

'Talking of cars, is that your Roller outside?'

'Yeah, why?'

'Do you have another car?'

'Why?'

'You'll see soon enough.'

'My wife has a little Mazda run-around. But I don't get why you want to know,' he said with an exasperated tone.

'You will,' I promised. 'But to get back to the arrangements for tomorrow. I'll be alone when I park my car on the roof and so will you. In case you try to pull a flanker, I'll have somebody watching the entrance of the car park. If there's anybody with you when you drive into the car park, they will contact me immediately and I'll be down that exit ramp and out of there before you reach the first floor. Understand?'

'Don't worry, I'll be on my own.'

I did not believe him. 'You'd better be, or you'll never see me or your drugs again.'

'I said I'd be on my own,' he said tetchily.

422

'Good.' I still did not believe him, but I left it and instead went on to set out my plans for our meeting. 'Is that clear so far?' I asked after I had finished.

'Very clear. What happens then?'

I smiled at him. 'That's easy. You'll drive my car away and I'll take yours. That's where your wife's car comes in, because I can't imagine you want me to drive off in your Rolls-Royce!'

Cassidy shrugged. 'It don't matter to me. I can get another Roller easy enough.'

I raised an eyebrow at him. 'The price of horse must be higher than I thought it was.'

'Street prices are driven by demand, and demand is currently sky high,' Cassidy explained.

'Lucky you.'

'The dosh ain't all mine. I have my partners and dealers to keep happy and bent cops to pay off.'

'My heart goes out to you. Now do we have a deal or not?'

'We have a deal,' he agreed unhappily.

I reached over and retrieved my spectacles from his desk and put them on. 'Good. Now get your goons to take me home.'

35

Monday 20th January 2020: London, England

When I got home, I poured myself two fingers of malt whisky and collapsed into an armchair in front of the electric fire in my sitting room. My ribs still ached from the punch Cassidy gave me, but I had experienced worse pain in my life.

I made three phone calls and then sat sipping my whisky whilst staring at the flickering artificial flames that lit up the plastic panel covering the bottom half of the fire.

I went over in my mind my plan of action for the next couple of days. It seemed fool proof, but I knew such confidence might be misplaced. I wasn't dealing with fools, so I was going to have to play very carefully the hand I had dealt myself.

Eventually, tiredness, the heat from the fire, and the whisky got the better of me and I felt my eyes drooping. I couldn't be bothered to move, so I fell asleep in the armchair.

36

Tuesday 21ˢᵗ January 2020: London, England

It had been raining most of the day, but by dusk the dark clouds had scuttled away to be replaced by a clear sky that saw temperatures plummet. By the time I arrived in Bermondsey, a bitter north wind had arrived, bringing with it Arctic air that quickly turned into ice any surface water it found on the streets of London.

I reached Knight Street at half past eleven and drove into the multi-storey car park. I stopped just inside the ground floor entrance and waited for Harriet to arrive, which she did, on schedule, five minutes later. It was a long enough gap to make it look as if we were not together.

She saw me and flashed her car lights briefly. I acknowledged her signal and watched as she reversed into one of the many empty spaces at the far end of the ground floor, close to the ramp to the upper levels. From her position she would be able to see any cars that came in. However, I hoped only one would arrive at that time of night.

When Harriet was parked, she gave me a quick thumbs up and turned off all her lights. Instantly the interior of her car was plunged into darkness, and I could no longer see her. That was good. If she was careful, and kept her head down, Cassidy would not see her either when he arrived.

I headed for the ramp and drove up six levels until I reached the parking area on the roof. There were only a handful of lights set into the low side walls and much of the far end of the roof was in darkness.

The car park looked as deserted as I had hoped, but, as a precaution, I drove the length of the roof, using my headlights to check the dark shadows. There were several patches of treacherous black ice on the ground, which earlier that day had been puddles of rainwater, but nothing else that I could see to worry about.

Satisfied I was alone on the roof, I parked the Prius next to the exit ramp, turned off my engine, and got out. I opened the boot to reveal a neat stack of polythene bags and plastic boxes. I got back into the car, took a wet wipe from a packet in the glove compartment and used it to clean any fingerprints from the steering wheel and plastic facia, then I settled down to wait.

At five minutes to midnight my mobile phone vibrated. It was Harriet.

'Cassidy has arrived,' she whispered. 'He's in his Rolls-Royce and has stopped at the entrance.'

'Is he on his own?'

'No, he's just let a man out of his car.'

Just as I suspected, Cassidy had brought along his own lookout to make sure I hadn't led him into a trap.

'Guess who it is?' she asked excitedly.

'We don't have time for guessing games, Harriet. Just tell me who it is.'

'Oh, sorry, it's Angelo Salvatori.' She sounded deflated, but I was not sorry for the way I had spoken to her. My reaction was an important lesson for her. She was young and new to fieldwork. She had to learn the importance of concise communication.

I was not surprised the Mafia were providing Cassidy with backup. However, it did make me wonder if Salvatori's presence meant Guiseppe Navarra was in town. I was not inclined to bet against it.

My guess was that they had reinforcements waiting somewhere outside the car park to ambush me when I left. I could not imagine that Cassidy and his Mafia allies would let me get away with £500,000 of their money. Once they had the drugs in their hands, all bets were off.

'Where's Salvatori now?'

'He went outside somewhere and now Cassidy is driving up the ramp to the next floor. There was nobody else in his car that I could see.'

'Okay. You know what to do now?'

'Yes, I'm onto it.' With that she was gone.

I smiled to myself. She was learning. A couple of minutes later I saw headlights coming out of the entrance onto the roof and then Cassidy's Rolls-Royce emerged. I got out of my car and waited.

Like me, Cassidy was suspicious about the dark area at the far end of the roof, so he drove the length of the parking area, lighting up every part with his headlights before turning around and driving back to park on the other side of the roof opposite me.

I watched as he got out of his car and opened its boot. He leaned in and I heard an audible click as he unlocked a large suitcase and raised its lid. He turned around to face me.

As we had agreed the previous night, we both raised our hands in the air so we could see the other person was not holding a weapon. Satisfied, he started walking towards me.

On his way, he carefully avoided walking across a large patch of black ice.

When he reached the Prius, he pointed at my overcoat. I knew what he meant. I pulled the lining of both pockets out to show they were empty, then I opened my coat and allowed him to check I was not wearing a holster and did not have a weapon tucked into the waistband of my trousers.

He nodded to indicate he was satisfied and then allowed me to go through the same process with him. He was clean.

'There's your merchandise.' I nodded towards the open boot of the Prius.

Cassidy looked at the boxes and bags full of white powder and grunted in satisfaction. He picked up one of the bags of heroin and carefully tore a small hole in the top. He stuck his finger into the bag, then withdrew it with white powder on its tip. He dabbed this on his tongue and nodded, before putting the bag back onto the stack from which he had taken it.

I slammed the boot closed and locked the doors with my electronic key fob. 'Okay, let's go see the colour of your money.'

We walked over to the Rolls-Royce where I counted the number of bundles on the top layer of used notes in the suitcase and then the number of layers. It was only a rough count, and for all I knew the lower layers could have contained bundles of plain paper. I didn't care. I was only going through the motions.

'It's all there,' I said as I closed the suitcase and pushed home its latches.

We exchanged car key fobs and Cassidy headed back towards my car. He had not spoken a word throughout the entire transaction unless the single grunt he had shared with me constituted a conversation.

By the time Cassidy had unlocked the Prius, and got the engine running, I was already manoeuvring his Rolls-Royce onto the down-ramp. However, as soon as the big car was off the roof I stopped and turned off the engine, effectively blocking the ramp.

I recovered my Glock, which was taped to my shin, squeezed out of the door, and positioned myself against the offside back wing of the Roller.

I heard the quiet hum of a car engine, as Cassidy drove towards the exit, then the noise of the engine was drowned out as the clatter of a helicopter rent the air above the car park.

The Prius was about to turn into the entrance of the down-ramp when Cassidy realised his exit was blocked. He slammed on his brakes, put the car into reverse, accelerated, and shot backwards with a squeal of tyres.

The car hit the ice patch and almost skidded into the side wall. Cassidy spun the steering wheel and somehow managed to stop the car just in time. Once he had the car under control, he accelerated again and headed for the entrance to the up-ramp.

I made my way out onto the roof and followed the speeding Prius. I did not run. There was no need. Cassidy did not know it, but he was going nowhere.

The rear lights of the Prius flared in the darkness as the fleeing man slammed on his brakes when he found there was now a car parked at the top of the up-ramp, blocking his way.

He jumped out of the Prius, leaving its engine running, and raced towards the roof door leading to the stairs, but he never made it, because I got there first.

But Cassidy never gave up, seeing the Glock I was pointing

at him, and realising he was trapped, he turned on his heels and ran back across the roof.

I had no idea what Cassidy intended when he reached the other side of the roof, but it was irrelevant, because in his haste he forgot about the patch of black ice. He ran onto it and immediately lost traction, gliding across the ice like an ice-skater for half a dozen paces, then his legs flew up in the air, as if somebody had pulled a rug from under him, and he crashed to the ground in a heap.

Cassidy managed to clamber to his feet just as a police helicopter landed on the roof in front of him. He looked around desperately for another escape route. But there was none because I was behind him with my pistol still pointing at him. Suddenly he was pinned to the roof by a bright spotlight from a second helicopter that was circling above the car park.

The spotlight lit up not just Cassidy, but the armed police officers who had already piled out of the first helicopter and were forming a semi-circle round him, with their Heckler & Kock MP5SF carbines raised and pointing at him.

That's when Cassidy realised the game was up. He put up his hands and looked at me as I approached him. 'You're gonna die, Statton,' he hissed.

'We all die someday, Tommy. So, let's just hope there's plenty of room left in Hell for you.'

37

Wednesday 22nd January 2020; London, England

'Are you telling me Cassidy didn't notice the boot of your car was full of powdered milk?' Sam Brewer asked when I had finished telling him what had happened the previous night.

'That's exactly what I'm telling you.'

'Didn't he test it?'

'Of course, he did. Cassidy might not be the brightest light on the Christmas tree, but he was clever enough to check one of the bags.'

'How come he didn't notice it was powdered milk?'

'Because it wasn't powdered milk,' I explained, trying hard not to sound smug. 'I knew Cassidy would want to check it out, so I made sure every bag on the top layer was full of heroin.'

'Didn't he think to check a bag on a lower layer?'

'No, he wasn't that clever. I think the Christmas lights' circuit breaker bulb blew after he checked the first bag.'

'What if he had checked one of the other bags?'

'I'd have been in deep poo.'

'You took one hell of a risk,' he said disapprovingly.

'A calculated risk.'

'Rather than take any risk, why didn't you just load all the heroin into the boot?'

'Switching the bags was my safety net just in case the operation had somehow gone tits up.'

'How?'

'Plenty of ways.'

'Such as?'

'Well for a start, I guessed Cassidy would have a carload of heavies waiting outside the multi-storey. If they had managed to capture me before Jane's boys collared them, I would have been able to use the location of the remaining drugs as a bargaining chip.'

'Would that have worked?' he asked sceptically.

'It did when I was picked up the first time.'

'So why put any heroin in the boot? You could have just filled it with milk powder and taken a risk that Cassidy wouldn't check any of the bags.'

'Doing what I did wasn't only about reducing the risk. It was necessary for a successful operation.'

'Why?'

'Because it was important to have a reasonable quantity of heroin in the boot of Cassidy's car when the police picked him up. It might have been difficult for plod to secure a conviction, if all he had in his possession was powdered milk.'

'But the drugs weren't in his Rolls-Royce, they were in your pool car. He could have said the drugs belonged to you.'

'He could have said that, but it wouldn't have done him any good.'

'Why not?'

'Because he was caught driving the Toyota and his were the only fingerprints inside it. In addition, the Prius is no longer a pool car. The DVLA[1] records show it's registered in Cassidy's name.'

'You arranged that?'

432

'Of course.'

It was Tuesday afternoon and we were sitting in Sam's office. Rachel Frewin had earlier brought in a percolator of coffee and it stood bubbling away on the modern glass coffee table that was positioned in the corner. Now she came back into the office carrying a blue plastic tray, containing equally modern looking retro style cups and saucers, with a matching cream jug and sugar bowl, and placed it next to the percolator.

'Smells good,' I said and it was not an exaggeration.

'Help yourself. I'll have mine black,' Sam said.

I poured two coffees, handed one to him and loaded mine with cream and sugar. Sam had offered me afternoon tea, but I insisted on coffee.

'I need a shot of caffeine. I only managed to grab a couple of hours sleep last night, and then I've spent most of the morning at Scotland Yard for a debrief about last night's operation.'

I explained that at the briefing I found out that when Harriet triggered the Special Operations action by ringing Jane Manning from the car park, she had reported also that Salvatori was somewhere outside. However, by the time the first squad car arrived the Mafia man had disappeared. Jane's team did manage to apprehend Cassidy's back-up team of heavies, including Vinny, but a second group of men escaped.

'And you think the men who got away were Mafia colleagues of Salvatori?' he asked.

'Yeah.'

'So, where is the rest of the heroin now?'

'In a lock-up.'

'Whose lock-up?'

'That's something it's best you don't know.'

Sam was not happy with this and it showed on his face. 'Where is this lock-up?'

'In Tower Hamlets.'

'Tower Hamlets covers a wide area,' he said with an exasperated edge to his voice. 'Can't you be more precise?'

'It's in Bethnal Green, but it's difficult to explain the exact location. However, I'm happy to take you there. You can help me collect the drugs and take them to the Met Police's Criminal Exhibits Store.'

Sam perked up at this offer. 'That sounds a great idea. I'd like to come with you.'

'In that case, can we use your wheels? I haven't had time to arrange another pool car yet, and Harriet is off work today.'

'Not a problem,' he said and then stared moodily into his coffee cup. 'You know you asked for Jane Manning to help yesterday?'

'What about it.'

'You should have cleared that with me first.'

'I didn't have time and you were at GCHQ.'

'There are such things as telephones.'

'I'm sorry, but it all happened so quickly.'

'Well it can't be helped, what's done is done.' He finished off his coffee and raised his empty cup. 'Would you like another?' he asked as he stood up. 'I think there's enough left in the percolator.'

'I don't mind if I do,' I said and then sat in silence as I watched him refill our cups.

'So, to be clear, Deputy Assistant Commissioner Manning and you planned the operation on your own.' He handed my cup back to me. It wasn't a question, but I answered anyway.

'That's right,' I said and added cream and sugar to my coffee, but took only one lump this time. I was trying to cut down on my sugar intake. 'I rang Jane as soon as Cassidy agreed to meet me.'

'Presumably, at that time you wouldn't have known exactly how long it would take to do the exchange, nor whether Cassidy would be on time?'

'Correct.'

'And if the helicopters had arrived too late, then Cassidy's sidekicks could have come into the car park, driven up the ramp and ambushed both you and Miss Barratt.' It was noticeable that Sam still couldn't bring himself to refer to Harriet by her Christian name.

'Correct again. As I explained earlier, that's why I switched the drugs.'

'On the other hand, if the helicopters arrived too early, Cassidy could have been spooked and might well have been able to escape before the exchange took place.'

'To be honest, that was my biggest fear,' I admitted. 'Choppers are bloody noisy machines.'

'So how did Jane know when to send in the cavalry? Wasn't that another risk?'

'Of course, it was. Which is why we decided to leave it to the last moment before activating the Special Ops squad. Jane already had her team in position by the time I arrived at the car park, and she was just waiting for a signal to send them in.'

'How did you contact her? You were on the roof with Cassidy.'

'I didn't give the signal. Harriet did that. After she blocked off the exit from the up-ramp, she watched what was happening on the roof and as soon as she saw Cassidy and I switch car fobs she contacted Jane. In the end, the gods were with us and everything went according to plan.'

'What happened to Cassidy?'

'He's safely locked away in Walworth Police Station.'

'How long can the police hold him?'

'Hopefully longer than last time. His brief is already trying to get him bail, but Cassidy has little chance of getting that because he was caught bang to rights with 6 kilos of heroin in the boot of his car.'

'So, when do you want to go pick up the rest of the drugs?' Sam asked.

'Whenever you're ready. The sooner we get them safely locked away, the better.'

'I'm off to a meeting with the Cabinet Secretary in a few moments to discuss my application for the position of D-G, but I'll be back by 3.30. Is that okay?'

'That suits me just fine. I have a couple of telephone calls to make and can catch up on some paperwork. I'll see you at 3.30 unless you get back earlier. Ring me when you're ready to go.'

'Will do.'

In the event, it was 4 o'clock when Sam's secretary rang me. 'Mr Brewer is on his way downstairs and asked if you could meet him at the entrance to the underground car park.'

'Was that a rhetorical question, Rachel?'

'No, it was a rhetorical order.'

'In that case, perhaps I should give him one of my well-practiced rhetorical responses.'

'I wouldn't wind him up if I were you.'

'Why not?'

'He wasn't a happy bunny when he got back from the Cabinet Office, and he was no better by the time he left the office.'

'What's wrong with him?'

'I don't know. But he's in one of his hyper moods and really on edge.'

'I'm shaking in my shoes.'

'I'm serious, Steven. You'll make him even worse if you're late. He hates being kept waiting.'

'He's not alone,' I said pointedly, but she had gone.

I opened my desk drawer and took out my Glock and holster. I strapped the holster into position so that the pistol was positioned handily in my armpit. Then I put on my jacket and headed for the door.

It took me only a couple of minutes to reach the entrance to the car park, but when I arrived it was obvious that Rachel was right about Sam being on edge. He scowled at me and made a point of looking impatiently at his watch.

'Don't you dare,' I warned him.

'What?'

'Tell me I'm late.'

'You are.'

'You told me you'd be back by 3.30,' I pointed out, 'but your secretary didn't contact me until 4 o'clock, so don't complain.'

'Do I look as if I'm complaining?' he asked with a forced smile as he opened the entrance door and stepped through into the small underground car park that was reserved for Very Important People who warranted such perks. This did not include me.

'Yes,' I replied as I followed him to his 2019 plated BMW 2 Series. There were a couple of other cars in the car park, but neither of them looked like a battered ten-year old Toyota Prius. That was hardly surprising. The car park was strictly for the use of people of senior management grade and VIP visitors, most of whom could afford expensive cars.

Sam responded with an irritable grunt, then lapsed into a sullen silence as he started his car and drove up the ramp and out of the car park into St James's Street. Every so often I gave him directions, but he did not respond.

We hit heavy traffic when we reached the Mall, and our progress was stop-start from there all the way to the A1208 Hackney Road. The heavy traffic, which forced us to crawl along at snail pace, only added to Sam's agitation. He tapped his fingers on the steering wheel in a continuous rhythmic beat, and every so often he glanced in the rear-view mirror, as if making sure no one had slipped onto the back seat uninvited.

Once we hit Hackney Road the traffic started to thin out and speed up, which seemed to settle Sam and he stopped his finger drumming, but he still glanced in his rear-view mirror from time to time.

'How did your interview with the Cab Sec go?' I broke the silence.

'It wasn't an interview; it was just a discussion about the future.'

'Of course it was. So how did the discussion go? Did you get the job?'

'No,' he answered.

'No?'

'Yes. Sir Mark said that a final decision had not been made yet,' he explained grumpily. 'He told me other candidates were being considered.'

'I thought you were a shoo-in. Particularly, with my letter of commendation in your pocket.'

'It seems you don't carry as much weight as my predecessor.'

'Dame Alexandra?'

'Yes.'

'What's her involvement in the selection process?'

'I don't know. However, my source in the Cabinet Office told me the old girl's been visiting Downing Street regularly.' He glanced at me. 'Don't you think that's a little odd?'

'Perhaps she was just dropping in for a cup of tea with the Cab Sec. They've been friends for years.'

'A cup of tea?'

'Yeah. I understand Sir Mark serves up a particularly delicious Estate Darjeeling.'

He glanced at me again. 'Are you serious?'

'No.'

'So you do think it's odd Dame Alex visits the Cabinet Office so often, despite being on gardening leave?'

'What I think is that you're being paranoid, Sam.'

He lapsed into silence and started tapping the steering wheel again. 'Have you spoken to her recently?' he asked eventually.

'Who?'

'Dame Alexandra of course.'

'Why would I do that?'

'You're pretty friendly with her niece.'

'That's irrelevant. I have several friends, but that doesn't mean I'm friendly with their families.'

'So, you haven't been in touch with the boss?'

'I thought you were the boss,' I said.

'Don't be difficult, just answer my question. Have you been in touch with her?'

'Why would I?'

'You would if you were plotting with her against me.'

I stared at him. 'You really are paranoid.'

'I'm not paranoid.'

'Okay, let me guess. You're not paranoid, you just think everybody is out to get you.'

He smiled briefly at that. 'Only Dame Alex.'

'And me by the sound of it.'

'Only if the cap fits, Steve.'

'I don't wear caps. I prefer beany hats because they keep my ears warm.' By now we were approaching Bethnal Green railway station. 'Okay, take the second turning on the left.'

When we arrived at Moore's lock-up, I glanced out of the back window and saw a set of headlights sweep past the end of the road and disappear, but apart from that vehicle, the area was deserted.

'Let's go,' I said and jumped out of the car. I unlocked the double doors of the lock-up and pushed them open. 'It's best if you reverse in, Sam.'

'Okay. See me back.'

'Give me a minute and I'll switch on the lights.' I went into the unit, flicked up the light switch and took up a position alongside the breezeblock partition. I waved to Sam and watched as he reversed slowly into the lock-up, prompting him on with my hand.

'That's it,' I called out and showed him the palm of my hand. I thought for one moment he was going to keep coming. 'Stop!' I shouted and thumped on his offside rear wing. That stopped him.

The BMW was wider than the Toyota Prius I parked in the unit the previous Sunday (it was only three days before, but it seemed much longer) but there was still plenty of room between car and furniture on my side of the unit, and enough room on the offside for Sam to open his door wide without worrying about scratching his paintwork on the metal shelves.

As Sam got out of the car, two men came charging into the lock-up. One was short and fat, and the other was tall and thin. I recognised them immediately. It was Guiseppe Navarra and Angelo Salvatori and they were both brandishing guns.

If they had arrived a few seconds later, Sam would have been out in the open, but now he was hidden by the driver's door and managed to drop to the floor.

I was not so lucky. I was exposed. Both Mafia men took aim at me, but, as they pulled their triggers at the same time, I managed to dive behind the partition. One bullet whistled through the air where my head had been nano seconds before, and the other ricocheted off the wall, chipping off a piece of breezeblock, and headed towards the toilet cubicle where it drilled a hole in Iman's smooth, brown forehead.

I sprang to my feet and pulled my Glock from its holster. I climbed three steps up the aluminium stepladder and peered over the top of the partition wall, looking through a gap between two dolls.

Salvatori was edging cautiously past the BMW with his pistol pointing at the place where he had last seen me. Navarra had taken refuge behind one of the wardrobes, and every few seconds he peeked out to see how his younger colleague was doing.

I could not see Sam and I guessed he was skulking behind his car. However, I still hoped he would be able to keep Navarra busy while I dealt with his underling, which was my first priority. I had a score to settle with Salvatori.

I went up the final two steps of the ladder, so I could take a shot at the Italian hitman, who was still focussed on the spot at which he had last seen me. I was just taking aim, when my arm brushed against one of the dolls, which slipped from the wall and dropped with a crash to the ground.

Salvatori looked up and saw me. His reactions were incredible; in the blink of an eye he dived towards an upended sofa, letting loose a shot as he flew through the air.

It is difficult to fire accurately when you are off your feet and luckily for me this was no exception. Salvatori's snapshot missed me by inches, instead, it hit one of the dolls between its baby-blue eyes, exploding its head in a shower of china.

But if the Mafia hitman's reactions were fast, mine were faster, and much more accurate, but then I did have the advantage of a prime firing position, with a secure stance, a clearly visible target, and the need for less than the blink of an eye.

I remember my small arms instructor at Sandhurst telling me to shoot with my heart, rather than my eye. That's what I did, and my bullet went through Salvatori's temple before his head disappeared behind the sofa. He was already dead when his long body crashed onto the cement floor.

Some fellow cynics might say it was a lucky shot and perhaps they were right. However, if it was luck, my good fortune ran out almost immediately after I pulled the trigger, because, without warning, and with a loud clatter, the aluminium stepladder buckled beneath me.

I crashed down on top of the bench, landing on my back with a thud that jarred my whole body. My spectacles were dislodged from my nose and the Glock was jolted from my hand. I saw it go spinning towards the Pirelli calendar just before my head struck a heavy metal vice that was fixed to the side of the bench.

I blacked out momentarily and when I came-to I was lying on my right side with my left arm behind my back. I was about to roll over when I heard footsteps. I changed my mind and stayed where I was, pretending to be unconscious.

I watched through slitted eyes as the short, rotund figure of Navarra appeared from behind the end of the partition wall. Although Navarra's pistol was pointing in my general direction it was not clear at what part of me he was aiming. My spectacles had fallen on the floor and my vision was blurred, in addition his hand was shaking, making the barrel of the pistol move erratically from side to side.

At first, I thought he was scared, but I soon discounted this. You do not get to the top of a Mafia family unless you are brave and ruthless. In addition, I did not represent much of a threat to him lying prone on the bench without a weapon.

As Navarra stepped towards the bench, I used the hand behind my back to search for something with which to defend myself. I found what felt like a screwdriver handle. I had no idea whether it was a Phillips, or a flat bladed screwdriver and did not care. Anything was better than nothing.

When Navarra reached the bench, he stood over me with the muzzle of his pistol pressed lightly against my chest. His hand was still shaking, and I guessed he was suffering from the early stages of Parkinson's Disease.

The Italian leaned down until his lips were almost touching my left ear. Because of his short stature, he did not have far to lean. Despite my blurred vision through almost closed eyes, I saw that his halo of hair had shed dandruff onto the shoulders of his black suit jacket.

I remained motionless and waited for the right moment to strike.

As Navarra leaned over me I could smell his aftershave, which, although it had a strong musky odour, did not hide the pungent smell of garlic on his breath as he whispered in my ear: 'Preparati per la tua morte, figlio di puttana!'

My knowledge of the Italian language is limited, but I know morte means death, so I guessed whatever Navarra was saying to me, was not designed to improve my health. I decided there would be no better opportunity, so the right moment had arrived.

I twisted suddenly catching Navarra by surprise. I reached up, gripped his wrist with my right hand, and pushed his arm aside before he could pull the pistol's trigger. He jerked upright and tried to step away from the bench, but I had his wrist tightly in my grip.

I twisted my body again and at the same time pulled my left hand from behind my back, lunging forward with the tool I had grabbed. It was only as it flashed through the air, that I realised it was not a screwdriver but a pointed wood chisel. I drove the sharp tool into Navarra's chest with all the power in my arm. I felt the metal blade spear straight through his body and into his heart.

I let go of his arm and he took several steps back from the bench and then crumpled in a heap like a punctured blow-up doll. He lay stretched out on the floor, face up, with the chisel protruding from his chest. Despite the terrible, fatal wound there was only a little blood because his heart had stopped pumping within a second of being pierced.

I half sat up, but had to stop when a jagged pain sliced through my head. I screwed up my eyes and tentatively touched the back of my head with my fingers. When I inspected them they were covered with sticky blood.

My head began to spin as I was hit by a momentary bout of vertigo. I lay back down on the bench and closed my eyes in the hope this would help clear my head.

I passed out again.

When I recovered a few seconds later, I opened my eyes and found that although my head still throbbed painfully, my vision had almost returned to normal. I closed my eyes again, forced myself to sit up, and this time I managed to stay up.

With my eyes still closed, I swung my legs over the edge of the bench and slowly lowered myself onto the floor. I opened my eyes and saw Sam bending over Navarra. He twisted the pistol to prise it out of the dead man's hand, slipped it into his pocket and turned to me.

'What happened to you?' he asked.

'The stepladder collapsed on me,' I explained weakly as I bent down and picked up my spectacles from the floor.

'Are you okay?'

'I hit my head.'

'You look all right to me.'

I held my hand up to show him the blood on my fingers. 'I'm bleeding.'

'Don't be a wuss, you're unlikely to die from loss of blood.'

I put my spectacles back on and Sam came into better focus. 'That's easy for you to say. It wasn't your head that hit the bloody vice.'

'You'll survive.'

'Thanks for the sympathy.' I stood upright, but quickly slumped back against the bench. 'Ouch,' I moaned and held my head in my hands.

Sam picked up my Glock from the floor, then came towards me. 'So, where's the heroin?'

'Over there.' I pointed at the stack of tea chests. 'But—'

'No buts,' he said, holding my Glock in his hand.

I thought he was offering me the pistol, so I held out my hand for it, but then I realised the muzzle was pointing at me.

'I don't have time for buts,' Sam was saying. 'I want those drugs in my boot pronto.' He nodded towards the tea chests. 'So, get moving.'

I massaged my temples gently. 'I have a pounding headache,' I told him with a groan. 'So, if it's okay with you, I'll pass.'

'It wasn't an invitation,' he said in a voice that was both quiet and menacing. 'Move, or I'll cure your headache permanently.'

I looked up and saw he was pointing the pistol at my head. 'Is that supposed to frighten me? If so, you're threatening the wrong person.'

'Why's that?'

'Because I've been round the block a few times and counted all the bricks in each building I passed.'

'What's that supposed to mean?'

'It means I'm experienced enough to know what's going to happen.'

'Which is what?'

'You're going to kill me anyway, whether or not I help you.'

'And why would I do that?'

'Because you can't afford to let me live.'

'That's not true. Once the drugs are in my car, I intend to tie you up…'

'Tie me up?' I interrupted him with a laugh. 'What with? Your socks?'

'No with the towrope I have in the boot of my car.' He nodded to where his BMW was parked. 'If you don't believe me, go check.'

'I'll pass on that too,' I said. He probably did have a towrope in his car, in case he broke down, along with a toolbox, spare tyre, hydraulic jack, first-aid kit, can of fuel, rubber torch, Hi-Viz jacket and reflective warning triangle. He was that sort of guy.

'Once you're tied up, I'm going to leave you here in the lock-up and return the drugs to their rightful owners. Then I'll head for Dover.'

'No doubt with a suitcase full of Euro notes from your Mafia friends.'

'One good deed deserves another,' he said with a wry smile.

'You don't really believe the authorities are going to let you get away with it, do you?'

'They won't know where I am. I'll be long gone.'

'And what about me?'

'By the time you're found, you'll be hungry and thirsty, but at least you'll still be alive.'

'I believe you,' I said, but I was lying and so was he. I pushed myself upright again. 'Okay. I'll help you.'

'Very wise,' he said and stepped well back to let me pass. He was taking no chances.

Half walking, half staggering, I made my way to the stack of tea chests. I reached up to grab the top one and winced in pain. 'You might have to help me.'

'No chance. You can do it. You're a big boy now.'

I struggled to lift the heavy tea chest, and groaned as the effort tore open the wound on my head. I felt blood begin to dribble down the back of my neck, but eventually I managed to lower the tea chest to the ground.

Still covering me with the Glock, Sam walked over to his car. He leant inside and flicked a switch without taking his eyes off me. Silently the boot lid of the BMW opened slowly, smoothly and silently. German engineering at its best.

'Drag the tea chest over here.' He pointed to a spot about two feet from his car.

I shook my head slowly and gently. 'I can't. The chest is too heavy to move on my own.'

'Just do it.'

'Okay, but I think there's something you should know first.'

'What?'

'Can I show you?' I pointed into the tea chest.

'Go ahead.'

I reached down and took out a one kilo bag of white powder. I weighed it in my hand and looked over at him. 'This isn't heroin, Sam. It's powdered milk.'

'I don't believe you.'

'Check it for yourself.' I tossed the bag across the lock-up to land at his feet.

He stared down at the package suspiciously.

'Test it,' I said.

'How do I do that?'

'Are you that stupid?'

He shrugged apologetically.

'Taste it, or smell it,' I explained.

'I have no idea what heroin tastes or smells like.'

'Have you ever used powdered milk?'

'Of course.'

'Well, heroin tastes and smells nothing like it.'

Sam picked up the bag, poked a large hole in it and sniffed the contents. He frowned. 'It's milk powder.'

'Bravo! Give that man a prize.'

He threw the bag down in disgust and a puff of white powder came out of the hole as it hit the cement floor and sprinkled the toecaps of his shiny black shoes. 'What about the rest of the bags?'

'They're all the same,' I replied.

'How do I know you're not bluffing?'

'Why would I do that?'

'You bluffed Cassidy and you could be trying the same trick on me. For all I know you prepared that bag specially.'

'That's true, I did.' I picked up another bag. 'But I prepared all these bags the same way.' I threw the bag towards him. 'Try that one as well, then you can come across and choose any of the remaining bags to check. But you'll be wasting your time because all you'll find is more powdered milk.'

Sam showed no inclination to pick up the second bag that lay on the floor in front of him, instead he poked it gently with the toe of his shoe. 'So where are the real bags of heroin?'

I didn't answer his question, instead I said, 'I feel dizzy. Can I sit down?' I didn't wait for permission, I simply perched myself on the edge of the tea chest with my head bowed and my arms hanging loose by my sides. I must have looked like a boxer who is slumped in his corner after a particularly brutal round. I certainly hoped that was the case.

'Where are the drugs?' Sam repeated his question.

'The Met's Criminal Exhibits Store,' I mumbled.

'So, what you told me about conning Cassidy was a lie?'

'Yeah. All the bags in the boot of my car that night were full of heroin.'

'So why the charade?'

'It was part of the plan.'

'What plan?'

'The plan to flush you out.'

He fell silent and I could feel his eyes drilling into the top of my head. 'How long have you known?' he asked eventually.

I looked up. 'I've had my suspicions about you since my trip to France to see Olsen. Somebody tipped off Navarra about my trip and only a few people knew about it, including you.'

'One of the other people could have done it.'

'That's true, which is why I needed proof that it was you in league with the Mafia. I got that proof when Navarra and his sidekick turned up tonight.'

'How did that prove anything?'

'Because only you and I knew we were coming here tonight. Somebody tipped off the Mafia, and it wasn't me. I suppose you have a device in that flash car of yours that allowed Navarra to track your route?'

He didn't deny this, so I guessed it was true.

'Does anybody else know about me?'

'No,' I lied. 'I wanted to nail you before sharing the information with anyone.'

He considered me thoughtfully. 'You know what this means, don't you, Statton?'

'Yeah. Now you really do have to kill me.'

'That's right.' He raised my Glock, so it was once more pointing at my head.

'Before you pull the trigger. There's one other thing you should know.'

'What's that?'

'One of those devices is recording everything that you say.' I pointed towards the camcorders.

He turned his head to look over at the shelves.

'Which one?'

'It's the one with the little blue flashing light,' I said and that's when he made a fatal mistake. He took time out to try and spot which camcorder was on. At the same time, he allowed his gun arm to drop a fraction and for a split second the Glock was no longer pointing at me.

It was all the time I needed. My right arm was already dangling into the tea chest, now I picked up the pistol I took from Vinny, which was uncovered when I took out the second bag of powdered milk, and with one smooth movement, I jumped to my feet and went into a classic side on firing position.

Sam must have heard the rustle of my clothes because he turned back to face me and raised the Glock again, but he was too late. I had already pulled the trigger of my own weapon before he could get a bead on me, and my shot hit him square in the forehead, giving him a matching hole to Iman.

It took only that one bullet because the top of his skull exploded outwards, covering the roof of his expensive BMW with bone and gore. Mercifully for him, death was instantaneous, which was more than he deserved. He collapsed silently to the cement floor in a blood-covered heap without ever knowing why.

By now, my headache was only a lingering reminder of my earlier fall. It was never as bad as I had led Sam to believe, which was just as well because I had no time for aches and pains. I had several important tasks to complete before I could leave the lock up.

I set to work.

I dragged the tea chest over to the car, avoiding the few splashes of blood on the floor, and transferred its contents into neat piles in the boot of the BMW. I then took the empty tea chest back to the stack and lifted down another full one. I took this halfway to the car and then turned it out onto the floor and kicked the bags, so they scattered.

Next, I dragged Navarra's body out from behind the partition into the main part of the unit, and laid it next to the upturned tea chest. I wiped the butt of Vinny's pistol and placed it in the Italian's hand. I pulled the chisel from his body and I wiped my fingerprints from its handle with the same paper towel.

I went back to Sam and took my Glock from his still warm hand and replaced it with the chisel. I slipped the weapon back into its holster, took Navarra's pistol from Sam's pocket, and slipped it into my own. It would be added to my illicit arms store.

Finally, I pushed one of the wardrobes onto its back and manhandled Salvatori's body into it. He lay there, on his back, as if lying at rest in a wide wooden coffin. I closed his eyes and crossed his arms. I took a black biro from the inside pocket of my jacket and used it to write Traditore across the Mafia hitman's forehead, then I closed the double doors.

When I had finished, I stood back and surveyed the scene behind me.

I very much hoped my precautions would be unnecessary, but if they were needed I wanted any police SIO[2] assigned to the case to think Sam and Navarra argued, had a scuffle during which my now dead boss had stabbed the Mafia man with a chisel, and in turn had been shot by the Italian as he died.

However, I was in little doubt that any SIO worth their salt would soon find lots of inconsistencies in the little scenario I had set up, and when Salvatori's body was found, the water would be muddied still further.

I left the lock-up, secured it with the padlock and waited in the dark for quarter of an hour to see if the police turned up. When I was sure no shots had been reported, I made my way to Bethnal Green Underground Station.

---

1   DVLA: Driver and Vehicle Licencing Agency.
2   SOI: Senior Investigating Officer.

38

Wednesday 22ⁿᵈ January 2020; St John's Wood, London

Dame Alexandra Nichols lived in a detached house in St John's Wood, close to Lord's Cricket Ground. The location was convenient for her husband, who was a long-standing member of the MCC[1], and was one of the reasons they bought the house in the first place.

It was by no means the grandest house in the quiet residential road, but it was large enough to have a price tag afforded only by somebody who can write a cheque north of £10 million. Somebody like Angus Nichols, who, in addition to inherited wealth, had made a fortune in the City of London.

It was almost seven o'clock when I pressed the shiny brass bellpush on the heavy oak front door of the house. Somewhere deep inside the house I heard the opening bars of *Jerusalem*.

As I waited for somebody to react to the bell's call to arms, I shivered uncontrollably. I suppose this could have been a delayed reaction to the evening's events, however, I preferred to tell myself it was because there was already an icy feel to the night air.

It was Angus who opened the front door. He greeted me with an amiable smile and a firm handshake. 'It's damned cold out here,' he said without preamble. 'You're shivering.'

'Tell me about it.' I stepped into the hall.

'You'll soon warm up. This way.' Angus led me down a long tastefully decorated hallway. 'The boss is in her study. She's expecting you.'

We stopped halfway along the hallway. Angus opened a door without knocking and ushered me into a room lined with book ladened shelves. 'She's all yours,' he said with a wry smile and then disappeared, closing the door behind him.

Dame Alexandra was sitting behind a desk. She was writing with the aid of a desk lamp, which had a tasteful green shade and was the only light in the room. She looked up, closed the file she was working on, screwed the cap onto her Montblanc pen and laid it carefully on top of the file.

'Take a seat, Steven.' She waved me towards the chair in front of her desk. 'Angus thought you might need that.' She pointed at a round silver tray on her desk, containing a bottle of Laphroaig malt whisky and a set of cut glass tumblers. 'Help yourself.'

She didn't have to invite me twice. 'What about you?' I asked as I poured myself a generous measure of whisky.

'No thank you. I'm not much of a drinker.'

'Everyone to their own,' I said and then took a long sip of my drink, relishing the distinctive iodine taste of the Laphroaig as it hit the back of my throat. 'Angus was right, I needed that.' I pointed at the file on her desk. 'You look busy.'

'It's my daily report to the Minister for State Security.'

'So Fletcher is still involved?'

'Yes. It's always useful to have a political shield when dealing with such delicate matters and Benedict has been particularly helpful.'

'I'm surprised you're still doing handwritten reports.'

'It's security. Even the Government's computers system can be hacked. My reports to the minister are hand delivered by Rachel, and are strictly for his eyes only. Once he has read my reports, Benedict destroys them immediately.'

'The Cab Sec would have a fit if he knew what was going on.'

'Don't worry, Benedict is very discreet. He understands that in the national security game it is necessary sometimes to do things that are not strictly by the book. Now how did it go?'

'It went just as we planned,' I replied as the Laphroaig started to warm me up.

'And were you right about Brewer roping in his Mafia pals?'

'Yeah.'

'How many turned up?'

'Two. Navarra, and his henchman, Salvatori.'

'And?' she prompted.

'And neither of them will be eating any more spaghetti,' I replied and related what had happened in the lock-up and how I killed the Italians.

'What about Samuel?'

'Dead as a dodo.' I told her how Sam had died.

'So everything went smoothly?'

'I wouldn't say that. A bloody stepladder collapsed on me after I shot Salvatori. I fell and hit my head on a metal vice, which is why I'm covered in blood.' I turned my head to show her what I meant.

'I can see dried blood on the collar of your shirt, but there is none in your hair. You've probably just grazed your scalp.'

'Thanks for the prognosis, doctor. I'll remind myself of it when I'm rushed to hospital with severe concussion.'

'Don't be so dramatic. It probably feels worse than it is.'

'You sound just like my mum. When I was nine, I fell off my bicycle and injured my elbow. I told her it was broken, but she insisted it was just a sprain.'

'Your mother has always been very sensible.'

'I didn't think so at the time.'

'What did she do?'

'She put ice cubes on my elbow for half an hour and then wrapped it in an elasticated bandage.'

'That's exactly what you should do with a sprain. Did it help.'

'Yeah.'

'There you are, your mum was right,' she said triumphantly.

'My mum is always right. Even when she's wrong.'

She laughed at that and then said, 'And so am I. However, as a precaution you'd better get your war-wound checked out by a doctor. You can't be too careful with head injuries.'

'I'm going to the hospital later to see Marion. I'll pop into A&E[2] afterwards.'

She raised an eyebrow in disbelief. She was right to be sceptical. I had no intention of waiting in A&E for hours, only to be told to take a couple of paracetamol tablets. I could work that out for myself.

'Now, about Samuel. Are you certain there is no chance of his death being traced back to the department?'

I shrugged. 'The only certain things in life are birth, death, and taxes. However, it's highly unlikely the police will discover the bodies before we get the lock-up cleaned up, but in case they do somehow find them first, I did my best to throw them off the scent.'

'How?'

I explained about the way I had arranged the lock-up to make it look like Brewer and Navarra had killed each other.

'But what about Salvatori? Which gun did you use to kill him?'

She was sharp, my boss.

I opened my jacket and patted the Glock, that hung in its

holster under my arm. 'This one.'

'But isn't that weapon registered to the department? Won't ballistics be able to trace it?'

I shook my head. 'No, to both questions. The pistol issued by the armourer was lost in that fire in France. This one is unregistered.'

'How did you get hold of an unregistered weapon?'

'You don't want to know.'

'You're probably right,' she agreed. 'Nor do I want to see an illicit weapon. So, please cover it up.'

I closed my jacket. 'Is that better?'

She nodded. 'Thank you. Now, is there anything else I should know?'

'Yes.'

'What?' She looked worried.

'Don't worry, boss.'

'That's not always easy when I'm dealing with you. Now what did you want to say?'

'I only wanted to assure you that any bullets fired by the Glock pistol you can no longer see, are completely untraceable.'

'Untraceable?'

'Quite.'

'And that is supposed to reassure me?'

'I rather hoped it might.'

She studied me carefully. 'You know, I think I might have one of those after all.' She pointed at my whisky.

'That's a relief,' I said as I reached for the bottle of Laphroaig. 'I hate drinking alone.'

'Is that true?' She raised a sceptical eyebrow.

'Nope.' I picked up a cut glass tumbler. 'The truth is that

intelligence agents spend a lot of time on their own, particularly when they're operating in the field.'

'And?'

'In my experience the only field agents who don't drink alone are teetotal and that doesn't include me.'

'You're just like your father,' she said as she watched me pour her two fingers of malt whisky before raising her hand to tell me to stop.

'You know my dad?' I asked as I passed the tumbler to her.

'Yes, I worked with him when I joined MI6. That was just after your father left the Army, and before he joined the department, although back then the SSA was just a small specialist intelligence unit called DFCO. It only expanded into its existing size, with its own Director-General, about ten years ago.'

'I know the department's history,' I said wryly.

'Of course, you do.' She stared thoughtfully into her whisky glass before taking a tentative sip. 'David Statton was already a legend when I met him,' she mused and smiled fondly as she mentioned his name. 'He was the original working-class hero. He was a hard-drinking, cynical, insubordinate, argumentative rebel, who only obeyed the rules when it suited his agenda.'

'Is that why I remind you of him?'

'Yes.'

'I'm not sure whether to feel insulted or proud.'

'The latter, Steven. Despite his faults, your father was highly regarded in Six. He was an excellent intelligence officer, who set up several successful networks, most of which are still active today.' She paused and took another small sip of her whisky. 'David was one of those men who was liked by everybody in our section. A very working-class spy.'

'Everybody? Knowing my dad, the way I do, I find that difficult to believe.'

'Yes, everybody. Back then he had bags of charisma and was very attractive, particularly to women.' She smiled again. 'The older women wanted to mother him, and the younger ones lusted after him.'

'I had no idea my dad was a sex symbol.'

'Your father was hardly a sex symbol, but he did break a few hearts when he married your mother.' She took another delicate sip of her whisky and then asked, 'By the way, how are your parents?'

'They were okay the last time I saw them. Mum is teaching languages part-time in the local college and Dad spends most of his time either gardening, or on the Wargaming Society website, trying to prove that Wellington would have won the Battle of Waterloo, even if Field Marshal von Blücher's Prussians hadn't broken through the French right flank.'

'Has he succeeded?'

'No, but he keeps trying.'

'Your dad was always very persistent.' She smiled strangely and I wondered what she meant, but did not ask. 'Can I ask you something, Steven?'

'I can't stop you asking, but I can't guarantee you'll be happy with my answer. It depends on the question.'

'It's about Harriet.'

'What about her?'

'I know you are having a relationship with her.'

'We're both consenting adults.'

'That's true.'

'So, what's the problem? We don't let our private life interfere with our work.'

'That's not the point.'

'What is the point?'

'I'm worried about Harriet.'

'Why?'

'Because she has fallen head over heels in love with you.'

'What do you want me to do? Shoot Cupid for firing his bloody arrow at her?'

The hint of a blush tinged her cheeks, or maybe the Laphroaig had hit her bloodstream. 'I knew this was going to be difficult.'

'Life is difficult, boss.'

'Yes,' she agreed sadly.

I felt sorry for her then. 'Do you want me to stop seeing Harriet?'

She shook her head. 'No, but I think it might be better if she leaves the department.'

'Because you don't like us working together?'

'Partly.'

'But my mum and dad worked in the department for years, and nobody complained,' I pointed out.

'Times have changed. These days fraternising between staff is frowned on more than it used to be.'

'Is that supposed to be progress?'

'The World has moved on from the age of the dinosaur.'

'I know, and personnel departments have metamorphosised into human resources departments, which recruit all those morons, with degrees in gender-studies, who devise all these new stupid rules.'

'That is not wholly fair, Steven. The rules are there to prevent predatory men from taking advantage of impressionable young women.'

'Is that what you think I'm doing?'

'Of course not.'

There followed another strained silence during which we finished off our whiskies.

'I'll have another small one.' She held out her glass.

I poured her a finger of Laphroaig and gave myself a double measure.

'So, if Harriet leaves the department, where will she go?' I asked.

'She could transfer back to the FCO. She is still highly regarded in King Charles Street.'

'Harriet won't be happy. She likes working here.'

'She liked working for the FCO too.'

'Well I think it's a shame. She's going to make a damn fine intelligence officer someday.'

'There is always Six. It comes under the FCO and I still have some influence in Vauxhall Cross. If you can persuade her to apply for a transfer, I will ensure her application is accepted.'

'I'll see what I can do, but your niece can be very stubborn when she wants to be.'

'I know. She takes after her mother; stubborn and headstrong.'

'We all have our faults. Now, is that everything you wanted to talk to me about?'

'No.'

'So, what else do you have?'

'I'm worried you are going to break Harriet's heart,' she said quietly. She stared into her glass and looked uncomfortable.

'I'm not the one insisting she should transfer out of Operations.'

'That is not my worry.'

'What is it then?'

'It's your relationship with her. I don't want to see you hurt her, the way your father hurt me.'

'I don't understand,' I said. 'How did my dad hurt you?' I asked, but she did not reply. Then I realised what she was suggesting. 'Are you telling me you had a relationship with him?'

She nodded.

I stared at her in astonishment. 'When was this?'

'A long time ago. When we were both working in Six.'

I was stunned and for a moment did not know what to say.

'I was just down from Cambridge University and was young and naïve,' she went on, but soon lapsed into silence again as she took a longer sip of her whisky.

'Are you suggesting my dad was a predatory man taking advantage of an impressionable young woman?'

She shook her head quickly. 'Oh, no. It was nothing like that. If anything, it was the other way round. I made all the running and did so knowing he was already in a relationship with Joan Thorvik.'

'You mean he was seeing you at the same time as my mum?'

'Yes, but our fling didn't last long.'

'Is that supposed to make his betrayal more acceptable?' I asked bitterly.

She shook her head. 'Of course not, but please don't blame your father. He was very clear from the beginning that our affair could never come to anything.'

'Oh! That's okay then.'

'Don't be harsh, Steven. It really wasn't your father's fault.'

'Of course, it wasn't. Just think, if the no-fraternisation rules had been in place forty years ago, my dad would've been protected from a predatory young woman.'

'Touché! Yes, it is true, I was a predator. However, although your father allowed himself to be beguiled by me, it did not make him any less committed to your mum.'

'How reassuring.'

'You sound bitter.'

'No, I just feel sorry for my mum.'

'There really is no need. Your mother is not stupid. Never has been. She soon worked out what was happening and gave your father an ultimatum. Her or me.' She paused for a moment and stared into a distance that ended at her beautifully wallpapered study wall. 'Of course, he chose her,' she finally said sadly. 'I was devasted when he ended our affair.'

'What do you want me to say? I forgive you?'

'No, I just want you to promise not to hurt Harriet the same way.'

'That's a very difficult thing to promise. I don't have second sight and have no idea what might happen in the future.'

'I suppose you are right. Nobody knows what the future will bring. It's just that I can't help worrying about Harriet.'

'You don't need to worry about her. Harriet might be young, but she's not naïve. She will never let me, or anybody else, lead her up the garden path with blinkers on. I think you'll find she'll only walk between the cabbages and carrots with her eyes wide open.'

She smiled. 'Thank you for being honest, Steven. Strangely, it makes me feel a little better than if you had simply told me what I wanted to hear.' She finished off the rest of her Laphroaig in one swallow. 'Now, back to what we were discussing before. Do you really think the police will believe that Sam and Navarra killed each other?'

'Not a chance. A rudimentary investigation of the scene won't fool even the most inexperienced forensic scientist for long, particularly when Salvatori is discovered in the wardrobe with a bullet in his head from a weapon that miraculously disappeared from the crime scene.'

'So, could that present us with a problem?'

'It might, except we have an ace up our sleeve.'

'What's that?'

'We probably have time on our side.'

'I don't get you.'

'It's easy. If we move quickly, we can get a clean-up team to remove the bodies and make them disappear. They can then remove Sam's Beemer and clean up the unit. Once that's done nobody will ever know what happened tonight.'

She looked at me with a puzzled expression. 'If it's that easy, why did you go to the trouble of setting up that charade in the lock-up?'

'It was just a precaution. There was always a possibility some-body heard the gun fire and called the police.'

'Is that likely?'

I shrugged. 'I don't think so. When I left the unit the area was deserted. I waited outside for fifteen very cold minutes, but there was no sign of the cops. I was pretty sure we were in the clear, but I didn't want to chance it.'

'Okay, but what about the owner of the lock-up? What happens if he decides to pay it a visit?'

'He won't. I've warned him off.'

'Can you trust him to listen?'

'On this occasion, yes. But if by some miracle he did summon up the courage to disobey me, he would be out of luck because I've changed the padlock on the door. He won't be able to get in without smashing down the door and he won't want to do that.'

Her look of bemusement turned to one of admiration. 'Very clever, Steven. I am genuinely impressed.' She nodded in satisfaction as she spoke. 'So, how quickly can you get a team in to remove the bodies and clean up the lock-up?'

'Unfortunately, that's not something I can do, or I would have arranged it already.'

'Why not?'

'Because we use the Five clean-up teams to do that sort of work, and they won't act unless a director level request is made in writing. That's way above my pay grade.'

'Is there no other way?'

'No. I do have contacts in Five, who I could ask for a favour, but the Cabinet Office would have a fit if I tried to bypass the system. No, I'm afraid it's down to you to sort something out, boss.'

'Hmmm. Would a deputy director have the necessary authority?'

'Yeah, but currently our Deputy D-G is lying in a lock-up in Bethnal Green with what's left of his brains decorating his Beemer.'

She took an envelope from her desk drawer and pushed it across to me. 'Our *previous* Deputy D-G.'

I picked up the envelope and saw its back was embossed with the crest of the Cabinet Office. 'What's this?'

'Open it and you see.'

I opened the envelope and pulled out a single sheet of folded paper.

'It's an appointment letter,' she explained as I unfolded the paper.

The appointment letter had been signed by the Cabinet Secretary.

'Congratulations, Steven,' she said with a smile. 'You are now the department's new Deputy Director-General.'

'Is this your doing?'

'It was certainly my recommendation.'

I read the letter. 'It says here that I'm the Acting D-D-G.'

'That is purely a formality. The Cabinet Office will want to negotiate your renumeration, and other terms and conditions, before offering you the position on a permanent basis. It's the way they operate these days.' She smiled again. 'So what do you say?'

'I'm not sure I want the job.'

She looked shocked. 'Are you serious?'

'Yes.'

'What's the problem?'

'All the D-D-Gs I've ever known have been desk jockeys and I hate paperwork. I much prefer operational fieldwork.'

'There is no reason why you cannot continue to head up the Operations Section and still be my deputy.'

'What about the paperwork? I hate paperwork.'

'You will have enough staff to handle all the paperwork.'

'Can I handpick my staff?'

'I'm sure that can be arranged.'

I raised an eyebrow at her. 'Wow! You really must want me badly.'

'I do,' she said earnestly.

I laughed out loud. 'Hang on a minute. Not long ago you inferred I was a hard-drinking, cynical, insubordinate, argumentative rebel, who only obeys the rules when it suits my agenda?'

'That's true, but you are also honest, dependable, loyal, and trustworthy,' she paused before adding, 'and don't look at me like that.'

'Like what?'

'Like you don't believe me.'

'As if.'

'I meant it, Steven. After Samuel's betrayal, those qualities are exactly what the department needs right now.'

'Is that all you want me for?'

'No, you have many other positive qualities. For instance, it was you who came up with the plan to defeat the Iranian conspiracy. And very effective it was too. By the way, I would be immensely grateful if Operation QS had no loose ends.'

'Don't worry. Everything has been arranged and all the loose ends will be tied up in the next few days.'

'Excellent work, Steven. That is the sort of efficiency that persuaded me to recommend your promotion. Now, will you accept it?'

'I'll think about it.'

'Well, don't take too long making up your mind.'

'I won't.'

'Meanwhile, will you at least agree to be my Acting-Acting D-D-G?'

'Yeah.'

She smiled. 'Thank you. That being the case, how quickly can you organise a team to remove the bodies and clean up the unit?'

'Bloody quickly.'

---

1   MCC: Marylebone Cricket Club.
2   A&E: Accident and Emergency.

39

Wednesday 22ⁿᵈ January 2020; London, England

For once my confidence was not misplaced. It took only a quick phone call to get things moving. I used my mobile and rang Joe Onura as I walked to St John's Wood Underground Station. Luckily he was on duty that evening.

'Not a problem,' Joe said when I explained in a low voice what I wanted. 'And you say one of the dead men is Sam Brewer?'

'Yeah.'

'What a bummer. It always hits harder when we lose one of our own.'

'It certainly does.'

'Is there a reason why you want Sam's body to disappear in the same way as the other two?'

'I'll explain later,' I replied, not wanting to give any further details over the phone.

'I understand,' Joe said. He was quick. 'Okay, I'll get onto the head of Section H straight away.'

'Is that still Jason McBride?'

'Yes, do you know him?'

'I do. Can you ask him to give this job top priority? We need the lock-up cleaned out before plod get wind of it.'

'I'll do my best, but I know a couple of Jason's team have gone down with some sort of chest virus.'

'There seems to be a lot of it about at the moment. But I'm sure Jason will be able to sort something out. Just remind him he still owes me a favour.'

'Will do. But one more question before you go.'

'What's that?'

'How do Jason's guys find the lock-up and how do they get into it?'

'That's not a problem. I'll send Jason a key by courier and will include directions to the lock-up. Was there anything else?'

'Well, there is one other thing.'

'What's that?'

'I'm going to need a request in writing. I'd usually do it for you without an official request, but I need to cover my arse. There have been accusations we've been guilty of breeching civil rights and the suits on the top floor are getting twitchy about procedure. We have to do everything by the book.'

'No problem. Our new Acting Deputy Director-General will email over a request straight away.'

'Has somebody already been appointed to replace Sam?'

'Yeah.'

'Who is it? Anyone I know?'

'You know him very well.'

'Who?'

'Me.'

'Are you winding me up, man?'

'No. It's true.'

'Okay, I believe you, but I'm not sure my boss will. He'll just think you're trying to pull a flanker.'

'Would I lie to you?'

'Probably,' he said with a laugh.

'Not this time, Joe.'

'Seriously, are you being straight with me?'

It was my turn to laugh. 'I really am the new Acting D-D-G

of the SSA,' I insisted and smiled to myself. I had not realised how good it would feel saying that.

'Okay, I'll find a way of convincing my boss.'

'That won't be necessary, Joe. I have in my pocket an appointment letter signed by the Cabinet Secretary himself. I'll scan the letter and attach a copy to my email request for the lock-up to be cleaned up. You can wave it under your boss's nose if he doubts my word.'

'That would be perfect, and congratulations!'

'Thanks.'

'Does this mean there won't be any more nights out with the lads?'

'I've only been promoted, Joe. I haven't been elected Pope.'

'Just as well. I'm not sure the Catholic Church would approve of some of the places we have been known to frequent!'

'That was when we were younger. I think we've moved on from those days, but I can offer you a curry on Friday night. My treat.'

'How can I say no?'

'You never have in the past,' I replied with another laugh. 'In return, you can make sure Jason gets his finger out and the lock-up job gets done tonight.'

'I knew there would be a catch.'

'There's no such thing as a free meal, Joe.'

'I can see why you've been promoted. You'll soon be as hard-nosed as the rest of the top floor suits.'

'God, forbid,' I said with feeling as I ended my call. I had reached the underground station, where I was likely to lose my mobile phone signal, so, before I went inside, I rang the Cabinet Office garage and asked the duty officer to arrange another pool car for me. After some huffing and puffing the man promised to have it delivered to the DFCO car park as soon as possible. However, he made no commitment to how soon that was, or whether delivery was even possible.

When I arrived at my office I quickly scanned my letter from the Cabinet Office and emailed it to Joe. I wrote out directions to the lock-up on SSA headed notepaper and put them in an envelope with the padlock key. I wrote Jason McBride's name on the envelope and added the Millbank address of MI5.

Next I rang Harriet and told her what had happened in the lock-up.

'I can't believe you shot Sam,' she said when I had finished.

'It was either him or me.'

'Are you sure he's dead?'

'I'm sure.'

She was silent for a few seconds, then she asked, 'What about you? Are you all right?'

'I fell and hit my head, but I'll survive.'

'Oh, poor you,' she said, and then asked, 'Are you still coming with me to see Marion?'

'Yeah, but I've got to sort something out first. It won't take long.'

'How long?'

'Give me half an hour.'

'Okay. I'll meet you at the hospital,' she said and was gone.

I rang the security office to arrange for a courier. My call was answered by Ken Paine. 'I was expecting a call from you, Mr S,' he said.

'Were you?'

'Yeah. Some bloke turned up here a few minutes ago with a car for you. He said you wanted it urgently.'

It was a pleasant surprise to learn the garage duty officer had delivered on his promise to me. 'Did the driver leave the ignition key with you?'

'Well he left some sort of plastic fob if that's what you mean.'

'That's what I mean, Ken. I'm on my way down to collect it,' I said and headed straight down to the night security office.

'The driver said you wanted the car parked in the underground car park,' Paine said when I arrived at the security office. He gave me a black plastic smart key with a Toyota logo on its face. 'That car park is for SCS[1] grades, Mr S, and you ain't supposed to use that one, but I let him park there, because it was for you.'

'You're a star, Ken' I responded, deciding not to challenge his trumpet-blowing boast by explaining that technically, as a newly appointed SCS Grade 1, I was now entitled to use the car park. 'I don't want my knuckles wrapped. I still have the scars from last time.'

'Don't worry, Mr S. I won't tell nobody if you don't.'

'My lips are sealed,' I promised. I pulled an imaginary zip across my mouth and handed him the envelope containing the lock-up padlock key. 'Can you arrange for a courier to take this to Millbank. It needs to be there in the next hour.'

'Not a problem, I'll get onto it straight away.'

'Thanks, I owe you one.'

'In that case you can buy me a pint,' he said as he picked up the phone. 'Maybe when we're in Grimsby,' he added, laughing loudly.

I left him to enjoy our running joke and headed for the hospital.

1   SCS grades: Senior Civil Service grades, EG: Deputy Director is SCS1 and a Director is SCS2.

40

Wednesday 22nd January 2020; London, England

Harriet was waiting for me in the hospital reception area. She waved to me as I stepped through the automatic entrance doors.

'You look a mess,' she said after giving me a quick hug.

'We can't all be born beautiful like you.'

She smiled at the compliment. 'I meant your clothes are a mess.'

'I didn't have time to change.'

'Did you know you've got blood on your collar.'

'Yeah. I hit the back of my head when I fell off a bloody ladder.'

'I know, you told me.' She studied me with concern. 'Are you sure you're all right?'

'Well, your Aunt assured me it's just a graze, so I must be okay.'

'You've spoken with Auntie Xandra?'

'Yeah, I've just come from a meeting with her.'

'I don't understand.' She frowned. 'Why did you meet her? I thought she was suspended?'

'It's complicated. I'll explain all later. Now, let's go see Marion. How is she?'

'They brought her out of the induced coma this morning. She's still feeling poorly, but at least she's conscious.'

'Where is she?' I asked, pointing at the list of wards on the plastic sign that was affixed to the wall behind her.

'She's in the private wing on the top floor. The police decided she would be safer there. Come on, I'll show you the way.'

She led me down a corridor decorated with colourful murals to the lifts and we travelled up to the fourth floor in a spotless-ly-clean, stainless-steel lined lift.

The private wing of the hospital was made up of indi-vidual rooms that would not have looked out of place in a posh hotel. Sitting on a chair outside one of the rooms was a young, uniformed policewoman. She got to her feet when we approached.

'This is Marion's room,' Harriet said unnecessarily when we reached the policewoman, who moved to bar our way into the room.

The cop looked me up and down with suspicious eyes, and then turned to Harriet. 'I'll need to see some form of identifi-cation before I let you in.'

'Not a problem,' Harriet said with a friendly smile. She pulled out her forged warrant card and showed it to the police-woman, who gave it only a cursory look.

When I showed the cop my warrant card, she studied it more closely, reading every word carefully. 'Sorry, Inspector. I wasn't expecting anyone else from the Force to visit Miss Jones this evening.'

'Who else from the Met has visited Miss Jones today?' I asked quietly, trying to keep alarm from my.

'A uniformed sergeant came to take a statement from her.'

'Did you check his identity?'

'No, sir.'

'Why not?' I asked uneasily.

'Because he was a she and I know her. We're both based at Kensington Police Station. It's in Earls Court Road.'

I relaxed at hearing that news. 'I know where the station is,' I said gently. 'What was *her* name?'

'Karen, sir. That is Sergeant Karen Brown.'

'And what's your name, constable?'

'PC Stuart,' she answered and then added: 'Tracey Stuart.'

'Well done, Tracey. You did exactly the right thing in asking to see our warrant cards.'

'Thank you, sir,' she said and finally rewarded me with a smile.

'Now can we see Miss Jones?'

'Of course, sir,' she stepped to one side, before pressing down on the door's lever handle and pushing it open. 'Just go in.'

I ushered Harriet through the door and was about to follow her when the young policewoman spoke again. 'Did you know you've got blood on the collar of your shirt, sir?'

'Yeah. I went for a haircut today,' I replied, before walking into the room and closing the door behind me.

'You are awful,' Harriet whispered with a stifled giggle. 'She probably thinks the barber cut your head with a pair of scissors.'

'It's better that, than the truth,' I said as we walked towards the bed.

My secretary was propped up on a mound of pillows and her battered face was deathly white against her hair, which framed her head in a cascade of jet-black curls. Lying there, with her eyes closed, she looked like a flawed Snow White, waiting for a prince to wake her with a kiss.

However, Marion needed no prince to wake her. Harriet and I did that without having to kiss her. She opened her eyes as she heard us approach her bed and smiled wanly when she recognised us.

Harriet pointed at the bottom of the bed. 'Can I sit there?' Marion nodded her consent and Harriet settled herself on the bed, leaving me the chair that stood alongside the bed.

'Hello, boss,' my secretary said in a hoarse voice as I sat down.

'Hello, Marion, or should that be Gwyneth?' I asked and her eyes widened slightly in surprise. I studied her carefully. There was a large purple bruise on her right temple, a smaller one on her cheek bone, and a vicious looking cut across her throat, which sported half a dozen stitches. Despite those external injuries, I guessed she was hurting more inside, than out. 'Or, what about Kylie?' I went on.

She nodded and then winced with pain. 'How did you find out?'

'Detective work and modern technology.' I explained about the photograph in the Evening Standard that linked Marion Dudley with Gwyneth Jones, and how the DNA test had linked Gwyneth to Kylie Wilder. I told her also how Harriet had tried to trace her address to send her a get well card, but had failed, which had rung alarm bells in my mind.

'You were going to send me a card?' Marion asked Harriet.

'Yes, but it was from both of us,' Harriet nodded towards me.

'That was very thoughtful of you,' Marion said to Harriet, no doubt guessing it had been her idea.

'It was nothing,' Harriet said with a dismissive shrug. 'We were worried about you.'

'I'm sorry about that.'

'There's no need to be sorry. I don't suppose you threw

yourself down the steps to your flat deliberately.'

Marion shook her head. 'No,' she mumbled as tears welled in her eyes. She pulled a tissue from a box stood on her bedside table.

I stepped in to move the conversation on: 'I understand you've made a statement to the police.'

'That's right,' Marion said as she dabbed her eyes with the tissue.

'How did the interview go? Was it traumatic?' Harriet asked.

'No, it was fine. The policewoman who interviewed me was understanding and very sympathetic.'

'I take it those bruises are Cassidy's handiwork?' I pointed at her face.

Marion nodded. 'Yes.'

'And the scar on your throat?'

'Yes, Tommy tried to cut it with a sliver of broken glass.' She touched the wound tentatively. 'The doctor said I was lucky the wound wasn't worse. If the cut had been any deeper I would probably be dead now.'

'This wasn't the first time Cassidy has beaten you up, was it, Marion?' Harriet asked.

She shook her head silently.

'Is that why you were off work in the first place? You didn't fall down any steps, did you?'

'Yes, to the first question and no, to the second.' She turned to me. 'The policewoman told me Tommy has been arrested for another crime. Is it true?'

'Yeah.'

'Were you responsible for his arrest?'

I nodded.

'I take it he was arrested for dealing in drugs?'

I nodded again.

'Good. I thought you would catch him.'

'How did you know?'

She smiled wanly. 'Because I was confident you would follow up on my tip-off about the horsebox going missing.'

'So, it was you who sent the article to me?'

'Yes. I've been keeping my eyes and ears open for ages. Recently I began to suspect Tommy was using horseboxes sent to his polo club as a means of smuggling heroin into the country. That's why I sent the clipping to you. I'm pleased you investigated it.'

'Harriet did most of the investigating,' I admitted.

'Well done, you,' Marion said to Harriet.

'Without appearing immodest, I'm pretty good at gathering information,' Harriet replied diffidently. 'However, that information is worthless without well trained intelligence officers, like the boss, analysing it and putting it to practical use.'

'What did you discover?' Marion asked me. 'Was he using horseboxes to smuggle in drugs?'

'That's what I thought, but I changed my mind after I found the remains of a horse in Cassidy's abattoir.'

'You didn't tell me about that,' Harriet said.

'That's because I didn't understand the significance at the time.'

'Was the horse slaughtered in the abattoir, or was it taken there after it died?' Marion asked.

'Almost certainly the former.'

'But that doesn't make any sense. Horses are valuable, and Tommy is really miserly. I can't believe he would willingly get

479

rid of something worth money.'

'He would if it was being used as a drugs mule.'

'You think he was smuggling heroin inside horses?' Harriet asked.

'Yeah.'

'Where inside horses?' Harriet asked. I could see from her eyes she was beginning to understand. 'No, don't tell me, let me guess. It was in their wombs. Am I right?'

I nodded. 'That's why only mares were imported.'

'So, another mystery solved?'

'Yeah.'

'How much heroin does a horse's womb hold?' Marion asked.

'I think I can answer that,' Harriet said. 'The foal of a large horse can weigh up to fifty-six kilos, so presumably that's about how much heroin can be packed into a mare's womb.'

'How much is fifty-six kilos of heroin worth?' Marion asked.

'Over ten million pounds at street value,' I replied.

Marion stared at me in astonishment. 'My God! That much?'

'That much.'

'I had no idea.'

'And you worked out how Cassidy and his pals were smuggling drugs into the country, simply because you found a dead horse in his abattoir?' Harriet asked.

'It wasn't only that. It was also something Jane Manning told me. Her team found traces of heroin in urine on the floor of the horsebox.'

'How did it get there?' Marion asked.

'I can only imagine a bag of heroin must have leaked inside the horse and then made its way into the bloodstream. I'm sure a forensic test on the horse's carcass would reveal heroin present in it.'

'Did the heroin kill the horse?' Harriet asked.

'I don't know. It depends how much leaked from the bag. The horse could have died of an overdose, but it's more likely Cassidy had it slaughtered to recover the drugs.'

'He probably butchered the poor beast himself,' Marion said. 'He enjoyed working in the abattoir.'

'Do you think Cassidy slaughtered all the imported horses that disappeared?' Harriet asked.

'Yeah.'

'That's awful. How could anybody do that?'

'We're talking about Tommy Cassidy,' I reminded her. 'They don't call him the Balham Butcher for nothing. Just look what he did to Marion,' I turned back to the injured girl. 'So, how are you feeling?'

'I'm better than I was, boss.'

'Are you up to answering a few more questions?'

'I think so,' she said bravely.

'If at any time you're uncomfortable with my question, you don't need to answer.'

'I'll be fine. Ask away.'

'To begin with, just tell us in your own words exactly what happened that night.'

A frown creased her forehead momentarily, and I thought she was not going to say anything, but then she began talking. 'Tommy organised a party at the apartment for a few friends and business associates.'

'Were there any women there?' Harriet asked.

'No, only me,' Marion replied quietly. 'We were in the

lounge and the men were all drinking heavily. I was on pain killers for my broken fingers,' she held up her right hand to show two of her fingers were bound together with a bandage, 'so I only drank lemonade.' She paused and took a sip of water from a glass that stood on her bedside table next to a jug.

'About ten o'clock I began to feel woozy,' she went on. 'At first, I thought it was the effect of the strong pain killers.'

'Did you take any other drugs that night?' I asked.

'Not knowingly, why do you ask?'

'Because traces of GHB and heroin were found in your blood.'

She looked at me thoughtfully. 'I think my lemonade must have been spiked,' she said.

I nodded. 'Probably with GHB.'

'It was Tommy,' she said with certainty.

'What makes you say that?'

'Because he wasn't surprised when I told him I felt dizzy.'

'Did he try to help you?'

'I thought so at the time. He led me through to the bedroom and laid me on the bed. I closed my eyes and passed out. When I came to, I felt something being injected into my arm.'

'That was probably the heroin.'

'If you say so. Whatever it was made me feel really bad. At first I felt disorientated and nauseous, then I got slowly worse until I was almost catatonic.'

'Heroin can have that effect on some people, particularly when it's taken for the first time.'

'It was a horrible feeling and all I can remember is that Tommy was on top of me. I wanted to push him away but I couldn't lift my arms. My head felt as if it was going to explode, and the last thing I wanted was sex. I tried to twist my body away from him but he punched me in the head and told me to lie still.' She paused and closed her eyes as if to rid herself of the memories my question had evoked.

I took her left hand and squeezed it gently. She opened her eyes and tears started to well up again.

'You don't have to go on,' I told her.

She shook her head and wiped her eyes again. 'I want to tell you everything,' she insisted.

I nodded but said nothing.

'Tommy tore off all my clothes and then raped me. When he had finished, I tried to get off the bed, but couldn't. I was paralysed. The only thing I could move was my head and I could only move that slowly and with great difficulty. When I did manage to look around me, I discovered I was surrounded by naked men.' She paused again and this time started to cry. 'They all had sex with me, sometimes two at the same time, and there was nothing I could do to stop them,' she sobbed.

Harriet slipped off the bed and went to hug the crying girl. 'It's okay, sweetie,' she whispered to her. 'You're safe now.'

Marion hugged her back and eventually stopped sobbing.

'Steve is right,' Harriet told her. 'You don't have to go on.'

'I want to,' Marion said as she disentangled herself from Harriet's arms. 'You need to know what happened so you can get those bastards.'

'Are you sure you're ready to answer more questions?' I asked. She nodded.

'I take it the men who raped you were in the lounge earlier?'

'I assume so.'

'Were all of the men from the lounge involved?'

'I don't know. I couldn't see their faces because somebody had turned off the bedroom lights.'

'Did you recognise any of the men in the lounge?'

'Only one of them, although one of the other men boasted that he was a member of Parliament.'

I glanced at Harriet who gave a quick nod of her head. We had the same thought.

'Have you ever met any of the shareholders of Cassidy's polo club?' I asked Marion.

'No.'

'Did Cassidy ever mention them?'

She looked at me thoughtfully. 'No. Why?'

'Because one of the shareholders is an MP,' I said. 'I'll arrange to have a DNA sample taken from him.'

'Can you do that? Won't you need his permission?'

'Don't worry about that. We have ways of obtaining a sample without him ever knowing. If the test gives a positive result, we'll obtain samples from the other shareholders.'

'What if the result is negative?'

'We won't have lost anything. Now what about the guy you did recognise. Who was he?'

'I'm not sure I should say.'

'Why not?'

'Because he's a friend of yours.'

'If he was one of those who raped you, he's no friend of mine. Now who was it?'

She hesitated.

'Who was it, Marion?'

'Mr Brewer,' she said quietly. 'Although, I don't think he recognised me and I didn't introduce myself. He just thought

I was Tommy's girlfriend.'

'Are you sure it was Sam Brewer?'

'Yes. Will you be able to get a sample from him?'

'Very easily,' I assured her.

'Will he provide one voluntarily?'

'He has no choice.'

'Why not?'

'Because he's currently lying in a garage with half his head missing.'

She looked confused. 'What do you mean?'

'Brewer is dead.'

'Dead?'

'Very. But we'll check out his DNA anyway, if only to add something else to the con side of his epitaph if it proves positive.'

'How did Mr Brewer die?'

I gave her a truncated version of what happened in the lock-up.

'So, you killed him?'

'Yeah.'

'Thank you, Steve.' She looked at me intently and tears welled in her eyes again. 'I'm pleased Mr Brewer is dead. Is that awful of me?'

I shook my head. 'Not at all. I'd feel the same way if I was you.'

'Quite right. Brewer deserved all he got,' Harriet added angrily.

'Do you think the same thing will happen to Tommy?' Marion asked quietly.

I shrugged. 'Who can tell?'

'I hope so. He's a vicious, sadistic animal.'

'I know. Which leads me nicely to my next question. How did you get involved with a hoodlum like Cassidy in the first place?'

'He murdered my family and tried to kill me when I was a little girl.'

'I know what he did to your family, but it doesn't answer my question.'

'How much do you know about my past?'

'Not much. Only that after your family died, you were placed on a witness protection programme and went to live with foster parents in Wales. I assume that's when you were given the name Gwyneth Jones?'

'Yes. Jones was the name of my foster parents. I was only nine at the time and because of my age nobody told me who had killed my family. I did try to find out, but my foster mum and dad always refused to talk about what had happened because they thought it might upset me.'

'So, when did you find out about Cassidy?'

'When I went to university. I didn't socialise much, instead I spent all my spare time in the library researching what had happened to my family. I went through the online archives of all the newspapers.

'That's how I found out Tommy Cassidy was suspected of murdering my family. It made me angry when I discovered the case against him was dropped when the only witness was killed. I was convinced Tommy murdered my family and that poor, defenceless witness. I decided to do something about it, so I set out to discover all I could about him.'

'How did your research go?' Harriet asked.

'It went okay. It took a long time, but it was worth the effort because I managed to find out about his background, his family, his friends, and his business interests.'

'Sounds as if you did well,' Harriet said. 'Perhaps you should have my job.' I thought she was joking, but I couldn't be sure.

Marion gave a nervous laugh. 'I like doing research, but I'm not strong or courageous enough for some of the other aspects of an intelligence officer's job,' she said.

'Don't underestimate yourself,' Harriet told her. 'So how did you use the information you gathered?'

'Well, the more I discovered about Tommy, the more certain I became of his guilt. That's when I decided to kill him.'

'Just like that?'

'Yes. Just like that. I put together a plan of action and when I graduated, I came up to London, changed my name, rented a tiny flat in King's Cross and got a job with the SSA.'

'Why did you choose the department?' I asked.

'I needed money and it was the only decent job available.'

'How did you meet Cassidy?' Harriet asked.

'It was easy. Once I had settled in, I started going to a night-club Tommy frequented and contrived to bump into him.'

'How did you know he would take an interest in you?' Harriet asked.

Marion smiled knowingly. 'In my experience, long legs, short skirts, big boobs, and a low-cut top are usually guaranteed to attract the attention of most red bloodied heterosexual males.'

'Obviously it worked,' Harriet said.

'It did. Tommy noticed me straight away. We started dating and within a month we were sleeping together. At first, Tommy used to visit my flat in King's Cross a couple of times a month, but he got fed up having his car scratched by the local yobs so he insisted I move into an apartment he owns in Knightsbridge.'

She paused and closed her eyes. I thought she was going to sleep again but she soon opened them. Once again they were wet with unshed tears. 'I'm sorry,' she said reaching out to pull another tissue from the box. 'It sickens me whenever I think about how I debased myself just to get close enough to Tommy to kill him.'

'But you didn't kill him,' I pointed out gently.

'That's true, but I promise you I planned Tommy's death so many times I lost count. I laid in bed most nights thinking of ways to do it. One night, after he was asleep in my bed, I went through to the kitchen and took a knife from the drawer. I went back to the bedroom and was about to stab him when I bottled it. I couldn't do it. That's what I meant earlier about not being strong or courageous enough.'

She looked at Harriet. 'I bet you would have done it.' Now there were tears glistening on her cheeks again.

'Maybe I would and maybe I wouldn't,' Harriet said softly. 'But then I've never had to decide whether to kill somebody.'

'Well I did and I flunked it. I soon realised I was never going to have the guts to kill Tommy, so instead I decided to get my revenge by having him put away for a long time.'

'Well, you've done that,' I said. 'With your help, Tommy Cassidy was already on his way to a lengthy stay in Wandsworth Prison for drug dealing, now, with your evidence, rape and attempted murder can be added to the charge sheet. That should be worth an extra ten years inside. He'll be drawing his old age pension before he's released.'

That prospect brought the first fleeting smile to Marion's

lips. 'Did you have any other questions?'

'Only one. Why did you choose the name Marion Dudley?'

'That's easy. Marion was my mum's name and Dudley was the town in which I was born.'

'You look tired,' Harriet told her. 'I think we'd better go.'

'Will you visit me again?'

'Yes,' Harriet said.

'Of course,' I added. 'But there is just one other thing. You never answered my earlier question. What do you want us to call you? Marion, Gwyneth or Kylie.'

'Marion,' she said without hesitation. 'It's the only one of the three names that's not tainted by the past. The other two will forever remind me of Tommy Cassidy. I never want to hear the names Kylie and Gwyneth ever again. As for him, the only time I want to hear his name is when he is sentenced.'

She was crying again, and Harriet reached out and squeezed her good hand. 'Let's hope he gets a whole life sentence without any chance of parole.'

'What does that mean?' Marion asked.

'It means Cassidy will probably die in prison.'

'I hope he does,' Marion said with some force. 'That would be my wish come true.'

As I listened to her, I was reminded what Bobby Moore had said about there being more than one way to skin a rat. At the time I thought he had misquoted but now I wasn't so sure. If I was right about what Humpy had in mind, then perhaps Marion's wish would be delivered sooner than she thought.

'I've missed you,' Harriet said as we went back down in the lift.

'And me you,' I said and realised it was true.

489

'Now tell me why you went to see Auntie Xandra. I thought she was on gardening leave?'

'That was just a ruse to get Sam into a position of power. She figured that if we gave him enough rope, he would eventually hang himself.'

'And she was right.'

'Yeah, she was right, except the rope was exchanged for my Glock.'

'So, you and Auntie Xandra have been working together all along?'

'That's right.'

'And the Cabinet Office were in on it too?'

'Yeah. The Cab Sec was a bit twitchy about the ethics of what we were doing, but he went along with the plan. He had no choice.'

'How is Auntie Xandra?'

'Happy to be officially back in charge. She hates gardening.'

'What else did she have to say?'

'She wants you to transfer back to the FCO.'

'Why? Is she unhappy with my work?'

'Of course not. She's unhappy at the thought of you sleeping with her deputy. She thinks it might by one fraternisation too far.'

'Sleeping with her deputy. What do you mean?'

'I've just been promoted.'

'You're the D-D-G?'

'Acting D-D-G.' I pulled my appointment letter from my pocket and waved it in front of her face. 'That's what this says anyway.'

She snatched the letter from me and began to read it out

loud: '"Dear Mr Statton. I am pleased to inform you that following a recommendation from the Director-General of the Special Security Agency, the Rt Hon Dame Alexandra Nichols, the Cabinet Office Renumeration and Appointments Committee has unanimously decided you should be offered the position of Acting Deputy Director-General of the Special Security Agency. Blah, blah, blah... Yours Truly..." and look, its signed by Sir Mark!'

'I know. I read the letter.'

'Have you accepted?'

'I said I'd think about it.'

'Are you serious?'

'Yeah.'

'Why are you hesitating?'

'I don't want them taking me for granted.'

'Do they take you for granted?'

'Not at the moment, but they could relapse.'

'So, does that mean you will accepting?'

'On one condition.'

'Which is?'

'I want you in my team.'

'Will Auntie Xandra accept that?'

'I think so.'

'But aren't you worried that working together might affect our relationship?'

'Why should it make a difference. We've been okay up till now.'

'But you weren't the Deputy D-G then.'

I shrugged. 'Don't worry. I'm not planning to throw you over the office photocopier and ravish you.'

'Not planning something is a management tactic to cover their backs in case they change their minds.'

'I won't change my mind.'

'That's disappointing,' she said with an impish twinkle in her eye. 'However, I think we should consider the implications should you be tempted by my animal magnetism.'

'Do you?'

'Yes, and I'll happily apply for a transfer if we decide it's the right thing to do.'

'OK. Let's go to the Red Lion and discuss it over a drink.'

'I would prefer to go home and discuss it in bed,' she said.

So that's what we did, except very little discussion took place.

PART FOUR

EXTREME RETRIBUTION

In our eyes this is rage
No apologies can return
The progress that's been erased
Retribution's on its way
Tonight

Steve Moore/Inner Surge

41

Jalaluddin Haqqani watched with hooded eyes as the young servant placed a plate of Qabuli pilau[1] on the floor in front of where he sat on a silk covered cushion. He had not seen the girl before.

'What is your name, little daughter?'

'Hooriyah[2], master,' she replied shyly, making sure she kept her eyes firmly trained on the ground as she placed a bowl of rose water next to the food.

'It is a pretty name and suits you well.'

'Thank you, master.' An embarrassed blush darkened Hooriyah's smooth young cheeks.

'How old are you, child?'

'Sixteen, master.'

Haqqani nodded in satisfaction; the girl was old enough for what he had in mind. Not that he had any scruples about having sex with a girl under the official age of consent, or to whom he was not married. No court in this beloved male dominated land would ever convict him of either offence.

For was it not the case that women were created by Allah (*may His glory be glorified*) to satisfy the needs of men, particularly powerful men such as he.

The old man stared intently at the girls bowed head. Good. Female servants should know their place and understand they can be used in any way their master chooses. 'You may go now, little daughter,' he told her.

'Yes, master,' Hooriyah said without looking up.

'However, I would like you to bring a warm glass of dugh[3] to my bedroom at ten o'clock tonight.'

'It shall be as you wish, master.' Hooriyah said softly as she shuffled backwards towards the door.

Haqqani turned his attention to his evening meal. He started by reaching down and washing his right hand in the bowl of rose water, then he took a ball of food from the plate and put it into his mouth. He chewed slowly in a preoccupied way.

Usually he savoured the taste of the lamb pilaf, which was flavoured with sweet and warming spices by his cook, but today was different. Tonight, he ate distractedly because he had something on his mind and it was not his young servant. This was something much more important. Something worrying. Something that meant he had a hard decision to make.

The previous day he had sent an encrypted email to that arrogant infidel, Guiseppe Navarra, notifying him the heroin he had ordered a week ago was now ready to be shipped.

This notification was part of the agreed delivery procedure and usually triggered a similarly encrypted email response from Navarra confirming the shipment should be sent immediately to Sabawi al-Barak in Baghdad for onward transit to the Mancini Polo Club in Treviso.

But Haqqani had heard nothing from the Italian, which was very unusual, puzzling, and worrying. However, he had received an email from Azad Nuristani in Baghlan, to let him know the Buzkashi pony he had ordered was now loaded into a horsebox and was about to leave. That email was sent at 2 pm local time.

Haqqani glanced at the Rolex Oyster watch on his wrist. It

would take the driver just under five hours to make the journey from Baghlan to Charikar. If there were no delays, the horsebox would arrive at Mazraea-e Jananjoy[4] within the next hour.

The usual procedure was that bags of heroin would be implanted into the horse as soon as possible, then one of Haqqani's men would tow Nuristani's horsebox almost 3000 kilometres to Baghdad. Now, in the absence of a confirmation email from Navarra, he had to decide whether to go ahead as planned.

Although half the amount the Italians were paying for the heroin had been paid into his bank account already, the balance would only be paid on safe arrival of the drugs at the home of Sabawi al-Barak, who would then be responsible for onward delivery of the horse to Italy, no doubt for a very large fee.

But what if an email eventually turned up from the Mafia instructing him to deliver the heroin to a different destination? Would Navarra still pay if the shipment was on its way to the usual address in Iraq?

Haqqani mulled over this conundrum as he chewed his food. He was reasonably confident the Italian would arrange for al-Barak to transfer the shipment to the correct destination, and then pay the balance anyway, but what if he was wrong? Was it worth taking a risk, no matter how small?

Of course, if he decided not to press ahead with the ship-ment, should he send the Buzkashi horse straight back to Baghlan tonight, or wait until the next day, in the hope an email would arrive overnight?

This latter option made more sense, because postponing his final decision until tomorrow would allow him all evening and night to receive instructions from Venice and give him longer to decide his course of action.

Although deferring the decision was unlikely to please Nuristani's driver, who would be forced to stay at Mazraea-e Jananjoy overnight, it would enable him to sleep in peace.

Haqqani smiled as he thought of what he would do later that evening, when sleep would come only after he had enjoyed the delights offered by the body of his pretty young servant. It was a prospect that lifted his mood and he finished off the rest of his dinner with renewed relish.

*

At about the same time that Jalaluddin Haqqani was eating his dinner, the man he knew as Yamin Abdullah was driving a Toyota Hilux down Afghanistan's Highway AH76.

Abdullah was pleased to be out of his chauffeur's uniform. Instead he was dressed casually in jeans and a heavy jumper, which he wore over a military style sweatshirt. He was looking forward to going home to Canada, where he would be able to revert to his real name, Sean MacDonald, until he was given another field assignment, when, no doubt, he would have to take on another alias.

Attached to the back of the pickup truck was a battered horsebox. Azad Nuristani always used old horseboxes for these trips, because he knew they were never coming back.

MacDonald could hear a high-pitched whine coming from the horsebox's back axel and was amazed a wheel had not fallen off as he navigated the pothole strewn highway.

It could still happen, he thought to himself and instinctively slowed down, although he knew this was unlikely to help. There was no lighting on the highway, and when he did spot a pothole or boulder he had very little time to avoid it. Most times he did, but sometimes he was not quick enough.

Despite his concerns about the reliability of the horsebox, MacDonald was making good time. He had already left behind him the Salang Pass, which traverses the Hindu Kush mountain range, and he was now following the highway down onto the fertile plains on which many of the region's crops were grown.

In the distance he could see the bright lights of Charikar sparkling in the dark night like tired fireflies resting in the grass before resuming their search for mates. When MacDonald reached the outskirts of the city, he turned left onto the Panjshir Road and headed towards Haqqani's farm, which was about ten kilometres further on.

Twenty minutes later he passed a sign, on which was written in Pashto the name: Mazraea-e Jananjoy, and seconds later he arrived at a metal barred gate, next to which stood two guards carrying AK47 assault rifles. One of the guards held up a hand to stop MacDonald, then ordered him out of the Hilux and made him stand with his back to the horsebox.

While his companion covered MacDonald with his rifle, the guard searched the cab. He opened the glove compartment, but it was empty except for a green plastic first aid box. He opened the box and found nothing except a bandage, a few plasters, a syringe, and a vial with a label printed in English.

'What is this?' the guard asked in Pashto.

'Insulin. I have type one diabetes,' MacDonald explained fluently in the same language, touching the crook of his left arm as he spoke.

The guard nodded his understanding and returned the box back to the glove compartment. Then, satisfied there was nothing else of interest inside the cab, he checked the back of the pickup truck, which did not take long, because it was clearly empty.

Next, the guard stood on tiptoes to look through the small window of the horsebox. 'He's a powerful looking horse,' he said admiringly to MacDonald. The Afghans love their horses, particularly those bred for Buzkashi, as this one was.

'It's a mare,' MacDonald responded.

'You don't say.' The guard sounded impressed. 'Well she looks like a stallion. Big and strong like you.' He pointed at MacDonald. 'You don't get many Buzkashi mares like that,' the guard added as he frisked the visitor carefully to ensure he wasn't hiding any weapons under the loose-fitting jumper. Satisfied the driver was not armed, he turned to his colleague and said, 'All clear.'

MacDonald watched as the second guard took out a two-wave radio from the deep pocket of his long goatskin coat and whispered into it. When he had finished talking, the guard pushed open the gates.

'You can go through. Do you know your way?'

'Yes. I've been here before,' MacDonald replied and clambered back behind the wheel of the Hilux. He wasn't put out or worried by the thoroughness of the search. He had visited Haqqani's farm on a number of occasions and the process to gain entry was the same every time. It was only the guards who changed.

He started the engine of his pickup and drove slowly through the gates and headed down the track towards the farm complex, which nestled at the foothills of the Hindu Kush.

As MacDonald made his way down the track, he drove

through acres of poppy fields, from which Haqqani's workers would eventually extract opium latex to be converted into a morphine base, which would be heated with acetic anhydride to make heroin.

Soon he reached a cluster of buildings, these included several storage barns; a small processing plant, where the drugs were produced; a stable block; a handful of primitive mud huts; and the more substantial, single-storey house where Haqqani lived.

The open courtyard separating Haqqani's home from the L-shaped stable block was lit up with floodlights and when MacDonald drove into the courtyard he found the owner in front of him, waving him to stop. He drew up alongside the Taliban leader and wound down the window.

'There is a problem,' Haqqani told him without preamble. 'You will have to stay here overnight.'

'I'm afraid I can't do that, sir. Mr Nuristani is expecting me back tonight. I am to drive him to Mazari Sharif first thing in the morning,' MacDonald explained patiently.

'Don't worry. I will contact your boss and explain the situation. He will understand,' Haqqani told him without further explanation. 'Park the horsebox by the stables. You will find fresh straw, oats, and water for the horse in the first stall…' he paused and pointed towards the far end of the block, '…and there is a camp bed in the last stall. You can sleep there. I will arrange for food and drink to be brought to you.' Haqqani headed back to the house without another word.

MacDonald was smiling to himself when he drove over to the stable block and parked. So far it was going as planned. He got out of the cab, pulled a sheepskin jacket from behind the driver's seat and slipped it on as protection against the bitterly cold night. He was a big man, but the bulky coat made him look even larger.

He uncoupled the horsebox, unbolted the back doors, and lowered the ramp to the ground. He walked up into the back of the box and untied the rope that tethered the mare to a rail fixed to the front panel.

He slowly coaxed the horse backwards down the ramp and then led her into the first stall of the stable block. The mare was hungry and soon had her head in the food trough containing oats that was positioned on the floor alongside a metal bucket of water.

MacDonald spread fresh straw on the floor and then left the stall, bolting the door behind him. He returned to his truck, opened the passenger door, and leaned into the cab. He took the syringe and vial of clear liquid from the glove compartment and put them into his jacket pocket.

He closed the passenger door and as he was locking it saw a young girl come out of the house and walk across the courtyard towards the stable block. She was carrying a tray. He guessed this was his evening meal and went to head off the girl. They met just before she reached the end stall.

'Is that for me?' He towered over the youngster.

'Yes, sir,' Hooriyah replied softly, keeping her eyes lowered.

'Thank you. Let me take it from you.' He held out his hands.

The girl passed him the tray and headed back to the house. She looked unhappy and preoccupied and MacDonald wondered why. He would soon find out.

*

Later that evening Jalaluddin Haqqani was lounging on a bed of plush cushions on the floor of his darkened bedroom. He was smoking charas[5] from a hookah that stood on the low table next to him.

He had heard nothing from Guiseppe Navarra, despite sending him an urgent chase-up email, and this lack of a response did not help his state of mind as he weighed up the risk of sending the shipment of heroin to Italy before he received the balance of his money.

He had tried to telephone Azad Nuristani to tell him he was keeping his driver in Charikar overnight, but the line to Baghlan appeared to be down, and when he rang the horse breeder's mobile phone it went straight to voicemail. In the end he sent his associate an email, but again he received no response.

Haqqani hated uncertainties in his ordered life and he became increasingly irritable as the evening wore on. His mood was not helped when his servant resisted all his attempts to seduce her.

He had started off being tender with her, but when the young girl tried to pull away from him, he scooped her up effortlessly and hugged her, with arms that were still powerful, despite his advanced age.

As Haqqani pressed himself against the girl's body, and felt her firm young breasts rubbing against his bare chest, he became aroused, stiffening in excitement as he tried to manoeuvre her into a position that would allow him to push apart her legs, but she fought hard to resist him.

Instead of being grateful that he deemed her worthy of his attention, the young girl screamed in protest, fighting him with a strength that belied her slight figure, clawing his face with sharp fingernails.

The heat of the old man's recently awakened desire quickly cooled, turning to frustration and then anger. He threw the girl to the floor in the corner of the room and proceeded to beat her into submission.

Now as Haqqani sucked on the hookah pipe he sighed with pleasure as his lungs were filled with more intoxicating charas fumes. He glanced towards the corner of his bedroom, where the broken-spirited young servant huddled, whimpering like a frightened puppy. He felt no guilt at having beaten her, nor did he have pity for her distress. She should not have spurned him. He was her master. He owned her. All of her.

Hopefully the stupid child would now realise she was only postponing the inevitable. He would not be denied. He was determined to take her to his bed tonight, but first he would enjoy the rest of his charas. The delay would give the wench time to reflect on what a further refusal might mean for her. He was confident she would see sense. They always did.

Haqqani closed his eyes and sucked again on the mouthpiece of the hookah hose. As a fresh infusion of charas was added to the drugs already being pumped to his brain, a swirling mist descended on him, burying his anger and sexual frustration deep beneath his subconscious. His mind was suddenly filled with a jumble of incoherent thoughts, abstract images, and disturbing fantasies, over which he had no control.

In one confusing vision, Haqqani found himself riding a horse onto a Buzkashi field where men on horseback were milling around attempting to grab hold of the headless body of a goat.

He urged his horse into the melee and headed for the pure white carcass, using the shoulder of his horse to violently push aside a prancing horse as he went. He grunted in satisfaction as its rider was thrown to the ground where he was trampled on by many hooves.

Haqqani pressed on regardless, barging through the riders until he reached the middle of the field, where a screaming tribesman was pulling the carcass along the ground on the end of a length of rope.

Haqqani reached across and pulled the rope from the rider's hand and then pushed his way out of the melee using one hand to control his horse and the other to hold the carcass up in the air.

Then he was free and with a jubilant cry of triumph he galloped towards a hole in the ground that was the designated goal. He pulled his horse to a halt and dropped the carcass into the hole. He looked down and realised that the carcass was not that of a headless goat, but a young girl who looked up at him with accusing dead eyes.

Without warning an eagle swooped out of the sky, sunk its claws into the girl's body, lifted it out of the hole and carried it up into its mountain eyrie, where a nest full of hungry fledglings were waiting to be fed.

Haqqani watched in fascination as the eagle pecked one of the girl's eyes from her head and fed it to a fledgling, but he was spared seeing more of the gruesome feast, because a thick mist suddenly descended on the mountain range.

When the mist lifted, Haqqani was leading a group of Taliban warriors as they attacked a Tajid village in the mountains northwest of Kabul. Once again, the images were vivid as the group made its way through the scattering of sun-bleached mud buildings, kicking open the rotten wooden front doors and shooting everybody they found.

When the carnage was over, there were no Tajid villagers left alive, except a pretty young girl they found, along with the rest of her family, in the last house they visited. As the terrified girl watched with wide eyes, the Taliban murderers gunned down her father, mother and two brothers.

When the slaughter was over, they stripped the girl and threw her on a kitchen table where two of his men held her down while the rest of the group raped her, one after the other.

When it was Haqqani's turn, he stared down at the young girl, spread-eagled on the table beneath him, and recognised her as the badly beaten servant who was now lying in a heap in the corner of his bedroom. He frowned in confusion. How was this possible?

He reached down and tenderly touched the girl's cheek, as if to reassure her, but discovered her skin was icy cold. That's when he realised she was dead. He used the same finger to slowly prise open the girl's eyelid, only to find that her eyeball had disappeared, to be replaced by wriggling maggots, some of which crawled out onto her cheek.

He stepped back hurriedly and stared down at the dead girl's naked body. Despite his disgust at the sight of the maggots rapidly spreading across the dead girl's face, he still found himself aroused by the sight of her tender young body. But could he really bring himself to have sex with a dead body? What did the Koran say? He could remember no mention of such a situation. He decided to stand aside and let the next man take over.

'She's all yours,' he mumbled and looked over his shoulder to see who was next in line. The man behind him was huge, like a big black bear, and he had to look up to see his face. He frowned when he realised who the man was. It was Nuristani's driver, Yamin Abdullah, but what was he doing here? When did he join the group? Haqqani couldn't remember.

'What's that in your hand?' the old man asked in alarm as he lifted his gun and pointed it at Abdullah. He pulled the trigger, but nothing happened. He looked down at his hand and saw he was not holding a gun, but the mouthpiece of his hookah hose.

Haqqani looked up at Abdullah again and finally understood that he was going to die. 'Verily we belong to Allah (*may His glory be glorified*),' he intoned quickly, 'and verily to Him do we return.'

*

Sean MacDonald cautiously pushed open the door to Haqqani's bedroom and stared into the darkened room. At first, he couldn't see the Taliban man, but then he saw him lying on a bed of cushions. In one hand he held the mouthpiece of a hose that was connected to a hookah. Haqqani looked as if he was comatose, which would make his job easier.

MacDonald took from his pocket the syringe, which was already filled with liquid from the supposed insulin vial. He held up the syringe and gently pressed the plunger to ensure the liquid was flowing. He walked over to Haqqani and looked down at him.

The old man mumbled something that the Canadian did not understand, then turned his head and looked up at MacDonald.

He frowned and asked, 'What's that in your hand?' This time MacDonald understood, but didn't reply.

Haqqani raised his hand and pointed the mouthpiece of his hookah hose at him, then he looked at his hand in puzzlement. He looked back up at MacDonald and understanding washed over his face. 'Verily we belong to Allah (*may His glory be glorified*),' he said quickly in Pashto, 'and verily to Him do we return.'

'Allah be praised,' MacDonald said in English, as he stabbed the syringe needle into Haqqani's carotid artery and pushed the plunger all the way home. The concentrated dose of deadly ricin poison quickly took effect, and within minutes the Taliban leader was dead.

MacDonald heard a noise in the corner of the room. He walked over cautiously and found somebody cowering on the floor. It was the servant girl who had brought his supper to him earlier that evening. He guessed immediately what had happened. 'It's all right,' he said gently in English. 'You're safe now.'

Hooriyah recognised the man's voice and looked up at him with tear filled eyes. She let him help her to her feet and then pointed towards Haqqani's body.

'He is dead,' MacDonald told her in Pashto.

'Can this be true?'

'It is true,' he replied and took her hand. 'Come. Let me take you home.' He started to lead her to the door, but she pulled away from him and walked over to Haqqani. She looked down at the dead man with hatred etched on her face, then she summoned up a mouth full of phlegm and spat it into the dead man's face.

Hooriyah stood for several seconds with a smile on her face as she watched the spittle dribble down Haqqani's long, grey flecked beard. She turned and looked up at MacDonald, who seemed to fill the room like a bushy bearded bear. 'Who are you?'

'It's probably best you don't know, ma'am. All you need to know is that I'm a friend.'

'Are you American?'

'What makes you say that?'

'Because you talked in English just now.'

He smiled at her. 'You're a clever girl,' he told her, but didn't answer her question.

'Are you?' Hooriyah persisted.

He shrugged and repeated: 'All you need to know is that I'm a friend.'

'Well, whoever you are, thank you. Can you take me home now, or is there something else you must do?' She nodded towards Haqqani.

'No. Let's go. My job here is finished.'

And it was.

As MacDonald was driving the girl home to the village in which she lived, just outside Charikar, he glanced at the digital clock that was set into the Hilux's fascia, just above the satellite navigation screen. The tiny display showed 23:59, but as he watched, it clicked over to 00:00. He smiled.

150 miles due north, in Baghlan, another clock silently registered that it was now midnight. That clock was hidden in a shoebox under the bed in which Azad Nuristani was sleeping. The horse breeder was alone. He was unmarried, and had never had any interest in sex, so nobody else would be sharing his bed.

As the clock signalled that a new day was about to start, it activated a battery that sent an electrical charge to a detonator, which, in turn, ignited a block of Semtex. The explosion that followed blew the bed apart, killing Nuristani instantly.

The beautifully decorated bedroom was destroyed, but the Canadian had used the right amount of plastic explosive and the rest of the house remained intact. None of Nuristani's servants were injured.

---

1   Qabuli (or Kabuli) pilau (or pulao) is an Afghani rice and meat dish.
2   Hooriyah means "beautiful and radiant angel" in Arabic.
3   Dugh is a drink of yoghurt, salt, cucumber and mint. It can be served ice cold or warm.
4   Mazraea-e Jananjoy is loosely translated as the Farm near Jananjoy.
5   Charas: a type of hashish or marijuana used in Afghanistan.

42

Sabawi al-Barak lived in Mansour, which is one of the more affluent administrative districts of Baghdad. It is also one of the safest. However, everything is relative, including personal safety. Mansour is not somewhere you would walk alone at night, unless you were happy to be mugged, kidnapped, or murdered.

Al-Barak had no reason to fear such threats to his safety. As head of the Iraqi National Intelligence Service, he was provided with an armoured plated car and a chauffeur to drive it.

Today he was being driven to Ramadi for a meeting with a Turkish contact who had an import/export business in the city. The Turk's enterprise was a perfect vehicle for handling the onwards shipment of the horseboxes that al-Barak received periodically from Jalaluddin Haqqani. It was the Turk's job to ensure the shipments were transported by road to Albania, and then onwards by ferry to Italy.

It usually took about 90 minutes to drive from Baghdad to Ramadi using the most direct route, which was Road 97 and Freeway 1. However, when they reached the slip-road leading to Road 97 it was blocked following a collision between two cars.

The driver wound down his window to talk to the policeman who was redirecting traffic. The cop advised them to head north up Highway 1, and then use Road 23 to reach Freeway 1.

When they were on their way up Rabie Street, towards the slip onto Highway 1, al-Barak slumped onto the backseat and loudly cursed the stupid drivers who had caused an inconvenience that would add at least half an hour to his journey.

Once they were on the Highway 1, which has been dubbed by many people the scariest road in the world, their speed increased as they made their way north towards Taji. Half hour later the car began to slow down, as they approached the Road 23 junction.

The driver swore loudly.

'What's wrong?' al-Barak asked, craning his neck to see why they were slowing down.

'Looks like there has been another accident, sir.'

Al-Barak looked ahead and saw a US Army vehicle transporter had jack-knifed at the entrance to the west-bound slip road off Highway 1. Standing behind the transporter was a uniformed US military policeman who gesticulated urgently with his hand in an obvious order that they should drive on.

'What will we do now,' al-Barak asked as they drove past the policeman.

'All we can do is carry on and do a U-turn at Taji and then use the east-bound slip road to get onto Road 23. I know just the place. It's not far.'

'Okay, but be as quick as you can,' al-Barak said grumpily. 'I'm going to be late as it is.'

'Not a problem, sir,' the driver said cheerily.

When they reached the next exit, the driver pulled off Highway 1 and headed down a road past a cluster of houses. He glanced in his rear-view mirror and saw that al-Barak had his eyes closed. He smiled to himself.

A few minutes later he turned left through a set of gates and passed a large sign that read WELCOME TO CAMP COOKE in faded red letters. He drove on for several more yards and drew up outside a low building which had a Stars and Stripes flag flying from a pole.

'Why have we stopped?' al-Barak asked.

The driver did not answer, instead he turned off the engine, got out of the car and used his smart key to lock the car. 'He's all yours,' he said to a young American army captain who stood outside the building.

'Good timing,' the captain said as half a dozen soldiers surrounded the car with their carbines pointing towards it. 'Your plane is waiting for you over there,' he pointed towards the Taji airstrip, which was less than a hundred yards from the building.

The driver went to the car's trunk and took a large holdall from it. With a cheerful wave at al-Barak, who was staring through the back window at him with a dumbstruck look on his face, he made his way quickly to the airstrip and went up the steps of the Gulfstream G150 that was waiting to take him to England.

Twelve hours later, Jamal Abbas was met at London City Airport by his cousin, Fraser Goran, who took him to the new home in North Kent he shared with his wife and two children.

Twenty-four hours after that, Sabawi al-Barak could be found locked up in a Guantanamo Bay detention centre, wearing bright orange overalls, and demanding to see a lawyer.

His demands went unanswered.

43

It was 5pm in Tehran when Raven finished work after another busy day. Before leaving her office she made sure the blotting pad, telephone and desk organiser were straight, and any unfiled documents were locked away in a drawer.

Satisfied she had once again finished the day with a tidy and paperwork-free desk, she smoothed down her smart office suit, put on an overcoat, tied a woollen scarf round her head, and made her way downstairs to the front foyer of the Ministry of Defence and Armed Forces Logistics.

When Raven stepped out onto the pavement she was greeted by a clear blue sky in which the sun was sinking rapidly towards its death. The temperature was heading in the same direction. It was only 3 degrees Celsius and a cold wind was blowing down from the snow covered mountains in the north, making her shiver despite her coat and scarf.

Raven lived alone, and was in no hurry to get home, so she headed for her favourite café and found a space at a table occupied by a handful of regular customers, who she had got to know well during the years she had worked at the ministry. Those regulars knew her as Sheema Azadi.

Sheema ordered a cup of coffee and whiled away an hour with her acquaintances. She never said much herself on these occasions, preferring instead to sit and listen to the local gossip and the many whispered complaints made about the regime. It was a good way of gauging the mood of the public, which was an important piece of information for any spy.

When Sheema left the café she headed home. She could have taken the Metro, but she preferred to walk, telling any of her acquaintances who queried her decision that she relished the fresh air after spending all day in a stuffy office. They rarely bothered to ask and today was no exception.

She walked briskly. Despite the cloudless sky, the air was becoming even frostier as dusk settled over the city. She strode down Ferdowski Avenue, to Imam Khomeini Street, and then down Khayyam Street, before she took a right turn into City Park.

This diversion was not on Sheema's direct route home, but she took it because she had another reason for preferring to walk home every day.

When Sheema reached an isolated area of the park, she sat down on a bench, took her mobile phone from her pocket, and checked it. There were no messages, but that was irrelevant. Checking the phone was an excuse to make sure she wasn't being followed.

Next to the bench was a low granite stone wall, behind which a tall, straggly hedge was crying out to be trimmed. Sheema looked around but could see nobody else in the park. It was well into dusk now and the temperature had dropped below zero. Few people would be out and about, but she was confident that anybody further than a few metres away from her would not be able to see her sitting on the bench in her black coat and scarf.

Sheema reached down behind the wall until she found a wide crack between two stones. The back of the wall was well hidden by the bushy hedge, and nobody would find the crack unless they knew it was there. This was the dead drop box that Eagle used to contact her.

Sheema used her fingers to explore inside the crack. She felt something in it and her heart raced as she was gripped by a surge of excitement. She checked the dead drop box every night, but there was rarely anything in it.

She looked nonchalantly around again and when she was certain she was still alone in the park, she quickly pulled a slip of paper from the crack and slipped it into the pocket of her coat. The whole exercise took only seconds.

With a growing sense of impatience, Sheema waited on the bench until dusk gave way to night, then, satisfied she was still not being observed, she stood up and made her way out of the park into Behesht Street. After another brisk ten-minute walk, she arrived at her apartment.

When Sheema was safely inside and the door was locked and bolted behind her, she pulled the slip of paper from her pocket and read the message from Eagle. It was short and dramatic: Leave Tehran immediately. Go somewhere safe. Do not return until I contact you.

Every good field agent has an escape route planned and Sheema was no exception. She opened the safe that was hidden behind the mirror in her bathroom, took out five-hundred 50,000 Rial banknotes, a thousand US dollars and a thousand Euros in mixed denomination notes. She also retrieved her passport, and other useful documents, in case she was forced to flee the country.

She stored the money in the false bottom of a large suitcase, along with all the documents except a national smart card in the name of Shirin Farahani. She put this identity card in her purse with twenty of the Rial banknotes, then packed the case with clothes and shoes.

When Sheema finished packing, she locked her apartment and took the Metro to Mehrabad Airport, where she caught a flight to Tabriz International Airport. Just under four hours later she arrived at the Northwestern Bus Terminal, which is located southeast of the airport, where she purchased a ticket for the hour and a half bus journey to the city of Ahar.

Sheema had relatives who lived on a remote farm located halfway between Ahar and the Iranian border with Azerbaijan. Her aunt and uncle would be waiting for her at the Islamic Republic Boulevard Bus Station in the city's southern suburbs to take her to their home, where she could stay for as long as necessary without fear of being discovered by the authorities.

*

The next day agents from the Ministry of Intelligence, otherwise known as VAJA, kicked down the door of an apartment in the Moniriyeh district of Tehran, but found nobody inside.

Raven had flown.

44

Steve Statton had just finished a phone conversation with Fraser Goran, who had briefed him on his cousin's successful operation in Iraq, and was about to pick up the phone again to ring the D-G's office, when it rang.

It was Rachel Frewin.

'That's spooky, I was about to ring you,' he said.

'What about?'

'I want to speak with the boss.'

'That's good because she wants to talk to you.'

'What about?'

'I've no idea.'

'I thought secretaries were supposed to know everything.'

'Not this time,' she said with a laugh and then changed the subject. 'How are you settling into your new office?'

'Great. It's much bigger than my old one and, praise be, I've even got a window.'

'Lucky you. I only get to see the sun at work if I look out of the boss's window. Talking of the sun, I hear your secretary is off to South Africa to get married. Is she coming back?'

'Not as far as I know.'

'Have you found anybody to replace her yet?'

'I'm in no hurry. Marion's out of hospital and will soon be fit enough to return to work. I can live without a secretary until then.'

'What if she decides not to return?'

'Then I'll find somebody else. What about you?'

'I already have a job, or didn't you notice?'

'I noticed, but you could always ask for a transfer.'

'Hmmm. I'm not sure Dame Alexandra would be happy if she knew you were trying to poach her staff.'

'It beats poaching kippers and eggs,' he said with a laugh. 'So when does the boss want to see me?'

'Straight away.'

'Is there coffee on offer?'

'What do you think?'

'I think I'm on my way.'

When Statton walked into the D-G's office it was filled with the rich aroma from the fresh ground coffee that wafted out of the percolator that was plopping merrily away in the corner.

It was the same percolator Sam Brewer used when he occupied the D-G's chair, but now the coffee maker was standing on an antique Queen Anne table, next to a solid silver tray on which were set expensive looking bone china cups and saucers, a dinky looking cream jug, and a matching sugar bowl complete with a pair of small tongs poking out from under its lid.

It was all very tasteful and typical of Dame Alexandra Nichols.

Statton's boss stood up and politely waved him to sit down. He watched as she walked over to the table and poured two cups of coffee. She added cream to both, then lifted the lid of the sugar bowl and put two lumps of demerara into one cup and handed it to him.

'Cream and two sugars. Rachel tells me that is how you take your coffee.'

'She has a good memory,' Statton said.

'That's why she's my secretary. I have very high standards.'

'So do I, particularly when it comes to coffee.' Statton made a show of sniffing his coffee as if it were a fine wine. 'This smells like Jamaican Blue Mountain Number One. Is it?'

'No, just bog-standard arabica beans from Brazil.'

'Ah, yes. Of course. An easy mistake.'

She looked at him with a knowing smile on her lips. 'Be honest, Steven. Have you ever had Blue Mountain coffee?'

He smiled back at her. 'No, I wouldn't know the difference between one coffee bean and another.'

Dame Alexandra picked up her own cup of coffee, walked behind her desk and sat down. 'Rachel tells me you wanted to talk to me about something. What is it?'

'Do you remember Fraser Goran?'

'Of course. He was the Afghan interpreter for whom I arranged permanent leave to remain. What about him?'

'Goran has a cousin.'

'Yes, but I cannot recall his name.'

'Jamal Abbas,' he told her and then took a sip of his coffee. 'What about him?'

'Three days ago, Abbas delivered Sabawi al-Barak to the American air base in Taji, from where he was shipped off to Guantanamo Bay.'

'Extraordinary rendition?'

'That's what the Yanks call it.'

'I take it this was something you organised as part of your tying up the loose ends exercise?'

'Yeah, with Goran's help.'

'Good work. Al-Barak might be able to provide some useful information about the current turmoil in the Iraqi Government.'

'I don't think so.'

'I'm sure the Americans have ways of making him talk.'

'That might be difficult. Even waterboarding won't work on al-Barak.'

'Why not?'

'Because he committed suicide on his first night in captivity.'

'Suicide?'

'That's the line the Yanks are peddling.'

'Do you believe them?'

'Why not? I believe in the Loch Ness Monster, Santa Claus, the Tooth Fairy, and that the President of the United States is an alien masquerading as a human being.'

'You do think it's true then?' she said with a twinkle in her eyes.

Statton acknowledged his boss's joke with a cynical smile. 'Suicide or not, al-Barak is dead and it's one loose end ticked off our list.' He used his finger to draw an imaginary tick in the air. 'And I don't suppose there are many people outside Iraq who will mourn his passing.'

'Or inside Iraq.'

Statton looked at her. 'There's something else.'

'What's that?'

'It's Jamal Abbas. I told him he could join his family in this country. He's with them now, but it would be helpful if we could arrange for him to remain here permanently.'

'I'm sure that's something you can sort out, now you're my deputy.'

'Acting deputy,' Statton could not resist pointing out.

'Yes, but it's only a matter of time before your permanent appointment is confirmed. In fact, I hear you have a meeting with the Sir Mark next week to discuss your terms and conditions.'

'Monday,' he confirmed.

'That's what I thought. Meanwhile, as Acting D-D-G you already have the necessary authority to discuss Abbas's case with the Home Office.'

'I know, but I wanted to clear it with you first.'

'Consider it cleared.'

'Thanks, I'll get onto it. Now what did you want to see me about?'

'I had three phone calls this morning.'

'Lucky you. Who were they from?'

'The first was from the CSIS Deputy Director Ops.'

'You mean your mate Lloyd Harper?'

'Yes.'

'Did he ring about Sean MacDonald?'

'Yes.'

'Is he back in Canada?'

'He is.'

'Was he successful?'

The D-G smiled. 'Yes.'

'So Haqqani is dead?'

'Yes. Apparently he injected himself with ricin.'

'What an unusual way to commit suicide,' Statton said with a cynical smile.

'Yes.'

'What about Nuristani?'

'Dead too, but I don't think his death can be passed off as a suicide.'

'Why not?'

'Because he was killed when a bomb blew up under his bed.'

'I like it. That really is extreme retribution,' Statton said and drew two more ticks in the air. 'That's another couple off our list,' he added before finishing off his coffee. 'That's great coffee.'

'Help yourself to some more and I will have a top up too.'

'What about the other calls?' Statton asked as he poured their coffees.

'The second one was from DAC Jane Manning. She wanted to give me the latest information about the security guard who tried to kill Benedict Fletcher on the House of Commons Terrace.'

'Have they discovered her real name?' Statton passed a coffee to her and then sat back down.

'Yes.'

'That's a surprise. I wasn't sure it was very high up on the Met's priority list,' he said.

'It's always top priority when a minister is involved, particularly if they are a Home Office minister.'

'Of course it is. How silly of me. So, who was she?'

'Her name was Aleah Mohammad.'

'The name means nothing to me.'

'She was the daughter of the Iranian Home Security Minister, Islam Houshian, who was killed by an American missile last year.'

'I know about Houshian's death. Benedict Fletcher mentioned it at our meeting on New Year's Eve. Do you think her father's death was the motive for Mohammad's attempt to murder him?'

'It was certainly one motive, although her attempt was at the behest of the Iranian leadership.'

'Was it connected to Operation QS?'

'No,' the D-G said with a shake of her head. 'Our friends across the pond in Langley believe the Iranians wanted to assassinate one our Government ministers in revenge for Houshian's death.'

Statton nodded his understanding. 'Who better to recruit for the job than his daughter?'

'Exactly.'

'But why did the Iranians target Fletcher?'

'For two reasons. The first was because he is our Intelligence and Home Security Minister. A like for like death.'

'That makes sense, but why target us and not the Yanks? After all it was their drone that killed Mohammad's dad.'

'The CIA suspect they chose Fletcher because our ministers are less well protected than the Americans and because of the Iranian's second reason.'

'Which was?'

'They think it was all about harnessing Aleah Mohammad's hatred of Fletcher.'

The mention of the Mohammad's hatred jogged Statton's memory and he recalled the way the woman had looked at the politician as she was about to shoot him. 'Why did she hate Fletcher?' Statton asked.

'Because she was Farrokh Mohammad's wife.'

Statton shrugged his shoulders. 'Give me a clue. Who's he?'

'Mohammad was a member of an Iranian sponsored insurgent group operating in Afghanistan. The insurgents ambushed a section of soldiers from the 5th Battalion, The Rifles that was patrolling in the Babaji area of Lashkar Gah district. Mohammad was killed during the ensuing skirmish.'

'The death of an insurgent is no great loss to mankind, but what's it got to do with Fletcher?'

'He was the officer in charge of the British patrol.' Dame Alexandra paused and sipped her coffee before adding, 'In fact, it was Fletcher who shot Mohammad.'

'Now you mention it, I remember the incident but I didn't realise Fletcher was involved. Wasn't there a bit of a fuss about the death?'

'Yes. The Iranians alleged Mohammad was killed while he was lying on the ground injured. The Human Rights law leeches in this country were all over the case and demanded a public inquiry.'

'I don't remember there being an inquiry.'

'There was no inquiry,' Dame Alexandra said. 'However Fletcher was quietly court marshalled and an internal investigation was held into the circumstances surrounding Mohammad's death.'

'And was he found guilty?'

'No, all charges were dropped when film from the body camera he was wearing proved he shot the insurgent in self-defence.'

'Despite him clearly being innocent, I suppose seeing Fletcher get off would have made the woman even more determined to kill him,' Statton said.

'Definitely, and she might have succeeded if it hadn't been for you. I understand the minister is still singing your praises.' She paused again and looked at Statton thoughtfully. 'Actually, I suspect Mr Fletcher had a hand in the speed with which your appointment as my deputy was approved by the Cabinet Office. Such appointments usually take weeks.'

'I'll put him on my Christmas card list.'

'I didn't think you sent cards.'

'I don't, but it's the thought that counts. Now, who was the last phone call from?'

'Bannerman.'

'What did Jimmy want?'

'To deliver some bad news. It seems the January 16th cell in Iran has been compromised again.'

'What happened?'

'Six were contacted yesterday by the Cell's Principal Agent.'

'The Principal Agent's code name is Eagle.'

'You know him?'

'Or her. Will Berry mentioned Eagle a few weeks back, although he had no idea whether the agent was male or female. He told me it was my dad who recruited Eagle and he has always refused to reveal the agent's identity, even in retirement.'

'That doesn't surprise me. Your dad had integrity and was always very protective of his agents, that's why they trusted him so much.'

'Why did Bannerman call you? I thought Berry was the January 16th Case Officer?'

'He is, but he has caught some sort of virus and is seriously ill in hospital.

'Jesus, not Will too. I didn't realise. How is he?'

'Not good. He's currently on a ventilator in an intensive care unit.'

'That's a bummer. He's one of the good guys.'

'I know.'

'So, what did Eagle tell Jimmy?'

'Apparently, somebody tipped off VAJA about one of his

agents, a woman whose code name is Raven.'

'I've heard of her too. Raven works in the Ministry of Defence and Armed Forces Logistics. It was her who told Six that Soleimani was in Venice.'

'Of course! Now you mention it, I remember reading that in a report somewhere.'

'So what happened to Raven?'

'Eagle was able to get a message to her and she managed to escape before she was arrested.'

'That's great news, but what does it have to do with us? Surely any problem with the January 16th cell is Six's headache, not ours?'

'Under normal circumstances that would be the case. It would be for Berry to sort out, but that is out of the question with him in hospital.'

'Six have plenty more agents. For instance, Bannerman could step into the breech temporarily.'

'He is already doing that, but there is an additional complication. Eagle has told Six he or she knows who tipped off VAJA about Raven.'

'Who?'

'Eagle would not say. All Bannerman was told is that the tip-off came from a member of our intelligence services.'

'Shit! Which service? Was it us?' Statton thought of Sam Brewer.

'I have no idea. Eagle insists they will only reveal the identity of the source in a face-to-face meeting.'

'So why doesn't Bannerman go to Tehran and meet with Eagle?'

'He offered to do just that, but Eagle insists that with Berry out of circulation, the only other person they trust is you, Steven.'

'Me?'

'That's right.'

'Why me?'

'Eagle seems to believe you have inherited your father's integrity.'

'The poor, misguided sod,' Statton said.

45

While Steve Statton was meeting with his boss, Tommy Cassidy was sitting in a small interview room in HMP[1] Wormwood Scrubs. He was not happy.

'I ain't got you on a ten grand a year retainer to sit on your fat arse doing sweet FA[2], Solly. Why ain't you got me out of here yet?'

'I've just explained that to you, Tommy. It's because you were refused bail,' Solomon Wiess replied patiently. He took a new roll of soft mints from his pocket, opened the foil wrap, and popped a sweet in his mouth. He offered one to his client, who took one without any thanks.

'But in the avoidance of any doubt let me explain again,' the solicitor went on, sucking gently on the mint in between sentences. 'The Met Police's brief convinced the beaks[3] you would abscond if given bail. That's why they turned down your application.'

'Couldn't you appeal the decision?'

'That's exactly what I did. I lodged an appeal with Southwark Crown Court, which the presiding judge took all of two minutes to dismiss. He too was convinced you would abscond.'

'What makes the bastards think I'll scarper?' Cassidy said angrily.

'Because you have been charged with a very serious offence and, if found guilty, face a very long prison sentence at Her Majesty's pleasure.'

'Since when was possession of a few drugs a very serious offence?'

'Tommy, we're not talking about a few drugs. You were found with fifty kilos of heroin in the boot of your car. It would be very difficult, even for you, to pretend that such a large quantity of H was for your own private use. Like it or not, no judge in the country is going to allow a suspected drugs dealer to go free.'

'So, no bail?'

'No.'

'Can't you find another way to get me out of this shithole.'

'There's only one way you're going to get out of here before your trial, Tommy.'

'How's that?'

'In a wooden box.'

'Are you taking the piss, Solly?'

'No, Tommy. I'm being upfront with you. There's nothing more I can do for you. You need to accept that you're going to remain in custody until you stand trial at the Old Bailey.'

'In that case you're fired, so don't expect any more dough from me, you little shit.'

Wiess stood up and signalled to the prison officer who was waiting outside the room to unlock the door. 'Don't worry, I wasn't anticipating any more money from you. All your accounts have been frozen, so you couldn't pay me anyway.' Weiss stared at his now ex-client. 'Look, Tommy. They have you bang to rights. You're going to be found guilty of drug dealing and will be put away for a very long time. By the time you get out of prison, you'll have more hairs on your head than pounds in the bank and that will be very few.'

He picked up the roll of soft mints and offered them to Cassidy. 'Here you are, Tommy, keep these. I know they're your favourites and you might not get any more for a while. No hard feelings, huh?'

'Piss off!' Cassidy told Weiss angrily, but he took the sweets anyway.

*

Mateusz Nowak let Solomon Weiss out of the interview room and locked the door behind him. He led him to the end of the corridor where he unlocked another door, this one led to a small area lined with small lockers that were used to store prohibited items temporarily taken from visitors. He opened one of the lockers and took out a mobile phone, a bunch of keys and a thick brown envelope.

The prison officer returned the phone and keys to the solicitor but slipped the brown envelope into his own trouser pocket. 'Is it all there?' he whispered.

'Yes. Five hundred quid in used notes.'

'And the rest?'

'It will be paid into your bank account once the job is done. As we agreed.'

'Don't worry. The job will be done.'

'So everything is arranged?'

'Tak oczywiście…' the prison officer started to reply in Polish and then changed it hurriedly to English. 'I mean. Yes, of course. Just as you asked.'

'Good, let me know when it's done.'

'I'll contact you later today, now let me escort you out before anybody sees us talking.'

When the solicitor was safely through the glass security doors, and out of the front doors, Nowak returned to the interview room and let the prisoner out.

'Come on, Mr Cassidy, I will take you back to your cell,' Nowak said as he ushered the prisoner out of the room.

The prisoner did not reply, instead he simply headed towards B Wing, which was where all new inmates were placed to receive induction into the prison regime.

Nowak escorted Cassidy along the corridors to his cell, unlocking and locking the succession of metal doors they encountered on the way. As they arrived on the wing, the prisoner swayed slightly, as if drunk, and for a moment looked as if he was going to collapse.

'Are you all right, Mr Cassidy?'

'Yeah, I'm just feeling a bit tired.'

'Don't worry, you'll soon be back in your cell and will be able to have a lie down before lunch.'

When they arrived at Cassidy's cell, they found a cleaner mopping the landing outside. When he saw the two men approaching, he pushed his metal bucket out of the way with his foot to let them pass.

Cassidy had left his cell door open, so he walked straight in and plonked himself down on the narrow bed. He looked up and saw the prison officer and cleaner staring at him.

He stood up and walked to the door. 'I don't need you two pricks watching me while I take forty winks.' He pulled the door closed with a loud metallic crash.

The prison officer made no attempt to lock the door. This was not necessary for remand prisoners who were awaiting trial, because technically they were still innocent until proven guilty. Instead, he gave the cleaner a knowing look. 'Okay, Mr Okoro, you can finish cleaning the landing now.'

The cleaner, who stood a good foot taller than the prison officer, and was wide and muscular after spending many hours in the prison gymnasium, nodded his understanding, shrugged his huge shoulders, and carried on mopping the floor outside the cell.

Cassidy sat on the narrow bed and stared at the cell wall, on which a faint message had been scrawled inviting the Governor to perform a self-sexual act that was physically impossible for any normal person.

Somebody had tried to remove the message (it might even have been the cleaner who was still mopping the landing), but had not succeeded because the message was still legible. Perhaps whoever that somebody was felt the same way about the Governor.

Cassidy felt rage forming bile that went from his stomach to his mouth, leaving him with a bitter taste. He was angry at his lawyer. Angry at the beaks for refusing him bail. Angry at the system that was keeping him cooped up inside this tiny cell. Angry at Vinny for allowing Statton to steal his merchandise, but, most of all, he was angry at himself for letting the four-eyed bastard sucker him into being ambushed by the rozzers.

Cassidy closed his eyes and concentrated on controlling his anger. He knew it would only make matters worse if he allowed his pent-up rage to explode into the open. If that happened, he was likely to tear apart his cell, and anybody who tried to stop him. That would not look good in court.

He took one of the soft mints, popped it into his mouth and sucked on it aggressively. As soon as the minty flavour had replaced the taste of bile, he crunched down hard on the sweet's hard shell until his teeth found the soft centre. Then swallowed it whole.

He ate another sweet in the same way, and another, feeling his anger slip away as he made his way through the roll of sweets until they were all gone.

Finished, he crumpled the wrapper and deliberately dropped it on the floor of the cell. Let that black bastard who was still on the landing outside his cell clean it up. He laid back on his bed, closed his eyes again and within seconds was fast asleep.

*

Adedayo Okoro finished his cleaning and stored his bucket and mop away in the small storeroom that was located at the end of the deserted landing, furthest away from the wing office, where he could see Prison Officer Nowak chatting to one of his colleagues.

As he headed towards the barred metal gate that separated the landing from the wing office, Okoro stopped outside Cassidy's cell and looked through the peephole. Cassidy was lying on his back with an open mouth, from the corner of which ran a dribble of saliva. He was snoring loudly.

Okoro glanced towards the office and saw that the prison officers were still engrossed in conversation. He gently edged open the door of Cassidy's cell, stepped inside and silently closed it behind him.

He opened his shirt and pulled out the short length of clothesline he had stolen from the prison laundry that morning. He quickly made one end of the line into a loop, using a slip knot, and then stepped over to the bed, where Cassidy murmured quietly to himself, but did not open his eyes.

Nowak had promised him the prisoner was drugged, and would be comatose for a couple of hours. It looked as if he was right. Okoro lifted the man's head and slipped the loop over it until the rope settled round his neck, then he pulled sharply on the rope until the loop tightened.

Still the unconscious man did not stir, even as the rope bit deeper into his neck, compressing both the carotid artery and the larynx, quickly strangling him. Within two minutes Cassidy was dead.

Okoro lifted the prisoner's heavy body from the bed, like a child lifting a rag doll, and propped him against the wall under the single window. He held him in position with one meaty hand, whilst threading the clothesline through the bars with the other.

Once the line was secure Okoro let the body drop, so it slumped halfway to the ground, looking for all the world as if the dead man had committed suicide. He left the cell, after checking he was not being observed, and made his way to barred door at the end of the landing.

This time Nowak saw Okoro coming and came out of the wing office. 'All finished, Mr Okoro?' he asked in a loud voice.

'Yes, boss.'

'And is the cleaners' storeroom tidy?'

'You can check if you like,' Okoro said.

'I think I might,' Nowak said, looking over his shoulder and giving his colleague in the office a wink. He opened the barred gate and stepped through onto the landing, locking the gate behind him. 'Come on.'

The two men walked to the other end of the landing where

they disappeared into the cleaners' storeroom. There was just enough space for them both. As soon as they were inside, Nowak pulled the brown envelope from his trouser pocket and handed it to Okoro, who stuffed it inside his shirt.

'Are you sure he's dead?' Nowak asked.

'He's dead,' Okoro confirmed confidently. 'Please make sure my wife gets the rest of the money you promised. She needs it to pay off my debts.'

'Don't worry. She will get it.'

'I hope so. It will make me very angry if you let her down and you really don't want to see me angry.'

'I said she would get the money,' Nowak hissed. 'Now get back to your cell. I'm going to check up on Cassidy in a few minutes and when I report him dead the shit is going to hit the fan. It's likely the Governor will order a cell check so hide that money somewhere it won't be found.'

Okoro pointed at his own huge backside. 'Don't worry, I have just the place,' he said with a wide smile.

*

Three days later Bobby Moore sat hunched over a glass of bourbon in a corner of the Cardigan and Balaclava. He had his mobile pressed to his ear and was talking into it in a husky whisper.

'Tell that big ape I gave his missus the wonga yesterday. If the bitch ain't paid off his debts he should sort it out with her.'

'That might be difficult, Humpy,' Solomon Wiess said. 'He doesn't know where she is.'

'You mean she's done a runner with his money?'

'Looks like it.'

'I wouldn't like to be around when he finds her.'

'That won't be for some time. Okoro has just been convicted on three counts of murder, and when he's sentenced next week, he's likely to be given a minimum thirty-years stretch.'

'What about Cassidy? Are they likely to pin his death on Okoro as well?'

'No. The police decided Tommy committed suicide and that was backed up by the autopsy.'

'What about the morphine? Didn't the autopsy pick that up?'

'Yes, the forensic pathologist spotted that, but he never made the link between the morphine and the remnants of the soft mints found in his stomach.'

'It was a smart move injecting the drug into the sweets, Solly. But how did you know the bastard would eat enough of them to make him unconscious?'

'Because I've seen him get through a tube of mints like that before, and people like Tommy Cassidy never change. Once a pig always a pig.'

---

1   HMP: Her Majesty's Prison
2   To do sweet FA, or sweet Fanny Adams, means to do nothing.
3   A beak is a slang word for a judge or magistrate.

46

The winter snow was late arriving in Tehran, but during the night it had dropped from the sky with a vengeance, leaving the city blanketed in a white overcoat that seemed to shimmer as the early morning sun started its climb up the ladder of cumulus clouds that had formed in the clear eastern sky.

When Steve Statton left the Bahar Hotel, he found the pavement on Enghelab Street covered in three inches of pure white snow, although the surface of the road itself had been turned into black slush by the rush hour traffic. As he made his way warily along the slippery pavement, he kept close to the buildings to avoid the occasional spray thrown up by passing vehicles.

Some of the cars had skis strapped to their roof racks. He guessed the owners of the cars were heading upcountry for a weekend at either Dizin, or Shemshak. The two ski-resorts were not to Statton's taste, but he was sure Jane Manning would love them.

At the first junction he joined a group of pedestrians who were waiting to cross the busy road. There were no traffic lights, so they had to wait for a temporary gap in the stream of vehicles before taking their lives in their hands as they splashed hurriedly across the road together like lemmings rushing for the cliff edge.

Once Statton was safely on the opposite pavement, he turned down a narrow one-way road that still wore an almost pristine covering of snow. Halfway down the road, there was a parked police car, blocking-off the entrance to Qaedi Street.

There were two cops standing by the car smoking cigarettes. They were both looking up the road at something Statton could not see, and took no notice of him as he turned into the blocked-off street.

As Statton trudged towards his destination he wondered what the cops were doing. He decided they were probably looking out for warning signs of another of the protest demonstrations that were a daily occurrence in Tehran.

A couple of minutes later Statton found the café for which he was looking. He entered and sat down at an empty table next to a window that was opaque with condensation. In the centre of the table was a menu printed in both Farsi and English, and set out in front of him was a placemat decorated with a colourful Persian design.

A waiter came over and placed on the mat some cutlery wrapped tightly in a paper napkin. Statton ordered a coffee and answered 'no' when the waiter asked whether he wanted any food. The waiter tried to hide his disappointment, but when he went off to get Statton's drink he did not look happy.

Statton unbuttoned his overcoat and settled down to wait for Eagle to make contact. He unwrapped the cutlery and used the paper napkin to wipe away some of the condensation from the window. He could now see anybody who came up Qaedi Street.

The café slowly filled up with customers who had snow on their boots and pinched expressions on their faces. None of the newcomers seemed to take much interest in him and none of them looked as if they could be the agent he had come to meet.

Time went by and Eagle still hadn't arrived. Statton ordered another cup of coffee and decided to have something to eat after all. He asked for some baklava and this time the waiter went away smiling. Perhaps he received commission on any food he sold.

Statton went back to looking out the window. He could see the police car still parked on the corner with the two cops standing next to it smoking fresh cigarettes. As he watched, a Safir military vehicle drew up behind the police car. One of the cops threw down his cigarettes, jumped into the car and moved it out of the way so the Safir could drive into Qaedi Street.

The Safir drove up the road and stopped outside the cafe. Two men wearing the bottle green uniform of the Islamic Revolutionary Guard Corps got out. One was a staff sergeant and the other a corporal.

The soldiers came into the café and headed straight for Statton's table, where they arrived just as the waiter was putting a coffee and a plate of baklava in front of the Englishman.

'Come with me,' the staff sergeant said in English. 'Now.'

Statton got to his feet and slowly buttoned up his overcoat. There was no point arguing. He could see the soldiers meant business and would not hesitate to use their pistols, the metal butts of which were just visible under the flap of the shiny leather Sam Browne holsters they wore.

The soldiers hustled Statton out of the café without giving him time to settle his bill. He felt sorry for the waiter who really was having a bad day. The staff sergeant led the way, with Statton sandwiched between him and the corporal, who was walking close enough behind him to make it possible to hear the rustle of his uniform.

When they arrived at the Safir the staff sergeant indicated

that Statton should sit in the back, then squeezed in next to him, leaving the corporal to drive. They had already frisked the Englishman, and knew he was unarmed, but they were taking no chances.

The Safir headed east up the one-way Qaedi Street and when Statton glanced over his shoulder he saw that the police car had disappeared. Obviously, the cops had completed their task of keeping him under surveillance, but what Statton did not know was how the authorities knew he was going to be in the café.

The journey to the headquarters of the Islamic Revolutionary Guard Corps took just over twenty minutes. There was no heater in the Safir, so by the time they arrived at their destination Statton was shivering uncontrollably, despite his overcoat.

Statton's stony faced military escort did not seem to mind the cold, nor did they waste any energy in idle chit chat. Statton was too cold to worry either way.

When the Safir drew up outside a side door in the sprawling building in which the IRGC headquarters were located, Statton was handed over to a different pair of soldiers. One of the new guards was overweight with a careworn face and steel grey hair, whilst the other was much younger, with the slim, hard figure of an athlete. But like their colleagues, both men had equally stony expressions and similar shiny Sam Browne holsters strapped round their waists.

Statton was in no doubt that they too would be more than happy if he gave them an excuse to draw their weapons. He did not intend giving them an opportunity to prove him right.

The two soldiers silently marched Statton along a series of passages and up several flights of stairs, until eventually they led him down a corridor lined with portraits of Iran's leaders, past and present, including a giant one of the current Supreme Leader, Ali Khamenei.

When they reached the end of the corridor the older soldier opened a door to reveal a sparsely furnished room. The younger soldier prodded Statton in the back to urge him in. The Englishman was about to turn around and whack his escort when he remembered the sidearm the man was carrying. Instead, he walked silently into the room.

'You stay here,' the young man ordered menacingly. They were the first words Statton had heard since he left the café. He smiled to himself as the door slammed closed and he heard a key turn in the lock. The guard's words were superfluous because there was no way out of the room. Perhaps the youngster just wanted to practice his English.

In the centre of the room was a table and two chairs. The top of the table was empty except for a battered metal ashtray full of cigarette butts. In addition, there was a small desk at one end of the room and a couch against the wall at the other. There was a large window set into the wall opposite the door and Statton walked over and looked down at the snow filled grounds surrounding the building.

There was a high wall enclosing the grounds and beyond the wall, to his right, was a large park in which the trees were heavy with snow that was slowly melting as the weak sun reached its zenith.

Statton watched as two people strolled arm in arm along the winding tree-lined paths in the park. Suddenly, the couple looked up in alarm as they were showered with water and snow as the strengthening wind shook the branches of a large conifer they were passing under.

In another part of the park could just see a young man who swept snow from a bench with his hand, then spread a newspaper over it so that he could sit down. He waved to a woman who was helping a child build a snowman. She paused from pressing small stones into the snowman's front to wave back. The child waved too, but the snowman just stood motionless with a crooked smile on its face.

To Statton's left soldiers were clearing snow from an area of the grounds that separated the IRGC building from the boundary wall. As the snow was shovelled to the edges, where it formed a low white bank, black tarmac was revealed. Statton guessed the area being cleared was either a car park or a parade ground. Maybe it was both.

A key turned in the lock and the door opened. Statton turned as a man strode into the room. He was tall and well-built with salt and pepper coloured hair and a matching thick, but well-trimmed, moustache.

The man wore the uniform of the Islamic Revolutionary Guards Corps and on his shoulder epaulettes were displayed gold crossed scimitars, laurel leaves, and an Iranian coat of arms.

The officer wore a badge above his right breast, which showed his name written in Farsi. Statton did not have sufficient knowledge of Farsi to translate the script into English, but that was unnecessary because he recognised the man immediately. It was Brigadier Ali Khadem.

The soldier was carrying a small recording machine in one hand and a thin buff file in the other. He sat down in one of the chairs and laid the recorder and file on the table. He pointed to the other chair and pressed a switch on the recorder.

'Please join me,' he said politely before speaking into the recorder. 'This is Brigadier Ali Khadem interviewing Mr Steven Thorvik who has been arrested as a suspected enemy of the Iranian State and its people.'

'What's this all about?' Statton asked.

Khadem ignored his question, instead he asked, 'Why are you in my country, Mr Thorvik?'

'I'm on a cultural visit.'

'A cultural visit?' Khadem asked with a wry smile.

'Yes. I'm looking forward to seeing all the interesting museums you have here in Tehran. In fact I was on my way to visit the Under-Glass Painting Museum when your men picked me up.'

Khadem opened the file and took from it a single sheet of paper. He took a pack of Gauloises from his pocket, tapped the packet until the end of a cigarette slid out of the end, and offered it to Statton, who shook his head.

'Thank you, but I don't smoke.'

The brigadier shrugged and pulled the cigarette from the packet. He put it into his mouth and lit it with a gold Dunhill lighter. He did not ask the detainee whether he minded him smoking.

As it happens, Statton had no objections, because the distinctive smell of the coarse French cigarette reminded him of his dad.

Khadem tapped the paper. 'It says here you were picked up in a café, not a museum,' he said this with the cigarette still balanced in the corner of his mouth.

'I stopped there for a coffee.'

'There is a café at the museum,' Khadem pointed out.

'I know, but it's located outside and I didn't want to sit in the snow.'

Khadem studied Statton with intelligent brown eyes, which narrowed as smoke drifted up from his cigarette. 'That is understandable, however, there is something else about your visit that puzzles me.'

'What's that?'

'Why are you travelling in the name of Steven Thorvik?'

'I don't know what you mean.'

'I mean, your name is not really Steven Thorvik.'

'Is that so?'

'Yes, it is so. I happen to know your name is Steven Statton and you are employed by the British Secret Service. You are a spy.'

Statton shook his head. 'I'm sorry, but you must be mixing me up with somebody else. I think you'll find his name is James Bond.'

'Do not waste my time with your little jokes, Mr Statton.' The soldier stubbed the remnants of his cigarette into the ashtray with such force that several butts spilled onto the table-top. 'What is it you English say?' he asked as he lit another Gauloises. 'I didn't fall off a Christmas tree?'

'I'm English and I don't say that, but I'll remember it for the next time I'm lost for words.'

'What about, I'm not stupid, don't take me for a fool? Would you prefer that?'

'I have no particular preference, but I'm impressed you have been able to pick up English idioms so quickly. Did they teach you that at the Iman Ali Officers' University?'

'No, I picked it up at your Royal Military Academy in

Sandhurst,' Khadem replied with another of his wry smiles.

This was news to Statton. 'What were you doing at Sandhurst?' he asked, genuinely interested.

'When I graduated from Iman Ali I was sent to the UK as part of an officer exchange scheme. That was back in nineteen eighty-eight, when relations between our two countries were much better than they are now. I spent two years seconded to the Military Academy, which, incidentally, is one of the best officer training academies in the world, second only to our own military academy here in Tehran.'

'I think there are many Sandhurst graduates who would argue strongly about that ranking.'

'I would expect nothing else. We all believe our own country provides the best of everything. Only, in my case it is true. Now, to get back to your presence in Iran. I know exactly why you are here, Mr Statton. It is all down here in black and white,' he tapped the sheet of paper again.

'And what does it tell you in black and white?'

'It tells me that you came here to meet with the ringleader of a terrorist group that is fomenting trouble in my country and planning to overthrow the democratically elected Government.'

'Would that be the democratic elections in which only candidates approved by your Guardian Council were permitted to stand?'

'They were all excellent candidates and they deserved to win.'

'Of course they did. However, it must have helped those excellent candidates to have had no opposition. As I recall, the Guardian Council disqualified any candidate who was opposed to the status quo. That's not my idea of democracy.'

'I see, so you do support those who oppose my Government?'

'I never said that.'

'But you do not deny the claims on this paper?'

'I didn't say that either. I certainly deny any involvement with a terrorist group, but I don't know about the other claims, because you haven't told me what they are? If the author of that paper says I have a soft spot for pretty girls; sometimes wear brown shoes with a black suit; don't suffer fools gladly; and drink too much, then I would have to plead guilty.'

Khadem slid the paper across the table to Statton. 'Read it for yourself. You might not be quite so flippant when you see what else we know about you.'

Statton quickly read the report and his heart sank as he realised how much Khadem knew about him and Operation QS. The report mentioned his involvement with the death of Aleah Mohammad; his trip to Afghanistan to meet Fraser Goran; his killing of Guiseppe Navarra and Salvatori; the kidnapping of Sabawi al-Barak; and the assassination of Jalaluddin Haqqanim. However, what really unnerved Statton, and made him feel physically sick, was that the report claimed he was in Tehran to meet with an agent by the name of Eagle.

'Do you deny those claims, Mr Statton?'

Statton had no choice other than to brazen it out. 'Of course I deny them, and stop calling me Statton. My name is Steven Thorvik and I am a tourist in Tehran to visit museums,' he protested, hoping the tension in his stomach was not betrayed in his voice.

'Of course you are, Mr Thorvik,' Khadem said, with extra emphasis on Statton's assumed name. 'So are you telling me all the information in that report is made up?' He took the sheet of paper, put it back in the file and closed it.

'Let's just say, whoever wrote that paper should be awarded top prize in the Fiction of The Year competition, because fiction is what it is!'

Khadem smiled at Statton coldly. 'Very well, if you insist on continuing to spout this nonsense, I have no other option than to escort you to the airport and put you on the first flight back to London.'

'But what about my visit to the Under-Glass Painting Museum? I was really looking forward to seeing some fine Persian art.'

'Don't push your luck, my friend,' Khadem said with more than a hint of menace in his voice as he violently stubbed out his latest cigarette. 'Just be grateful I'm letting you go home and have not handed you over to the boys from VAJA. However, let me be very clear for the record, Mr Steven Thorvik.' Khadem pointed at the recorder. 'If you ever step foot in my country again, you will be arrested immediately, charged with being a spy and when found guilty, you will be shot. Do you understand?'

'I understand,' Statton said. What else could he say? Khadem's use of the word "when", rather than "if" made quite clear his intent.

Khadem switched off the recorder and stood up. He put the machine in his pocket and picked up the file. 'Let's go,' he said and ushered Statton from the room.

The brigadier led Statton back down the network of corridors and out of the building. There was no chauffeur waiting for them in the long black Mercedes saloon that was parked close to the front door. Instead Khadem opened the front passenger door himself to let Statton in. He then went round to the driver's side and settled himself behind the steering wheel.

Khadem drove the car through the narrow side streets, showing a natural skill that is acquired by somebody who eschews the use of the chauffeur to which they are entitled and prefers instead to drive himself.

The sun was high in the sky now and much of the snow had disappeared from those parts of the roads and pavements that were no longer in the shadow of the surrounding buildings.

Fifteen minutes later Khadem navigated the car onto a wider highway, from which the snow had been cleared, and headed at speed south-west down the Persian Gulf Freeway.

Khadem said nothing throughout their journey, he just concentrated on avoiding the many potholes that littered the road and smoking a succession of cigarettes.

Statton sat looking out of the window, as the suburbs of Tehran gave way to open fields and scattered settlements, and thought about the implications of the Iranians knowing all about Operation QS.

Eventually Statton spotted in the distance the modern buildings of the Iman Khomeini International Airport and a few minutes later they left the Freeway to join the North Beltway, the circular road that services the airport complex.

Khadem drove past the turning for the set-down area, instead he headed towards the short-term car park, which is the only parking with direct access to the main terminal. The car park was half empty and he parked as far away as he could from the entrance and those spaces that were already occupied.

They got out of the car and Khadem opened his boot. He took out Statton's travel bag, which he had last seen in his hotel room, and put it on the ground. The soldier lit yet another cigarette and stared at Statton in silence for several seconds. 'I apologise for the way I treated you back there,' he said eventually. 'However, it was necessary to avoid suspicion.'

'That's okay,' Statton said, but had no idea what the soldier was talking about.

'You are indeed your father's son,' Khadem said.

'I hope so,' Statton replied, still wondering where this was going, 'or my mum has been deceiving me all my life.'

'You are like two halves of the same apple.'

'You know my dad?'

He smiled and waved his cigarette in the air. 'It was your father who got me smoking these Gauloises. He was addicted to them.'

'I know and that smell reminds me of him. My mum hated him smoking and nagged him endlessly until he gave it up.'

'In Iran, women are not allowed to nag men,' Khadem said and then lit another cigarette from the dying embers of his last one. 'The only problem is that nobody told our women,' he added with a sad laugh.

'How do you know my dad?'

'I first met him when I was at Sandhurst. He took me under his wing and was like a father to me. He used to insist that I spend the weekend with him and your mother, who at the time was pregnant with you. It was during those weekends that he converted me from Marlboros to Gauloises.'

'So if you know my parents, what was all that nonsense about earlier? Why didn't you tell me then?'

'Because I have to be careful. All the rooms in the building are bugged and monitored at all times.'

'I see, and I assume that's why you said nothing in your car?'

'Yes. I don't think it is bugged, but it is better to be safe than sorry. That is another of your English idioms, is it not?'

'So they tell me,' Statton said and then asked, 'but what is it you have to be safe about?' although he was beginning to understand.

'I think you know. It's why you are here in Tehran.'

'You're Eagle?'

Khadem nodded.

'I was told that recruiting you was the last thing my dad did before he retired,' Statton said.

'Yes.'

'But he didn't retire until the year two-thousand. That would have been twelve years after you first met.'

'Yes, he was very patient. He waited until he knew I would say yes, before asking me to head up his January 16th cell.'

'So why did you agree?'

'Because, by then I was a major in the Revolutionary Guards and had witnessed at first hand the corruption that lies at the heart of my country's government. In many ways, the theocracy under which we live, is worse than communism.'

'Tell that to somebody who lives in Beijing or Pyongyang.'

'At least in China and North Korea women are treated as human beings and not chattels. My own wife was put in prison for supporting a group that was campaigning against the law that makes it compulsory for women to cover their hair.'

'But you're a brigadier, weren't you able to arrange her release?'

'That might have been possible, but only if she had agreed to stop supporting her friends. I didn't bother asking her to do that because I knew she would refuse.'

'Is she still in prison?'

'No, she died two years ago without being released.'

'I'm sorry to hear that.'

They stood in silence for a while, with Khadem puffing on his cigarette and Statton remembering the fug of Gauloises whenever he was allowed into his dad's study.

'I understand you have information about a leak from our intelligence service?' Statton asked.

'Yes.'

'Is that where all that stuff about me came from?'

'Yes.'

'Which service? Was it my department?'

'No. It was MI5.'

'And do you have a name?'

'Yes. Gerald Draper. Do you know him?'

'Oh, yes. I know him all right. But do you have any proof of his guilt?'

Khadem pulled a sheet of paper from his pocket. 'I knew you would ask me that. This contains details of the bank account into which a monthly sum is paid to Mr Draper. I believe you call it a retainer?'

Statton nodded.

'The bank statement also shows several much larger amounts that were paid to Draper whenever he provided our Ministry of Intelligence with information. I am sure you have clever people who can use that statement to prove a link between Draper and VAJA.'

'I'm sure we do.'

'And when you satisfy yourself of Draper's guilt will you be able to deal with him?'

Statton thought about that for a few moments. 'I think so.'

'And what are you thinking?'

'Something you said to me earlier gave me the idea,' Statton said and then explained his plan.

'Truly you are your father's son,' Khadem said with a smile of admiration. 'By the way, I have written my personal telephone number on the bottom of the statement. If you need to contact me use that number. It is safe.'

Statton took the sheet of paper from Khadem. 'Thank you. Now what about you? Do you want us to arrange for you to defect? We could ensure it was done in such a way that it doesn't affect your family and friends.'

'I have no family. My mother and father are dead, and my wife and I had no children. As for friends, somebody in my position has few of them. Superiors, subordinates, colleagues, associates, allies, and enemies, but no real friends.'

Statton knew what he meant. He was in the same kayak, trying to navigate a personal life that was permanently buffeted by the choppy white waters of active service as a field agent. 'Then you have nothing to stay for. We can give you a new identity and enough money to see you comfortable for the rest of your life.'

Khadem picked up Statton's bag and handed it to him. He then took an airline ticket from his pocket. 'It is a very tempting thought and I am very grateful for your offer.' He handed Statton the ticket. 'However, I still have unfinished business here in Iran. I will not be content until I avenge the death of my wife by helping to bring about a change in our government. The current regime is destroying everything that was good about my country.' He held out his hand. 'Goodbye. I hope to meet Mr Steven Thorvik again soon.'

'I'm sure you will,' Statton said as he shook the brigadier's hand. He watched as Khadem got into his car and started the engine. The soldier was about to drive off when he opened his window.

'Can I trust you to keep my identity secret?'

'Of course.'

Khadem nodded. 'I believe you. Your father must be very proud of you, Steven.' With that he drove out of the car park.

'I hope you're right,' Statton thought as he watched the brigadier go.

47

Gerald Draper looked out of his apartment window and watched as the heavy rain, which had started a few minutes before, suddenly turned to hailstones, which now hammered down on the cars that were parked in the tree lined road outside, bouncing off their bodywork like demented white locusts committing hara-kiri.

'I don't know where that came from, Tinker Bell,' he said to the Russian Blue cat that lay in his arms. He looked up at the black cloud that drifted slowly across an otherwise clear blue sky.

In response Tinker Bell raised its head to be stroked. Draper obliged by running his fingers through the fur on the cat's long neck.

'It looks as if it's passing,' he said, as the shower of tiny balls of ice began to ease and the setting sun escaped from the bottom of the black cloud, and was reflected in the windscreen of a car further up the road.

Draper laid Tinker Bell gently on the Navajo Indian decorated towel, which covered his plush Willow and Hall sofa to protect it from the cat's hairs, and walked through to the entrance hall.

He opened the small cloakroom next to his front door and exchanged his velvet Albert slippers for a pair of handstitched Oxford shoes from Foster & Son in Jermyn Street. He placed his slippers neatly on the wooden shoe rack that stood on the floor of the cloakroom and slipped rubber galoshes over his shoes.

He pulled a waterproof stockman's coat over his blazer, taking care not to dislodge the rainbow coloured badge that was pinned to his lapel. He wore the badge with pride. Gay Pride. He put on his wide leather drover's hat and looked at himself in the full-length mirror that was attached to the inside of the door. He did a little twirl and liked what he saw. The coat and hat made him look so butch.

'I won't be long, darling,' he called to Tinker Bell. 'Daddy is just popping out to the shops to get you some din-dins.' He went out and closed the front-door quietly behind him.

It took Draper about twenty minutes to walk to the parade of shops in the main road. The black cloud had disappeared, heading off towards South London, taking the rain and hail-stones with it.

However, the earlier storm did leave behind several deep puddles on the pavement, which Draper found difficult to avoid, so he was pleased he had taken the trouble to put galoshes over his expensive Oxfords. He was also grateful for the waxed coat and hat because there was an icy wind blowing from the north that made his exposed face tingle.

By the time Draper arrived at the shops, dusk was beginning to draw in and the light was fading fast. His first stop was the cash dispenser outside his bank. He mainly used debit or credit cards, but being old fashioned he still liked to have real money in his pocket. He put his debit card in the dispenser slot and waited for the machine to prompt him to provide his pin number, but no message showed up on the screen and the machine appeared to have swallowed his card.

He decided there was no option but to go into the bank and complain, but when he tried the door, he found it was locked. He checked his watch and discovered it was past the bank's closing time.

Cursing to himself he made his way to the little supermarket where he usually bought his groceries and cat food. He filled a basket with goods and headed to the checkout point with his purchases.

When the cashier had finished scanning the assortment of tins and packets, Draper used his credit card to pay, but the machine would not accept it. He pushed up the sleeve of his coat and rubbed the back of card on his shirt. He tried again, but the machine still rejected it.

A short queue had built up behind him and the cashier was getting restless, so, to avoid any further embarrassment, Draper took out his wallet and found he had just enough cash to pay for his purchases.

Draper left the shop and headed home. As he trudged up the dark streets home, he was already composing in his mind the angry email of complaint he would be sending to his bank.

However, by the time he arrived home he had begun to wonder if perhaps his debit card had been confiscated because he had insufficient funds in his account, and whether his credit card was rejected because he had reached his limit. Both were highly unlikely, because he was very careful about such things, but being a fair man, he was prepared to give his bank the benefit of the doubt. So, before emailing them, he would check his account online.

'I'm back, my little darling,' he called to Tinker Bell, who came slinking through from the lounge. She sat on the hall floor and watched him with inscrutable eyes as he took off his hat, coat, galoshes, and shoes, and put on his slippers.

'Don't look at daddy like that, you naughty girl,' he scolded the cat. 'He's had a rather distressing time and must check something on his computer before he prepares your din-dins.'

Draper went through to the lounge, with the cat following close behind him, and sat down at the side table where he kept his laptop computer. He lifted the lid, powered up the laptop and clicked on the link to his online bank account. He went to the log-in page and punched in the fourth, second and first numbers from his pin that were requested, this was followed by the third, fifth and sixth characters from his password.

The following message was displayed on his screen:

The log-in details have been entered incorrectly. Please re-enter carefully to avoid losing access to Online Banking and Telephone Banking.

Draper frowned and put in his pin numbers and password characters again, this time taking extra care to get them right, but again his details were rejected. He tried for a third time with the same result. When he went to try yet again, a message came up telling him that his account had been frozen, and he should contact his bank.

For the second time that day Draper cursed his bank. He decided to try his other bank account. This account was one that was used only for the special payments that supplemented his Government salary. Those payments made his life worthwhile, as did his beautiful Iranian boyfriend, who he met whilst on holiday in Turkey and to whom he more than willingly provided information.

But when he tried to log onto his second account, he had

exactly the same problem as he had with his normal account. As he sat staring at his computer, trying to work out what was going on, his doorbell rang.

'Who can that be, Tinker Bell?' he asked distractedly. He got to his feet, went through to his front door and opened it.

'Oh! It's you?'

*

Gerald Draper lived in one of those leafy roads in Islington where the residents vote Labour and complain about the government doing nothing to help poor people whilst washing down their guacamole dip and tomato flavoured chorizo bread with bottles of nicely chilled Chablis Grand Cru.

Draper's apartment was on the first floor of a sprawling Victorian building, which had once been owned by a peer of the realm, but whose family were forced to sell on his death when they were hit by an Inheritance Tax bill they could not afford to pay.

Steve Statton stood on the doormat on which was printed the risqué legend: My favourite pussy lives here… Ooer!

Statton wiped his shoes on the mat and pressed a shiny brass bellpush and a couple of minutes later the door opened.

'Oh! It's you?' Draper said.

'Yes, it's me, Gerry.' Statton pushed past the MI5 man's half raised arm and walked into his entrance hall.

'What are you doing here?' Draper spluttered in outrage.

'I'm here for a little chat,' Statton said as he made his way into the lounge.

Draper scampered after the intruder. 'You can't just barge into my home,' he protested.

'I think you'll find that I just did. Do you have a problem with your computer?' Statton pointed at the screen of Draper's laptop, on which could plainly be seen the logo of a well-known bank.

'It's none of your damn business,' Draper said and quickly closed the lid of his laptop.

'That's where you're wrong.' Statton pulled a pistol from his shoulder holster and pointed it at him. 'This makes it my business.'

'God help me!' Draper raised his hands in front of a face from which the blood had drained.

'I don't think that even your God can deflect a bullet from a Glock 17. You'd be better praying to this.' Statton switched the gun to his left hand and waggled his trigger finger in the man's face. 'One squeeze from this and you're dead.'

'Are you going to shoot me?' Draper stared at Statton's finger.

'Not if you're a good boy.' Statton transferred his pistol back to his right hand. 'Are you going to be good?'

Draper lowered his hands and nodded hurriedly. 'Yes.'

'In that case, you have nothing to worry about,' Statton assured the MI5 man, but he kept his pistol trained on him.

Statton's words seemed to satisfy Draper because he recovered some of his confidence. 'So, why are you here?'

'I told you, I'm here for a chat.'

'Chat about what?'

'Sit down and I'll tell you,' Statton pointed to one of the two armchairs in the lounge.

Draper sat down and stared at Statton as he settled himself in the other chair and parked his pistol on its arm.

Draper stared at the Glock in fascination, as if he thought it might go off at any time. 'What is it you want to chat about?' he asked truculently.

'This and that, but first I want to tell you what your problem is.' Statton nodded towards his laptop.

'I don't have a problem,' Draper insisted.

'I'm afraid you do, and it's much bigger than you think.'

'Okay, I'm listening.' Draper still sounded truculent, but now Statton detected a hint of nervousness in his voice.

'Let's begin with your bank accounts.'

'That should be in the singular,' the MI5 man said haughtily. 'I only have one bank account.'

'Really?'

'Yes.'

'Very well, let's begin with that one. This afternoon you attempted to withdraw money from your singular bank account using an ATM in the High Street.'

'How do you know that?'

'Gerry, we know everything about you,' Statton paused before emphasising: 'Everything.'

Now Draper really did look nervous. 'Like what?'

'Like you couldn't access your money because the ATM didn't recognise your card. Then you tried to use your credit card at a local supermarket, but that card wasn't recognised either.'

Draper frowned. 'If you know that, then presumably you also know the reason my cards were declined. Have you done something to my account?'

Statton shook his head and smiled. 'No, because the bank account you insist is your only one, no longer exists.'

'What do you mean?'

'It should be easy for a man of your supposed intellect to grasp what I mean, but let me explain again slowly. Your. Singular. Bank. Account. No. Longer. Exists.' Statton smiled coldly at Draper. 'Is that clear enough for you?'

The MI5 man nodded but said nothing.

'And the reason your account does not exist is because you do not exist.'

'I don't understand.'

'It's quite simple. There is no such person as Gerald Draper.'

'What do you mean?'

'There you go again. Are you really that stupid or are you just pretending not to understand what I'm saying to wind me up?'

'I do understand what you're saying, but it doesn't make sense,' Draper protested. 'I'm here and you are looking at me. I do exist.'

'I know that, and you know that, Gerry, but the State system doesn't know that and, as far as the authorities are concerned, Gerald Draper has never existed.'

Draper looked stunned.

'Would you like me to explain?'

Draper nodded silently.

'Okay, it's quite simple. If you go to Somerset House and ask for a copy of your birth certificate, you'll find your birth was never registered. Similarly, your passport is no longer valid, because there is no record of one being issued in the name of Gerald Draper. There is no record of a National Insurance Number in your name. There is no record of you attending school and university, or ever working for MI5. You have never paid tax and never been in hospital. You are not registered with a GP, or a dentist. In fact, all traces of your life have been erased from the records.' Statton let that information sink in. 'Now do you understand, Gerry?' he asked eventually.

Draper nodded. 'Did you do all that?'

'With a little help from my friends, to coin a phrase.'

'But why?'

'Because if you no longer exist, nobody will notice when you disappear.' Statton smiled coldly at the MI5 man again. 'What you need to understand, Gerry, is that you are now a non-person.'

'You can't do that,' he protested.

'Sadly for you, I can and have done that.'

'But that is outrageous. What about my human rights?' He was so agitated he almost leapt to his feet, but thought better of it when he saw Statton's hand move closer to the butt of his gun.

'Your human rights?' Statton mused. 'I'm sorry, Gerry, I must have missed that particular chapter when I read the *How To Deal With A Traitor* training manual.'

'Who are you calling a traitor?'

'Surely that's obvious.'

'I am not a traitor. How dare you even suggest such a thing?' Draper protested hotly.

Statton did not respond to the rhetorical question.

'Let me tell you something, Statton. I shall be seeking legal advice with a view to suing you for defamation of character,' Draper blustered, becoming red in the face as he spoke, 'and whoever sent you here to intimidate me.'

'Who said anybody sent me?'

'I know they did, and sitting there with a snide smile on your face only makes matters worse. But then that's typical of you,

Statton, isn't it? You've never liked me, have you?'

'Not much,' Statton admitted.

'I suppose it's because I'm gay?'

'Not at all. Who, or what, you shag is no business of mine. In fact, I don't care if you take your cat to bed with you each night.' Statton pointed at the Russian Blue that had perched itself on the back of Draper's chair and was staring at him with interested eyes.

'That's disgusting,' Draper snapped.

'So are you,' Statton retorted. 'But where we differ is that you are also a slimy, two-faced, little shit, who is a traitor for good measure.'

'I told you I am not a traitor,' the MI5 man protested.

'Well, you would say that, wouldn't you? However, we have evidence that proves you have been passing classified information to the Iranians.'

'You're lying. There can be no evidence because I'm innocent,' Draper insisted, still trying to brazen it out.

'That's where you're wrong. We have more than enough evidence to prove your guilt. For instance, I have bank statements from the second account you denied having. Now, why do that if you have nothing to hide?'

Draper did not answer, but much of the colour had drained from his face again.

'Those bank statements show regular monthly payments, and several much larger payments, which were transferred from a bank account belonging to the Iranian Ministry of Intelligence. The payments were authorised by Teymour Rashidi, who is your controller.

'I know nobody of that name,' Draper insisted quickly.

Statton took a photograph from his pocket. He leaned over and handed it to the MI5 man. 'Perhaps you know him as Davoud Parsa, Gerry. That is you with Parsa in that photo, isn't it? I believe it was taken while you were on holiday in Turkey. It looks as if you're having a whale of a time.'

Draper stared down at the photograph. 'Where did you get this?' he asked weakly.

'You posted it on Facebook.'

'But I deleted that post months ago.'

'Come on, Gerry, you're not that naïve. You work for MI5 remember. You must know that posts are never completely deleted from Facebook, they are just cached on a remote server to which only a handful of people have access.'

Draper stared at Statton and it was obvious this was news to him.

'No?' Statton went on. 'In that case you also won't know that numbered amongst those privileged few, is the UK government and its security agencies.'

Draper shifted uncomfortably in his seat and Statton guessed he was starting to understand the serious trouble he was in.

'You still haven't told me why you're here.'

'That's easy. I'm here to offer you a deal,' Statton said.

That perked Draper up a bit. 'What sort of deal?'

'Basically, you have two options.'

'Which are?'

'Either you come clean about passing information to the Iranians, at which time you will be allowed to do a Kim Philby and defect, or…'

'Oh, that option is definitely out,' Draper interrupted his uninvited guest. 'I don't want to live in Moscow.' He gave a nervous titter, as if trying to make a joke of it. 'Russia is far too cold at this time of year.'

Statton ignored him and carried on with what he had been about to say: '...or, we will use all the evidence we have against you, to prove your guilt...'

'What other evidence do you have?' Draper interrupted again.

'Oh, lots of it. For instance, we have several other very interesting photographs, which are even more intimate than that one.' He pointed at the photograph Draper was still holding. 'But trust me, Gerry, with or without evidence you are going to be found guilty. Do you understand what I'm saying?'

Draper nodded miserably. He understood all right. 'I didn't know the information was going to the Iranian Government,' he mumbled eventually.

'So, you admit passing information to Teymour Rashidi?'

'Yes, but Davoud told me he was a writer and wanted the information as background for a novel he is writing.'

'Are you really that stupid?'

Draper shrugged. 'It's the truth, and I'm happy to let a court decide my fate.'

I shook my head.

'What's wrong?' Draper asked.

'Gerry, every time you open your mouth you seem determined to prove how stupid you are.'

'What do you mean?'

'I mean, do you really think that you'll ever see the inside of a courtroom?'

'But I thought you said I would be found guilty?'

'Come on, Gerry, get with It. We're living in the real world.

No government likes to see its security deficiencies exposed to the glare of the publicity that surrounds a court case. So there will be no open trial. Instead, Her Majesty's Government has appointed me as your judge and jury.'

'But that is not justice,' Draper wailed.

'There is more than one form of justice, and because of your admission, I have found you guilty. Which is why, the two options you have been offered are a one-way ticket to Tehran, or this.' Statton picked up his pistol and pointed it at him.

'So you *are* going to shoot me?' he clasped his hands together tightly in a vain effort to stop them shaking.

'Only if you refuse to defect to the Iranians. Personally, I think you're lucky to have a choice. If it was my decision, I wouldn't have given you that option in the first place. I hate traitors and would be more than happy to put a bullet through your head.'

'You would do it too, wouldn't you?'

'You'd better believe it, Buster. So, what's your decision?'

'I'll go to Iran.'

'That's a real shame. I was looking forward to seeing what passes as your brains decorating those fancy curtains behind you. However, there is one other condition.'

'What's that?'

'You couldn't have got all the information you passed to the Iranians on your own. So before I put my pistol away again, I want to know who you were working with. We know it was somebody in the SSA, but who?'

Draper hesitated, and at first Statton thought he was going to refuse, but eventually he said, 'It was your colleague, Sam Brewer.'

Statton shook his head, as if in disbelief. 'It's easy to blame a dead man who can't defend himself.' He did not tell the MI5 man his own suspicions about Brewer, or how he had died. 'So who was it really?'

'I swear it was Sam,' Draper pleaded.

'So what did Brewer want in return?'

'Money. Davoud paid us both for the information we gave him.'

'How much?'

'You've seen my bank statement. Davoud paid the same amount into a bank account set up in Sam's name.'

'Just like that?'

'Yes.'

'And neither of you wondered how a bloody writer could afford to hand over thousands of pounds a year?'

'Davoud said he had a wealthy father.'

'And you believed him?'

'Yes,' Draper said miserably. 'Honestly, it's true.'

'You don't know the meaning of the word honesty, but on this occasion I'll give you the benefit of the doubt. So go pack a suitcase.'

'What now?'

Statton stood up. 'Yes, now.'

'But what about Tinker Bell?'

'Don't worry about your bloody cat, I'll find it a good home. Now, up off your backside before I lose patience.'

When Draper had finished packing his case, he wheeled it through to the lounge. 'I just have to get my passport from my desk drawer.'

'Don't bother. As I told you before, that passport is no longer valid. It has now been placed on the Red Notice list and you wouldn't get past security at Heathrow without having your collar felt.' Statton took an envelope from his pocket and passed it to Draper.

'That contains a new passport, your plane ticket, two hundred Euros and a debit card that will allow you to access a bank account with a balance of five thousand pounds in it. That should keep you going until you sort something out with your boyfriend, Teymour Rashidi, or whatever name he's using when you track him down.' Statton was confident Draper would never see Rashidi again, but he thought it best not to tell him that.

Draper stared down at the envelope but did not open it. 'Thank you,' he mumbled and then stroked his cat. 'Bye-bye, my little darling. Daddy is going to miss you.' He turned to Statton with tears in his eyes.

Statton thought Draper was going to plead with him to change his mind, but he said nothing. It was just as well because Statton had no sympathy for his plight. Draper had brought it on himself.

'Let's go, Gerry, but first, take off that bloody badge. If you're wearing it when you arrive in Tehran, you won't last five minutes.'

*

Gerald Draper joined the queue that was winding its way through the Arrivals Hall at Iman Khomeini International Airport towards the booths in which immigration police were greeting passengers with expressionless faces, and flicking through passports with suspicious eyes, perhaps hoping to find somebody who had previously visited a hostile enemy state, such as Israel.

Draper had already studied his forged passport and was pleased to find that the only countries he had visited was Iran and its allies, including Iraq and Afghanistan. He was impressed that whoever had produced the passport, which had a rather pleasing photo of him staring out with a superior expression on his face, had done their homework.

When it was his turn to have his passport checked, it was done by a handsome young policeman, who studied him with obvious interest. Momentarily, Draper studied the youngster with equal interest and wondered what his body looked like under the Khaki uniform. Sadly, he was not able to ogle for too long, because the cop stamped his passport, handed it back to him and waved him on.

Draper made his way to the baggage claim area where he recovered his suitcase from the carousel and headed for the exit. He was just about to make his way through the double doors under the green Nothing To Declare sign, when he was approached by two soldiers wearing the dark green uniforms of the Islamic Revolutionary Guards Corps.

'Can I see your passport, sir?' one of the soldiers asked, holding out his hand and turning the request into an order.

Draper handed over his passport, which the soldier checked but did not hand it back. The second soldier took his case from him without asking permission first. Draper knew better than to complain.

'Come with me,' the first soldier said and this time he did not bother to dress his order up as a request. He led Draper to a small office situated close to the baggage reclaim area.

Once inside the office, he was told to sit down at a table.

The first soldier sat opposite him, whilst his colleagues wheeled Draper's suitcase over to a desk at the other end of the office and opened it. He slowly and carefully rummaged through the case's contents.

The first soldier showed Draper his passport. 'Is this your passport?'

'Yes,' Draper confirmed.

'And your name is Steven Thorvik?'

'Yes.'

'Are you sure?'

'Of course,' Draper replied, feeling the first twinges of alarm.

The soldier stood up, took a mobile phone from his pocket, punched in a number, and spoke rapidly in a language that Draper did not recognise, but guessed was Farsi. The soldier then went and stood by the door, making it clear this was to prevent Draper from leaving.

Five minutes later a third soldier strode into the room. He was a big man, with the aura and bearing of an officer. If the man's superior rank was in any doubt, this was immediately dispelled when the first two soldiers stood to attention as he entered the room.

The officer waved his men to stand easy and then sat down opposite Draper at the table. He took a pack of Gauloises cigarettes from his pocket and offered them to the Englishman, who shook his head.

'Do you mind if I smoke, Mr Thorvik?' The officer asked politely in impeccable English.

'Do I have a choice?'

'We all have choices, Mr Thorvik. Some people make the right choice, but other people make a bad choice. One of my bad choices was to start smoking. It is a disgusting habit, but it helps to calm me. If I don't smoke, I have this dreadful tendency to lose my temper and make even worse choices. It is for you to decide what is in your best interests when you make your own choice. So, do you mind if I smoke?'

Draper shook his head again.

'An excellent choice, Mr Thorvik.' The officer lit his cigarette and sucked the smoke deep into his lungs in satisfaction. 'Aaah, that's better. Now down to business.' He pulled a small recorder from his pocket and put in on the tabletop next to the Englishman's passport. He pressed a switch and the recorder started humming.

'This is Brigadier Ali Khadem interviewing Mr Steven Thorvik,' the officer said to the recorder, 'and follows on from the previous interview with Mr Thorvik, the transcript of which can be found in his file.' He turned to Draper. 'Mr Thorvik, why have you come back to Iran and why did you not heed the warning I gave you at our last meeting.'

'I don't know what you're talking about. This is my first visit to Iran, and I have never met you before in my life.'

'Come, come, Mr Thorvik, you will have to do better than that.' He picked up Draper's passport. 'This is yours, is it not?'

'It is,' Draper confirmed, but his sense of alarm was deepening, and a worm of nervousness began to eat at the lining of his bladder.

The Brigadier flicked through the passport and stopped at a page. He turned the passport round so that Draper could see the entry. 'This shows that you visited Tehran one week ago. Surely you remember our interview?'

Draper shook his head dumbly as he began to realise what

was happening.

'No? Well let me remind you. I said that if you ever returned to Iran you would be arrested immediately, charged with being a spy and when found guilty, you would be shot.'

Suddenly Draper realised four things. The first was that the Brigadier's two soldiers were now standing much closer to him, on either side; the second was that Statton had set him up; the third was that he was going to be executed; and the last was that he needed the toilet urgently.

'The interview is over,' Khadem said as he turned off the recorder. 'Take him away.'

The two soldiers yanked Draper to his feet and that was when he suffered the final humiliation. He wet himself.

48

'Do you like cats?' Steve Statton asked Dame Alexandra when he finished telling her how once Eagle had identified Gerald Draper as the informant he had visited the MI5 man, got him to confess his guilt, persuaded him to defect to Iran, and then arranged to have him arrested by the Islamic Revolutionary Guard Corps.

'Not much. We have always been a dog family. Why do you ask?'

'Because I have a Russian Blue at home, which seems to spend its time sharpening its claws on my bloody furniture.'

'I didn't know you liked animals.'

'I don't. Tinker Bell used to belong to Draper. I promised I'd find a good home for it.'

She laughed. 'Tinker Bell? Isn't that the name of a fairy.'

'Yeah, a bit like its master.'

'I'm not sure that in our current politically correct world you can make jokes like that anymore.'

'Who said I was joking? Anyway, Draper can hardly complain about me. Can he?'

'You are sure he's dead?'

'Yes.'

'That happened very quickly, I thought you said he only flew to Tehran three days ago.'

'He did, but he was picked up on his arrival; was tried by a military court the next day; found guilty of spying and executed by a firing squad the same day.'

'So how did you manage to arrange for him to be arrested

by the Iranians in the first place?'

'I tipped off a brigadier I know in the IRGC,' Statton told her, which was true, but not the whole story. 'In exchange, he told me what information Draper had leaked to them. He knew pretty well everything about Operation QS, including what happened to Sabawi al-Barak and Jalaluddin Haqqanim.'

'Did he indeed?'

'Yes.'

'This brigadier of yours seems pretty clued up.'

'He is. I wouldn't want to get on the wrong side of him.'

'He certainly sounds formidable,' she looked at Statton with eyes that were far too shrewd for his liking. 'I don't suppose it was your contact Eagle who put you in touch with this brigadier?'

'You could say that, but I couldn't possibly comment. Remember, Eagle isn't my contact, he is controlled by Six.'

She gave me another of her piercing looks. 'Talking of Eagle. You haven't told me his identity. I seem to recall that was why you went to Tehran in the first place. Did you actually meet him?'

'Or her,' Statton said.

'Or her,' she agreed.

'Yes, I met him or her. However, I promised to keep his or her identity to myself.'

'Like your dad did.'

'Yes.'

'And Draper told you it was Sam Brewer who passed our classified information to him.'

'Yes, but I'm not convinced.'

'How so?'

'Because Draper told me money was paid into an account

in Brewer's name, but we have checked with all the banks and there is no record of any such account.'

We sat in silence sipping our drinks.

'Are you thinking what I'm thinking?' she asked.

'It depends on what you're thinking.'

'I am thinking that some of the information Khadem possessed related to events after Brewer died.'

'That's what I was thinking.'

'So there is another traitor somewhere in the camp?'

'Either that or Brewer was not the traitor at all.'

'Is that possible?'

'Yes.'

'You think Draper was lying?'

'Let's just say that I'm not convinced Brewer was his accomplice.'

'Why?'

'Because Sam didn't need the money. He was receiving more than enough backhanders from Cassidy and his Mafia mates. The one dodgy bank account we did find in his name contained a couple of hundred grand, all of which was traced back to Cassidy.'

'Perhaps Brewer was greedy.'

'That's possible, but not likely.'

'But likely or not, we know somebody else must have passed information to Draper after Brewer died.'

'Yes.'

'So you know what your next task is?'

He nodded. 'You want me to find him.'

'Or her,' she said with a grim smile.